AT ANY COST

CARA ELLISON

Diversion Books
A Division of Diversion Publishing Corp.
443 Park Avenue South, Suite 1004
New York, New York 10016
www.DiversionBooks.com

For more information, email info@diversionbooks.com

First Diversion Books edition May 2013.

Print ISBN: 978-1-62681-094-5
eBook ISBN: 978-1-62681-066-2

AT ANY COST

COST

CARA ELLISON

DIVERSIONBOOKS

ONE

The law office of Johnson Sloan Pruitt occupied three floors in an elegant steel and glass temple on G Street in the center of the District of Columbia. The sleek décor and furnishings were modern to the point of minimalist, allowing the astonishing view from the massive fan windows speak for itself. A postcard-perfect view of the White House reminded clients—as if they needed reminding—of the firm's literal and metaphorical proximity to power. As old as the Constitution itself, with alumni attorneys who had gone on to the Supreme Court, the Attorney General's office, and various other outposts of power, Johnson Sloan Pruitt was among the most prestigious and best-connected white-shoe law firms in the District of Columbia.

The young, attractive associates who populated the hushed and storied hallways were scions of America's ruling dynasties, endowed with rich family legacies, six-figure educations, and important social connections that guaranteed an effortless rise to the top of whatever field they ultimately chose, whether it was law or something more interesting and inevitable, like politics.

In contrast to her coworkers, Fallon Hughes grew up on a horse ranch in Shelby, Montana and earned her law degree from Pepperdine, an institution her peers thought was roughly equivalent to a second-rate community college. Unlike the other associates who had been selected for their bluest of blue blood, Fallon's family was nouveau riche.

Ranchers and oilmen could not impress the posturing-and-maneuvering snobs at Johnson Sloan Pruitt or the senior partners who ignored her from their massive corner offices, and they never let her forget it.

She blended in like baby powder in oil.

• • •

Knowing she was never going to win over her detractors, Fallon rarely discussed herself at work and tried to stay out of office politics entirely. Instead, she attempted to earn the respect of her bosses by producing excellent work. Currently she was tethered to her desk ninety hours a week trying to defend a multi-billionaire hedge fund manager who had been indicted on forty counts of fraud, conspiracy, and obstruction. The Department of Justice alleged that Robert Chandler was operating a ponzi scheme, defrauding wealthy widows to fund his lavish lifestyle, which included a fleet of twenty Ferraris, a yacht the size of a football field, and a French chateau featuring a bubbling fountain of Cristal champagne that flowed twenty-four hours a day, whether he was in residence or not. When he was indicted, he finally shut the spigot on the champers and sought the services of Johnson Sloan Pruitt, desperately attempting to save himself from a life sentence in federal prison.

Though Fallon had only a miniscule aspect of the case, it was a plumy assignment, high profile, with lots of opportunity to impress the partners. Certainly all those billable hours made for happy management committees, especially during bonus season. So with her career in the balance, Fallon swallowed her certainty that her client was *guilty, guilty, guilty* and went about defending him with zeal that was almost religious. For weeks now, Fallon had ignored the grinding fatigue that infiltrated her body like a virus and kept up the pace, living on coffee and grit.

As she deleted two inelegant sentences from the motion she was working on, the phone on her desk warbled discreetly. She shifted her gaze just long enough to see the word UNKNOWN flash on the caller ID.

"Fallon Hughes," she answered distractedly, her concentration already returning to the motion.

"Hello?" a husky, unfamiliar male voice rasped.

"This is Fallon Hughes. Can I help you?"

Dead air hissed for several seconds, then the trembling voice said, "Good, hi. I need to talk to you … to a lawyer."

His breath was labored, as if he were in the middle of some physically demanding activity. "Is this confidential? Like attorney/client confidentiality …?"

"Um … No," Fallon replied, confused enough to pause her work on the screen and focus on the call. "Attorney/client privilege only extends to actual clients. Is there something I can help you with?"

"I need to talk to you but I can't do it on the phone. This phone is tapped and I don't have much time. They're trying to kill me. They're right behind me …. This is a matter of national security." He sounded like he was forcing himself to speak clearly and calmly, tightening a tourniquet on his emotions so that he might be taken seriously.

"I'm serious, ma'am," he added, correctly interpreting her silence as skepticism. "They're gonna kill me."

Even taking into consideration the very real possibility that she was talking to a mentally unstable person, the urgency in his voice sounded genuine. She picked up a pen. "What is your name?"

"Antoine Campbell."

"What's the national security issue?"

"I can't talk about it on the phone. Can we meet somewhere?"

"Tell me what's happening, then if I think it's necessary to meet, we can set up an appointment."

"Please, they're trying to kill me. If they know I'm talking to you …. Shit! I don't know … I'm really scared, man, these guys are psycho …. Please help me!"

"Who is psycho?" Fallon asked, noting the mounting hysteria in his voice.

"The guys chasing me! I have to talk to you."

"Where are you calling from?"

"I'm on the Beltway right now, heading to D.C. They are right behind me. They're going to kill me! Richard Mullinax is giving away the map to the keys! You have to help me!"

Fallon did not know what a *map to the keys* was, but the name Richard Mullinax stopped her short. As Deputy Director of the National Security Agency, his was not a name that many people outside the government would just casually know. Fallon's attention sharpened.

"What does Richard have to do with this? How do you know Richard Mullinax?"

"Please, I can't ... in person ... I will tell you everything."

"Do you want to come to my office?"

"No. Somewhere public."

"There's a coffee shop, the Daily Grind, at the corner of 15th and K Street."

"K?"

"Yes, K. As in *kilo.*"

"I'll be there in about fifteen minutes." The call abruptly disconnected.

Placing her pen on the yellow sticky note she'd scribbled on, Fallon mentally replayed the conversation. National security? More likely, he was off his medication. The District of Columbia was ground zero for paranoiacs. St. Elizabeth's Hospital was full of poor broken souls who thought they held national security secrets or that the president was beaming secret messages into their dental fillings. On the surface, Antoine Campbell didn't seem so very different from those people.

And yet ... Fallon had grown up around actors and had a good ability to intuit when someone was being artificial; she had an ear for the rehearsed, the overdramatized. The terror in Antoine Campbell's voice sounded genuine with an edge not even Meryl Streep could pull off.

Fallon glanced back at the motion on her computer monitor, realizing she'd inadvertently spelled their "there"—a clear sign she was not on her game. Even if Antoine Campbell turned out to be a loon, now was a good time for a coffee break. She pulled on her long cashmere overcoat and scooped up her handbag.

Over her protests, Johnson Sloan Pruitt had accommodated her Secret Service detail with an adjoining office, a concession that irritated her coworkers—and frankly, her too. She always felt like she had to apologize for their presence. But it was better than the alternative: letting the agents loiter in her office. If agents were glued to her, there would be no such thing as attorney/client privilege when she was discussing cases, so this was a good compromise. It kept the agents near but not on top of her. The firm had also supplied a computer, which the agent was using when Fallon rapped her knuckles lightly on his door. The agent looked up from the monitor.

Then Fallon abruptly stopped breathing, struck dumb.

Her eyes laserlocked on the man who was sitting where she expected someone else—anyone else—to be sitting. She regarded him with the uncomprehending stare of a sleepwalking child, transported into another dimension by shock.

That was ... Tom Bishop.

Wasn't it?

She saw him in pieces, a Pointillist illusion: his eyes, his smile, his cheekbones, his hair. The pieces came together in one astonishing flash, creating an image of a man she had known once and never thought she would see again. The man who had haunted her dreams for four years. She was staring at a ghost.

He was staring back at her calmly and kindly. If he was experiencing any degree of shock, it didn't show. His expression remained composed and unsurprised, though a private and tentative smile had begun to tease the corners of his mouth.

"Ma'am," he said, and rose to his feet.

Fallon blinked, trying to focus so that his appearance in her Secret Service detail's office would make some sense. *Was* that Tom Bishop? Quick up and down assessment: jungle-green eyes, light brown hair, killer physique under that crisp business suit so black it looked like a weapon. Devastatingly handsome. Oh yeah, no doubt. Her racing heart was tertiary confirmation.

Tom Bishop stepped from behind the desk. His tall, solid-looking frame was clothed in a beautifully cut suit that emphasized his broad shoulders and narrow hips. She noticed the glint of the badge on his hip, then his gun in the holster, and she belatedly made the connection that he was her Secret Service detail.

A rush of questions bubbled to her consciousness, but she could articulate none of them. She felt thrown, upended. She could not think ... except ... except the last time she saw him was on the island of Paxos, in their hot little room above the quay. He was holding her in a vast white bed, languid after lovemaking. Face to face, breathing in each other's breath. Her leg was slung possessively over his hip, his warm chest burned against hers; they couldn't get close enough. His eyes, brimming with intensity, bore into hers in the shadowed darkness of the bedroom, as if he were trying to convince her of something important, something she must remember.

"I love you," he whispered, his low, smooth voice roughened by emotion.

Then his lips found hers, brushing against hers with such tender softness that it took her breath away.

In the morning, he was gone.

And now he was here, as if summoned by a wish or a dare. Haplessly she stared at him, so utterly unprepared for his appearance that she didn't actually know what she felt other than pure shock.

"What are you doing here?" she finally blurted.

"Dan Rizzuto's wife gave birth this morning so he is at the hospital with her. I've been temped over."

Fallon's mouth dropped open like a carp. She made an effort to shut it but ended up saying, for clarification, to make sure she understood correctly, "So you're … you are … my … detail leader?"

"Special Agent in Charge. Temporarily."

She struggled to iron her face into bland impassiveness, but her physical response was impossible to control. Her cheeks were stinging though she didn't know why; she'd done nothing to be ashamed of, yet she felt weirdly embarrassed and caught *way, way* off guard. Her body was trembling uncontrollably; her knees had turned weak as water.

Oh this was bad. She looked away, unable to hold his gaze. She bit the inside of her cheek, hard, to try and keep herself grounded.

"Are you okay?"

Was that a real question? She couldn't even fathom where *okay* was on a map. Through the confusion, she heard Sam Cahill's voice carry from down the hall. Her boss was generally friendly and supportive, but she didn't think it wise to attract his attention at the moment, not when her whole reality was suddenly warped. She had to get out of here.

Struggling to effect a neutral expression, she murmured, as calmly as she could, "It's time for a coffee run."

Tom spoke into the tiny mic in his cuff to notify the control room and the limos outside: "Avalon is en route."

Fallon sleepwalked through the office to the bank of elevators in a small alcove that provided a smidge of privacy. At least she could die of shock without all her coworkers observing. She pressed the elevator button and forced herself to breathe calmly. Deep breath, in through the nose, out through the mouth. Pranayama yoga: the art of breathing control. She'd practiced yoga for years, but that calm feeling that came over her when she was in the corpse pose in a peaceful sunlit studio was as far away as Mars.

Stupid yoga.

Shock was doing weird things to her body, but it was doing even worse things to her brain. She perceived a weird giddy happiness starting to blaze through the murk and that weird thigh-tingling attraction that was so familiar when he was around. She mentally tried to ward that off before it took hold. So inappropriate. One should not greet marauding pirates with joy. That was what he had been—a pirate, plundering all she had. Leaving her utterly pillaged.

She didn't lift her eyes until the elevator doors slid closed, sealing them inside together. Tom's big, hard body dominated the small space. He was still dangerous-looking, with strong features and the physical presence of a man who was accustomed to wielding authority. He looked almost the same. Not older, exactly, but somehow harder. Like he'd become refined in some unidentifiable way. She realized with a start that it was possible he saw changes in her too.

She felt unspeakably vulnerable. Scared of his power to jilt her, to leave her a heartbroken fool. And scared of herself when she was around him, because she let him.

The elevator doors slid open in the bright atrium lobby. On

the street beyond the glass walls, two enormous black Chevy Suburbans idled at the curb. The armored SUVs that comprised her motorcade were immediately recognizable as official vehicles on the streets of Washington D.C., conspicuous by the light bars on the roofs and the multiple antennae. Plus, there were always two of them: a primary and a follow-up.

The possibility of being trapped in the car with Tom Bishop and her own tangle of confused emotions made her throat close and oxygen seem like a suddenly rare resource. She had to physically move, clear her head and give herself an opportunity to get a grip.

"We are going to walk, if that's okay." Not that she needed his permission.

"Yes, ma'am," he replied. He lifted his wrist and spoke into his sleeve to notify the motorcade that Avalon would be walking.

"We're going to the corner of 15th and K, if you want to let the drivers know."

Tom Bishop radioed the information to the vehicles. As they walked in the direction of McPherson Square, she was acutely aware of Tom beside her. Normally her Secret Service detail was part of her background, but not today. He was pretty much the only thing she could think of, though she tried not to look terribly interested in him. She was still scrambling for the resources to pretend this was perfectly normal. She wasn't a particularly good actor though, and the best she could muster was a neutral expression.

Pedestrian traffic was heavy, despite the blustery cold, and Tom stayed close. As he walked abreast of her, others were forced to move aside. When Fallon tried to step out of the way of a harried businessman, Tom smoothly grabbed her arm, keeping her next to him and forcing the businessman to step into the grass with an annoyed grunt. Tom's quick contact felt jarring, even impolite. The pressure where his fingers clasped her bicep was solid and thrilling, and she hated that she liked it so much.

Fallon chanced a glimpse of his stoic profile. Even with his game face on, the man was startling attractive.

His dark hair was maybe just a tiny bit longer than the Secret Service officially approved of, carelessly swept off his smooth forehead and emphasizing the cold distrust in his eyes. He was the kind of agent who makes you feel good about paying taxes, all polished angles and cold, hard competence.

She wasn't usually attracted to the buttoned up type, considering she was one herself. She liked the artists and the brilliant academics—the ones who made her see more of the world than what was right in front of her. But Tom defied all her conventions and rules.

She had never seen him working before and despite the questions and miasma of shock, she decided she liked it. He might be an incompetent jerk when it came to relationships, but she had no doubt that if a bullet came whizzing in her direction, he'd jump in front of it. Professional obligation and all that.

"I got a strange phone call," Fallon said.

"Strange how?"

"Somebody called needing a lawyer but wouldn't meet at the office. We're going to see this mysterious caller at the coffee shop. He sounded distraught."

"Did he say why he was distraught, or why he wouldn't meet at your office?"

Fallon paused before answering, judging how much to say. She didn't want him to think she was naïve for agreeing to meet someone who might very well be a recently released St. Elizabeth's patient, or worse. "He said he was being followed and wanted to meet in a public place. Plus, he mentioned a rather obscure government official. I want to find out what is up with this guy."

Tom reached the door before she could and held it open for her. She slid past him, noticing the slightest whiff of his cologne as she passed. The Daily Grind was warm and overstuffed, infused with the aroma of roasted coffee. Fallon took quick account of the customers, seeking out anyone who might be Antoine Campbell.

"I guess he isn't here yet," Fallon murmured, as much to herself as Tom.

At the counter, the barista recognized her and asked if she was having her usual, a soothing raspberry tea. "No, not the usual. How about a jumbo pumpkin spice latte with double whipped cream, caramel sauce, and can you dump some of those chocolate covered espresso beans on top?"

"Bad day or good day?"

"Honestly, I just don't know," Fallon replied, still trying to get the mental feng shui right. She spontaneously added a plain cup of coffee to her order. Black coffee, neat scotch: Tom Bishop was a man with simple tastes, luxurious tastes, things distilled to their purest essence. She wished she didn't remember that.

After paying for the drinks, she handed the cup of black coffee to Tom. His eyebrows lifted in surprise at Fallon's casual act of thoughtfulness.

"I thought you might like something warm." When he still hesitated, she added: "It's not poisoned. Too much."

Tom smiled then. The smile transformed him. It softened his whole face, giving him an aspect of sudden sweetness that she found disarming. White, straight teeth signaled that he had perfect genetics, but the lines around his smile, like little parentheses, reminded her that he loved to laugh. Under that Secret Service poker face was a man who loved life.

"Thank you," he said, taking the cup.

"Let's sit down."

"Yes, ma'am."

She bristled at the formality. "Why are you calling me 'ma'am'?"

"Protocol."

Of course. Protocol. The system people relied on when they could not be themselves.

She sat down to wait. Tom sat across from her. He periodically glanced beyond her forehead to the door, or the large side windows, but otherwise he seemed perfectly content in the silence.

His calmness had to be a facade. There was no way he wasn't acutely aware of the shared past that lay between them, the questions that were circling around her head like a cartoon corona.

Well, she wasn't going to be the one to mention Paxos. She had moved on. She'd finished law school, found a real job, made a life for herself. She barely recognized the bohemian yoga hippie she'd been, wandering through Europe with no thought to the future. It was embarrassing, really, recalling how utterly stupid she'd been back then.

She was smarter now. Certainly sharp enough to play this cool.

Fallon took a sip of the pumpkin spice latte and used the opportunity to study Tom again. He seemed like an abstract concept, a miracle and a curse at the same time, sitting in front of her. Within nose-punching distance.

That was probably not an idea she wanted to pursue.

"Antoine Campbell sounded really upset. I hope he's okay," Fallon said.

"Maybe he's stuck in traffic," Tom suggested.

True, traffic on the Beltway might be heavy; it often was, even in the middle of the afternoon.

She wanted to ask how he was doing, or what he was doing, but those questions would be ridiculous. They would only emphasize how strange this whole arrangement was—how utterly artificial they were being with each other, as if they'd never met before.

She realized with dismay that she hoped he might give her some kind of small, private signal that he remembered their shared past in Greece and he respected their time together. But when her gaze once again met his, she saw only cool, vast, imperturbable nothingness. Pristine Siberian wilderness.

He was blocking her out intentionally. She recognized the blankness as a defense. Once, she'd been able to vault past it, to the impossibly sweet, generous, gentle man inside. There was no sign of that guy today and never would be again.

The logical lawyer side of her personality insisted she should despise him after the way he left her. But she hadn't loved him logically. She'd loved him passionately, with searing, aching intuition—all heart, no brains. Gwen Atwell, her best friend, would tell her she was an absolute fool, which was probably true.

Jangling bells signaled the opening door and Fallon looked up, expecting Antoine Campbell. A curious old man with a sporty felt cap and a red muffler entered the shop with a stack of newspapers, bringing a gust of cold air in with him.

"How is your family?" Tom asked, surprising her with the personal question. "I hear your brother is keeping his agents pretty busy."

Fallon spontaneously smiled, touched that Tom mentioned Evan, her six-year-old autistic brother; he was the one person she could honestly say she loved unconditionally. "He's amazing," she said with more passion than she had intended. She was never much good at keeping her feelings a mystery. "Why, what have you heard?"

"Not much. I've heard he goes to the Air and Space Museum every day."

Evan was fascinated with airplanes and math. The Air and Space Museum was one of the only places he would talk. It was like he could relate to people only through airplanes. Fallon tried to juggle her weekend schedule so she was at the office in the evening through the night so she her days were free to take him to the museum. She knew her parents wouldn't do it, and it was important for the boy to actually spend some time with family instead of Secret Service agents, babysitters, special needs teachers, personal assistants, minders, and the various pols who orbited around her parents like buzzards.

At the thought of the little sandy-haired boy and all his haunting complexity, her heart squeezed. She loved him very much, painfully and protectively. She hoped she loved him with enough breadth and intensity to make up for the fact that her parents were less than loving toward him.

Her mother felt overwhelmed by his needs, and her own, so she drank to make all of it irrelevant. Since she'd abdicated her parental responsibility, Fallon stepped in. Nobody else was going to. Certainly not her father.

"I heard he toured Andrews Air Force Base. Ran away and slipped into the pilot's seat of a C-130. The agents were panicked, thinking they'd lost their protectee."

Fallon giggled, remembering the incident that had scandalized her parents, though they were more angry than amused. They thought of him as a problem child, someone who refused to yield to discipline, instead of a boy who could no more alter his love of aircraft than he could change the color of his eyes.

"He's very self directed. If there's an airplane within Frisbee distance, he's going to find it, and he's not going to wait for you to catch up."

"How about your parents? How are they?"

"Good," Fallon said automatically. She didn't think Tom would gossip if she told him the truth, but she felt protective of her family, however crazy they were. In fact, the less uttered about them, the better.

She'd had a rocky relationship with her parents for most of her life. It had something to do with feeling like she wasn't living up to their expectations. Her airy-fairy love and peace and butterflies existence seemed trivial to them. Over the years, they'd all settled into a mutually disappointing relationship.

It had reached a breaking point during the campaign; even now, things between them were more strained than usual. She was emotionally estranged from both of them now. Like most presidential campaigns, her father's had become ugly.

From his earliest days as an oil executive, Preston Taylor Hughes had flouted his marriage vows, and though his team was prepared to handle a whisper campaign that questioned his morality, they had been stunned by how hard President Ballard's people had hit on the theme that Hughes was a ladies' man and serial adulterer, and therefore could not be trusted with the presidency. Ballard's reelection team was headed by his longtime political guru, Gil Parry, who had masterminded Ballard's political climb from his earliest days. To a man like Parry, Hughes's personal life was a gift on a golden platter. His surrogates had leaked reports by "knowledgeable sources within the Hughes campaign" that Hughes and his wife were close to splitting. These same "knowledgeable sources" reported late-night screaming matches that featured thrown objects, vile language, and threats of divorce. No matter how many times Hughes denied marital problems, or his wife Elizabeth tried to laugh off the rumors off on daytime TV shows, the story had legs.

Accusations and tabloid tell-alls by women from Hughes's past added momentum and energy to the gathering storm.

Hughes fought back with an "above it all" strategy crafted by Jerry Chambliss, an inside-the-Beltway veteran of many political wars and Hughes's closest friend and advisor. It had been Chambliss who made sure the loudest of the Montana ladies with stories to tell quietly went away with large sums of cash.

Despite his full-force smear campaign, Ballard's henchmen missed the larger scandal, the real scandal that would have likely torpedoed Hughes's aims for the presidency. Six-year-old Evan Hughes was not Preston Taylor Hughes's child. For all his political muckraking and caterwauling about ladies on the side—which was true—and all his millions spent on opposition research, Gil Parry missed seeing Elizabeth Hughes's vulnerability.

Fallon was thankful for her mother's ability to hide in plain sight, and prayed that Evan's parentage remained a closely held family secret, not for the sake of her father's career, but for Evan. As a special needs child, he needed to be protected and cherished for the person he was, not used as a token in a bitter political battle.

It had been Fallon who noticed something odd about him when he was still a toddler. She pointed out to her mother that instead of playing with his small toy cars, he would line them up by size. Instantly defensive, Elizabeth Hughes dismissed Fallon's concerns; she'd taken Fallon's prompt as a baseless attack on her parenting.

Evan had been slow to walk and to talk, but when he began to exhibit poor motor skills, Fallon grew alarmed. She consulted Evan's pediatrician, but he said that Evan was too young for these symptoms to mean anything. Finally, two years ago, he'd been diagnosed with autism.

When Evan and her parents moved to D.C. after the

election, Fallon felt relieved. She'd be able to see him more often, and she'd be able to see to his health care.

Meanwhile, she devoured every book she could find about autism, and it was she who played with him and loved him and took joy in his accomplishments. Her life might be a little constrained and dim right now, but Evan was definitely one for the plus column.

Fallon glanced at her watch. "It's been almost an hour. If he's coming at all, he's very late." She looked around the little coffeehouse in case she had been so confounded by Tom Bishop that she missed her mark. Disappointed, she sank against her chair back. "I guess I've been stood up."

"Maybe he called your office," Tom suggested.

Fallon dialed her office voicemail, entered a passcode, and was informed by an electronic tube voice that she had two messages. The first message was from Gwen, who asked if she might join her at the club tomorrow morning for a swim. The second message consisted of rushing air and fuzzy background noise. It lasted only three seconds. Puzzled, Fallon replayed it, but only dead air echoed through the line.

Huh. Well, maybe it had been a hoax. She dropped the phone back into her purse.

Her cup was almost empty, but she did not feel inclined to leave. She wanted to see what might happen if she simply stayed here indefinitely. Would Tom offer an apology, or beg forgiveness, or explain why he acted like a complete ass and left her on Paxos without a word?

She noticed his hands, now flat on the table. They were large and good looking, with short clipped nails. No wedding ring, though that was not a reliable indication of a man's marital status anymore. Particularly for agents: none of hers wore wedding rings.

The possibility that he might be married gave her pause. That would certainly explain why he'd dropped her like a bottle of anthrax in Greece. Or maybe he was called back to D.C. on a super secret mission. Or maybe he was dying and needed an emergency heart transplant.

Ugh, a girl could go mad trying to guess at the motives. And she wasn't going to waste all her emotional energy on trying to puzzle out some douchebag who left her heartbroken years ago.

"I should get back to the office."

Walking back was tempting—the bracing air might help clear her mind—but she was acutely aware of how long she'd been gone. Her competitive, backbiting, sharky coworkers undoubtedly noticed her absence too.

Fallon gathered her things and walked outside, flinching at the cold. Pausing thoughtfully on the curb, she peered back down 15th Street, hoping to catch a glimpse of someone who could be Antoine Campbell. Pedestrians huddled in their coats and scarves trudged back to their homes and offices, but there was no one who appeared to be looking for her, nobody who desperately needed her help.

Fallon reluctantly climbed into the heated leather interior of the limo. Although she did not look at Tom in the front seat, she was acutely aware of his presence, registering his tiniest shift or movement in the confined space of the vehicle as it inched through traffic. So strange that she still felt magnetically attracted to him when she should despise him for his bad behavior. Surely if she confided in Gwen about the affair in Greece, her friend would advise Fallon to demand a new detail leader and never deign to speak to Tom again. Gwen was very certain about how things should work in a relationship, but Fallon wasn't. Her relationship with Tom had existed outside the jurisdiction of normalcy; there was lots of room for interpretation. She still clung to the belief that their time together had meant something important, that it had been real and honest, which made his vanishing act even more perplexing. He was, she thought, like a subtly provocative professor—the one whose class was supposed to be an easy A but accidentally changed her life.

The limos edged to the curb on G Street in front of Johnson Sloan Pruitt, nearly skinning off a hubcap, and Tom radioed the follow-up vehicle, instructing one of the agents to walk with

Avalon up to her office.

He glanced in the rearview mirror, taking measure of the street behind them. Media had been following Avalon since her father's victory, but today they seemed to have picked up some other story, which made his job easier. No threats. He stepped onto the sidewalk and swung open Avalon's door. As she stepped out, she glanced up at him with a sweet smile that made him wonder what the hell he was doing here. A gust of wind tousled her blonde shoulder-length hair, sending it flying across her face. She used her knuckle to push the tresses out of her eyes and blinked up at him with big round eyes the color of the earth as viewed from space. In the past, one flash of those babies made him go goofy. Now they made him queasy with guilt because her fundamental goodness was so obvious in them, and he had dimmed that glow a little bit with his stupid, bad behavior.

This was never going to work, not when he was still as attracted to her as he'd ever been. He slammed the door closed. Another agent walked with Fallon inside the building, Tom following a few paces behind.

As Fallon and Kevin White strode toward the elevators, Tom diverted to the small room, called a down room, that sufficed as the Secret Service command center while their protectee was upstairs in her office. He ignored the two other guys in the room and grabbed his laptop. He didn't actually have any pressing work to do but he wanted to emanate harried busyness to give out the distinct vibe that small talk was not welcome.

He felt a little breathless, a little antisocial at the moment.

He had not been sure how it would play out, seeing Fallon again. She looked different than the young free-spirited girl he had once known. Her radiant innocence, he recognized at once. The work-worn lawyer in a sleek Chanel suit, not so much … but he liked her anyway. Her face was framed by thick platinum hair and defined by high cheekbones and those enormous cobalt eyes that reflected everything going on inside her. When she saw him, all the questions and confusion played across her face like shadows, and he'd wanted to blurt out an apology right then. He felt ashamed of himself in that moment, but he covered it well, as he always did. Fallon, however, was still incapable of playing it cool; every flickering emotion was right there on the surface for anyone to see—one idiosyncrasy, among many, he had loved once upon a time.

Fate. Karma. Words Fallon used to say came back to him now, mocking him. Yeah, maybe being here really was some universal retribution. After the way he left her, he definitely deserved to get his ass kicked by fate; there was no profit or use in denying that.

He tried to rationalize away the chemical ramp-up of excitement and the sudden spike in his heart rate when he saw her face. Just a reflex from long ago established patterns, that was all. Totally normal. Cause and effect. Man and woman.

No, that wasn't true. Other women didn't turn him into a raiding sexual Hun, leave him aching, his body thrumming with adrenaline and amped up on testosterone. Her beauty and sweetness still spoke to a part of himself he had long ago locked away—the part that once understood poetry and love and gentleness … the human part. She still had the ability to momentarily jolt him out of his self-imposed exile.

Four years of uneasy celibacy had not been easy for him; he was naturally highly charged and enjoyed the company of women. But total abstinence, after Fallon, had been necessary for his survival. What had begun right after 9/11 as an attempt to prevent himself from ever feeling as cracked and vulnerable again solidified into an inability to feel anything at all. He was quite content to live in a world of cold, hard reality.

But seeing her again had just about obliterated the barriers he'd erected around himself. Just one look and he felt that warm expansion in his chest, his cock twitching and lengthening in his pants, and the silly, puppyish desire to make her happy.

He slumped in his chair and rubbed his temples, trying to figure out how the hell he would make it through the day.

To his dismay, Tom found himself using his old trick—the 9/11 trick—of focusing on a small, quiet place inside himself. The place where he could look at the bodies and think, *okay, get to work*. Or look at the vast empty nothingness that was his life and think there has to be a reason not to fucking blow your own brains out. *Your job is to find that reason.*

He had managed to keep his shit together through 9/11, through losing Bethany and leaving Fallon. He could get through seeing Fallon Hughes again too, even if it killed him.

TWO

Claudia Wells, the vice president-elect, lifted herself from the damp, quivering body of her much younger lover and enjoyed the view. His perfectly muscled body was the stuff of cologne and European car ads, every silken inch of him sculpted and hard, with a light sheen of sexual perspiration glistening on his skin. All that raw masculine power, his youthful endurance, and his charming submission to her every whim … it was all just perfect. God, she loved her life.

Richard Mullinax was breathing heavily, his hands still poised over his head, where Claudia had been pinning his wrists. His gaze dropped to her full swaying milk-white breasts and he licked his lips. She had not allowed him to climax in several days, and he was no doubt nearing the end of his compliance—a state of tension that Claudia found almost unbearably exciting.

"Amazing," Claudia whispered, and lifted herself from Richard. He moaned with a little protest as he slipped from her body and lifted his hips, trying desperately to stay inside.

"Have some mercy," Richard muttered.

Claudia flopped down beside him with indifferent insolence. She was thoroughly satisfied, glowing from the inside out; Richard's plaintive mewling did not even register through the cone of sublime happiness. She reached over to the bedside table and grabbed her BlackBerry.

Stacks of emails had collected since she'd been off the radar for the last two hours, secreted with her lover at the dingy Motel Fifty on Route Fifty in Arlington, Virginia. They always chose shoddy, cheap motels—places they would be unlikely to be recognized and allowed quick getaways. Plus, they were honest: dirty places for dirty deeds. Had Richard ever suggested a pleasant location with clean sheets and adequate amenities Claudia would have been insulted. It would have felt like a lie.

A text from Claudia's husband reminded her that their daughter was coming home from England and asked that she make arrangements to pick her up from the airport since he had been called to do an emergency angioplasty for a German diplomat. Claudia typed an acknowledgement then set the small device back on the faux-pine table.

Richard placed his hand on the flat plane of her belly, allowing the shaft of his penis to press insistently against her taut thigh. "I need you," he breathed into her sweet-smelling hair, and then took her mouth as his hand moved down between her legs. "I need this."

Claudia calculated the time she would need to get to National Airport and decided to take mercy on him. Sort of. She gently gripped his penis, and as always when his eagerness was so apparent, she felt the sensual spark of excitement in the simple acknowledgement of all that youthful exuberance so beautifully disciplined for her.

She had not always liked younger men. Indeed, she had been shocked and flattered when Richard Mullinax approached her at a gala six months ago and introduced himself as the Deputy Director of the National Security Agency. The youngest official to ever hold the title, he told her with unmistakable self-satisfaction. His cockiness both grated and amused her.

"How old are you?" she'd asked bluntly, her candid gaze unflinching.

"Twenty-seven."

She suppressed a teasing smirk and tried hard not to roll her eyes.

"Is that too young for you?" he asked, equally blunt. His eyes liquidly dark, striking against his Chesapeake-tanned skin, seemed impossibly beautiful. Cherubic, except for the sexual energy that emanated from him like an irresistible cologne.

Claudia felt her face flame. Her mouth felt dry so she lifted the drink to her parched lips. "No," she replied and took a sip.

The champagne made her unusually loose, willing to

entertain a flirtation. But the alcohol could not be blamed for her willingness to be seduced. She saw them suddenly with a third person's eyes: a powerful woman in her late forties and the young, tall man teasing her, getting away with it in the middle of a party where her husband stood only few feet away, chatting with the Secretary of the Interior. She knew then, with great certainty, what would happen. Saying no was never in the cards.

She'd meant it to be a one-night stand, a quick, forgivable indiscretion. But what began as a secret summer fling had evolved to an all-encompassing sexual obsession.

Richard's position gave her confidence that the affair could go on for as long as they wanted it to. Politically, he was her equal.

On January 21, she would take her oath of office in front of millions of people on the west steps of the US Capitol. Less than two weeks away. Thus, her position in the administration was not something she could afford to risk. She had worked many years to cultivate an All-American public image, Ms. American Professional and Family Woman and Mother. To succumb to a sex scandal—the most clichéd kind—with a man twenty years her junior would make her the laughingstock of the nation and destroy everything she had worked for. Her famous cardiologist husband, astronaut son, and Rhodes Scholar daughter would be humiliated. What would her children think of their mom having kinky sex with a man their own age? It was too awful to contemplate.

Richard Mullinax had no desire to embarrass her by posting pictures of their trysts on the Internet or bragging to friends about their rendezvous. With his high-level job, he had as much to lose as she did if this thing went public.

Claudia called the shots in this relationship because she did not want to fall into the same boring holding pattern she had with her husband, so she pushed for control. Her husband worked all the time, she felt neglected, and the world tasted like gravel when he was around. Richard added color and movement. And actual *fun*. She could not remember when or how she'd simply stopped having fun, but now that it was back in her life, she wanted it all the time. Controlling this sexy man was as pleasurable as climaxing for her. It was kinky fun and her private secret ... and it was the best part of her day.

Claudia gently pushed him back onto the thin pillows. Grasping his shaft, she slowly began to stroke. She bent down and took him in her mouth, which made him groan. He slid his hands into her hair, and she grabbed his wrists, holding them down by his side while she sucked. He began to thrust faster into her mouth, and as his moans became low and gasping, she knew he was there. She simply pulled back, letting semen shoot helplessly onto his belly and chest. Without friction contact, he cried out and instinctively reached to finish himself off, but Claudia, hovering over him, used her leverage to keep his wrists pinned securely at his sides. She watched with cool fascination as his chest and throat and face beat bright red, veins popping out in his throat and arms, an expression of agony scrawled across his face.

Finally his climax ended, but his penis was still ironhard, and he was nearly sobbing with frustration. Claudia giggled and kissed his mouth. "Sweet boy," she cooed. "You are so beautiful when you're hurting like that."

"Oh my God ..." Richard was speechless, in torment. He had climaxed, but not to completion. His whole body was confused and sensitized, infuriatingly still needing more release.

Claudia stood up by the side of the bed, posing with her hands on her hips. "Where did you throw my panties?"

"Claudia, please ..."

She found her nude satin underwear on the filthy carpet by the television and stepped into them.

His expression pleaded with her to be reasonable. "You aren't going to leave me like this ..."

She smiled. "Yes, I am. I have a life to return to. So do you, ostensibly."

He looked down at himself as if he could not comprehend the cruelty that had befallen him. Claudia wondered if he saw himself as she did. Adorable, sexy. There was simply nothing she enjoyed more than a man on the very cusp his ability to control himself.

Claudia finished dressing, then collected her chic leather handbag from a horrid puce chair with torn stuffing bursting from the ragged seams. "I will call you tomorrow."

"Okay," Richard replied huskily.

"Don't sulk."

"I'm not." He allowed a soft smile to prove he was a good sport about Claudia's casual cruelty.

She blew him a kiss and sashayed out the door.

Richard waited until he heard the low growl of her Mercedes engine and the tires crunching over shale as she piloted onto of the lot onto the highway. When he was sure she was gone, he gripped his penis and began to stroke himself. Just as he felt he might be close, his phone began to ring from under his pants on the floor. He tried to blot out the annoying noise and concentrate, but Beethoven's Fifth ringtone kept penetrating into his fantasy.

"Fuck!" His shout echoed off the walls and he got up to answer the phone. The number that flashed on the screen made him instantly lose his erection. A dart of trepidation pierced his chest. "Yes?" he answered tersely.

"An issue has arisen," the cool voice replied. "We need to meet."

Richard looked around the shoddy room. Though it was private, it was also secret; he wouldn't invite him here. "Let's meet at Lincoln's steps in half an hour," he suggested. Nobody had yet figured out how to bug a park; it seemed safe.

"Fine." He hung up without another word.

Richard tossed his phone back onto the pile of clothes and considered the situation. Whatever Omar Koss had to tell him would be bad; they almost never met face to face. Richard wanted to postpone the confrontation for as long as he could.

He had enough time, he thought, and lay back on the bed to finish the job Claudia started.

• • •

It was four o'clock: a cold, blustery afternoon with bleached skies and the sparkle of snow hinting in the air. Bundled-up tourists and determined joggers moved through the west end of the National Mall in a buzz of constant, light activity, seemingly oblivious to the landmarks around them.

Richard, ten minutes early, walked past the Vietnam Memorial, regarding with the required solemnity the names etched on the black granite wall. The nature of war had changed since those men died. Modern war was won by knowing more about your enemies than they knew about you. For all practical purposes, the United States was at war with every country on earth, doing battle twenty-four hours a day. At the front lines of this invisible war was Richard Mullinax. Tip of the spear.

There was no country Richard did not have access to, no system so secure that he could not penetrate it. The world's secrets flowed into his office every day. It was somewhat ironic that despite the United States government's extensive ability to monitor every other country in the world, it actually had very poor infrastructure for monitoring itself.

Richard gazed over the Mall, seeking out Omar Koss. He felt certain that Omar was already here, watching him. Koss lived and breathed surveillance and covert activities; he would not be seen until he wanted to be seen.

Richard huddled in his coat and strolled to Abe's Greek Doric temple. Few tourists had braved the nasty weather, one reason he'd chosen this place to meet. Abraham Lincoln gazed into the modern world with calm, steely resolve. Like an ordinary tourist, Richard began to read the Gettysburg Address etched into the marble walls.

"We agreed to meet on the steps," Koss said from behind him. He had approached with predatory silence. Cool as a cobra. His silence was positively unnerving.

"I didn't like being in the wind," Richard answered, hating the whininess of his answer. He used a blank expression mask the unease he felt from being in the other man's presence.

"Surveillance cameras are all over the place," Koss replied, stepping alongside him.

Richard risked a glance. Koss had an elegant, granite-sculpted face with a hawkish nose and an exotic hooded slant to his eyes that reminded Richard of shark's eyes. He was a big, solid guy who even in jeans and layered shirts and coats managed to convey supreme strength, like he could effortless destroy anyone or anything in his path. His true identity was something of a mystery; not even Richard, with all the world's resources at his fingertips, had been able to derive a complete and satisfactory answer to that issue. Mullinax smelled ex-spook or commando on him, but from what agency, he couldn't even hazard a guess. Presently, Koss operated his own intelligence service, the products of which he sold to whomever would pay the highest price. He had a network of buyers and sellers all over the globe. Anything you wanted, he could provide. Nukes, diamonds, babies, weapons, blackmail material. He was the middleman, making money on every transaction.

Koss said, "Let's walk."

They strolled down the steps and continued down the pathway toward the Washington Memorial obelisk. The flags around the monument snapped in a sudden gust of stiff wind. Beyond that, the white marble cupola of the US Capitol loomed like an accusation.

"There's been a complication," Koss said. "The kid … my partner had to neutralize him."

Richard winced. The first stirrings of genuine concern began low in his gut. There were not supposed to be any "neutralizations." Killing people would bring scrutiny—the one thing that Richard must avoid.

"The bad news …"

"There's more?" Richard blurted.

Koss continued as if he hadn't interrupted. "He told someone else what he'd discovered. I heard him on the phone taps."

Richard's stomach began to cramp. "Just … take care of it," he said.

"I will. But the person he told is Fallon Hughes. Considering this is somewhat more complicated than we planned, I want a bigger cut. Twenty-five percent."

Richard, stunned to silence, risked another sidelong glance. He could not fathom what Koss was implying. That he was planning to kill the daughter of the president-elect? Ridiculous. Only Omar Koss was crazy enough to even conceive of a project so reckless, stupid, and audacious.

It was possible this was all a ruse to squeeze him for more money. In fact, the more he considered it, that seemed the strongest possible explanation. Richard answered with forced confidence. "No way."

Koss shrugged, the movement emphasizing his big shoulders. "Suit yourself."

The consequences of being discovered were so great that Mullinax wondered which was worse: a twenty-five percent cut of half a billion dollars or going away to prison for life. They didn't hang people for treason anymore, he didn't think. He didn't want to find out. "Okay," he growled.

Koss did not reply, but Richard knew he was pleased. Koss thrived on money and violence. He was like an animal, a base creature whose only method of survival was to eat what it killed. He was as cold and logical as actuarial tables.

"I will call you at the end of the week," Koss said. Then for the first time, a smile crept into his voice: "To collect."

THREE

Collin Whitcomb had passed the late afternoon in anonymity, staying out of shopping centers, government buildings and other places where surveillance cameras were common. Not that he expected anyone to be searching for him, but he was a little anxious. Nothing wrong with being a little extra careful. He'd meandered through the Virginia suburbs—at the speed limit—checking the rearview mirror for cops. He eventually found himself at a quiet bar in Falls Church, where he'd finally mustered the courage to call Omar Koss.

He'd spent the last two drinks trying to anticipate what to say to Koss when he finally got here and was no closer to an answer. He glanced up at the television suspended over the skyline of liquor bottles where CNN was featuring a story about Preston Taylor Hughes. The footage of the president-elect hadn't ceased since November, and Collin was sick of looking at his cheesy campaign smile. He was tall and trim, with a full head of brown hair and calm blue eyes. He had that way of speaking that made every person feel as if he were speaking directly to them. News commentators said he was one of the best public speakers in decades, but Collin rolled his eyes at all the platitudes. That Americans ate this guy up spoke to their intelligence—or rather, lack of it.

He focused as Fallon Hughes briefly appeared on the screen with her mother and father. The wide-eyed girl glanced at the camera and stepped back awkwardly, as if the cameras surprised her.

The young president-elect was now in front of a lectern, showing some of the easy charm that had won the election. With that smooth confidence you just knew he'd never had a moment's doubt about his own ability. No sleepless nights wondering if he really was up for the job of being President of the United States. He seemed born for the role. He spoke extemporaneously, with calm certainty. Collin read the closed captioning.

"It is my hope and intention that the United States will continue to improve relations with Russia, but under my leadership, the United States will not be held hostage to any regime anywhere in the world."

The news anchor returned. "Despite assurances from President Ballard that the US was dedicated to diplomacy, tensions between the US and Russia continued to mount today when the president-elect said that Russia must cease supplying Iran with nuclear materials. Moscow's reply was less than reassuring. The Russian foreign minister said that Washington was provoking Russia and any display of force would be met with force. This could signal two different strategies with dealing with both Russia and Middle East, a possibility that concerns some experts."

One "concerned expert" spoke for a few seconds in a monotone that could anesthetize surgery patients about how confusing it must be for Russia to receive two conflicting political agendas. Outgoing President Ballard put his full faith in diplomacy, while the incoming president-elect, a rock-ribbed Republican, had begun to talk openly of "stopping the threat with direct action."

Screw that, Collin thought. He wanted to see more pictures of the daughter. Images of her never failed to pique his interest. Prim, even prudish looking, he bet she was a wildcat in bed. The buttoned-up ones always were.

The door opened and with a gust of frigid air, Omar Koss stepped inside. Finally. Collin tried not to look too relieved. He was dressed like an American in jeans and a sweater. Collin was clothed similarly to avoid notice, but it still seemed odd to see Omar in jeans instead of his Armani suits, handmade Savile Row shirts, and a platinum watch. Claiming the bar stool beside him, Omar ordered a Negro Modelo from the attractive bartendress. Another American affectation, and one that Collin could not bring himself to commit; he chose a dignified Irish whiskey.

The bartendress slid the beer across the bar with a little smile.

Koss didn't acknowledge the friendliness. He stared at her coldly until she turned away and busied herself behind the bar.

"I'm delivering the map of the keys to Europe tonight. After today's mistake, we can't wait."

Though he tried to suppress all reaction, like Omar himself, Collin felt annoyed by the rebuke in Koss's words. Collin was, after all, a professional; he felt no guilt for what he had been forced to do this afternoon to that kid. He had foolishly hoped Koss might be pleased, ebullient even, that he had so masterfully handled such an enormous problem. He had been forced to think quickly; the improvised death of Antoine Campbell had seemed both efficient and elegant. Why didn't Koss appreciate it?

Collin lifted his whiskey, holding it under his nose for a second. "You're delivering the map of the keys yourself?" He sensed a lie in Koss's words, though he would never confront him directly. He swallowed the shot, enjoying the fire on the way down, then set his empty glass on the bar. Only then did he dare regard him directly. Koss's blue eyes were so pale they were nearly the color of water. Collin involuntarily shivered, despite the soothing heat from the whiskey.

"This is important enough to handle myself."

"What about the Hughes girl?"

"I'll take care of her when I return from Europe."

"Why wait?"

"Because I want to do it myself," Koss replied with ice in his voice.

Collin shifted his gaze back to the television. Did Koss think it was too big a task for him? Was he losing confidence in Collin's ability? The possibility angered and frightened Collin. His inability to ask Koss directly shamed him.

They drank in silence, and after a short time Omar slid off the bar stool and then dropped a hundred dollar bill on the bar. Wordlessly, he left.

Collin stared after him, wondering how someone could

be so utterly inhuman. His cryptic silences and cold, deliberate demeanor were terrifying because Collin knew it wasn't an act, like some suburban guy's interpretation of a badass. It was real. *Psychopath* was the word that rocketed to mind.

Frankly he wasn't sure Koss had his priorities straight. Fallon Hughes knew about the map of the keys; that was a certifiable emergency in Collin's view. He considered calling Koss back to argue the point but stopped himself. Koss had no appreciation for what he had done, and it was likely he would have no appreciation for what he knew must do about Fallon Hughes.

FOUR

Fallon Hughes sliced through the warm blue water, her breath coming in deep, fast gasps. She gripped the ledge of the pool and flipped on the return lap, glimpsing the athletic figure of Gwen Atwell in the lane beside her. Gwen was suddenly half a body ahead—Fallon could match Gwen's arm strokes but not her perfect leg kicks. Fallon pulled herself through the water, struggling to stay even.

Fallon and Gwen had been friends since they were children in Montana. Their long friendship had survived the period when Gwen, one year older, had left for medical school in D.C. and Fallon stayed on at law school on the West Coast. As they grew older, the differences between them became more marked; they could exasperate each other. Gwen, older by almost a year, enjoyed bossing Fallon about offering professional advice, sometimes relationship advice, though that, admittedly, had not been required lately. Work subsumed any possibility of dating, and she just wasn't very good at it anyway. Her discomfort only intensified when her father began his run for the presidency.

Fallon was amused by Gwen's big sister act and tolerated it—to a point. Each retained an obstinate and unshakable love for the other.

Since she had not seen Gwen in over two weeks, Fallon had agreed despite intense fatigue to join her for an early morning swim at the club. Gwen promised that after an hour in the pool, she would feel featherlight, invigorated, refreshed, and ready to take on the world. The promise of ecstasy was the only thing that kept her going because after another late night at Johnson Sloan Pruitt, she was exhausted. She stayed until after 10 p.m., trying to compensate for her hour at the coffee shop yesterday.

By the time she got home, she was jazzed from the adrenaline of seeing Tom again and starving but too tired to eat. She collapsed on the bed and was asleep within seconds.

Cameron Chapman, her midnight-to-six agent, was standing near the doors. Except for the Secret Service, they had the whole pool to themselves. All the smart people were still in bed. Warm and cozy under mountains of blankets and cottony-soft sheets with nary an alarm clock anywhere in sight. Sleep porn, Fallon called it. Lust for the one thing she could not have.

When she reached the opposite end of the pool, she was unsurprised to see Gwen had beaten her.

"You okay?" Gwen asked, teasing her, challenging her fitness.

Fallon rolled her eyes. "Unlike you, I am a busy woman with precious little time for swimming practice."

Gwen playfully splashed her. "Ten more laps. Let's make it count."

Fallon lined up at the wall. "Ready."

"Set," Gwen said.

Together they chanted, "Go," and vaulted for the other side.

At the end of the ten laps, with a last mighty heave of breath, Fallon touched the edge of the pool and lifted off her goggles. She was startled to see Tom Bishop talking with Cameron Chapman. Even before the sun was up, Tom looked ready for action. Somehow, he managed to project athleticism even in a formal dark business suit. Tom acknowledged Fallon with a polite smile, then turned his attention back to Cameron.

It was going to be a long while before she got used to seeing him around.

Fallon had not yet had a moment to talk to Gwen about Tom. She didn't know how to bring it up anyway. She'd been too embarrassed to mention him when she returned heartbroken from Greece, so Gwen didn't know about the disastrous affair four years ago that had left her reeling. Small mercy.

Fallon climbed out of the pool, acutely aware that she was nearly naked in front of him and that he seemed to not care less; his focus was intently on Cameron Chapman. Fallon picked up a towel from the chair where she'd placed flip-flops and white terrycloth robes for herself and Gwen.

"I'm going home to shower and change. Do you want a ride to the hospital?"

"Yes, please," Gwen said, savoring a glance at Tom Bishop, still chatting with Cameron. Under her breath she uttered, "Yes, I definitely would like a ride to the hospital."

Fallon rolled her eyes. Gwen was engaged; shouldn't pre-marital women have more control? "No sense walking in the cold and dark when there's a nice warm car, right?" Gwen smiled.

And it *was* cold. Snow was forecasted late tonight; the air was black and pure as menthol in the lungs. The two women piled into the backseat of the SUV with their gym bags and purses, grateful for the instant, luxurious warmth of the leather seats. The drive to George Washington University Hospital took only two minutes. Agent Rowland drove the truck directly to the emergency room entrance. Gwen gathered her belongings and jumped out. "I'll call you later," she said and slammed the door shut.

As soon as Gwen was inside the electronic double doors, Fallon's phone buzzed, indicating a text. Fallon fished it out and read: OMG, HE IS PISTOL HOT!

No kidding, Fallon mentally answered as she put the phone away.

Presently, the motorcade arrived at Fallon's redbrick building on K Street in the riverfront sector of Georgetown. It was a new building set in an old, stately community of patrician doctors and lawyers and lobbyists. At this hour, the neighborhood was dead silent, dark, and with damp cobblestone streets looked like a place from a different, gaslit era. Fallon pulled the robe tighter around her body and stepped outside with Cameron, who would walk with her to her door to make sure she was safe. Intense halogen headlights of the follow-up SUV illuminated her in the dark morning. She blinked back toward the limo as she hefted her gym bag onto her shoulder, able to make out the silhouettes of the agents—one of which was Tom Bishop—in the front seats. It was nice to have a fantasy, she thought, and walked inside.

After a hot shower, Fallon filled a teakettle with water from the tap and placed it on the stove. Waiting for it to boil, she set out the milk and searched for the tin of chocolate biscotti in her larder she'd bought last time she was in Italy.

She'd like to go again, one day. She missed her travels.

Engrossed in preparing breakfast, she nearly missed it. Something uttered on the television in the living room snapped her attention. It took only a second—a satellite uplink pause—for the name Antoine Campbell to penetrate her erotic daydreamy memories about Tom Bishop. She wandered into the living room, upping the volume with the remote, but the live action segment was finished and the newscasters were back in the studio.

"A terrible tragedy, Plymouth," the blond news anchor said.

The male counterpart nodded in agreement. "Indeed, Greer. Up next, Dr. Marge tells us the extraordinary story of treating a woman for breast cancer, only to learn it was her own birth mother."

Fallon switched channels, hoping to catch the name again. The story had evaporated.

She sat down at her computer and navigated to the television station's website. On the right column of the screen, beside a headline announcing president-elect Hughes would be visiting Walter Reed Medical Center today, was a list of local headlines:

Big Rig Falls Off Freeway Ramp, Killing 3
Caught On Camera: Man Takes Toddler To Robbery
After High-Speed Chase, District Man Commits Suicide

Her breath suddenly a little restricted, Fallon clicked the last link and read.

Antoine Campbell, 22, committed suicide yesterday in Washington, D.C., witnessed by midday crowds. After a high-speed chase through Southern Maryland, Mr. Campbell drove to the corner of M Street and 21st Street, where he abandoned his vehicle, then ran into a skyscraper where he leaped to his death. Witnesses say he was yelling incoherently at the time he leapt.

"He was being pulled over for a routine traffic violation but he refused to stop," said a source familiar with the case, who spoke on the condition of anonymity. It was learned that methamphetamines and an ounce of marijuana were found in his vehicle after his suicide.

The suicide occurred at about two o'clock, police said.

If the early morning swim had calmed her and grounded her firmly into the sockets of her own body, this news unraveled the work. She was alarmed and unnerved, trying to make sense of the report while Antoine Campbell's desperate voice reverberated in her skull. *They're going to kill me.*

The sun had not yet risen over the Potomac when Fallon arrived at Johnson Sloan Pruitt, yet the office was busy as if midday. A pile of phone messages and emails had accumulated overnight, but Fallon ignored them and Googled the name "Antoine Campbell." Finding three more local news articles about the suicide, she was dismayed to see that each was a repeat of the original Associated Press story with no new details. That was odd. If the story was big enough for the AP, why wasn't it big enough for some enterprising local journalist to dig into?

Fallon began to gnaw her bottom lip. The shock and disbelief had begun to fade, leaving her acutely aware of her own emotional center, a deep reservoir inside her, filling with nervous guilt. *What more could I have done?* The fact that the answer was *nothing* offered no comfort.

She slouched in her seat and looked at her phone, foolishly willing it to ring with Antoine Campbell the other end, telling her it was a hoax or a mistake or something. Shutting her eyes, she could hear his voice again. *They're going to kill me.*

Glancing at the clock on her computer screen, she figured she had at least two hours before her boss, Sam Cahill, arrived and her day became devoted to the hedge fund case. Now or never. She pulled on her coat and scarf and walked into to Tom's office.

Seeing him sitting at the desk made her heart kick up a notch. He looked so in control of himself and everything around him. She wished she felt that calm. She operated at a very high frequency, naturally uptight and anxious. It would be nice to simply know, in her bones, that she could handle whatever life threw her way.

"Miss Hughes," he said amiably.

"Good morning. First, call the limos please. Second, I need to talk to you."

"Sure," he replied and called the limos using the radio. "Avalon is departing; line up the cars." Avalon. She liked her code name, she supposed, but found it a little silly how they named the First Family like pets.

He smiled at her sweetly, as if he were a servant waiting for her next order. "And what would you like to talk to me about?"

"The guy I was going to meet, Antoine Campbell, killed himself yesterday afternoon while we were waiting for him at the coffee shop."

Tom's face registered mute surprise. His lips settled into a firm straight line and gravity darkened his eyes.

"I heard it on the news this morning," Fallon continued uncertainly. "Maryland State Police were chasing him and he leaped to his death just three blocks north of us. But that's not really ... I don't think that's what really happened. I didn't tell you everything yesterday. Tom, he told me he was being chased. He said they were going to kill him."

"Who?"

"He wouldn't tell me. He said that Richard Mullinax was giving away the map of the keys. Do you know what that means? Map of the keys?"

"Never heard of it," Tom replied.

"Well, he was panicked. He said they were going to kill him. That was why I agreed to meet him. He sounded so scared."

"Why did he call you? Had you ever met him before?"

"No, I never met him and I have no idea why he called me. But I felt strongly that it was a legitimate call, not a hoax or ... whatever."

"So he called you, said someone was going to kill him, and then he killed himself while we were waiting for him ..."

Fallon shook her head. "He didn't kill himself," she said, surprised at the conviction in her voice. The fear in Antoine Campbell's voice, and barely controlled hysteria, came to her again clearly, clanging in her skull. She'd never forget that sound, however much she would pray to. "I heard his voice. He was desperate for help. He was not suicidal. He said they were going to kill him, that they were chasing him."

Tom's scowling gaze was solidly fixed on her, seemingly with undivided attention. The angular planes of his face made her think of arrogance, but arrogance born from pure, cold competence. She admired that quality. His fair-mindedness was admirable, but it was also frustrating; he was not cheerleading her. The impartial observer was allowing her to figure this out herself, which, she supposed, was the appropriate role of a Secret Service agent assigned to protect her.

He pressed his fingers to his earpiece, then looked at her. "The limos are ready for you downstairs."

The building where Antoine Campbell leaped to his death was adjacent to the Four Seasons Hotel. It was a six-story historic building of red brick and shining windows; a Chase Bank branch occupied the ground floor.

From the backseat Fallon said, "Stop here, please. I want to walk."

The SUV stopped and Tom jumped out, glanced down the street with his Death Glare, then determining there was no immediate threat, opened her door. Fallon stepped out, scanning the front of the building, relieved there was no lurid blood or gore marking Antoine Campbell's death on the snow-specked sidewalk. In fact, there was no tarp or police tape. Nothing at all remained of the man who had leapt to his death in this very location only seventeen hours previous. It seemed unreal, except for the faintly buzzing sadness in her chest that confirmed it had really happened; he had called; he had pleaded with her to help.

Fallon proceeded inside and to the elevators.

"Miss Hughes, may I ask what you are hoping to find here?" Tom asked, unerringly polite as always.

"I don't know." She nursed an irrational hope she would find a note or something that would confirm Antoine Campbell was crazy and his suicide had nothing whatsoever to do with pernicious people following him, tapping his phone, and some mysterious thing called *map of the keys*.

They rode up to the top floor, which was dominated by a glitzy international law firm. Fallon and Tom walked toward the red exit sign at the extremity of the hall. There was no access to the roof. At the other side of the hallway, they were confronted by the same problem: it was impossible to get up to the roof.

Puzzled, Fallon tossed up her hands. "What in the world?"

"Fallon—Miss Hughes—I wasn't sure at first but now I am. I was on the advance team when the Vice President visited an office in this building two years ago. The blueprint for the building showed there were escape routes on every floor except this one. I remember it because it threw the advance team into havoc trying to figure out how to get him out of the building in case of emergency."

Fallon suddenly grinned. "You are so bloody useful."

As they exited the elevator one level below, they walked to the end of the hall to the exit sign. Opening the door, Tom presented a narrow metal ladder welded to the wall that led to the sixth floor. Behind that, in a narrow crawlspace, a ladder went all the way to the roof.

Fallon mused aloud, "How would Antoine Campbell know about a secret pipeline from the fifth floor to the roof?"

"I'm wondering the same thing."

"If police were chasing him, they would have stopped him on the sixth floor and he'd never have jumped."

"Maybe he had some connection to the building," Tom said, his voice low and thoughtful.

Fallon adjusted the purse on her shoulder and stepped up to the rungs.

"Hold on," Tom said, and lightly gripped her by the waist.

Fallon yelped with surprise as he effortlessly lifted her off the ladder and set her on terra firma, leaving her a little giddy from the unexpected contact.

"I'll check it out," he said.

Fallon watched him climb the ladder, admiring his body in action. At the top, he pushed open the hatch roof. A wedge of gray sky appeared over Tom's head. "All clear."

Fallon climbed up and emerged on the roof. The strange perspective of the city rooftops spread out before her was exhilarating. The Gothic spire of the National Cathedral glimmered through the low clouds to the west. The rest of the city looked strangely anonymous—a grid of grayness.

Fallon walked to the edge of the roof and looked down at the vertex where M and 22nd Streets met. A queue of yellow taxis was shockingly bright in the pale pearl-gray morning light. Around the corner, her two glossy, bulky black limos were idling.

This is where Antoine Campbell would have jumped, from this very spot. Relatively speaking, the distance down didn't seem too terrible. Curiously, if Antoine Campbell had chosen to cross the street, he would have been able to jump from one of the District's few actual skyscrapers—the Verizon Building. Jumping from that building would have been much more certain to cause death than the relatively short six stories of this building. Fallon studied the cell antennae on the roof of the Verizon building. In addition to the height, it was also newer than this one, meaning it would have a modern fire code, one where the top floor would lead directly to the roof.

A dark certainty passed over Fallon. Tiny pinprick tears stung her eyes. She looked to Tom. His expression was soft and compassionate and she felt that he knew it too, that the truth had somehow been shown to them both in that instant.

"Somebody ... did that to him ...." Her voice was a trembling wisp.

Tom's lips tightened into a grim line.

"Come here," she said. "Look."

Tom shook his head.

A slow, bitter smile touched her lips. "I remember. You're

afraid of heights."

He looked at her evenly—reading her mind, she thought. Fallon felt her face heat, embarrassed to have mentioned her past knowledge of him, which opened up the subject that both were politely avoiding.

A dry, kind smile of acknowledgement came to his lips. He reached for her arm, gently urging her from the edge of the rooftop. "Come on."

Fallon stepped away from the edge. She wrapped her coat tighter around her body, trying to fight the cold and confusion.

"You got two calls yesterday."

Fallon blinked in surprise, jostled by his businesslike words. "Pardon?"

"At the coffee shop, you said there were two calls. One from your friend Gwen and another. Do you still have the message on your phone?"

"Yes, but it recorded just dead air."

"We can send your phone to Electronic Crimes. The geeks might be able to get some info from that. Maybe a number, maybe the origin of the call if it was made from a cell."

She shrugged. "Would they do that?"

"Someone who said he was in imminent danger of being killed called my protectee, then he dies under mysterious circumstances. That puts you in danger."

"I'm not in danger," she replied lightly. She found the whole Secret Service apparatus a little absurd; she was a struggling attorney—not a political operative. She still bristled when she wanted to jog and they were right behind her or when she went shopping with Gwen and they were just out of her peripheral vision. She didn't feel like anyone's "protectee," though she was amused to find herself in that role with Tom. It felt like an act. Antoine Campbell's death might have been wicked, but she felt too far removed from it to be in any actual peril.

"It's my job to decide when you are in danger," Tom said sharply.

She was taken aback by his seriousness. In that moment she saw a glimpse of his real life, the life she had not been able to see in Paxos. He cared about his job, obviously, but so did all of her other agents. Tom cared somewhat uniquely, she thought. He cared with a particular intensity, and it stoked her curiosity.

He was very near. His green eyes were intense, concentrated full of distances and heat. *Yep, I am in danger. Code Red. DEFCON 5.* But it had nothing to do with Antoine Campbell. It had to do with the man whose job was to protect her.

She felt herself becoming dangerously close to overstepping her boundaries and asking him straightforwardly what he remembered about her in Paxos, if she ever meant anything to him. It was a curse, her inability to hide her emotions—or even control them very well. But to ask would be to open herself to the possibility she really did not want to face: that he had simply not cared about her the way she had about him.

She looked away, suddenly frustrated with herself and with Tom Bishop. How absurd that she should feel guilty for wanting some clarification about what happened between them.

"Miss Hughes ..."

"Stop it," she said with sudden force. Adrenaline pumped through her. "Stop the *Miss Hughes* and *Avalon* and *Ma'am* stuff. You know who I am."

He looked surprised by her outburst, and it gratified her. His stoicism had a crack.

"I want you to relate to me as a human being, not a protectee," she continued in a rush. "This is weird for me and I'm sure it is for you too. There aren't any social rules for this territory. But it would be easier if we just acknowledged that we know each other from ... from before. You don't have to pretend you care about me ... you just ..."

A wash of pink appeared under his cheekbones, and she was pretty sure it wasn't from embarrassment though she couldn't tell what he was feeling. His jaw tightened. A cord in his throat twitched. She'd slalomed right over the line. Touched that sensitive bruise that existed between them. The Past. Paxos. It was her chance though. If she didn't just get it out in the open it would antagonize her forever.

"We should at least be ... friends," she finished lamely.

He did not reply. His gaze was cold and level. Back to the stoic Robot Man, his de facto state. He couldn't even stomach the thought of being friends? Stunned, Fallon forced herself to mimic him, remaining perfectly still, looking back at him with what she thought was proud impassiveness to disguise the acute disappointment that caused her heart to accelerate and tears to pinch the corners of her eyes.

He glanced behind her, then met her gaze again. "I cared about you back then." The words came out in a halting whisper. Everything about him seemed reluctant, restrained. "I still do. I have to ... maintain ... some sort of ..." His voice trailed off and he looked out toward the dramatic spire of the National Cathedral in the silky gray sky. Fallon stood quite still, watching him, trying to ignore and control the welling wave of expectation that was struggling to break through her feeble emotional ramparts. He swung his gaze back to her. "I have to maintain some formality. For work."

"Why?"

His green gaze met hers levelly. The Siberian wilderness flickered with signs of life. "You know why."

Shots of light began to dance in her mind. Yes, she did know why—she knew it instinctively. He still felt it too: the wild, ungovernable attraction between them. In his indirect way, he was acknowledging it—confessing his feelings. The sudden shock of elation nearly knocked her to her knees. She wanted to dance. To laugh. She had to think of something to say but had no idea what it might be. She looked into his eyes and saw the old unmistakable longing there, the raw emotion, and before she could say anything, her body answered for her. She stepped closer and pressed her lips to his.

Worst idea ever. But oh God, he could not stop kissing her. How had he lived this long without having something this good? After the initial shock of the sweet contact, his body shifted gears, plunging into overdrive. Her lips were silky soft, yielding to him instantly as he deepened the kiss. She tasted as luscious as he remembered—like vanilla. Delicious and sweet. She felt even better. Soft and warm and scrumptious all pressed up against him.

His inner resistance was gone, demolished in a torrent of kisses and searching hands.

At the worst possible time. Not that he was in much of a position to care at the moment because for the first time in four years, every single one of his cells was vibrantly, fully alive.

Fallon pulled back, her blue eyes dazzled, color high on her cheeks like a child with fever. Her glossy blonde hair whipped back in the wind. So heartcrackingly beautiful. She was shaking violently and he wanted to embrace her, to share the heat boiling under the surface of his skin, but she resisted. She met his gaze squarely, then slowly, deliberately placed her shaking hand over the massive bulge in the crotch of his pants. Her eyes slightly widened and her breath caught in her throat. "Oh God … Tom …"

Pleasure licked up his nerve endings, swirling and spiraling through him. Some dim voice in the recesses of his mind valiantly urged him save himself. Remove her hand. Protect the life he'd created for himself—the stark independence that he'd come to treasure more than even love or intimacy. But the voice was getting smaller until it was only a faint, indiscriminate din in the cacophony.

Fallon gently scraped her fingernails up the length of his cock; even through the barrier of his clothes, it nearly brought him to his knees. It had been a long time since he had felt this out of control of his own body and yet so fully inside his own body, so aware of every breath, every nerve ending being stroked and teased. He couldn't think about anything but getting her in bed. Didn't even have to be in bed. A wall, a floor, anything. Just needed to be melded against her soft, strong body. Inside her. It was thirty fucking degrees out and he was burning up. He could vaporize the polar caps like this.

"You have three seconds," he said levelly.

A smile teased the corner of her mouth. "Three seconds for what?"

He didn't trust his voice.

"One," Fallon breathed softly against his chin. "Two." She lifted her face and pressed her juicy pink lips to his, then dragged the kiss down his jaw to his neck. Her velvety warmth felt like a luxury he shouldn't be able to afford. Fallon pulled back, a little breathless, and met his gaze candidly. Her teasing smile vanished. "Three."

For a moment nothing happened. Then Tom grasped her wrist and firmly removed her hand from his groin.

An expression of mortification swam across her pretty features. She pinched her lips together and tears sprang her eyes.

"Come on," Tom said.

"Oh my God," Fallon whispered. Humiliated, she hid her face with her hands.

"Come on." He grabbed her elbow and edged her toward the exit.

Tom climbed down, ensured there was no ambush lying in wait, and then signaled for her to come down. Careful in her high heels, Fallon delicately climbed down and then stepped into vestibule with him. It was warm down here, and private. Not quite private enough to fall apart though. She struggled to bury the embarrassment at having thrown herself at a man who really, *really* didn't want her. Her lips were trembling. She could not meet his intent gaze.

Tom crowded her, so her back was against the ladder. Only then did she look up at him, the hope and light coming back into her huge cobalt eyes. That naked vulnerability crushed him. *Don't look at me like that*, he wanted to plead with her, but in the next instant, the words no longer existed anywhere in the world because he pressed his lips to hers.

Heat leaped and flared between them on contact, like throwing gasoline on a fire. The kiss was wild, out of control. Fallon was moaning beneath him, crushing her strong, small trembling body against his in her innocent eagerness. Her fragrance and female sweetness were intoxicating, sucking him in to a storm of sensations that felt shocking and new. It was like everything before this moment had been in black and white, and now there was color and flavor and texture.

Abruptly, he pressed his face to her neck, smelling the light, soapy, clean fragrance of her skin and wrapping thick silky locks of her blonde hair around his fist, then pulling her head back so her smooth white neck was totally exposed to him. He kissed her jugular with sudden gentleness, loving the fragrant, pulsing warmth against his lips and the way she sighed and whispered, "Yessss." His hungry mouth moved lower, to the swell of her cleavage, and he pressed desperate kisses to the soft flesh. In those demi-cup bras she wore, it was like her breasts were being offered up to him—a thought that pleased him very much. He began to kiss lower, licking and sucking the erect nipple over the lace of her white bra. Fallon arched her back, pushing herself toward him. Then, with a finger, she slid the cup down, exposing her pink-tipped breast to him.

Perfect, soft, bouncy tits. Absolutely stunning. Magnificent. His heart thudded in his chest as he nuzzled into her, then eagerly took a petal-soft nipple between his lips.

Fallon's hands fumbled at the button of his pants. In the next second, he felt her reach into his black briefs, and her small, warm hand gripped the iron club that was his cock. The sensation was shocking—almost blinding. He grew even thicker in her hand, fearful that he would not be able to control himself. "Oh God …" he groaned desperately into her ear. "What are we doing?"

"I have to," she said quickly, like it had become a matter of life and death that she have him.

"You deserve better … this is a … closet …." The last shredded strands of good sense were thrumming, about to sever. If she didn't have the presence of mind to stop them and demand better—a bed, for instance—it was going to happen. Against his better judgment. Against every precept he'd erected for himself. Against all odds.

"I want this. Now. Please. Please …." She slid her hand over the shaft of his cock and began to pump in slow, methodical strokes that felt absolutely fucking fantastic. "I swear I won't ask for more. Just this."

He swallowed her words, catching her lush lips with his. His palms slid up the impossibly smooth, soft skin of her thighs until her skirt was bunched over her hips. Tom blindly felt the soaked crotch of the panties, drawing out a moan of pleasure from them both. Fallon needed to be treated gently, but he could no longer be gentle. The new life he'd built based on rigid control and strict denial of all pleasure was a far, distant shore. He'd gone into combat mode. Adrenaline was pumping, and out of control lust was focused entirely on her. Both panting, their bodies were pressed together, hell-bent on fusion.

"Take 'em off," Fallon breathed, her mouth still grinding against his. "Just pull 'em down."

Tom took her at her word and peeled the panties down over her hips, so they fell onto the cold cement. Fallon shifted to step out of them, kicking them aside with her witchy looking stilettos. Tom slid his hand between their bodies to the plush wetness of her cunt, and he slid two fingers inside. Fallon shook violently, welcoming him with hot, wet, squeezing slickness. "God, yes," she muttered against his mouth.

Fallon shoved his pants and underwear down. He no longer cared where they were; he just had to be inside her. Desperately and urgently, with a keen focus he'd never known before. Effortlessly he lifted Fallon and shoved her against the wall. She wrapped her legs around his waist. The engorged head of his cock slid against the hot wetness. The contact was electric. With a slow, gentle thrust, he slid the head of his cock inside and they both froze. Fallon's abs contracted with the shock of his smooth entry. She tightened around him eagerly, her arms and legs holding him tightly. Trembling with his own effort to hold himself in check, he kissed her again and slid all the way home.

Oh, God. Nothing could have prepared him for it. Not memories, not wishes. For one blazingly beautiful moment the past evaporated—only this existed. Fallon's heart fluttering and pounding in her chest, her soft, hitching breath, her thin arms around his neck, soft lips trembling against his. She was so exquisitely soft and slick and sweet that he felt like tears might well up in his eyes. Unacceptable. His body jerked and he buried his face in her neck to hide his expression from her; he didn't want her to see just how lost he was. He began to pound inside her. Hot, hard, deep strokes that were only possible because she was so wet. She was kissing his face, kissing his mouth, breathing half-muttered words that could be prayers or curses, but which he finally realized were his name. Over and over again.

Oblivious to everything but her own careering pleasure, Fallon cried out, and Tom, with the very last vestige of sanity, covered her mouth with his so they wouldn't be heard somewhere out there in the real world. As her tongue touched his, he felt his own inevitable orgasm, which he'd been fighting for what felt like hours, days, years, well up with impossible intensity. He could no longer tell if it was an emotional or physical sensation. Too intense for mere pleasure. Sheer piercing pleasure shot through with terror. When it thundered through him, it felt like a rolling avalanche. All the memories, the missing four years of unanswered desire wrenched everything out of him. It was like running a marathon. In the emptiness formed a great gathering peace that left him dazed and exhausted.

When he came to, Fallon was gently kissing his face, stroking his hair. He willed his heart to slow from the frenzied gallop. He locked his knees by sheer force of will and let his weight prop their shaking, sweating bodies against the wall. Slowly he eased out of the hot clasp of her body, not quite ready for the contact to end but aware of the clock ticking. She staggered to the ladder, and her head flopped backward against the hard rungs, as if she didn't have the strength to hold it upright.

Tom cringed. "You okay?"

She laughed a low, giggly laugh. "I am fucking amazing."

She looked amazing. Her face was flushed pink and gold. Her new complicated hairstyle was mussed the way he liked it. Her skirt was hitched up over her hips, the pink lips of her pussy visible. Come dripped between her pale, shapely thighs.

"No condom," he said. He didn't carry them—he had no reason to since he'd given up sex.

"Pill," she replied.

Tom began to pull up his pants and try to force himself

into some semblance of a normal mindset. He noticed Fallon's pretty mauve panties on the floor and handed them to her.

"I could stay like this forever," she said silkily.

"We're in an office building," he reminded her, only half joking.

Fallon giggled and worked on getting herself together, stepping into her panties, pulling down her skirt.

Tom waited, tensing, for the self-hatred to come back, for the countersurge of disgust he expected. It was like he'd made a deal with himself that he only just now acknowledged—in order to pay for breaking his own rules, he'd live with the inevitable regret and disgust and rage for not being able to exert control over himself.

But the disgust didn't come. He felt only great, sweeping peace.

At least for a moment.

He had felt that sweet, searing sense of well-being on Paxos after making love with Fallon … but the darkness would creep up on him, tackle him when he wasn't looking.

He expected the same thing to happen. Maybe not right this minute, but soon … and much worse. Here, he had to see her every day. She was his job.

Remember this, he told himself. *Remember this feeling because you will have to live on it for the rest of your life.*

Fallon pat her hair into its normal smooth arrangement and affected a neutral facial expression. "How do I look?"

She looked like a beautiful woman who had just been extravagantly loved by a man. She glowed. Roses bloomed in her cheeks. Everything about her was soft and happy. "You are the most perfect thing I've ever seen," he replied honestly.

The pink in Fallon's cheeks deepened with embarrassment, which he found endearing. "I meant my clothes. Do I look normal? I feel like I must look like a disaster."

"You look great," he said. "You ready?"

She nodded and then in an awkward, adorable gesture, she grabbed his hand and squeezed it. After what they'd just done, the action felt unbearably intimate. He smiled at her and then opened the door, her hand naturally dropping his as they entered society once again.

Did that really happen? In the state of blissful shock in the backseat of the SUV, Fallon's head was dazed and her body pulsed as if Tom touched her still. She felt the wetness between her legs and shut her eyes, reliving every sensual, crazy, frantic second of it. Oh yes. It was very real.

She felt precious after being deprived of human contact for so long. Her crazy parents, the brutal, exhausting campaign and constant media scrutiny, her brother—the constant fight between love and guilt that she struggled with every day over him—and her career that demanded more than she had. It felt depleted, like she was stalled, perpetually running behind, being buried beneath the garbage of her own life. She barely had five minutes in any given day for herself. But this ... this was just for her. Sex with Tom served no greater purpose; it was not meant to assuage any lingering guilt or accomplish anything practical. It was a marvelously selfish act.

And it had felt *so fucking marvelous*. She'd not felt anything like it since Paxos. Not just the exquisitely sharp pleasure which left her weak but the connection, being seen and chosen and cherished by another human being.

Paxos intensified that emotional aspect—the act had a patina of familiarity, of completion. Maybe reconciliation. Not that she harbored hopes that they were now a couple—he'd seemed a little standoffish right afterward—but some of the questions had been answered. He had cared about her. He still did. And the sexual *crash-bang-pow* was still fully in effect.

The SUV stopped at the curb in front of her building on G Street. Tom swung open the bulletproof door for her. She stepped out and looked into his face, startled to realize that he was locked into Secret Service mode.

In the elevator, however, he put his hand at her neck and pulled her into him. He kissed her with a savoring sweetness that made her melt against him. "I don't know who I am around you," she murmured softly just as the doors opened.

Tom had no reply, which was just as well because the elevator doors opened.

Fallon straightened her shoulders and forced her face into calm, pleasant blandness, trying to get the sex vibe off her as she strode into her office.

As soon as they were in her office, Adam Johnson appeared in her doorway. This was unprecedented. Adam Johnson was the most senior partner at the firm, the direct descendant of the two-hundred-year-old firm's founder. Fallon had never met him; she recognized him only by the enormous portrait that hung in the grand hallway. The warm, dazzled glow Tom had imparted inside her began to perceptibly cool: Adam's presence could only signify something huge, and possibly awful, and so Fallon attempted to brace herself even as a dull, sick ache lodged itself in her stomach and around her heart.

"Miss Hughes, may I have a word?"

"Of course," she replied, forcing her voice to remain neutral and confident. Meeting Tom's eyes, he discreetly stepped out of her office.

Her spacious office suddenly seemed too small. Fallon felt trapped, like a rat in a cage. Adam Johnson said, "Miss Hughes, while you were on your errand, the police were here to see you."

"The police?"

"Indeed, they executed a search warrant."

"Search warrant? For what?"

"I do not know, Miss Hughes. But I assure you that it was an unpleasant intrusion to the other employees of Johnson Sloan Pruitt."

That was the first moment she understood the police had executed a search warrant on *her office*. Her laptop computer was gone. It had been on her desk this morning and now it was gone. Vanished. Her file cabinet was open, though files were still color coded and in place as far as she could tell in her state of accelerating confusion. "Oh my God," she murmured. She felt like she was sinking. Her legs were dissolving beneath her.

"We have made certain allowances for you, but if you are

involved in some sort of malfeasance, Johnson Sloan Pruitt will not continue to employ you."

She sank into her chair. "Mr. Johnson, I have no idea about any search warrant. I don't understand what is going on. Do you have a copy of the search warrant?"

"I believe they left it in the custody of the office manager, Ingrid Breyer."

"What are they accusing me of?" she asked desperately.

"I do not know."

"Mr. Johnson, I can't imagine what this is about. I've done nothing wrong."

"If I might offer one suggestion, Fallon, you might employ a criminal attorney. As an attorney yourself, I am sure you are aware that once probable cause has been established for a search warrant, an arrest warrant is not far behind."

"I did nothing wrong," Fallon said again, feebly. Her body hurt; every muscle in her body was pulled tight as power lines. Alan Johnson blinked slowly, like a turtle. His patrician bloodlessness set her teeth on edge.

"As I said, Fallon, we will give you a few days to get this straightened out, but we will not continue to employ an attorney who cannot foster trust among our clients."

A fine perimeter of sweat had broken out at her hairline. She feared she might start to cry. Thankfully, before the tears came, Alan Johnson exited Fallon's office. She looked helplessly to Tom as he came inside. "I did nothing wrong, Tom. Nothing."

"Let's find the search warrant and see what you're being accused of."

Fallon's mother had been an actress before she married Preston Taylor Hughes. She had been celebrated in both film and theatre and had won two Academy Awards. It was an inherited ability to act that enabled her to walk calmly through the unnaturally silent office to find Ingrid Breyer.

Since Fallon's first moment of employment at Johnson Sloan Pruitt, Ingrid's response to Fallon had been no more complex than that of bigotry or racism: she hated her on sight. To Fallon, the animus was mystifying. At first she attributed the conflict to political differences since Ingrid was an outspoken, proud Democrat while Fallon was from a Republican family, but that theory was disproved when one of the other associates was seen holding a Rush Limbaugh coffee mug and Ingrid flirted with him like a fourteen-year-old girl. The hostility was very definitely about Fallon Hughes and nothing else.

Fallon found her on the telephone. Ingrid's indifferent gaze flicked over Fallon, dismissed her, and then went back to her phone call. She chuckled softly. "You have no business even considering the idea," Ingrid murmured. "You have such a lovely bosom."

Fallon instantly lost all capacity to fake courtesy. She grabbed the receiver from Ingrid's slack hand and hung up. Bright red splotches appeared in Ingrid's pale cheeks as her eyebrows floated dramatically upward.

"Give me the search warrant," Fallon demanded.

Ingrid stood up. "You have no right—"

"Give me the search warrant," Fallon repeated with ice in her voice.

Ingrid stiffly turned to the credenza behind her and waved it at Fallon. "I am sure Alan has spoken with you …"

Fallon snatched the document from her hands. Ingrid, inflamed for missing an opportunity to milk the moment for all its glorious humiliation, reached for Fallon as if to strike her.

Tom grabbed Ingrid's wrist. "Don't," he said.

Fallon couldn't stay to argue or play games with this office sociopath. She had to get out. Quickly, before the tears came.

Back in Fallon's office, her hands were shaking so violently she kept dropping the warrant. "Calm down," Tom said soothingly. "Do you want me to read it?"

Fallon handed the document to Tom and shut her door.

She could not sit. She could not stand. She paced, finding a little comfort in the nervous movement. A search warrant! It was ridiculous—unthinkable. Her mind reeled at the sheer craziness of it, while at the same time, knowing that no matter how crazy it was, her life would have to be about this now. On top of an insane amount of work and the friction caused by her father's transition into the presidency, she would now have to spend every day defending herself, explaining every decision, and opening her life not only to prosecutors but to the public. Another wave of nausea coursed through her.

Staring at the empty desk where her laptop was supposed to be, she tried to imagine if the search warrant would actually reveal something incriminating. In law school, one of her professors said that nobody was innocent of everything. If any authoritarian party had the ability to search freely, they would eventually find something that could prove either embarrassing or illegal. Fallon had not believed him at the time. But now that the FBI was searching her computer, trepidation forced her to think twice. What was on the hard drive anyway? Emails from law school friends. Jokes. Bookmarks, research notes. She tried to remember if she had ever looked at porn while at work. She certainly did not think so, but sometimes friends sent links that didn't exactly pass the white glove test.

Realizing this could be the end of her career, a fresh upsurge of panic washed over her. It was over before it really began.

"It's an FBI warrant," Tom said. "They're accusing you of selling a fatal dose of cocaine to a Leo Jacobellis of Malibu, California five years ago."

Fallon felt the blood drain from her face, her expression slacken. The words were so true, she could not even keep up the pretense of innocence. Hearing that name had the strange effect of making everything very clear and very quiet, as if something inside had been struck with a tuning fork. In the silence, she could hear the muted typing from the office next door and her heart outpacing it. She saw Tom's confused face and wanted to explain, but her throat closed and no words could squeak through.

The last two weeks of the campaign, in a classic October surprise, in between the onslaught of insinuations about her parent's marriage and accusations from women who would swear to meeting Preston Taylor Hughes in some trashy motel, an opposition research consultant turned up something juicy for the Ballard campaign about Fallon Hughes—and Gil Parry used it to maximum political advantage. The Ballard campaign ran scary ads with the announcer warning in a swoopy timbre, "If Preston Taylor Hughes can't run his own house, how can we trust him to run the White House?"

Her father could only answer that politician's children were off limits and there were serious issues facing the nation that needed our attention; energy wasted on gossip was better spent schooling our children, helping our neighbors, and making the United States a better place to live. Despite his tepid response, the election results resolved—barely—in Hughes's favor.

This was going to reignite the scandal.

Fallon was suddenly thirsty. Her whole body felt desiccated, and she recognized it as life being drained out of her. This was only the beginning. It would only get worse. As an intensely private person, she would have to see her life and her family torn apart, examined, criticized. Her whole life would be about this now. Fighting some prosecutor, trying to prove her innocence.

"FBI agents are probably at my house with a search warrant," she said stiffly. "Come on, I need to go home."

Tom radioed the vehicles that Avalon was en route downstairs. A knock at the door startled her. Tom opened it, and she was relieved to see it was Sam Cahill, her boss, not the FBI prepared to arrest her.

He looked at her with genuine concern. "Are you okay?"

She nodded, instantly clicking into professional mode.

"You look like you've swallowed a tack."

"It's bad," she whispered.

"I heard. Take the rest of the day. I'll run interference for you."

The gratitude nearly knocked her sideways. "I didn't do anything ..."

"I know. Go take care of this."

Scrabbling in her handbag, she found her phone and, with shaking fingers, dialed her father's cell phone. Blake Henley, her father's chief of staff, answered. "Hi, let me talk to my dad," she exhorted, alarmed at how breathless she sounded.

"I'm sorry, we're in the car, just arriving at the fireman's union for his speech about ..."

Disappointed in herself for having to say it, she cut him off: "Interrupt, please Blake. This is a family matter."

"Just a moment."

After some back and forth, her father's voice came on the line.

"Daddy," Fallon gushed, and to her horror, her voice broke. "Somebody has a search warrant for me and they issued it at work."

"A search warrant for what?"

"The ... Jacobellis incident. They're accusing me of murder."

Preston Hughes inhaled a shocked little breath. Fallon squeezed her eyes shut, feeling his disapproval emanating from the phone. "Ballard has stacked that goddamn agency with cronies and supporters. It is the most politicized Justice Department in history. This is beyond the pale and ..."

"Dad ..."

Keeping his voice level, he said, "I'll call Max."

"I'm heading home because the FBI is probably there right now. Have the lawyer meet me at my place."

"I'll have Max meet you there. Do not speak to anyone until you have counsel."

In shock, Fallon nodded, then realized her father couldn't see her on the phone. "Okay. Daddy?"

"Yes?"

"I'm sorry."

"Stay calm," he answered. He mumbled, "One minute," to someone else—a personal assistant, press secretary, chief of staff. This was just another to-do in her father's long list of action items. She was interrupting him with her problems. She hung up and turned to Tom.

"I need to go home." She moved toward the door of her office, but Tom grabbed the sleeve of her coat. "Hold on," he said. "Let me get the limos lined up first."

In the haze of terror that had enveloped her, she recognized, dimly, that he was trying to protect her. No doubt word had spread through the office that a search warrant had been served, but if she ran out, white with shock, and he was issuing orders into his cuff mike, it would only excite more gossip.

"Okay," she nodded. She shut her eyes, trying to find some equilibrium between extreme happiness and *pure fucking hell.*

Tom quickly conveyed the information and then opened the door for her, walked with her to the elevators, pushed the buttons, and got her the hell out of there.

At the door of her loft, Fallon was shaking so violently she could not fit her key into the lock.

"Let me," Tom said, and inserted the key. "Check it out. I'll wait here."

Leaving the door open, she disappeared inside. Tom pushed the door wide on its hinges, looking for any obvious sign of disturbance in the apartment. He watched Fallon hurry up a staircase of wide, broad glass or Lucite stairs— they were clear, which Tom found unsettling for some reason. Entering a protectee's home was beyond the purview of his job. Nevertheless, he took a step inside the foyer to get a better look around. Everything looked normal, but his neck was crawling weirdly.

"All clear?" he called from the doorway.

From the interior depths of the loft, Fallon called, "I'll be right there." After a few tense moments, she descended the stairs. "Would you come inside? I don't want to be alone. I'm scared they're going to show up any minute."

After a moment of hesitation, he entered, leaving the door open.

Fallon's loft was full of Bohemian charm. Overstuffed cream and jewel tone furniture was spread over what seemed to be an acre of clear space, made more dramatic by the cathedral ceiling and a sinuously curved glass wall extended the entire length of the loft, admitting a sweeping view of the Potomac

River and green-gray hills of Arlington, Virginia. She was a woman who needed to see the world—literally. African masks and several good pieces of modern abstract art hung on the walls. Colorful vases and figurines were placed unobtrusively throughout the room—collectibles from the farthest reaches of the world. On one wall, an assortment of black and white photographs showed Fallon in various exotic locales: Fallon in a Jeep with a family of giraffes behind her; Fallon at the Taj Mahal; Fallon and her friend Gwen with their arms around each other's shoulders, grinning into the camera with the Eiffel Tower behind them. Several pictures featured Fallon with her young brother Evan. He was tow-haired with a stiff, lopsided smile. Tom averted his eyes from those pictures, unable to tolerate the creamy sweetness of them.

Fallon's jittery, unsettled movements and restless energy reminded him of a hummingbird or bumblebee. She looked beyond scared as she whipped open the cabinets in her immaculate, modern kitchen. Even terrified out of her wits, she was so stunning that Tom's breath arrested in his chest. He wasn't sure he would ever be able to think of her as just a protectee.

Fallon poured two glasses of soda, then added a generous splash of rum to one. She kept that one and offered the soft drink to Tom.

She took a long swig then set it on the counter. "Tell me again what the warrant says."

"It says the Department of Justice has probable cause to believe that five years ago you sold a fatal dose of cocaine to Leo Jacobellis."

Fallon frowned and shook her head pensively. "I never sold him anything. I've never done any illegal drugs at all. But … Leo was my boyfriend. And he did overdose on cocaine. You probably heard about it during the campaign. Dad's opponent made sure that every person in America believed I was a drug-addicted whore."

Her voice had turned bitter; he saw that Fallon had been genuinely hurt by the attacks. But voters apparently believed that nasty gossip had nothing to do with the ability of Preston

Hughes to govern, which made the timing of the search warrant even more curious. If the incumbent administration was going to harass the opposition with a murder investigation, why wait until it was too late to affect the outcome of the election?

Fallon was still visibly shaking. She was so pale that for the first time, he noticed

fine, coppery freckles sprinkled over the bridge of her nose. Had they always been there? He tried to remember.

Lifting the drink to her lips, she swallowed the rum and coke in huge, fast gulps. Then poured another. She still had that scared, glittery look in her eyes, like shaken dice offered in a cup.

"I didn't kill him," Fallon said. "Though I think … I think it will be difficult to prove that."

Tom could have laughed. The thought of Fallon killing someone was actually amusing. But he only said, "It won't get to the stage where you have to prove it. "

A loud knock at the door was followed by an authoritative male voice saying, "Miss Hughes?"

Fallon stiffened. Kevin White, the agent posted to the control room all morning, peered inside. "Ma'am, please pardon the interruption. Max Hall is here to see you. He says he has an appointment."

"Oh thank God," Fallon muttered, visibly relieved that the reinforcements had arrived. "Let Max in, please."

Max Hall had been the president's personal attorney for thirty years. In all the time Fallon had known him, even on social occasions, he never lost the patina of supreme competence. In a town full of attorneys and politicians, Max Hall had a monopoly on composure; he simply did not lose control, ever. It was this element of his personality that permitted Fallon a faint glimmer of hope that this nightmare would be handled well and quickly.

"Max, they served a warrant on me at work," she said, thrusting the document at him. "It's not true. I've never bought or sold or used cocaine. I don't know how this happened. Why now?"

Max let her babble while he scanned the document. He flipped to the back page and read the signatures of the FBI

CARA ELLISON

agents and judge. "This is shit," he said calmly. "They haven't been here yet?"

"Not yet."

"They will be," he said. "They are looking for indications of drug transactions, financial records, and narcotics and narcotics paraphernalia."

"Oh God," she groaned.

"Where I can make a call?"

Fallon indicated the back of the house, toward the office area. She took another gulp of her rum and coke, then stood very still at her black-granite bar, looking bewildered, as if she recognized nothing about her own life.

The burning anxiety in her eyes activated all kinds of protective instincts in Tom. It went beyond the rote throw-yourself-in-front-of-a-bullet training to something altogether more personal. Fucking his protectee in a hallway was the epitome of bad judgment, but it also helped clarify just how intensely he was committed to keeping her from harm, whether it was a bullet, an indictment, or a map of the keys, whatever that was.

Max Hall returned to the kitchen, where Fallon was still guzzling her rum and coke. "I am meeting Ben Lambert to find out where the warrant originated."

Lambert was the current director of the Federal Bureau of Investigation. Tom felt a little better about the situation—anyone who could demand an audience with the director on five minutes' notice was good to have on the team.

"I will see about getting your computer back, but that will depend on their evidence and what they are willing to let me know about their investigation."

"Are they coming here?"

"No. If that changes, I will let you know before they arrive."

"Are they going to arrest me?"

"Not until after I meet with them, if at all."

"Oh my God," she murmured. Fresh tears spilled from her eyes. She looked desperately to Tom.

"I doubt it, Fallon," Max Hall replied. "It would be very unusual."

"In the current administration, the vice president's son was arrested for marijuana possession," she said numbly. "It's not as if having a dad in the White House can protect me from this administration's Department of Justice."

"Actually, Fallon, you're wrong. Though I cannot speak for certain, I would bet if you were arrested and convicted of anything, your father would immediately pardon you. It would be a nonissue."

That was cold comfort, but Fallon didn't reply.

Max Hall excused himself.

"I have no idea what to do," Fallon said softly. "Should I go to the Blair House?"

"I don't know, ma'am."

"Are you ever going to stop calling me ma'am?"

Tom smiled gently. "It's the appropriate term during work hours."

Fallon perched a shapely buttock on a bar stool and looked mournfully into her drink. "Why are they dragging this up now? I'm not a drug dealer or user ... I never even drink! Except now ..."

"I believe you," Tom replied. And he did. Fallon was honest as bean stew.

"Thank you," she said.

"I haven't done anything."

"You're being very good to me." Fallon took another gulp of her rummy coke. "Earlier and now."

He smiled gently at her.

She got up to splash more rum into the soda. Because she looked genuinely lost and in need of direction, Tom stood up, gently took the bottle from her, and set it on the counter.

"You've had enough."

She looked up at him with wide, true-blue eyes framed in long, sooty black lashes. Her soft vulnerability made his heart constrict with empathy.

"I'm just really upset," she whispered.

"I know. But you've had enough."

The glittery panic that had been lurking in her eyes softened.

Fallon drew in an unsteady breath. "I keep thinking shock troops are going to bash down my door."

"They're not. Mr. Hall is meeting them now, remember?"

"Yes. But still."

"I tend to believe him," Tom offered.

She averted her eyes and listlessly began stacking a collection of exotic coins on her counter. Tom picked one up and studied it. An olive branch wreathed the words *20 Aenta*. Greek drachmas.

His heart sank. He was never going to be able to escape Greece.

"I don't want to stay here but I don't want to leave, because I feel like I need to protect my belongings. The thought of the FBI storming in here, pawing through my private space makes me ill."

"If the FBI showed up with a warrant, you couldn't tell them what they can and can't look at."

"I know. Strange to feel so helpless against this wall of government." She actually smiled. "How ironic is that?"

"Pretty ironic," Tom agreed.

"Maybe I should go to the Blair House." With just two weeks until inauguration day, the Hughes had moved from their suite of rooms at the Willard Hotel to the Blair House, officially as guests of President Ballard. It was both traditional and practical for the president-elect to live just across the street from the White House for the harried two weeks preceding his own presidency.

"I'm sure your father would like to see you."

Fallon rested her head on the bar. Her bereft, aimless expression made her appear much younger than her twenty-seven years. Tom gently pushed a lock of silky blonde hair out of her eyes and tucked it behind her ear. She looked up at him with an inscrutable expression. The glow he'd created in her face was gone now, replaced with fear.

"You're a nice guy under all that hardware," she said softly.

Tom smiled. "Just trying to keep my protectee sober during office hours."

Fallon stepped off the bar stool. "I guess let's go to the Blair House."

Tom used his walkie-talkie to alert the control room.

Kevin White replied, "Standby."

A moment later, White returned to the reserved frequency. "Rowland advises that a large crowd of media has gathered in the front of the building."

Fallon blanched. "How do they already know about the warrant?"

Tom said, "Standby." To Fallon he asked, "Do you still want to go?"

"Yes, but I want to avoid the media."

Tom radioed his counterpart. "Avalon will go all the way down to the underground parking garage, level two. Line up at the elevator there."

"Roger that."

They left her apartment, Fallon taking special care to lock up. In the parking garage, the limos were idling. Tom opened the door of the primary vehicle and Fallon jumped in. The limo proceeded slowly through the electronic gates. Tom took in the scene through the windshield. Agent White had not been exaggerating; it was not just a single photographer or a reporter with an inside wire to the Department of Justice. It was *the media*, what seemed like *all of them*.

Tom looked in the rearview mirror to Fallon, who sat up straight and tall, her sunglasses shielding her eyes, focused straight ahead. As the Suburban nosed out of the garage to prepare to turn left, cameramen swarmed the SUV, pressed their cameras to the windows, and snapped. Flashes of light and sound penetrated the black windows of the limo, but Fallon appeared not to hear. She might be a scandal waiting to burst open wide, but the photos that would inevitably end up in the tabs and online gossip sites would depict only a dignified woman on her way to an ordinary errand, oblivious to the chaos surrounding her.

FIVE

"How could you do this to me, Fallon?"

Fallon stood in the stately yellow Lincoln Room in the Blair House, feeling an invisible wave beneath the beautiful Aubusson carpets capsizing her, erasing all equilibrium. Her father was angry … *at her*. As if she had asked the DOJ to swear out a search warrant and take her computer deliberately to antagonize him. Blindsided, she had no answer. She just blinked, dumb as a cow.

Preston Taylor Hughes was a media dream. Able to deliver a prepared speech as if it were impromptu, with natural body language, and an excellent sense of timing, he was a quintessential politician. He also had the widest, most engaging smile ever to appear in Washington, which he used with ruthless precision. An imposing height, rich baritone voice, and full head of brown hair all created a potent package. Fallon detested the political animal he had become. He didn't know when to turn it off. He never seemed to realize that she was not an *audience*. She was his daughter.

With his polished political packaging ripped away, Fallon saw an angry man, weltering at her in exasperation and disappointment: her father in his *de facto* state of address. His manner of napalming political weeds to get to the heart of the matter might be respected by his political enemies and colleagues, but his aggressive, accusatory style was completely detrimental to actually relating to a member of his family.

"Do you ever think of anyone but yourself? Do you not realize what is going on here? A drug and sex scandal involving my daughter is not exactly how I wanted to begin my administration."

"It's not a sex scandal." Fallon took pains to avoid the glint of accusation in her words.

His mouth flattened into a grim line, well aware that was one area where both he and Elizabeth were vulnerable. At any moment, some bimbo could creep up from the sewers with risqué photos for sale at the right price.

His body looked tense, like he wanted to launch himself at her and shake her. "Fallon, do you realize the position you've put me in?"

Now he was playing hardball. Even as she heard the words, she wanted to shout *what about me?* But she couldn't muster a defense. The one place she desperately hoped would calm her shattered nerves would be here, in this nexus of power and family. How stupid. Ancient family dynamics didn't change just because she was in trouble or her father was about to become the most powerful man in the free world. How naïve to believe that just because she needed him, he would view her as his daughter, not put her on some political scale and determine whether she was more an asset or liability, and how to best spin this so his approval numbers stayed high. Since she was twelve, the first time he ran for governor of Montana, she had been expected to act always with her father's career first in mind. Like her mother, she was expected to care about her father's career more than anything else. But she didn't care. At least not like he wanted her to. She wanted a father, not a governor or president-elect.

Blake Henley, her father's chief of staff, paused in the entry with a phone to his ear. "He says it will be fifteen minutes."

"Fine, but tell him it is an emergency." Preston replied. Then to Fallon, he said curtly, "I've spent the morning appointing lawyers and making phone calls all over Washington." His lips were pursed in disgust.

She blushed from being rebuked in front of her father's staff. Heart tripping, she turned and walked away.

"Where are you going?" he demanded.

"To see my mother," she replied without looking back.

Fallon walked up the stairs to the suite where her parents were staying until the inauguration. She hadn't planned on her father accusing her of practically begging to be accused of murder, but she was prepared for her mother's reaction to be even worse.

Fallon hesitated outside the bedroom door to gather her courage, and then knocked. After a small silence, her mother called, "Come in."

Fallon entered the Principal Suite Bedroom. A large four-poster bed featuring a dusty rose floral print canopy dominated the room. This morning, a fire crackled in the fireplace, lending a cozy English cottage mien to the room. On the opposite side of the room, two tall wooden doors were flung wide to admit a view to the Principal Suite Sitting Room. There, Elizabeth was sitting at the antique desk, her head bent to a stack of documents. As Fallon entered, she stopped writing and rose to her feet.

The woman who would be First Lady wore slim Chanel sailor pants that emphasized her long legs and a form-fitting cashmere sweater with a cowl at the neck. Her mother was always flawlessly dressed, as if she'd stepped out of the pages of *Vogue* magazine. Her silky blond hair was pinned back with a tortoiseshell clasp, curling under her earlobes, which were dotted with small diamond studs. Her face was flawlessly made up. Her fine pale skin was seemingly untouched by time, luminous, lit with some unseen depth like the surface of the moon. Her gray eyes were calm and penetrating, famously able to cry on cue; her lips remained youthfully plump but avoided the "trout pout" so often sported by the overzealous users of fillers. Her mother was ageless and dazzlingly beautiful.

She smiled at Fallon, embracing her. "Hello, darling." Fallon shut her eyes, trying to detect the scent of alcohol, but it was futile to try to spot her mother's weakness that way. Elizabeth Hughes was too smart to allow herself to be accused of being drunk; she smelled of Bulgari perfume and spearmint breath fresheners—the same as always.

"Are they serious about that warrant?" Elizabeth asked smoothly. She took Fallon's hand and led her to a sofa.

"Yes," Fallon replied. "They're accusing me of murder."

A faint smile came to Elizabeth's lips. "That is so absurd. It is difficult to understand."

It was not difficult to understand for Fallon. Indeed it seemed to her very frank in its aims to cause her embarrassment. She chose not to belabor the point, and her mother said airily, "Perhaps it will go away when we get into the White House."

Elizabeth Hughes lived in a world where things simply went away when they were inconvenient, dispatched by unseen assistants, attorneys, and publicists.

Fallon frowned, wanting to explain to her mother that federal investigations do not simply go away; her work computer had been seized in a search warrant, and her life currently resembled all the order of a Jackson Pollack painting. But it didn't matter; her mother seemed to have lost interest already. She suddenly smiled, grasping Fallon's hand. "Come here. I have something to show you." She rose from the sofa and walked into the bedroom, Fallon following a pace behind.

She stood near the vaulted canopy bed in the large feminine room. Her mother flung open the closet doors, revealing a nearly empty interior. Most of her clothing was already in storage at the White House, waiting to be moved into the residence. The pieces hanging in the closet were her mother's staples: exquisite yet understated clothing selected by stylists to convey "casual yet supremely elegant First Lady." Elizabeth was preparing for her role as First Lady as she would a movie part. After relying her whole life on box office numbers to judge whether she was successful or not, she now cast the same importance on political approval numbers. They had been stratospheric since Preston Taylor Hughes won the election. Yet the wide-ranging approval had not imbued Elizabeth with instant happiness and on several occasions, Elizabeth voiced her dismay. Fallon had wisely held her tongue. Her secret reply was nothing would make her mother happy. For as long as she could remember, her mother's life had been a grim protraction of seething rage and disappointment.

Her parents despised each other and, at least in private, made no pretense otherwise. They both wanted to flee the scene of their marriage as if it were a fiery car wreck. Despite Elizabeth's acting ability, she was no expert at understanding or managing her own emotions and was adrift in trying to express the darkness that beat inside her.

In ten years, they had not eaten a meal together unless it was for some diplomatic function. Their interactions immediately took the form of fighting, as if it were one long fight, continuing for years with small respites to sleep or attend to business, only to be resumed, even more passionately, again the next time they saw each other. The veneer of calm in the lulls of their near-constant fights was almost as terrifying as the crashing, screaming battles because Fallon knew the untapped depths of her mother's cold fury and the incredible strength it took to maintain that controlled demeanor. One day, that thin veneer of composure, pulsing with resentment, was going to break.

It had not always been this way. In her teenage years, Fallon had loved to look at old romantic photographs of her parents. Their pictures were splashed on every magazine and newspaper: a beautiful movie star with her handsome, rich husband, nuzzling into each other, holding hands, sharing a kiss in Central Park one snow-covered Christmas, holding Fallon as a newborn as they gazed at each other like the whole world beyond them had faded to black.

They had not been faking their love. Something horrible but not dramatic had happened in the intervening years—the love that had once been all-consuming had slowly disintegrated. After it was gone, they could not even respect one another. In the space where happiness and contentment and commitment had once existed, hatred and resentment had thrived. Now they could not stand to look at each other.

Elizabeth guided a rolling garment rack from the closet. Gently holding up the plastic, she revealed a stunning one-shoulder silver ball gown. "What do you think?" she asked. A dreamy smile of pleasure appeared on her face as she lightly caressed the delicate fabric.

Fallon reached for something to say, but failed. Elizabeth had been looking forward to the inauguration because it was a connection to her movie star days—the glamour of beautiful styling, the veneration of the masses. Her mother craved *spectacle* and longed for her former life of acting and magnificent parties. So when she rolled out the gown, Fallon understood that the search warrant was nothing more than a passing inconvenience to her mother. She suddenly felt very small.

"It's beautiful." Fallon murmured the statement her mother no doubt wanted to hear. She watched Elizabeth feign happiness at Fallon's approval, then look again at the gown, seeing in her mind's eye how beautiful she would look in the pictures after the inauguration. The pictures were more real to her than the experience.

"I should go," Fallon said. "Dad is calling an attorney for me."

"Not yet," Elizabeth said with a little smile. "I have a secret to tell you."

Fallon instinctively backed away. "Mother, we've discussed—"

"Not that kind of secret," she said coolly. She walked back into the sitting room and collected the document on her desk, the one she had been working on when Fallon arrived.

"My agent has sent what has to be the finest script I've read in fifteen years," Elizabeth said. "It's titled *Kill Shot*, directed by Quentin Tarantino."

The room fell silent and Fallon realized she was waiting for some kind of disclaimer. Such as: "Wouldn't it be a hoot to actually do this?" Or: "Can you imagine?" Or, said with a smile of genuine depraved pleasure: "It would destroy your father to see me do this."

Instead, it became painfully clear that her mother was serious. The excitement about the prospect of making the movie manifested in the glow of her eyes, the slight Mona Lisa smile on her lips.

"What did Dad say?" Fallon asked. It was the first thing that came to mind, and she instantly recognized that she had miscalculated. Elizabeth's eyes darkened as her mouth tightened, injured by her daughter's lack of instant support.

"You're just like he is," she said with a soft, low tone. She said this without any apparent anger; they could have been discussing the weather or diminishing rainfall averages in Peru for all the emotion she conveyed. But Fallon's blood ran cold. "Why must everyone in this family have something for themselves but me? It seems terribly unfair. You have your career. Lord knows your father has his. Why is it that I am expected to simply sit quietly in the background? Am I nothing but a mother?"

This was the primary battle her parents had been waging for at least two years. Her mother's ardent desire to continue to make movies conflicted with Preston's desire to appear to be an average American husband and father. It did seem rather strange and unseemly for a First Lady to continue her career, a fact that puzzled Fallon. Women, after all, were expected to have careers and lives. Still, she knew that any hint of neutrality would be seen as fierce opposition. Suddenly the banality and appalling pointless predictability of the argument in the face of much graver concerns seemed ridiculous to her. At this moment, very powerful forces were conspiring to accuse her of murder. And her mother simply went on, murmuring delicately about her desire to act, how unfair it was for Preston to intervene in her career, how life without acting was dreadful and unfulfilling.

"I see you no longer require my presence for this argument," Fallon said blandly.

Her mother blazed at her with a silent, cutting stare, yet oddly hurt.

Fallon walked away, shutting the bedroom door behind her. Alone in the corridor, she paused, revolted yet pitying her mother, and waited for the feeling to pass. When she was sure she was in control of herself once more, she walked down the long hallway to her brother's room and softly opened the door.

At the sight of him in his airplane-themed bed, her heart lifted. But in the next instant, she was disturbed because he was asleep. It was nearly two o'clock in the afternoon. Why was Evan asleep?

At his bedside, Fallon knelt down. His innocence and beauty made her ache with sadness. Growing up in this family was a curse. Even now, as he lay there, he was being abused. He was six; he didn't need a nap every afternoon. But it was easier for her parents and keepers to let him sleep than actually take care of him.

Fallon kissed his cheek and he startled awake.

"Hi, sweetheart …"

Evan woke with a little start, blinking at her.

"Hi, honey, how are you doing?" She wanted to cuddle him, hug him close to her heart, and he usually allowed her to, but if she did it too quickly, he would become irritable. So she merely sat by his bedside, petting back his soft, baby-fine hair.

He sat up and looked around as if trying to remember why he was there.

"Where is Kendra?" Fallon asked.

"Don't know," he said sleepily.

"Come on, let's go find her," she said. She stood up and held out her hand. Evan took it and scooted out of bed.

With every step, she grew more furious at Kendra for leaving him unattended and her mother for not caring. At Kendra's room, Fallon knocked loudly on the door. No answer. She could hear her father's voice from the library asking, "Where the hell is Fallon?"

"Have you seen Kendra?" she asked the Secret Service agent posted at the foot of the stairs.

Just then, Kendra's voice floated over to her. "Here I am! Is Prince Charming awake?"

Fallon turned to the young caretaker with death in her eyes. "Where were you?"

"I just went to the bathroom."

"If you don't want this job, there are others who do," Fallon said coldly.

Shock stained Kendra's cheeks pink. "Miss Hughes …"

"Do not let him sleep in the middle of the day. His wake up is seven in the morning and his bedtime is eight thirty. Do you understand?"

"Yes," she said weakly.

"I have a meeting to attend," Fallon said. "But you will take my brother upstairs, play some games with him, take him to visit my mother, and keep him entertained for the rest of the day. Am I clear?"

"Yes."

"Good." Fallon turned to Evan, her manner instantly softening. "I will come see you tonight. We'll have dinner together, okay?"

"Okay."

Fallon bent down and kissed him. "Okay, Sport, I'll see you later."

He nodded and offered a tight smile that created a gap in the day—a little moment where nothing existed but his innocent goodness. What she wouldn't give to live a normal life, in a normal town, where she could make sure that Evan had a life that would be worthy of his sweetness. She'd love to be able to simply enjoy those smiles for what they were instead of feeling that they were too few. She made a mental note to talk to her mother about getting another nanny, but knew she couldn't do it now, not after their fight; her mother's silent treatment was legendary. When she got back to the office, she thought dully, she'd make some calls, see if she could find a replacement nanny. Someone with more experience with special needs children. And more common sense.

She was still shaking with fury and fear when she sat down on the green brocade silk sofa in the meeting room with her father, a defense attorney, and Jerry Chambliss, her father's advisor. The room felt crowded with all the big personalities bearing down upon her.

As her father stood glowering at her, resentment wafted from him like microwaves. How dare she take him from his important work, stealing his energy and time on something as trivial as murder, and then waste even more of it on Evan?

There was no support or love in this house. She had long ago accepted the familial arrangement, but now she felt the loneliness acutely. She was on her own. Normally, the reality of her family life would not have bothered her. She valued independence and self-reliance above all other virtues. But in this one instance, as she stood accused of taking a person's life, she had feebly hoped that her mother might offer some practical, loving advice, or her father might use his significant power to help her.

The criminal attorney wore a double-breasted blue serge suit and a red power tie. His thinning silver hair showed a pronounced widow's peak, which gave his face a hawkish look. It took several minutes to realize she had seen him before; he was a former Attorney General of the United States, now returned to private practice. It would be easy to mistake this for a grand gesture of assistance, but Fallon understood her father, at least better than she understood her mother, and so she knew that his ability to summon the former Attorney General was an ego trip. He demanded the most famous attorney in the USA because he wanted to feel powerful and to give the former AG an opportunity to become useful to this administration.

Capital murder would be negotiated down to manslaughter, he said, then hastened to add: even that would be the very worst scenario. "The DOJ will drop the case as soon as it becomes obvious that it's a political ploy. They'll be embarrassed for having launched this attack."

"Murder is rather on the nose, isn't it?" Jerry Chambliss said with a patrician chuckle.

Fallon barely heard him. The word "murder" kept chanting through her mind, obscuring any other cogent thought and paralyzing her with dread.

"You might as well get it all on the table now," the attorney said. "Tell me everything about Leo Jacobellis and why the DOJ thinks you gave him a fatal dose of cocaine."

Why? Because I did. Or rather: I didn't stop him.

Her last year of college, she had a disastrous affair with an engineering Ph.D. student. She liked him because he was smart and funny in a geek-endearing way. He was one of the first guys she'd ever met who was oblivious to her name. Hughes in Montana meant an empire of cattle, oil, and oceanic exploration equipment going back a hundred years. In the last ten, it had been the name of the governor. And Elizabeth Baker Hughes was not only an actress, she was a movie star, one of the most photographed women in the world. Leo was indifferent to all that. He pursued her with an intensity that overwhelmed her and left her dazzled. But at school, he was under pressure to finish his program and complete his thesis, the subject of which Fallon could not even begin to comprehend. His thesis was based on research that required long hours in the lab, and after a while, she began to suspect that he was taking cocaine to give him stamina.

She confronted him, and to her surprise, he admitted it. The fact that he did not attempt to deny his problem gave her hope. Even as an addict he was different—he was strong and *so* brilliant. He had so much to live for. He swore he would stop. Yet the addiction accelerated.

He began to oscillate between elation and desperate depression. As he fell further behind in his research and thesis work, he simply did not realize how much he was taking. Or that was what Fallon had said to the doctors when they told her that he'd taken a massive overdose and his heart had stopped.

They did not say the word. They did not say, "He died," or, "He is dead." They said, "His heart has stopped."

All these years later, the sadness never really abated. She had not loved him, not really; she knew that now. But she had liked him a great deal, and his death had informed almost every single major decision in her life.

She looked up at the attorney and said, "That's all." That would be the story she stuck with.

The hidden truth was more complex and it was not relevant to the Department of Justice's case against her.

She had been angry with Leo for a long time, so when the news came that "his heart has stopped" she didn't feel the dagger-stab of grief right away. Rather, it crept in slowly, over a period of weeks. As her anger melted, profound sadness took its place, filling her, weighing her down as if her blood was made of mercury. Her whole world narrowed and darkened. She carried the guilt like an anvil, certain that every person she encountered could see that she was marked with death.

When she finally graduated with a degree in art history, she had moved back to the family ranch in Shelby, Montana to be near Evan. His sweet presence was enough to help her start to see the light of life again. She longed to travel, and for a few months, she wrestled with her desire to see the world and the desire to make sure Evan was cared for. Her mother convinced her that Evan would be fine, so Fallon traveled to France, then Greece. There, on the isle of Paxos, she met Tom Bishop.

When she returned to the States, her father announced his plan to run

for president in the next election. It was time for her to settle down, and if she couldn't do it for herself, she should at least to do it for the sake of his political career.

The guilt card. Her father's irresistible gambit. As always, it worked. And as she expected, companies were not rushing to offer jobs to a woman who had an art history degree. Realizing not much else was available to her, she decided to take the LSAT. To her own surprise, she was admitted to Pepperdine.

Now she was in the weird bubble of D.C., being accused of murder. And some guy killed himself yesterday. She shut her eyes for a moment, wondering when life was ever going to let up.

Her father wrote a check to pay the lawyer's retainer fee. He glanced up at her with acute disappointment in his face, as if she were going to use the money for fancy shoes or some unnecessary trinket. *Sorry, Dad. I didn't mean to interrupt your day as I got accused of murder. My mistake.*

Her father thanked the attorney for coming on such short notice and asked to be apprised of any developments. He then walked with the attorney out of the Lincoln Room.

Fallon sat alone on the sofa, looking around the beautifully appointed sanctum, feeling it held no more significance to her life than a hospital waiting room or some stranger's foyer. A tumble of images bumped through her mind: Leo Jacobellis's funeral, Paxos, the search warrant.

A scuffing sound in the marble hallway caught her attention, and she glimpsed a dark figure step away from the entry.

Secret Service.

The heels of her shoes tapped and echoed across the

polished marble floor as she approached. Tom's head was bent to his BlackBerry, the smooth lines of his body backlit by a far window. How she wanted to feel him close to her and lose herself in his strength and his life-giving energy.

Tom looked up from his BlackBerry. Seeing her troubled expression, he put the device away and approached. "Are you okay?" His voice was low and soothing.

Fallon could not meet his eyes for fear she might do something mortifying like cry or reveal the tenderness she felt for him. Instead, she intently studied the sharpness of his white shirt against his black suit.

"Fallon?" He placed his fingers under her chin, forcing her to look up into his eyes. "Are you okay?"

His obvious concern incited more riots of affection through her. How unbelievably sweet it would be to give in to the impulse, to lay her head against his chest and let him gently soothe away all the bumps and bruises. But acting like she wanted to make up for lost time with him or allowing him into the emotional vortex that was her life would be madness. Seeking comfort from him was the wrong strategy. In that crazy moment in the vestibule when they were pawing desperately at one another, she'd babbled that she would never ask for anything more. It was unlikely he even heard her—he certainly hadn't acknowledged the comment—but she thought it wise to keep her word. Not just for his sake but for hers. She simply did not ever want to go through the heartbreak of Paxos again. She would try to keep things light between them. She'd never been able to do that before, but she had to make it work this time.

She inched back. "Yes," she answered firmly. "I am okay."

Tom looked dubious.

"Come on," she said, steeling her spine. "I have to get back to work." She paused and frowned. "I wonder if they actually want me back at work."

"Maybe you should call Sam Cahill? He seems like he's on your side."

Fallon scrabbled for her phone in her big, slouchy purse. Within seconds, Sam Cahill's voice came on the line.

"Hi, Sam, it's me. I don't know how to ask this discreetly so I'll just come out with it. Should I come back today?"

After a thoughtful pause, he answered. "I would give it a day to die down. Just take it easy for the rest of the day. Show up tomorrow and if you get any friction, come to me."

Secretly relieved, Fallon thanked him and hung up. "I guess we're going back to my place," she said.

In the back of the limo, Fallon checked the news on her iPhone. Breathless reports of her search warrant were all over CNN, Drudge Report, Fox News, and the networks, covering like it was worse than Watergate. She opened Facebook and saw her friends' posts asking what happened; what was the warrant about?

If she had been an alien who just landed from Mars, she would have thought only two things were happening in the United States: the daughter of the president-elect was being accused of murder, and the USA and Russia both feared increasing tensions.

The harsh rhetoric between the two nations had been ongoing since summer, but over the past few days, it had intensified to a frightening degree. The stress of handling such a delicate situation might explain her father's disregard for her well-being, but she doubted it. He was always abrasive and self-centered, even when the political landscape was calm.

Vice President-elect Claudia Wells was coy when asked at a press gaggle to give her impressions, saying only that she would leave diplomatic matters to the current person in that role.

Fallon's experience with Washington told her one thing: politicians never came out and bluntly told the whole truth. Everything out of their mouths was a talking point drafted by a press secretary. There were always deals being done out of the public spotlight, sleights of hand, trickery, white lies, and polls to confuse voters. Trying to make sense of it all was often impossible. So whatever was happening in Russia was probably only half known to the intelligence operatives on the ground and even more opaque to the general public. No matter how many media hours were dedicated to the situation, the truth was going to stay well hidden.

Not for the first time, Fallon felt apprehension about her parents' instincts for political gamesmanship. With tensions increasing by the day and serious foreign policy issues requiring deep thought and considered analysis at the forefront of every talk show, newspaper article, and blog post, Preston Taylor Hughes was expected to address a threat he simply did not understand. Her father had no real experience in diplomacy, though he believed his interactions with various heads of industry and lobbyists was substitutable. His overestimation of his abilities was going to be a very rude shock.

Normally when Fallon worried about her parents it was because there was something at stake that involved her. In this case, the entire United States of America was depending on a man who had got where he was because of raw ambition rather than any genuine political talent. He had hitched himself up the ladder step by step without any clear idea of what to do once he got to the top. A grimmer prognosis for a successful resolution, Fallon could not imagine.

When the world discovered what kind of man her father really was, it was going to be a disaster, and not even Jerry Chambliss was going to be able to salvage it.

She shut her eyes, trying to order her thoughts. When she felt the car stop, she opened them and found she was at home.

Once inside the elevator where they had a little privacy, Tom leaned in and kissed her. A flood of mellow joy coursed through her body, softening the tension. When she pulled back and looked into his eyes she felt like it might all be bearable. "You and I ... I know its crazy, but it's the also the sanest thing in my life right now."

"That's really sad," Tom said with a little smile.

His expression and sweet sense of humor coaxed a smile from her. She followed him down the hallway and he playfully took her hand, pulling her along.

At her door, she turned to Tom. "So you're just going to stand out here?"

"Yes."

"For how long?"

Tom shrugged. "About an hour. I'll call one of the other guys to come up, and I'll go to the control room."

"Can you come in?"

"No. Today was a onetime thing because you thought the FBI was in your house. I can't do it again."

She frowned. "Okay. I'll be right back." Inside her loft, Fallon set her purse on the bar and got herself a bottle of water and one for Tom. When she handed the bottle to him, he shook his head. "I can't. My hands have to be free."

"In case someone is going to come out of the apartment next door and attack?"

Her neighbors were doctors, lawyers like herself, and lobbyists who led quiet, discreet lives. The co-op board would frown on terrorists and assassins.

Tom looked at her carefully. "You should be more cautious. Walking yesterday was unnecessary. You're a little too available, in my professional opinion."

"You really think I'm in danger from someone besides the FBI?"

"I think something is happening that neither you nor the Secret Service has a handle on yet. I did some checking while you were meeting with your father," Tom said. "Antoine Campbell had an old conviction. He was prosecuted for hacking into the Army's network a few years ago. The fact that he mentioned the deputy director of the NSA when he called you and he has a background in hacking computers is interesting."

"Electronic surveillance ... hacking ... seems like there might be a connection."

"Do any of your clients have something to do with hacking? Is that why he called you?"

"My clients steal money, not information. I don't know why he called me."

The elevator doors opened and a neighbor stepped out. Fallon coolly said hello to the older woman, hoping she and Tom looked completely ordinary standing outside her door, chatting.

After the door closed, leaving them alone again, Fallon

looked back to Tom. "Today completely sucked except for the time with you."

A strained look crossed his face, and Fallon tensed in response. "Today was nice," he replied slowly. "I just …" He looked toward the door where the woman had gone. "This is very dangerous."

Fallon smiled. "It's okay. We can be careful."

After a moment he nodded. "We have to be."

SIX

Sixty-five miles west of Washington, D.C., on a black top road that wound through the vast, bucolic horse farms that populated the rolling hills of Front Royal, Virginia, Collin Whitcomb turned onto a winding private drive until he came to a small gray stone gatehouse. The security guard and surveillance cameras were mostly for show; the real security regime began half a mile back when sensors placed in the asphalt conveyed to whomever was working security that a car was approaching. The redirected microphones at the gate would record any conversation inside the car. Cameras placed in the trees and bushes were the size of bumblebees, so even if an intruder damaged the ones at the gate, the people inside still had eyes.

Collin tapped in the security code on the keypad and the heavy black gates swung open. A long treelined driveway winded to a stately Georgian-style manor. He drove to the rear and parked in the garage, a precaution in case helicopters or satellites happened to be hovering overhead.

He grabbed Fallon Hughes's laptop from the passenger seat and hurried inside the safe house.

A guard standing at the kitchen door had watched him on the monitors as he approached. They were former security forces mostly from Georgia and Bosnia. A few were Chechen. Collin was the only official American, but he was not the leader of the ragtag group of soldiers from the former Soviet republics. He was a follower, a role he was outgrowing very quickly. It could have accurately been said that Collin took his orders from Omar Koss, though that was becoming uncomfortably constricting, like a costume that no longer fit. Koss was good—but he was too careful. Koss occasionally admonished him and reminded him that to create real change, one must be patient. One should not simply jump at the first chance to kill. One must have a plan and a strategy to maximize every strike at the heart of the enemy. Everyone respected Koss—even Djvebe Malkhazi, who had fought the Russians with his own two hands and had been the leader of a group who had taken eleven hundred people hostage in September 2004 in Beslan. Malkhazi was famous for his exploits, and every time he opened his mouth, Collin sat, rapt, listening, thrilled by his passion and his vision.

Presently Malkhazi sat on the sofa, watching the news on a giant plasma screen television. This safe house belonged to him, purchased with the profits from a small arms dealing operation.

Collin's parents had been Chechen. When Collin was seven years old, his parents uprooted him to immigrate to California, where they Americanized the family. They changed their names; young noble Kaskyrbai, meaning *wolf*, morphed to Collin. They bought a minivan and watched baseball games and for most of his formative years, he was fully integrated into middle class American society. Collin certainly looked like a San Diego surfer kid with his blond hair and golden skin, but he was not one of them. His looks were a gift from Allah, a weapon to be used against the infidels. By blending in with them, he would perform jihad in the United States from the sheltering arms of the Commonwealth of Virginia—the heart of the beast.

He was devout, of course, but the fight had become less about Islam and more about the simple pleasure of war. He enjoyed having some big, overarching objective. It could be dressed up as Chechen independence, or Islam, or any number of things but when it came right down to it, what he really wanted to do was blow stuff up. He was a natural born radical.

Koss and his infernal urging to slow down made Collin crazy with impatience. Koss was born with what Collin's mother would have called an "old soul." He had the patience of rock. Collin didn't know how he could stand it, knowing the world was becoming more and more obscene every day, and still he urged patience.

But that might change now that Collin was in possession of

Fallon Hughes's laptop. This was very powerful leverage indeed.

It had been simple enough. Impersonating an FBI agent consisted of being stiff and wearing polished shoes. His network of contacts had come through for him in procuring FBI identification and an authentic FBI search warrant. It would be a few days until they figured out that the judge's signature was from an autopen and by then, they'd have absolutely no clue how it got on a warrant for Fallon Hughes's computer. With all the work that went in to it, surely Koss would give credit where credit was due.

If Fallon had told anyone what she had learned about the map of the keys, it was imperative to shut her up—sooner rather than later. Collin planned to kill her before Koss returned from Europe. Koss had demanded to do it himself, but he would thank Collin later. It was so urgent that it could not be left to Koss's ever-patient, ever-delaying leisure.

Not that he really believed Koss was in Europe handing over the map of the keys. Antoine Campbell had caught them too late; the contacts in Europe already had it. The mission was now in play.

Collin said hello to Malkhazi, then proceeded upstairs to the lab where electronics were kept and tested. While booting up Fallon Hughes's computer, he found a thumb drive to copy her hard drive.

He navigated directly to her email program, the very soul of a computer's user. In this case, the soul was a little more cloaked than he'd have liked. Most of the correspondence in Fallon's email went to others at the law firm of Johnson Sloan Pruitt. There was some discussion about Robert Chandler, the hedge fund manager who had bilked investors out of billions of dollars. Various defense strategies were discussed. Collin smirked. Only in the USA would the obviously guilty have a shot of evading the punishment that they so richly deserved. Personal email was sent to someone named Gwen Atwell. Fallon also corresponded with her parents.

Collin didn't see anything to do with Antoine Campbell. Maybe she used a personal account for that. Spontaneously he typed gmail.com into the URL bar. Instantly, Fallon Hughes's private email popped up. She didn't even have it set to ask for a password. A cakewalk.

And there, in an email to Gwen, was a question that sent his blood racing: "Do you know what a map of the keys is? I've gotta talk to you. Tonight?"

Whoa.

Collin exhaled with a hiss, seething at Omar Koss. He simply could not allow this girl to run around with this information. It was dangerous, and if he did not act, his negligence would get a lot of his people killed.

A rather ingenious idea had begun to coalesce. The perfect set of circumstances had presented itself. Easy access to Djvebe Malkhazi. Omar safely out of town.

Fallon Hughes would be perfect leverage to force the US government to hand over Mahomet Ayrzu. Ayrzu had fought with Malkhazi. After the war for Chechen independence, he had organized enormous terror attacks all over the globe, targeting full soccer stadiums, embassies, cruise ships, and skyscrapers. His most notorious act, however, was the unsuccessful attack on Air Force One. From Roosevelt Island, a tiny thumb of land in the middle of the Potomac, while Air Force One was climbing from Andrews Air Force Base, he shot at the giant aircraft with a Stinger missile. He winged it, but it had been a decoy and nobody was killed. The expert pilot had flown the burning wreckage to Reagan National Airport and landed safely. Nevertheless, his followers were awed and the public was mortified—the audacity alone was dazzling.

Ayrzu had been captured in Pakistan after the start of the War on Terror, though the United States denied it. The attack on Air Force One was blamed on someone else, someone already in custody who had been involved in the Bojinka plot, a story that satisfied most people. Americans felt safer. Airlines began to make a little money again with the terrorist in custody.

Meanwhile, Mahomet Ayrzu languished in custody unacknowledged. He was locked in one of the CIA's infamous black sites, possibly Gitmo, or perhaps a Navy brig, but nobody knew for sure.

Djvebe Malkhazi burned with a cold fire to see him free. Collin himself would enjoy watching the United States attempt to deny Ayrzu's existence while they held Fallon Hughes hostage. A delightfully roguish game, made all the more enjoyable because he knew the USA would blink first.

He would have to work around Omar, however. Not an easy thing. Collin had been Koss's protégé; Koss trusted him, or to put a finer point on it, Koss trusted him not to be a reckless fool when he wasn't around to clean up Collin's messes.

An opportunity like this came along once in a lifetime. An opportunity to move politics, to become his own man and operate on his own terms. The notion appealed to him. But actually betraying Koss would be another matter altogether. Could he do it? To his surprise, he actually felt a little guilty even considering it. It would be difficult for Koss to see the brilliance of this plan, but he felt certain that it would work.

Collin looked warily at the open door. At that moment it appeared to be an invitation. He could not hear the television from the far reaches of the mansion, but he knew Djvebe Malkhazi was downstairs watching news and growing fat on American food. Yes, Collin thought, Malkhazi would go for it. He would even admire Collin for thinking of it.

Downstairs, Collin took a bottle of water from the fridge and wandered into the living area. One guard with a Borz automatic weapon stood at the rear of the room. Another stood beside the terrorist leader, also armed to the teeth with a long gun, a hip holster, and probably a knife or another gun strapped to his ankle. One could never be too careful.

"Father," Collin said in Chechen, using the term of utmost respect. "I must speak with you about an urgent matter."

SEVEN

Tom cruised up G Street in his bland government car, past Fallon's office, and took a left onto 15th Street. To his amazement, he was able to nab a rare parking space. Standing at the trunk, he pulled off his jacket and tie, then placed his Sig Sauer in its holster and covered it up with his jacket. He waited for a few cars to pass then jaywalked across the street to Old Ebbit Grill.

As soon as he entered the elegant bar, he recognized lawyers and feds. Agents were easy to spot because they kept their jackets on while they were drinking, mindful of the weapons on their hips. Lawyers looked like self-congratulating assholes. Except Fallon, he thought miserably. Thanks to her, he might have to revise his opinion of the second oldest profession.

Brett Hitchcock, a friend who worked in Electronic Crimes, was seated at a banquette with a young woman that Tom didn't recognize. He wasn't expecting Hitch to bring anyone else tonight. She was pretty with huge brown eyes framed by a fringe of long dark hair. She looked young enough to be an undergrad at Georgetown U. Upon seeing Tom, she flashed a quick, genuine smile. Hitchcock introduced her as Lisa and said she was a new trainee at the Washington Field Office.

Tom sat down across from them and politely inquired how Lisa's training was going. She chatted about her weapons retention class then asked who he was protecting.

"Fallon Hughes," he answered, surprised at the little starburst of pleasure at saying her name out loud. Just saying it made his insides ping and light up like a pinball machine. He was in serious trouble.

Her eyes rounded with lurid excitement. "Oh my gosh, what is the deal with that search warrant? Did she really kill her boyfriend?"

Tom looked around for a waitress.

"Seriously, I read on Drudge Report that she's about to be arrested."

"She's not going to be arrested."

"She is so pretty," the girl was saying. "Is she that pretty close up?"

Tom was glad she didn't really expect an answer. She continued uninterrupted. "I also think the First Lady is gorgeous. I am dying to meet her. Can you imagine? Elizabeth Hughes. I swear, *Moneymaker* is one of my favorite movies. Did you see it? She won an Academy Award for it. She is so versatile …"

He couldn't talk about Fallon in front of Lisa the Trainee, so when it became obvious that she was here to stay, Tom excused himself. In the men's room, he sent a text to Leah Lennox to tell her he'd be home earlier than expected this evening: DO YOU WANT TO RUN TONIGHT?

Tom washed his hands and returned to the table. A moment later, his phone buzzed. It was Leah: RUN SOUNDS GOOD. CALL WHEN YOU GET HOME.

"Work," Tom said, palming the phone into his pocket.

"Dude, are you serious?"

"Is it Avalon?" Lisa asked, a little too eagerly.

"I have to get going. I'll catch up with you guys later." He dropped some money on the table to cover the beer he'd ordered but not touched and left.

Leah Lennox and Tom Bishop met their freshman year at college. Though romance had never sparked between them, they often joked that they were fated for one another—words so true that they felt like a bolt from the divine blue.

Leah was like a sister to him. A sweet, complex, troubled little sister. Stalked by periodic black depressions that would devastate her for weeks at a time, Tom had appointed himself on call for her suicidal fits. Tom believed he could rescue her, though he had no idea what to do. Mostly, he just held her. His presence did seem to calm her. A few days or weeks later, the blackness would lift, and she would once again be the fantastically engaging companion he loved.

When he met Bethany Cabrerra their junior year, Leah was happy for them. She liked Bethany and the two women got along well. When Bethany died, Tom suddenly understood, in horrifying detail, how completely *alone and sad* Leah felt in those desolate canyons of despair. He understood it so well that it shook the very bedrock of his life. Friends assured him the pain of losing Bethany would subside in time, but it was Leah in that permanent midnight who never uttered a platitude. Instead, she listened to him talk in halting, agonized speech because sometimes he literally had no words. It was Leah who cooked meals, and made sure he ate them, and reminded him to sleep. Her friendship during that horrible time was the most solid, tangible thing he possessed.

She now lived across from his condo in an apartment where he sometimes paid the rent for her. After six months of unemployment, she finally secured a position as a journalist at the *Washington Post*, fulfilling one of her lifelong dreams. Because of that, she had been in a great mood lately, but Tom still watched for the signs of depression.

The Court House Plaza was a large, cobblestone square surrounded by lunch shops, with benches for people watching. In the center of the frozen square was a beautiful fountain, though tonight it was turned off and silent. Leah was jogging in place on the steps of the fountain, trying to keep warm.

In companionable silence, they jogged a seven-mile tour of Washington that was Leah's favorite route. Back in the plaza, they returned to the fountain steps and stretched.

"Anything interesting happen at the newsroom lately?" Tom asked. He grabbed his ankle behind him to stretch his quadriceps.

Leah shrugged. "You mean besides us being on the precipice of war with Russia and Fallon Hughes being fingered for bloody murder?"

Tom ignored her piquant sarcasm. "Did you see the story about Antoine Campbell?"

She shrugged. "I heard something about it, but I was focused on the Russia situation all day. He was the suicide, right?"

"Yeah." Tom scrutinized her face for any sensitivity. Leah didn't wince at the subject. She had never had been particularly ashamed of her suicide attempts. She was even toying with the idea of writing a "memoir of suicide," as she called it.

"What was your first instinct about it?" Tom asked.

"I don't know. I hadn't thought about it."

"Allow me to fill you in. A guy commits suicide in the middle of D.C. Broad daylight. But the interesting thing? He chose to jump from a six-story building."

"Six stories?" A frown crossed her pretty features.

"Exactly."

"I wouldn't do it from six stories," she said. "There is no guarantee of death. If you do it and survive, you have to deal with the fact that you're going to be hauled off to the psych ward. But most importantly, I think that if you jumped and survived, it would cut off one of the available avenues of death. You don't want to experience the fear of impending death before you actually do it. You'd probably never try again."

As always, he was amazed at the fearless way Leah discussed death, particularly voluntary death. He admired her openness, even as he did not understand how she could stand to spend so much time fantasizing about her own oblivion.

"So if you were going to jump …"

"Tall building, definitely," she finished for him.

"You're not going to jump though, right?"

She smiled. "No thanks, not tonight. Jeez Louise, you don't have to ask me that."

"I know," Tom said, and spontaneously hugged her, enjoying her thin frame in his arms. "I want you around for a long time, that's all."

Leah stood on her tiptoes to kiss his nose. "I'm here. I have no plans to go anywhere."

"Promise?"

She rolled her eyes. "Do you really need a promise right now?"

"I really do."

"Then I promise."

It was nine o'clock when Tom Bishop said goodbye to Leah at her apartment and walked across the street to his condo. At the small desk in his bedroom, he turned on the ancient gooseneck lamp and scrolled through his phone for any Maryland State Police numbers. He had worked with Joe Bennett on a drug task force a few years ago and considered him a good guy, though they were not exactly friends.

After a few minutes of catching up, Tom asked what was going on with the Antoine Campbell case.

Bennett sniffed. "What do you mean, what's going on with it? Suicide, cut and dry."

"How do you know it was suicide?"

Tom could hear the sudden curiosity on the other end, that distilling of attention. Undoubtedly Bennett's territorial instincts were tweaked by the question. The fact that Tom was federal law enforcement would either relieve Joe because it would mean there was no competition from the feds to make a case, or it would cue him that he should be looking for wider implications in the case. No cop wanted to be caught out of the loop by another cop.

"There were eyewitnesses," Bennett said. "He'd stolen something, led the Maryland State Police on a chase, and then jumped off a building. Hundreds of witnesses verify it."

"Hundreds?"

"Well, plenty."

The witnesses could be anyone who worked in the area. Coming or going into the building in the course of their regular business, they would have seen Antoine Campbell ditch the car, run through the building, somehow knowing to enter the roof from the fifth floor, and then leap. Tom needed to talk to one of those witnesses.

"What did he steal, by the way?" Tom asked.

"I don't know. Drugs probably, but it's not my case so I don't have all those details."

Seeing there wasn't going to be a lot of revealing info forthcoming, Tom thanked him and ended the conversation.

If drugs were in the kid's system, it would be persuasive evidence that he really was out of his mind when he called Fallon. Tom wasn't quite sure what to do think yet. He was not one to jump to conclusions, especially when the conclusions were horrible.

He stood and paused, looking around the bedroom as if suddenly seeing it for the first time. It was very Spartan. After Bethany was killed, he'd gotten rid of all the pieces she had lovingly collected from showrooms and antique shops and replaced them with cheap, anonymous stuff. It had been a mad effort to divest himself of Bethany—but the joke was on him. The absence of her effects just made him miss her more.

After today with Fallon, the guilt was very near the surface. It felt pervasive and suffocating; he wished he had more self-control. He missed Bethany with a sudden acute jab to the chest that left him dizzy.

He could feel the despair gathering, then the spiral downward was swift and certain. He despised this ache, and, as he always did, he tried to fight it.

There were several palliatives but no remedy. Work, often. Driving, sometimes. But now he needed air, needed to breathe and think and try to dislodge the locomotive of guilt that was bearing down on him.

Spontaneously he grabbed the house key and ran down the two flights of stairs to the lobby. Straight out of the lobby doors, he began to run. Faster and harder than he had been able to with Leah, he ran through the plaza and along Wilson Boulevard. Legs pumping, heart pounding, he ran like he was being chased, the fury and missing and all the soft, sweet things he felt for Fallon building into a vortex of energy that fueled him through the neighborhood in a mindless, furious rush. He was two miles away, in front of the Key Bridge Marriott, before he allowed a single complete thought into his head.

Key Bridge would take him straight into Georgetown. Straight to Fallon. Somehow all roads led to her even when he didn't want them to. He'd been so sure that he would be able to simply say no when that attraction flared between them—yet his resolve had crumbled almost immediately. Four years, and he'd managed just fine. He'd turned down how many women? When Bethany died in those towers there was something about his grief that proved irresistible to women; they'd bring over cakes and casseroles, sweetly lingering, asking if he wanted company. He'd become adept at evading questions designed to prompt personal revelations, quite skilled at gracefully but firmly allowing women to know that he was permanently unavailable.

He missed sex grievously but he didn't want love or a relationship and he just wasn't built to have casual sex. It had never appealed to him and was unthinkable after knowing the intimacy and love he'd experienced with Bethany. Between the morning Bethany died and the day he met Fallon Hughes, he'd slowly hardened to quartz. Then Fallon melted him down to lava. With her, he was voracious, wanting her in every possible way, all the time. But that had been the opposite of a casual fling. He had been completely "in" with that one. Heart, mind, and body.

The experience with Fallon had burned him to the core. It had finally cured him of wanting intimacy with anyone in any degree. He'd learned to control his sex drive instead of it controlling him. He thought it very Zen.

After Fallon, he knew better than to play with fire. No sex. No flirting. Messy entanglements served only to protect fools from the reality that world was ultimately meaningless. He didn't need to be protected from that fact. He didn't even want to be. Even so, one had to pass the time and he chose to do so with work.

Once again, all she had to do was show up and his grip on his steely resolve vanished, like sand through a fist. It was much worse this time because he could not leave her without leaving his job—the one thing that sustained him at his lowest point and the one thing he lived for. He had to figure out a way to be close to her without giving himself completely over to her.

With Fallon, he could not muster the ruthless streak that enabled him to simply dismiss women without another thought. God no, even the thought of hurting her like he had on Paxos filled him with revulsion. How was he going to untangle this?

The memory of this afternoon's indiscretion left him dismayed. How had he just thrown away all his the resolve he'd acquired, year over year, not to mention professionalism, to fuck her in a small, dank little closet space in the middle of an office building? That risky behavior was seriously out of control and not like him at all. He was filled with disgust at his own lack of self-possession even as he undeniably wanted her again, right now. Maybe not like this afternoon, as hot and wild as it had been. He wanted her slower, so he could luxuriate in the experience. She would twine her slender limbs around him, press those petal-soft breasts against his face, let him nuzzle and kiss and lick. She would cradle his head, croon comforting things, and he would melt into her. Dissolve into her tender warmth.

Fucking disgraceful. He shook off the fantasy, revolted with himself.

She was too sweet to get involved with him. He was too cold, too cynical. A depressed, closed-off bastard; he had nothing to give her or any woman. Knowing this about himself, he should be mature enough to simply convey that to her. By keeping that fact hidden, he was only hurting again—the very thing he wanted to avoid.

He could sense how badly she had wanted him to reach for her after he fucked her in the vestibule. It was the worst part of the day, when he disappointed her.

But what skidded him into panic was that he wanted to reach for her, too. Wanted it bad. She'd woken up feelings he'd forgotten about, closed off with razor wire and "Keep Out" signs.

Goddamnit, he could not afford this frivolous bullshit.

Wet snowflakes had begun to swirl through the black air. The cold wetness felt good against his feverish face. Helped clear his head. He began to run back toward Rosslyn, slow and easy, trying to work out the problem of Fallon Hughes.

When he reached the empty Court House Plaza, he slowed to a walk. As he approached the steps that led to 14th Street, he noticed a car on a narrow side street. The red brake lights were on but the headlights weren't, and later, he would think it was that odd arrangement of lights in the snow that drew his attention. It seemed, in that instant, that he recognized the car. He had seen it this afternoon parked across from Fallon's apartment when they returned from the Blair House. It was possible that it was a different car, of course. He struggled to make himself believe that. Surely black late-model Volvo SUVs were not rare in the suburban soccer mom enclave of Arlington, Virginia. Nevertheless, Tom's sixth sense pushed him back against the wall, out of the reach of the decorative faux streetlights. He slowed his breath so it didn't puff in the frigid air, knowing it was possible the driver was watching him in the rearview mirror.

Yeah, he was a paranoid cop who suspected the worst in any given situation. But after Fallon's search warrant and Antoine Campbell's murder, anything less was suicidal.

Thickening snow made it difficult to see details like the license plate number or even which state the automobile was from. Suddenly the headlights flared, the brake lights went off, and the engine fired. The buildings were close together and in the canyon, it sounded very loud, like a roar. The car swerved from the curb and proceeded up the hill.

Tom took a long, slow look around him and behind him to make sure nothing else was out of the ordinary. He noticed nothing but snow and the dark windows of the shops.

He stepped out of the darkness and jogged across the street. The security in his building was good: it required both a key fob and a code to get in. On the second floor, he opened his front door and paused in the entry, waiting, scrutinizing the darkened kitchen and living room. In the hallway, he turned on the light, moving stealthily from room to room, finding nothing out of place. His Secret Service weapon, an extra magazine of ammo, and badge were on his bedside table, where he normally kept them.

Everything was normal.

Except for the wet snowy footprints on the carpet, left from the person who had been in his bedroom.

EIGHT

The next morning, Fallon was working diligently on the Chandler case until Tom's voice tore through her concentration. She heard him in the office next door, exchanging pleasantries with Cameron Chapman. After several moments of chitchat, Cameron walked by Fallon's door, heading back to the command center on the first floor.

Fallon waited about thirty seconds, then jumped out of her seat.

Tom smiled warmly as she entered his office. "Hello, Avalon."

"Good morning, Agent Bishop. Call the limos, would you please?"

"Yes, ma'am."

"Is that necessary?" she asked with fond exasperation.

"Yes, ma'am."

Fallon rolled her eyes.

At the elevator bank, out of earshot from the other employees, Tom asked, "How is it in the office today? Everyone curious about the warrant?"

"You could say that," she said. "Two people actually paused to chat with me today, for the first time ever." It had been rather embarrassing, trying to stiffly make small talk with people who so transparently wanted to know *what was going on*.

"How are you?"

"Fine," Tom answered. There was something stiff in his delivery though, and she thought he was brushing her off.

The elevator doors slid open where a somewhat nerdish woman was scrabbling in a giant patchwork handbag. She glanced at Fallon as they stepped inside. Fallon saw the sudden click, that burst of light in the eyes when people placed her, and she smiled politely as she pressed the button for the lobby.

Fallon could feel the woman burning holes in the side of her face. She hated those random moments when people recognized her because they always made her feel awkward. She was known for no reason of her own. Unlike her mother and father, she didn't crave the glamour of the camera or seek out opportunities to be photographed or filmed or interrogated about her parents at any given moment. Once in a while, she'd run into someone who believed that they knew her just because they'd heard her voice support for some issue or another or saw her on television. Those were the worst. Trying to get away from a discussion about something she really didn't care about with people she didn't know … yuck. It was very awkward.

Fallon saw the woman pull something out of her purse, then there was a blur in the corner of her eye, and in the next instant Tom had her arm twisted painfully behind her back. "Drop it," he ordered in a tone of voice Fallon didn't recognize. He was yanking the woman's arm painfully back and up, so she was on her tiptoes, her face distorted with pain and panic. Something silver dropped to the ground with a clatter. A camera. The back battery panel had broken off.

Tom blinked, as if not believing what he was seeing, and quickly let the woman go. Fallon reached down to pick up the camera. She replaced the battery panel, thinking like a lawyer that she might now be sued because her detail broke the lady's camera.

"I'm so sorry," she said, handing the camera to the frightened woman.

Her eyes were huge behind red-rimmed glasses. She looked with stunned, wide eyes from Tom to Fallon.

"Secret Service," Fallon said weakly.

"It looked like a weapon," Tom replied. Fallon was shocked at how calm he sounded. He was pumped up from an adrenaline burst, she could see that, but his voice was steady, his inherent politeness returning. Her heart was still pounding.

"It's not a weapon," she said. "My camera …. Can I have a picture?"

"Of course," Fallon said, doing her best to smooth over the situation. As the elevator doors opened in the lobby, the woman indicated a spot beside the security desk. Fallon stood in front of a potted plant and grinned broadly for the picture, aware that it would end up on Instagram in about three minutes.

Clusters of media people were waiting outside, cameras at the ready as they chased the search warrant story. Tom walked beside her, slightly behind, and another agent opened the door. When she came out, there was a cacophony of clicking cameras and a swell of voices shouting questions. If it had been her client accused of murder, she would advise them to keep their mouth shut, which is what she did. Pretending to ignore them, she climbed in the back seat of the limo.

Looking up at Tom, he seemed like a stranger as he slammed the door closed. She wanted to ask what was wrong but couldn't in the presence of the driver.

"The Four Seasons Hotel again, please, Agent Rowland."

"Wanna tell me what that confrontation was all about?" Fallon demanded as soon as they were alone in the building. She led him to a corner hidden from view by an escalator, then turned to face him.

"Just doing my job, ma'am," he said neutrally.

She flinched at the formality. Something really was off today. He seemed hypervigilant, looking around them, still on the clock.

"Look at me," she whispered.

When he did, his dark gaze was unapologetic.

"Something has happened," she said flatly. "Tell me."

"Not here," he said.

Fallon relaxed a smidge, pleasantly surprised that he wasn't stonewalling her. Still, the fact that he wouldn't just say what was on his mind irked her. Clinging to her dignity, she turned away, but Tom caught her sleeve and tugged her back toward him. The glib expression was replaced with something softer. Maybe regret for being so closed off, she thought. Not expecting that from him, certainly not here at this place and time, she felt disarmed. Just that one look brought to the shining, vivid surface just how many silly, hopeful fantasies had been bubbling at the back of her mind since yesterday. It was kind of pathetic actually. She'd fucked the guy yesterday and today was dying for a kind word, a gentle expression. Shame flamed her cheeks. Really, she had such low expectations of men. Tom too, she reluctantly admitted.

She tried to hush the internal criticism of him. She knew what kind of man he was from those days locked in each other's arms four years ago. He was capable of intense emotion, gentleness, joy ... genuine intimacy. She'd experienced it firsthand. To put it mildly.

"Meet me tonight," Fallon said spontaneously. "At Gwen's house. She's engaged and spends all her time at her fiancé's house. We can meet there and ... talk." She hoped they would do more than talk. Even just standing close flooded her with girlish awareness of him.

For a moment, he seemed to be thinking about it. Fallon braced herself for some lame excuse: he had to walk the neighbor's dog or something. To her surprise, he nodded subtly.

"I have to arrive first so my coworkers don't see me."

Wow. That sounded like a yes. "I'll set it up with Gwen."

"Okay," he said, without happiness, as if it had cost him a great deal to acquiesce.

Fallon smiled. "This will be nice."

"We'll see," he replied.

Fallon's expression must have revealed the little hurt of his words. He shook his head and ran his hand through his hair in a gesture. "That sounded wrong. I'm sorry. Of course it will be nice. We just have to ..."

"Be careful. I know."

"Okay. Good. Now let's go, Nancy Drew."

She rolled her eyes, but a smile did curve her lips.

Fallon led the way to the law firm that took up the entire fifth floor in cherrywood and gilt luxury. She mentally shifted gears as soon as she walked in.

The lacquered blonde at the receptionist desk looked up.

After a little pause she smiled, as if sharing the joke.

"Good morning. Agent Tom Bishop here is investigating the suicide of a young man who leapt to his death two days ago. We were hoping you might be able to tell us if there were any witnesses in this office to that tragedy?"

"Oh, it was horrible, wasn't it? I didn't see the actual jump, thank God, but when he came in here, I was leaving to use the ladies' room. He was shouting. He came running right toward me. I was really scared; he looked crazy. Out of control. I was relieved when the police officers came up. They grabbed him, but he got loose and then ran up to the roof."

"Were the officers in uniform?" Tom asked.

"The first one wasn't. Two more showed up, and they were in uniform."

"What was Antoine Campbell shouting?" Fallon interjected.

"That they were going to kill him." The receptionist actually looked traumatized. "He said it's a national security matter and that they were going to kill him."

"Did the officers interview you?"

"One of them briefly asked me what I saw and what Antoine was saying."

"Do you remember the detective's name or perhaps he gave you a card?"

"No, sorry. I didn't think to ask. I was quite shaken by the whole experience."

Tom switched angles and asked if there was anyone in the office who actually saw Antoine Campbell jump.

"Karen Schwartz did. She was on her way inside after a doctor's appointment and she saw the whole thing."

"Is Karen here?" Tom asked.

"I think so. I can page her if you'd like."

"That would be great," Tom replied. The receptionist paged her on the intercom but after several minutes, Karen still hadn't responded.

"She must not be at her desk," the receptionist said.

Tom handed her a business card. "Could you pass this to Karen and ask her to call me at her convenience?"

The receptionist looked at the card with the embossed five-point star that was the Secret Service emblem.

"I'll give it to her as soon as I see her."

Tom thanked her for her time. The door had barely closed behind them when Fallon said, "The police are chasing Antoine Campbell from Maryland, and only one detective and two officers follow him inside the building?" It seemed to her that in every police chase she ever heard about or saw, there were a dozen police cruisers with lights and sirens blazing, maybe a helicopter or two.

"It is odd," he agreed carefully.

Back inside the limo, Fallon's phone buzzed, indicating a text. From Gwen: HOW IS THIS FOR REHEARSAL DINNER? and a link, which Fallon didn't bother clicking. But the name Gwen Atwell on her phone triggered a sudden thought so absolutely brilliant that she was ashamed for not having thought of it sooner.

"Agent Rowland? I need to go to George Washington Hospital."

He glanced in the rearview mirror.

"I'm fine, I need to talk to a friend."

The hospital was only three miles away, but it seemed to take forever to get there. Since Gwen sent her a text about a rehearsal dinner venue, Fallon surmised Gwen was on a break. Gwen's break would be brief—ten, fifteen minutes—and Fallon had to reach her before she returned to her rotation and the business of birthing babies.

The limo swung into the circular drive only moments after the text. Tom jumped out and held open her door, and Fallon rushed inside the automatic double doors with Tom following. At the reception desk, she asked the attendant to page Dr. Gwen Atwell. "Tell her Avalon is here," she added.

The receptionist looked dubious.

"Please," Fallon said. "It's important."

"Avalon?" The woman frowned. "Names get stranger every year."

Over the loudspeaker, the receptionist announced, "Doctor

Atwell, you are needed at central admission."

Within a minute, Gwen appeared, looking alarmed at Fallon's presence at the hospital. She charged up to Fallon and clutched her in a tight hug, her eyes closed. "I was so scared for you."

"I'm okay. Dad has some people fighting the warrant, but I have to talk to you," Fallon whispered, extricating herself.

Gwen looked over to the Secret Service detail out of earshot and asked, "Are you really okay?"

"I'm fine. I need your help."

Gwen said, "Come with me." They walked beyond the reception area to a hallway that led to pediatric trauma center. Perversely, the walls were covered with cheerful yellow, pink, and blue flowers and bumblebees. Who were these walls trying to fool?

"A young man named Antoine Campbell committed suicide yesterday," Fallon said. "His autopsy would have been conducted here. I need the autopsy report."

Gwen's eyes widened. "What the hell is going on?"

"Please, Gwennie. It's complicated. I need the report."

"I can't do that," Gwen replied. "Why do you even want it?"

"Because he called me minutes before he died and I don't think he committed suicide."

Gwen looked deeply puzzled. And concerned. And just plain tired. Her coppery hair was yanked back in a sloppy ponytail. Her face was pale and devoid of makeup. Purple circles smudged beneath her eyes from days without sleep. Her lips were chapped.

Suddenly Fallon's bright idea didn't seem so bright anymore. It seemed like she was burdening her friend who had more than enough going on in her life right now without Fallon adding conspiracy theories and suicides.

"What happened yesterday with the search warrant?" Gwen asked.

"I don't know," Fallon said with a mystified little shake of the head. "But I think it's connected to the suicide call."

"As your friend, I'm telling you, you sound nuts."

"Granted. But Antoine Campbell is dead. If he really did

commit suicide, I will back off. But I need to know for sure because if he didn't kill himself, I am somehow a part of all this."

Gwen folded her arms over her chest. "Fallon …"

"Worst case scenario, you get arrested and my dad pardons you."

Unexpectedly, Gwen smiled at that. "You're asking me to do something really unethical."

"I know. I will never ask you for anything else again." Fallon said this with trepidation, aware that she was not only asking her friend to do something slimy, but betraying her own character. Honesty, truth-telling, and fairness were Fallon's reining virtues: she neither tried to create illusions nor indulged them in others. That might have been a reason the practice of corporate law did not come naturally to her.

Gwen sighed. "Okay. If I can get my hands on it, I will make you a copy. No promises though. I expect your dad to pardon me, Fallon. Seriously."

Fallon kissed her friend's cheek. "You won't need a pardon but if you do, you have my word." Two pardons, actually. One for her friend, and one for her. Because she was pretty sure she was breaking the law—even if there was no search warrant for this crime. Yet.

NINE

At Nordstrom in Pentagon City Mall, Leah Lennox stared at herself in the full-length mirror. The gown she'd bought earlier in the week had been tailored, and the result was just perfect. It was a long black silky-looking dress, sleeveless and slinky. It was the most sophisticated dress she had ever worn, and she felt as chic as a supermodel—poised, stylish and queenly. Of course her hips weren't exactly snake-like, and her skin looked a little blotchy … *Stop it*, she commanded herself. Not today. Not right now. This was a happy occasion.

Excitement would jolt her in sporadic starts, surprising her when she least expected it. She would be working and suddenly remember that she, Leah Lennox, was invited to an inaugural ball as part of the official White House press pool. It felt like a dream come true.

After being unemployed for months and feeling like her career was going nowhere, she was finally getting some traction. In a big way.

Leah stepped off the pedestal she'd been standing on. "It's perfect," she said to the seamstress. "I just need to change out of it."

In the spacious dressing room, Leah changed into her well-worn jeans and a black turtleneck. After she collected the dress on a hanger, she wandered downstairs to the floor with accessories. A bracelet and some earrings would work well with the dress—and Tom, who was paying for this because it was far outside the reach of her paycheck—had said to get whatever she needed for this occasion. Her gaze wandered over the array of sparkly things and landed on an extraordinary gold filigree cuff. She picked it up, surprised at the lustrous weight, and clasped it on her wrist. The gold cuff looked striking with her freshly manicured deep crimson fingernails.

"That is very fetching," a man said from beside her.

Leah looked up, surprised.

A raffishly handsome young man was looking at her with a pleasant smile on his face. He looked to be in his thirties, with wavy blonde hair and a sensual face. With light blue eyes and a pointed chin, he had a dashing quality about him, like a European prince. "Your bracelet. Very pretty."

"Oh," she blushed and took it off, suddenly feeling a bit awkward, like she'd been caught daydreaming or humming or something equally as private. "I just … yes, it is pretty."

She indicated to the saleslady that she would take it. Suddenly shy, Leah busied herself looking at earrings.

"Is there a special occasion?"

Leah smiled. "I'm going to the inauguration." She glanced up at him to see his reaction.

He looked surprised. "How did you finagle that?"

"I'm a member of the media," she replied casually, delighting in the sound of it. How long had she yearned to say those words and to achieve her dream of writing for a major newspaper? After many hard turns, it was her life now. Finally.

The man smiled, clearly impressed.

Leah picked up some beautiful gold and garnet chandelier earrings, watching the facets dance with light.

"Those would look very nice with your coloring. You have a beautiful olive tone to your complexion … the red works very well."

Before Leah could stumble for an appropriate response, the man held out his hand. "My name is Collin."

"Leah Lennox."

"It's very nice to meet you, Leah."

She felt a tingle of excitement. Was he hitting on her?

She indicated to the saleslady that she would also take the earrings.

"So what kind of media are you in? Television?"

"I'm a writer," she said, unable to contain her pride at being able to say those words.

"Fascinating."

"What do you do?" Leah asked nervously.

"I work for a political consulting firm," he replied smoothly.

Interesting. Besides the fact that he was gorgeous, he was also possibly an important contact. As a journalist trying to make her name, it was wise to keep her contact list growing.

The saleslady handed Leah the bag with her new jewelry.

"Pardon me if this is too forward, Leah, but you are beautiful, and I'd like to get to know you better. Would you consider having a drink with me?"

Leah, knocked for a loop, wondered if she'd just heard correctly. This never happened to her. Never. "I'd like that," she said.

He opened his wallet and searched through it. "I can't seem to find a business card. Why don't you give me your number, and I'll call you to arrange something?"

The saleslady handed him a pen and he jotted down Leah's number. He folded the piece of paper and then placed it in his jacket pocket. "I'll call you," he said.

"Okay," Leah replied. She watched him walk away.

Trying to shake off the strange, and kind of wonderful, encounter, Leah strolled over to the elegant handbags. She immediately locked eyes on the perfect evening clutch. It was black satin with discreet mottled platinum hardware, perfectly matched with the dress and the new cuff. And it was on sale, discounted enough that she could pay for it with her own debit card.

Today just could not get any better.

TEN

Should I or shouldn't I?

Tom asked the question a hundred times, walking past the address that Fallon had given him. He walked to the end of the street, pausing as if he were going to cross while discreetly checking his environment. It was a habit forged from his work, but it was more than that. Since his home had been broken into, he had the feeling he was being watched, that something was happening just beneath the surface.

Which was just one of a million reasons it was foolish to be meeting his protectee long after his business day had concluded. He still wasn't sure what he felt about Fallon, and the guilt was heavy as ever. Yet he couldn't really say no.

Gwen Atwell lived in a pricey but understated neighborhood about four blocks from Tom's condo. The Cape Cod-style house was small, and like its neighbors, it had a very large front yard with mature oak trees. Heliotrope and honeysuckle vines climbed up the walls at her front door and rambling rose bushes would be blooming in front of the porch if it were spring. For all her sophistication, Gwen's taste in architecture tended toward the twee.

Though he understood he was welcome, Tom still felt strange arriving at a woman's dark, empty home at night. After glancing around again to make sure he was not being observed, he found the key on the window ledge under a rock, where Fallon told him it would be. Unlocking the door, he entered the foyer and turned on a lamp.

Gwen's house reflected a cozy life. Inspired by the colors of the East Coast, she'd created a pretty home with blue, white, and beige furniture. Candles, candid snapshots, some in frames and some without, and knick-knack-covered shelves showing a full life of friends and travel. He was standing at the photos when he heard the low hum of the limos' engines on the street outside.

Tom walked farther into the house, careful to stay out of the sight of any agent who followed her to the door. Such a weird feeling, hiding from his teammates. The deception rankled.

Fuzzy radio traffic crackled faintly, then the car door slammed.

Tom's heart was racing; he could hear his own breath. It was a dangerous game he was playing here.

After a moment, a soft, rapid knock was nearly indistinguishable from it opening.

Fallon came inside, bringing with her a gust of cold air. She shut the door and locked it, then turned to face him, a bit rigid with uncertainty.

Tom was momentarily knocked for a loop. She looked like a girlfriend.

That was a fatal way to think of her, but it was the first thing that popped into his rattled head. In Paxos, she had been his idea of physical perfection. But now she seemed even more beautiful. Ethereal. He could appreciate the intelligence in her eyes and the character in the set of her lips in a way that maybe he didn't back in Greece.

She wore soft, well-fitted blue jeans that showed off her slim legs and a black cashmere sweater under an unbuttoned navy pea coat. Her shoes were simple black ballet flats, which made her look even more petite.

Definitely girlfriend material.

She took off the pea coat and hung it on the coat tree, then kicked off her shoes. Then she fussed with her hair, then put her hands on her hips as if she didn't know what quite what to do with herself, then finally clasped them in front of her, apparently settling on waiting to see what Tom would do.

They regarded each other warily. Tom's mind swirled, and he had the sensation for a second that he was falling from a great height: exhilarating and also terrifying.

All this was so out of context. This strange, sweet house,

his protectee, and being so powerfully attracted and so unwilling to break free of the spell she'd cast … it was like he'd been hypnotized. Exactly like the first time. He'd been carried along on the current of her vivacious energy, helpless to resist it after the dark years that followed Bethany's death. Like the first time, clanging disclaimers and warnings marched through his mind, but they drifted and became so inconsequential that they faded to background noise.

He wanted her. It was now the only impulse he could act upon.

He walked across the room to stand in front of her. "You look so beautiful," he whispered.

She smiled and shook her head. "I was tired after work. I guess I should have …"

Tom shook his head. "You're perfect."

Fallon looked up at him with wide, liquid blue eyes that were both vulnerable and hopeful. Cupping her face in his hands, he traced her sharp cheekbone with his thumb, then caressed her trembling lips. They parted beneath his touch. So beautiful. Delicate. Tom bent his head and lightly touched his lips to hers. A questing kiss. Her lips were warm and silky, inviting him to more.

And he wanted to take more. He locked his arms around her, drawing her to him, pressing her soft body against the hardness of his own. He deepened the kiss, running his hands up her back until they were laced in her thick hair, eliciting a little cry of surprise. Of hunger. Fallon's back arched, her soft breasts pressed against his chest.

She stepped back and looked at him with pure need, with a forwardness he would have found unnerving in any other woman. Her unique, confounding mix of boldness and vulnerability struck him as almost painfully sweet. She really was vulnerable and he knew, shamefully, that she had real reason to be scared—much more than he did. She was risking herself. The fact that he had disappointed her once before hovered between them like a dare.

She was so brave. She trusted him. He was a foundering,

lost soul. And she still saw something in him that made her think she could trust him. Amazing.

"Do you want to talk?" he asked, his voice sounding strangled to his own ears.

"Later." Her hand was warm over his. "Come on."

He followed her down a hallway to what appeared to be Gwen's guest bedroom. Fallon flicked on the recessed lighting, throwing the room into illumination. She turned to him, staring at him like a combatant, and began to tug at the button of his jeans. He stood motionless, watching her. Fascinated by the focused concentration on her face.

She buzzed down his zipper, then looked up uncertainly into his face. Like she was giving them both one final opportunity to back out.

Tom grabbed her close to him, kissing her lips, then sliding his hands under the soft, fuzzy-looking sweater, spanning his hands over her ribcage and up over the cups of her bra. Fallon stepped back and pulled the sweater off, dropping it on a nearby chair.

She wore a white cotton bra this time, with a tiny bit of lace on the cups. Functional—not a rich girl's lingerie. He loved it. Loved how her rounded breasts were severely restrained in the cups, creating sumptuous, teasing cleavage. Her jeans sat low on her lips, showing her narrow waist and flat belly.

She slid her jeans off her hips and discarded them, exposing her well-shaped legs to his voracious gaze. White undies. Plain and prim and perfect.

Her graceful hands went to the bra clasp between her breasts and then pulled the garment off her shoulders. The undies went next.

All those gorgeous landmarks of her naked body angling for attention sent his brain into a spin. Out of control, car-sliding-on-the-ice feeling.

"You're shaking," she whispered and placed her hand on his burning hot chest. "Why?"

As if he would have to explain that he was a little amped up when a beautiful, brilliant goddess was naked in front of him.

Everything about her was exquisitely sweet, divine, like she was created just to drive him out of his fucking mind.

That was the problem.

He couldn't think when he was around her. He acted on instincts activated by her magic, and the consequences were catastrophic.

Fallon smiled and lifted her arms around his neck, coiling her sensuous body against him like a siren. Oh God. No fucking way was he going to be able to resist this.

"If you don't fuck me right now, I will scream," she whispered, her smile deepening, her face utterly guileless.

If she just wanted sex, he could do that, maybe. His entire adulthood had been spent refining the art of compartmentalization, so there was no reason this couldn't be the same.

She placed her hand over the erection that bulged painfully, eagerly against his clothing.

Tom was mute, still paralyzed with the combination of unbearable desire and his knowledge that he should not act on it.

"I want you to fuck me," Fallon whispered.

He was not prepared for the effect of hearing those filthy words come over her beautiful teeth. It ricocheted through his body, rendering him nearly helpless to resist much longer.

"What do you want?" she asked back.

Tom answered with a careful kiss, calibrated to try and understand his own answer to her question. He felt every detail intensely: her velvety softness and heat, the plush interior wetness of her mouth, her slender body quavering in his arms.

Fallon gently pulled away, her expression ecstatic. Her eyes were wide, her pupils huge. She seemed lit up inside, like a nun burning with holy fire.

"You."

Fallon smiled then, a slow and naughty smile that he remembered from Paxos—oh yes, he knew where that led.

Tom unbuttoned his shirt, took it off, and dropped it on the ground. Fallon watched, her expression impassive except for the slight intake of breath at the sight of his chest.

He pulled off his pants and his black boxer briefs.

"Oh God," Fallon whispered. She dropped to her knees and took him in her mouth.

Oh Jesus. Not at all what he'd planned. He was knocked out with her sweetness, the way she immediately began sucking, her hands cupping his balls. She swirled her tongue around the head, then drew the shaft into her mouth as deeply she could. She glanced up at him, all big doe eyes, thick curling lashes, and huge blue irises. His heart was going to explode in his chest. All her tentative little touches and licks and sucks, the way she moaned, holding him in her mouth as deep as she could take it, then slowly pulling back, like she couldn't get enough of him, left him helpless in her thrall. An unusual feeling. Too late now though.

He shut his eyes, enjoying the plush, hot slide of her mouth on him. She licked the underside of the head, making him shudder against her, and he had the strange realization that she remembered he liked that. Gently, he pushed her back on her heels and she stayed, looking up at him.

"Come here," he said.

Fallon stood up and positioned herself in front of him, so his hard cock was pressing hopefully against her belly, the top of it grazing her belly button. She gently began to tug him with long, milking strokes. He had to do something to get away from the stimulation overload.

He moved out of her grasp and slid his hand between her legs, finding that her wetness had smeared onto her inner thighs. Gently his fingers brushed her slickened lips, relishing the outrageous wetness, her obvious desire. Capturing his mouth to hers, he kissed her again and slid two fingers inside the cushiony heat of her sex. Hot, wet heaven.

She made a husky little noise against his lips and arched toward the contact.

"How long have you been thinking about me?"

"Since the first moment I saw you in my office," Fallon replied.

God, he loved the way she surrendered completely to him. There were no games with Fallon, no obfuscations or hedging;

she was open and exposed. More generous than any woman he'd ever known, more fascinating, more interesting. How was it that someone who was so open was the most mysterious woman he'd ever met? It was a paradox.

He removed his fingers and pulled her closer so the length of her body burned erotically against his. Skin on skin contact. Nothing like that velvet smoothness to make his mind go to mush.

He walked Fallon backward to the bed and eclipsed her body with his own. Fallon shoved his shoulder, pushing him aside, and rolled on top of him.

He remained propped up on his arms as Fallon straddled him. He was thick, so Fallon slicked the fat bulb of his cock with her juices, then slowly eased herself down on him. He shuddered and groaned involuntarily as every inch was squeezed in Fallon's slick grip. Penetration. Nothing like it. All that sweet womanly heat … her sex was a silky wet glove around his cock.

Their gazes locked. Fallon exhaled slowly, her lips trembling. He wanted to lean forward and kiss her so he wouldn't have to see the open adoration in her face. Instead, he leaned forward and took a piquant pink nipple in his mouth and lavished the little bud of flesh with insistent sucking. Fallon wrapped her arms around his neck as he sucked.

"Oh God …" she whispered. She began to move up and down on his cock, drawing him in deep with every down stroke.

He leaned back, watching her, delighting in the details of her body as she became increasingly excited. Her breasts bounced, the flat span of her belly contracted with little muscles. Her thighs squeezed as she grinded on him. He wrapped her in his arms, gently pushing her hips down on him to take him even a little deeper on the downstroke, so he was pressed as deeply as he could possibly go, right up against her cervix. Fallon gasped, her unguarded eyes wide. "I'm going to come," she moaned.

"Do it. Come. Over and over again. I want to watch you."

Fallon arched her back and cried out as the pleasure began to surge through her. He felt her tiny muscles clench his cock. No matter how distant he tried to remain during sex, he couldn't watch her climax without feeling like he was going to either come or cry. The emotion wrapped around his heart and yanked. She was so sweet, so perfectly wonderfully sweet. She was lost in the torrent of sudden bliss and he was thankful for it. He could not bear the possibility that she might see the raw intensity in his face so he held her close, letting her use his big body as ballast.

After she stilled, she tossed her hair back and looked him in the eye. Wordlessly she began to grind against him again. He could do this all night: let her break herself against him, use him for her pleasure. She seemed content to grind herself against him, working herself up to one of those heart-racing, soul-quaking orgasms that seemed to bolt through both of them, like she was sharing it with him. Her energy was intoxicating.

She lolled her head against his chest. "How do you want me?" she rasped.

Tough question. He wanted her in every position, sweet and filthy, slow and fast and frenetic. He could think of approximately two thousand ways to fuck her that would be just perfect. But he needed to prove to himself that this was a fuck, purely physical. Two animals fucking for pleasure. Best way to do that was …

"From behind," he said.

Fallon looked surprised. "Oh. Okay… " She slid off him. "How …"

"Hands and knees," he said.

"I'm not really … I mean …"

"You'll love it," he said, ignoring the timid look on her face. "You have such an amazing body. I want to see it while I'm fucking you."

Fallon kneeled up to kiss him. He gently kissed her but didn't linger. After watching her crack open like that, he couldn't luxuriate in the aftermath. Slowly, Fallon lay down on her tummy, then came up on her hands and knees. Tom positioned himself behind her, admiring the bright gold of her hair brushing her upper shoulders, drawing attention to her strong, straight back, tiny waist, and the high, round globes of her perfect ass. So pretty. Everything about her was so feminine and beautiful.

Her sensitive pink slit was wet, glistening. He rubbed the head of his cock up and down, his whole body preparing for that hot, tight glide into her. He drew in a sharp breath, his muscles trembling with restraint.

"I feel … Tom … this isn't what I wanted."

"Relax, Fallon. I promise, it will rock your world."

"Tom …" He heard a note of genuine distress in her voice. "What is it?"

She sat down and turned around to face him. "You seem different," she whispered. She looked scared, and his heart split. Was she seeing that ruthless side of him, the side he'd done his best to hide because he knew it was ugly and he was ashamed of it?

He wanted to believe he had succeeded in erecting an emotional wall between them, but it was suddenly obvious that the pretense was only self-delusion. Fucking her from behind like she was anonymous and acting like an uncouth rogue would not mitigate the emotion he felt. Wouldn't subtract from the intensity he felt. It would just be another lie.

He suddenly lunged at her, pushing her back against the mound of pillows. He covered her mouth with his, trying to apologize with his kiss. He lifted his head, then slid down her body, caressing her soft breasts, kissing her belly. He shifted between her thighs and pressed his face into the soft, tender flesh, inhaling her scent. He licked up the syrupy slit, intoxicated by her taste. Honey. He would be content to simply lick her all night if that was what she wanted. He wanted to prove something to her, something about his character, and this was the only way he knew how to do it.

After several long moments, Fallon whimpered. "I want to come."

"Come, baby," he growled, licking her with feverish, tender ferocity.

"No, with you inside me. Hurry, please."

He tore himself away and looked up at her. The naked desperation was obvious. "Please," she whispered.

Fallon reached for him, and he hovered over her. "Hurry,"

she said against his mouth guiding him into the slick sweet grasp of her body. Pure heaven. She wrapped her legs around his waist and held him tight.

He was astonished at her kindness, her generosity. He did not deserve her. He did not deserve this. But Fallon kept giving it to him. He didn't know how to make her stop. And now he didn't want her to. God, he wanted all of her. Her forgiveness, her sweetness. He tried to convey all this in the feverish thrusts of his cock inside her.

Fallon's eyes fluttered open. "I'm going to come again, Tom. Come with me, please …"

The beg in her voice is what did it. That sweet, plaintive "please." He nuzzled into her honey-scented hair and finally let himself be swept away in the frenzy. Fallon held on to him, but he was also holding on to her, clinging to her, to the past, to the present, afraid if he let go, it would be gone forever. The pleasure seemed to belong to both of them at the same time, an incredibly powerful force pushing them into each other.

It took a long time to remember himself. Fallon clung to him, her face in his chest, her arms around his back. He gently rolled over to his side, holding her close. She folded into the crook of his arm naturally. He pet her silky hair, rubbed her neck, anything to keep his hands moving over her shaking, sweating body. She held him tight, like she was afraid to let him go.

Tom pressed a tender kiss to the top of her hair and shut his eyes. He'd given this up, he reminded himself. Women, sex, love. He'd abandoned that particular brand of trouble. Except for Fallon. A deep thrum of constant anticipation had hummed in the back of his consciousness all day. Now that he had her, he wanted more. Wanted to play with her, to really enjoy her. Not just in snatches of time but for an extended period of time. Like in Paxos. She was right; he was different. But until this moment, he didn't realize just how different. An ache in his gut felt remarkably like fear. Fear of knowing that he was breaking his own rules, and he was exposing himself to Fallon's magic. The savageness was gone now. Only tenderness remained.

His cock twitched, lengthening and thickening

between them.

Fallon made a soft, approving sound and then gently gripped the thick shaft. She pressed a kiss to his throat. At the caressing warmth, Tom moaned.

"How can you be ready for more after that?" Fallon whispered.

"It's you," he replied honestly. "You do this to me."

Tom gently rolled her onto her back and then propped himself between her legs. He wanted to look at her. To admire her.

Gently, he slid his fingers over the plush labia, wet with their juices. She bit her lower lip, but as his thumb began to caress her clit, she sighed luxuriously, letting her knees fall open in trusting surrender. Wide open. Defenseless. The look of gentle hope and admiration and pleasure on her face made him want to be worthy of that esteem. He touched her reverently, tenderly.

Her hips rolled eagerly as he dipped a slick, gleaming finger into her. He glanced up at her face to see if he was pleasing her. Her face was very grave. Her lower lip, swollen from his rough kisses, trembled. Her gaze met his evenly, then her eyelashes fluttered closed. Her flushed cheekbones, the sooty sweep of her lashes, her trembling mouth were intensely erotic. Fragile and strong at the same time.

She found a rhythm, working herself against his thrusting fingers with increasing urgency until her hips were rolling sensually against his hand as she was straining for release. She shook with shuddering tension.

"Can I have it," she rasped out. "Your … cock … please," she panted, her thighs clenching desperately around his hand.

Tom hooked her knees around his elbows and began to rub the swollen head of his cock against her slit. She was dripping like an exotic fruit, but even so, it was a slow, tight entry. Inching in by slow degrees, she quaked and sighed. He leaned forward, kissing and nuzzling into her neck as she stretched around him.

He held himself inside her, letting her get accustomed to him again. Tom pressed kisses to her forehead, her jaw. Fallon began to move against him, her breath coming in slow, hitching gasps. Tom looked down at her gorgeous breasts, her tummy, the trim nest of curls between her legs where they were joined. Physically and emotionally joined, he thought. They'd always been joined. Always had these fine interconnecting wires between them, and no matter how far away, they were always aware of the other. He gently let her legs down, and her arms came around him, holding him tight.

He felt her body ramping up to orgasm, and he forced himself to hold his own back. She gripped his upper arms, wrapped her legs around his waist, and cried out. He felt the soft fluttering of her inner muscles hugging his cock, watched her face transform as she began to climax.

He felt his own climax gathering at the base of his spine.

"Wait," Fallon gasped.

Tom, breathing hard, stopped thrusting, afraid he'd hurt her. He pulled back and looked into her flushed face.

"Wait, get up," she said, shoving at his shoulder.

Confused, he shook his head. "Why?"

"Just do it," she said.

Reluctantly, he slid from the sweet hotness of her pussy and sat up on his ankles.

Fallon turned over, getting on her hands and knees. Tom swallowed hard against the emotion that was twisting through his throat.

"Like this," she said.

"You don't have to ..."

"I want it," she said. "I want to give you what you want."

He couldn't argue. He had to be inside her. He positioned himself behind her, then slid inside. He tried to be gentle but he was already on a knife's edge.

"Oh God," he thought she whispered as she clenched around him.

"You're so beautiful," he said.

"Do you like it?"

"Mmm-hmm." The physical sensation was intense, but the emotional component was much more compelling. He recognized this was a risk for her, and it was a test for him. It was a sneaky opportunity to switch off, to look at her like a faceless, meaningless fuck. But he couldn't do that now. She was Fallon, and she was trying to make him happy.

He gently grasped her hips and began to thrust. Fallon began to rock against him. The sensation was outrageous. Silky, sweet friction. Her sensual energy driving him deeper and deeper, further away from himself.

When he came, Fallon cried out. That was the last thing he remembered before the long soul-smashing orgasm seized him. Fallon fell forward, and he lay down on top of her, unable to move.

Fallon giggled, with her face smushed in the pillow. "That was crazy. I could feel your ... um ... semen." Tom gently rolled off her. She turned and looked at him. "I mean, I normally feel it, but that was really intense."

Tom smiled, pushing her hair back so he could see her face, which suddenly grew serious. "Is it always like this?"

Tom shook his head slowly. "Not in my experience."

It was little more than an hour later and Tom was walking home. It was cold and it had rained earlier in the day; he hardly noticed the chill. His legs felt weak, but his chest felt strong. Hell, he felt like he could run down the street, take off, and fly. His phone buzzed and Leah's phone number appeared on the caller ID. He discovered right this instant that he was eager to talk to her. "What are you doing?" he asked by way of greeting.

"Writing and watching television. What are you doing?"

He avoided the question by asking one of his own: "Want to meet me at the sandwich shop for a late supper?"

Leah, always a little hungry either because she couldn't afford food or because she was dieting, enthusiastically agreed to meet him in the Plaza in five minutes.

As he turned the corner, Leah came into view. She stood in the plaza looking up through the rain-lashed air to the invisible sky. At this distance, in that pose, she appeared to be a very young girl. Her hands were tucked deep in her pockets, her face lifted in three-quarters profile against the muzzy background.

Leah wore a black knit cap, which mashed down her brown hair and forced pretty copper curls to explosively emerge from her temples to her shoulders. Her narrow silhouette reinforced his impression of a twelve-year-old child.

When she noticed him, she smiled broadly and jogged toward him. Tom hugged her warmly, inhaling her sweet female scent, as she warmed up next to his big body. Together they walked toward the sandwich shop where Leah could get the sandwich she liked: turkey with no mayo and plenty of hot peppers on "skinny bread." She was phobic about carbs this month.

The little café was nearly empty with only one other patron, an older gentleman hunched over a newspaper open to the business section. Tom and Leah sat down with their trays of food.

Tom intended to ask Leah more about her thoughts on Campbell's suicide, but before he could start, he noticed a dark blue late-model Volvo idling across the street, ghostly plumes of exhaust visible in the cold, wet evening.

Leah waved her hand in front of his face. "Hello? You okay?"

"I'll be right back," he said, but he was already halfway to the door. As he opened the door, the car speeded away.

Tom stared after it, seething, his adrenaline pumping.

"You okay?" Leah had appeared beside him.

Tom dragged his focus back to Leah. "Yeah, just … thought I saw a friend." Leah looked at him thoughtfully. She knew him well enough to know he was lying, but also knew him well enough to not to probe—not when he was in that focused, scary state.

"Come on," she said, pulling him back into the café.

"Why did you want to meet me?" she asked.

He looked out the window, dragging his attention back to her.

"You okay, Tom? You look … electrified."

He felt it too. From Fallon. From that Volvo.

"I need a favor," he said grimly.

Leah chuckled. "It is strange hearing you say that. Usually I'm the one asking you for favors."

Tom leaned in close. "Fallon received a call from Antoine Campbell right before he jumped. He said he had some national security information and he urgently needed to speak to her. Fallon and I went to meet him, but he never made it."

Leah's features sharpened and intensified. Her attention was total. "And then he leaped from that short building," she whispered.

"It doesn't make sense," he said. "Right after the jump, the FBI served a search warrant on Fallon at her office accusing her of murder, which has contributed to the general state of paranoia."

Leah's eyebrows knit prettily together. "And you think they're related?"

"It's all very strange." He hesitated, trying to decide whether to tell her about the Volvo and the snowy footprints in his bedroom.

"What can I do?"

"I'm not sure. Just keep your eyes open, I guess. If you hear anything …"

Leah grinned. "I'll start in the morning," she said. "I'll tell my editor that I got a tip and …"

"No," Tom exhorted, "No, Leah. There's more news out there for you to chase, like the situation with Russia. But if you hear anything …"

She made a face.

"I'm serious. Please."

"Okay," she sighed dramatically. She shrewdly scrutinized him. "Why are you looking at me like that?"

"I'm thinking what a great girl you are."

She rolled her eyes.

He smiled gently at her and lifted a chip from her paper plate. Eager to get his mind off both Antoine Campbell and Fallon, he asked, "Are you excited about the inauguration?"

Leah could not suppress a giggle of glee as she launched into a discussion of how amazing this experience would be. Her excitement was palpable. Life really was improving for her, and Tom was glad to see it.

When they finished the meal, Tom walked with her back to her apartment building. "You don't have to see me up," she said.

Tom didn't show it, but he was thankful. After tonight with Fallon, he felt something that needed contemplation and reverence and solitude. He said goodnight to Leah, kissed her cheek, and walked home.

ELEVEN

As soon as she was back inside her apartment, Leah got back to work. Visions of Bob Woodward-level fame danced before Leah's eyes as she pulled together copious public information on the crisis with Russia. Her handwritten notes took up several pages but no names were on the record. Nobody worked harder than Leah Lennox at developing sources for news and leaks. One of her weekly tasks was to call the VP's office or senators' offices, getting to know the press secretaries and chiefs of staff, anyone who might give her an inside story, or at least an exclusive. Her perseverance paid off, giving her access to several good sources for top-flight information. One person who trusted her, and who had given her some good information in the past, particularly during the presidential campaign, was Claudia Wells, the former senator of Virginia, who would be vice president in a week.

Leah thought of her now, as she looked up from her notes to the news conference replaying on the nightly news. Leah had been at that news conference this afternoon, sitting way in the back, and even then she could feel the tension between Hughes and his predecessor. Russia's potential threat to United States was mounting, and the competing viewpoints of the current and imminent administrations were causing as much anxiety as the issue itself. Ballard wanted dialogue. Hughes, determined to make an impact from his first moment in the Oval Office, was making demands.

Leah had managed to fire off one question. "Mr. Hughes, during the campaign you said—I quote—the United Nations is an organization as impotent as the Nevada Gaming Commission. You've said that you want sanctions against both Russia and

Iran. My question is, would you use UN forces to enforce those sanctions, or do you have a plan for the United States to handle this crisis on our own?"

A few titters of laughter moved through the press pool. Putting feet to fire of a new president was a right of passage, but nobody had expected the pointed question to come from the upstart. Leah did not dislike Hughes and the question wasn't intended to embarrass him. It was intended to prove to the other journalists that she knew her stuff.

Hughes answered, "Everything is on the table." A nonanswer. Next time she would push harder for a definitive answer. She would have to if she ever wanted to reach her goal of being the doyenne of political correspondents.

Leah had learned about the Cold War in middle school. She could remember the roll-down maps in her social studies class and the giant white space that took up the USSR, spanning the Arctic like a cape. The teacher discussed peace talks at Reykjavik and the threat of nuclear war. The lessons imparted a dull feeling of dread in her belly, which had returned with the renewed crisis. The standoff between the two countries seemed an awful lot like history repeating itself. The United States wanted Russia to immediately cease selling nuclear materials to Iran. Russia scoffed; they were sovereign people and could engage in diplomatic and economic ties with whomever they wanted.

Iran had begun to openly proclaim its intentions to destroy the USA. By assisting Iran in its nuclear capabilities, Russia appeared to be less an ally every day. Their diplomats assured the USA that they remained committed to a friendly relationship with the USA. In fact, they were dependent on the USA economically and did not want to sour that relationship even as they assisted in Iran's nuclear ambitions.

Leah glanced at the time on her cell phone and decided it was not too late to call Claudia Wells to ask if she had any inside information.

She sounded preoccupied from the first moment. Leah offered to call back tomorrow, but Claudia declined. "Actually it's only going to get more crazy as the week progresses, I fear."

"What do you think of this Russia situation? Is there any serious threat of the USA going to war with Russia? It's starting to be talked about openly by unnamed sources in the current administration."

Claudia paused, obviously judging whether or not to reveal what she knew. "This is off the record?"

Leah frowned. Damn it, she was hoping for an on the record comment. Still, she wouldn't turn down free information. "Absolutely. I'll call you a 'government source.'"

"Don't screw me on this, Leah," she warned.

"I won't," Leah replied emphatically. A keen sense of discovery was at hand. She knew better than to betray her sources.

"I don't have all the facts yet but it appears we might have a mole in our government," Claudia said. "Someone working for the Russians."

"A spy?" Leah was nearly breathless. She had heard nothing about a spy.

"Why do you think that?"

"Because two of our extremely highly placed assets in Moscow were murdered today."

Leah was stunned to silence.

"The current secretary of state is debating whether to kick all the Russian diplomats out of D.C. If he does that, the Russians will kick ours out of Moscow. That will only ratchet up the tensions."

After asking questions for fifteen more minutes, Leah hung up and began to type up her report, carefully avoiding any hint of where the information originated. Two dead Americans in Moscow … Her knowledge of history reminded her wars had begun over much less than that. She shivered with a sudden, horrible thought: those were the first dead of World War Three.

She abandoned her original piece and began writing the story about the two dead Russians. She would not wait to turn it in tomorrow; she would call the office and get it filed to the *Washington Post* website tonight.

• • •

No answer. Richard Mullinax folded his phone, tucked it into his pocket, and paced the plush white carpet of his luxury apartment in Chevy Chase. Anxiety had been building and gnawing at him all day because he could not get hold of Omar Koss. Emails, phone calls, it all vanished into a sucking black hole with no response at all.

Since he learned that two Russian assets were murdered in Moscow, he had begun to feel honest fear. Resonating down deep in his bones, a suspicion that his fate was sliding out of his own hands. The map of the keys had been delivered to Moscow as they had planned, but he did not expect the Russians to respond so quickly. He had hoped for time to distance himself from his involvement in the scheme. And now Omar was AWOL.

In frustration, he again dialed the number Omar had given him. An automated phone voice said, "The person you are trying to reach is unavailable." Then it hung up without even giving him an opportunity to leave a message. Omar must be screwing him, but why? The money had been wired to Omar's offshore account; there was no reason to leave him in the cold.

Multiple scenarios of revenge floated through his mind. Perhaps he should warn Fallon Hughes that her life was in peril. Of course he wouldn't actually do that. It would expose his relationship with Omar and that must be prevented at any cost.

Where are you?

His body felt sick and weak, like he was missing some essential vitamin. Perhaps he should call Claudia for a quick romp. No, he was too distracted even for Claudia. This wasn't supposed to happen. He was the Deputy Director of the National Security Agency; he should be able to track Omar on his cell phone. The secret truth, admitted only in the privacy of his own mind, was that he was a bureaucrat, not one of the hotshot code breakers. He had run Omar's phone through a simple GPS tracking system, but nothing showed up. He could not risk asking an underling to try some more advanced probes, such as trolling for email messages, texts, and the like. To do so would bring attention. All it would take was one stupid insignificant code jockey to remember that Mullinax knew

Omar's name and it would be Game Over.

Omar Koss was so discreet his name had never appeared on any of the internal watch lists or terror org. charts, sometimes called Terror Trees, that crossed Mullinax's desk every day. That alone spoke to his skill. The thousands of threads that connected one terror group to another were full of auxiliary names, but he appeared nowhere. He was a ghost. He would not be contacted until he wanted to be contacted.

It had only been one day, Mullinax told himself. His panic was eating at him, warping his senses. There was still time for Omar to explain himself.

He tried to remain calm. The investigation into the deaths of the two operatives would logically start in the CIA. They would be looking for someone who had access to identities of US sources in the KGB and Russian military and probably someone who directed the analysis of Russian intelligence operations. It would take time for the CIA to clear those people. They may never come to the conclusion at all the NSA was involved at all.

Stupid thinking. He knew from his earliest training at the NSA that arrogance was the Achilles heel of most spies. They believed they were smarter than everyone else. Richard certainly did not feel that way now. Having actually committed espionage, his confidence in the abilities of the US government to track his illicit activities had grown exponentially.

Perhaps he could leave. He would go to Costa Rica or Panama. No, no, now he really was thinking crazy. If he left there would be no doubt of his guilt. The CIA or his own organization would send teams after him, they would steal him in the night, wrap his mouth in tape, and drag him back to the USA with indictments and handcuffs, lawyers and trials, and ultimately the needle, sliding under his skin, thin deadly streams of venom shooting into his veins; he envisioned a pale light tracing from the needle insertion up his arm to his heart. They said you don't feel it; they give you a drug to make you unconscious, then your heart stops beating and then you're dead.

He shivered despite his profuse sweating. He had to talk to Omar. He had to get Omar to help him cover his tracks. Omar would help him erase his involvement in the deaths of those diplomats. If Omar could do that—and he had to do that—then Richard would resume his ordinary life and forget the billions of dollars that he had planned. He would one day be the director of the National Security Agency. He would be the best director in the history of the agency: squeaky-clean.

He felt for the phone in his pocket and dialed again.

TWELVE

Fallon told herself that she was not dressing for Tom, but never could Fallon recall wearing a sexy jersey wrap dress and knee-high boots to the office. She'd woken up feeling amazing, with well-being glowing like sunshine in her veins. She never felt sexy and happy anymore. She wanted to wear something that reflected her newfound attitude.

When she stepped into the corridor where Tom was waiting, she saw that the dress had been the right decision. He took a slow, sensual visual tour of her outfit—and her body—and her heart fluttered. She had the feeling it wouldn't have mattered what she was wearing. He seemed to like to look at her, no matter what.

"Good morning," she said.

"Good morning, ma'am."

"We're back to *ma'am*?"

"You will always be *ma'am* during work hours." He radioed the drivers that Avalon was en route.

They stepped into the elevator, and the doors glided closed. Tom leaned in to kiss her: smooth, all male, and totally hot. The delicious contact ended too soon as the elevator arrived in the lobby.

Beyond the wide glass windows, a few reporters were gathered on the sidewalk, even as a picturesque sugary snow fell. Across the street, satellite trucks were queued up. Suddenly the dreamy pleasure of Tom gave way to the cold reality that her life was in shambles, and she was still accused of murder. That knowledge had a way of making everything seem small and insignificant by comparison.

Tom asked, "Do you want to go through the garage?"

The motorcade was idling at the curb. It would be quicker to run the gauntlet. "Let's just go."

Two agents positioned by the doors kept the media from getting too close, but she could hear them barking questions, the word "murder" spiking the cold, still air.

She climbed into the backseat and the doors slammed closed behind her. Fallon shut her eyes, listening to her heartbeat and trying to find some semblance of calm.

Fallon lightly thumbed the keypad of her iPhone, trying to decide whether to call her father and ask what was going on. Obviously, he didn't especially want to hear from her. He had not called back with any information about the FBI warrant or the impending charges against her. He certainly had not called to ask if she was okay after being scared witless by a search warrant. Perhaps this silence was his way of disowning her. As disownments went, this one was pretty low-key. Disavowal by ignoring.

Spontaneously she dialed her mother's cell.

"Hello, dear," Elizabeth answered crisply.

"Hi. I just wanted to find out how Evan is doing today."

"He's having breakfast," she said.

"Mom, you need to hire a better minder. Kendra is completely irresponsible."

"Oh good Lord, Fallon. I am so tired of you criticizing me—"

"This isn't about you. It's about Evan."

Elizabeth wasn't listening. She had gone off on a tangent about how mean everyone was to her.

Same old routine. Frustrating as hell.

"I'm at work now, Mom. I'll call later." She hung up and jumped out of the car.

At her desk, Fallon got to work on the Chandler case. She'd only just begun to review the updates when her cell rang. It was her mother again.

"I wanted you to know I thought about what happened yesterday and I've decided that I need to confront your father about the movie."

Oh God, no more. No more of this craziness. Fallon made

a noncommittal "hmmm."

"You really helped clarify that for me yesterday. I forgot to ask while you were here. Have you bought your inaugural gowns? I wanted to make sure we're coordinated."

Fallon wanted to mention that she was presently under suspicion of murder and thus pretty inauguration frocks had slipped her mind, but she knew better than to antagonize her mother.

She squeezed her eyes shut, trying to figure out how to handle this. Finally she diverted herself from the issue like she did every other time it confronted her. "Have to go," she said and hung up.

In that moment, she felt pity for the people of the United States who had elected her father. Her parents were clueless, selfish people whose naked lust for power was embarrassing to witness. Her father was a politician, so he, at least, had the polish. He spoke the political language, even if he was badly prepared for life in Washington, D.C.—a fact he would never concede simply because he was ignorant about how national politics worked. Her mother, on the other hand, was a Hollywood actor who had absolutely no concept of what normal people expected and deserved from their politicians. Beautiful gowns? Nobody cared about her gowns. There was a potential war with Russia looming on the horizon, a shaky economy, the fact that Iran was getting nuclear weapons, and terrorism, and a thousand other things that normal people cared about before they cared about what color her mother's gowns were.

Fallon understood her mother's strangeness to some degree. Her mother had not worked in five years. She was an artist. She needed to create, which had to be why she was so excited about *Kill Shot*; it was an opportunity not only to act but to do something dangerous. There was a fission of excitement about it. Her father would—rightly, in Fallon's opinion—put the kibosh on that idea. While Fallon loved Tarantino films, she could not imagine her father would countenance the First Lady actually acting in one.

The role Elizabeth presently occupied was not one she took

to easily. Her wings were clipped; she was suffocating.

The drinking, though, had begun when they moved full-time to Helena. What was she supposed to do all day in Helena? She tried to work in Los Angeles as much as possible, but by then Preston was making noises about it being improper for her to work. "The First Lady of Montana does not make movies," he had bellowed at her when Fallon was home from Pepperdine one Christmas. Soon after, Fallon noticed the subtle change in her mother. Then the changes grew dramatic. Her mother seemed to float through long, heavy days not constructed out of anything solid as a meal, a telephone call, an appointment with a friend.

Drinking helped the days go by faster.

Fallon had once mentioned it, subtly, to her father. His only comment was that he would take care of it. Fallon could just imagine the magnitude of the fight that ensued if indeed he reproached her drinking habits. Her parents could not change each other or take care of each other. Theirs was a model for every relationship Fallon did *not* want to have.

Her parents apparently enjoyed squabbling and even screaming fights: that was the only way they related to each other. Fallon did not want that for herself. Though she had never argued with Tom about anything, she did secretly still harbor some rather dark emotions after his rejection of her in Paxos. They'd not discussed it, and it was starting to bother her.

Would she one day blow up at him? Would she one day say terrible, hateful things to him? The thought made her sick. But she also knew she couldn't keep quiet about his abandonment forever. She hungered for him with a great yearning need, but she also wanted to protect herself.

She stood up to close the door but Tom appeared in the doorway. "Kevin White will be up in a moment. I'm heading to WFO to do some paperwork, which is grievously overdue. Whoa. Are you okay?"

"I'm fine," she said warily. "My mother ..."

"Is she okay?"

"Drunk but otherwise fine," Fallon spat out. She shook her

head and covered her face with her hands. "I'm sorry."

His big hands gently tugged her wrists down and he looked into her face. "Is this a crisis?"

She laughed despite herself. "No, I'm okay."

"You sure?"

"Yes. Nothing I haven't handled before."

Tom glanced down the hall. "Okay. If you need anything, text me and let me know."

"Thanks," she said as Kevin White appeared in the hallway. She stepped back into her office and shut the door. Solitude. Silence. She needed it. It was time to work. She opened an email that had just arrived. It was a note from Robert Chandler sent to both her and Sam Cahill. "Please don't let me go to prison," it said. "I wouldn't do well in prison."

"You and me both," Fallon whispered and opened his file.

Tom did go to the Washington Field Office to complete overdue paperwork, but his real purposed was attended after that. The address listed on the police report for the incident resulting in Antoine's suicide was an attractive redbrick townhouse in the lively Adams Morgan neighborhood. Antoine Campbell was listed on the top floor of a four-floor building that looked much newer than its neighbors, which was curious. It was not exactly the residence he expected for a twenty-two-year-old kid with an arrest record and no official occupation. How, for starters, did he afford it?

Tom knocked and waited. When the door cracked open, a face pale from lack of sunlight looked at him with an unfocused stare. "Got a warrant?"

Funny how they could just smell authority on you.

"Is this the residence of Antoine Campbell?"

"Used to be."

"Can I talk to you? Secret Service." He showed the kid his badge.

"Secret Service? I don't give a shit about the president," he said.

"I'm investigating the suicide of Antoine Campbell. I don't think he had anything to do with the president, either."

The door opened and Tom entered what looked like an office after a massive bankruptcy. The living room was full of tables of monitors, speakers, keyboards, miles of cabling. But no computers. Interesting.

"They took them all," the guy said as Tom scanned the room. "They took my servers and laptops, Antoine's, everything."

"Who took them?"

"FBI. They were investigating him for hacking and they took all our boxes."

Hacking? Again? Tom's blood raced for more info, but he would stick to the plan.

"Did they leave a copy of the warrant?"

"No. They just came in here and took all the hardware."

"When did this happen?"

"Two days ago." The day Antoine supposedly jumped off the building.

"Is there some place we can sit down?" Tom asked.

The guy pulled out two metal folding seats. Dust imprints were still on the table where the computers had been.

"What's your name?" Tom asked.

"Jake Wilson. I already told the FBI everything I know."

"What was Antoine involved in?"

"Nothing."

Something was off. Tom could detect it. The nervousness, the quick, breathy answers.

"Look, Jake, I'm not here to get you into any kind of trouble. I need to know what Antoine was involved in."

"I told the FBI—"

"Fuck the FBI!" Tom shouted, surprising him. It was a move calculated to get him to talk. If this guy was involved in hacking at the same level Antoine appeared to be, he'd probably resent law enforcement. He would see himself as an outsider. Tom attempted to bond with him on that basis.

"Fuck them," Tom repeated in a normal tone of voice. "I'm not the FBI. Let's talk about Antoine. Was he a hacker?"

Jake shrugged.

"He was arrested three years ago for breaking the Army's servers. Was he still involved in that?"

"He was a computer security consultant. He penetrated systems to show companies where their weaknesses were."

"Okay. Did the Army ask him to do that?"

"No."

"Okay, so was he still involved in hacking?"

"No."

"Why did the FBI think he was hacking? What did they think he took?"

Jake looked at him with wide, blank eyes. "He was a consultant ..."

It occurred to him that Jake wasn't protecting Antoine, who was now dead. He was protecting himself. He was scared. Of the FBI.

"What were the agents' names?" Tom asked.

"There was only one and I don't know."

"Did the agent give you a business card?"

"No."

"What did he look like?"

"I don't know."

"White guy? Black guy? Hispanic? Asian?"

"White guy."

"What color hair?"

"Dark blond."

"Eyes?"

"I don't know. I don't go around staring into guys' eyes."

"Was he tall or short? Fat or thin? Give me something here."

"I don't know. Average. Everything about him was average."

"Was he dressed well?"

"As I said, he looked like you. Polished shoes, hair trimmed every nine days, the whole G-man stereotype."

"Did Antoine ever talk about the map of the keys?"

Jake winced. It was subtle, and he recovered quickly, but Tom caught it. He shook his head. "No, man, I don't know what you're talking about. The FBI wanted to know that too. I told them just like I'm telling you: I never heard of that before."

Tom kept his expression neutral, but he was going to get nowhere with Jake Wilson. Either he really didn't know or the FBI had worked him over to keep him silent.

Tom stood up and handed him a card. "Please call me if you feel like talking about Antoine."

He looked down at the card and slipped it into his pocket.

Tom returned to the blustery, cold afternoon. Funny, the agents who served a warrant on Fallon didn't leave a card either. The agents who spoke to the receptionist at the law firm where Antoine died likewise didn't offer a business card. It could be just a coincidence, but it seemed very odd. As public servants, securing the trust of the public they served was critical with every interaction. Part of that was being accountable—allowing citizens to know your name and how to reach you was very basic.

It was possible they did things differently at the FBI, but Tom doubted it. If the person who took Fallon's computer wasn't an FBI agent, who was he? Probably the person who chased Antoine Campbell to the rooftop and threw him off. And the same person who broke into Tom's house.

What the hell were you involved in, Tom silently asked Antoine Campbell. He climbed inside his car and steered away from the curb, feeling instinctively that he shouldn't spend too much time in front of Antoine Campbell's former house. He knew something bad was happening, and that he was probably being watched, but he couldn't figure out why or what they wanted. He only knew there was danger in paying that instinct too little attention.

THIRTEEN

Richard Mullinax finally broke down and asked to see Claudia because Omar Koss still had not contacted him and the stress was overwhelming. He figured Claudia would clear his mind for a little while, or rather fill his mind, displacing the images of destruction that continued to plague him. And he was correct. Claudia had taken control, as she always did. He simply did as she asked. With straightforward efficiency, Claudia removed her pants, then her jacket and blouse. His erection twitched at the sight of her pretty plum lingerie. It clashed pleasantly with her red hair. Claudia reached behind her and unclasped her lacy bra. Her milk-white breasts bounced forward. Large and full, the wild-rose nipples already puckered … Richard desperately wanted to take each of them in his mouth and suck. But, of course, she would tell him what she wanted from him.

As she removed her purple lace panties, Richard glimpsed her trimmed red muff before she turned to place the panties neatly on a chair with the rest of her clothes. Her command was total. It occurred to him that she knew exactly how much he was aching for her as she dallied with the correct folding technique for her underwear. His penis throbbed uncomfortably.

She walked gracefully to the edge of the bed, then sat down. "Come here," she said and opened her long, shapely legs.

Richard crawled to her. He was shaking with lust, the desire to taste her so intense that he licked his lips. Her cool hand gently lifted his chin to force him to gaze into her eyes. "You're very handsome when you're so obviously horny. A man in such pronounced need …" Her sentence faded away as a slow, sexy smile spread over her lips.

She liked him in this state. His arousal was as sexy to her

as her own release—a fact that Richard understood put him at a distinct disadvantage.

She had not allowed him to remove his clothes. She knew it was killing him that his penis was throbbing and aching in the confinement of his pants, a presence that made itself known no matter how he tried to concentrate completely on Claudia.

She understood male psychology so well it scared him sometimes. He had to allow for the possibility that she was on to him, that she knew what he had come here for and was using his weakness against him. He startled at the thought. Glancing up at her, he saw only her usual expression of satisfaction and expectation. There was nothing nefarious in her gaze. No, he could trust Claudia. She might be the only person he could trust. A good ally. A strong, well-liked woman, respected on the Hill by friends and enemies alike. He must be careful not to push her away with his mounting paranoia. She might be the only friend he had who could save him.

Gently, she pushed his face between her legs, and all thoughts of her possible betrayal vanished. Claudia began to move her hips against him, bucking wildly as he drove her closer to orgasm. He wanted to reach down and stroke himself but knew that Claudia would be furious. She told him when, and how, he could have release—it was part of the fun. Plus, he felt guilty for bringing himself to orgasm two nights ago when he'd last seen her. That was partially her fault, of course. Making him jerk into the air … it frustrated him just to remember it. In any case, he was determined to do better now.

Claudia reached down and shoved his face hard into her. With a wrenching cry, the climax bore down on her. Her moans blunted in his ears as her thighs squeezed around his face. As she squirmed against him, he relished the heat of her pussy and the furious tight clutch as the muscles contracted, her clitoris insistent, swollen, needing so much attention in that moment.

It was over too fast. She pushed him away but kept her feet on his shoulders. Exhausted, she lay on the bed, silently recovering. Richard took advantage of her lassitude and, with his fingertips, gently caressed the soft red hair and velvety lips.

So pliant and slick, so ready for him. The anticipation of not knowing whether she would actually allow him to enter her, or if, indeed, he would be allowed to climax at all, was infuriating.

Claudia finally sighed deeply and propped herself up on her elbows. Looking down at him, she smiled sweetly. "That was wonderful," she murmured. "Get undressed."

Not believing his luck, Richard's whole body vibrated with lust. He moved quickly, aware that she might change her mind any minute. Once naked, she scooted to the pillows and then gestured for him to join her.

He lay down beside her. She rolled onto her belly. "Give me a backrub," she murmured drowsily.

His chances for actually being granted any satisfaction just diminished greatly. He found himself taking her deltoid muscle in hand, gently rubbing it with long, fluid strokes, alert for any tightness or signs of stress.

She sighed, content, and her eyes fluttered closed.

It became clear that she would not allow him to climax today. The fog of desire began to clear and his anxiety returned. Omar Koss, who had vanished utterly for a while, returned to consciousness with force. It felt like a cold knife twisting in his gut. He had a horrible premonition that Omar was betraying him and the investigation into the mole would soon reveal him.

As casually as he could, he asked, "Claudia? What do you think of the Russian assassinations?" He gently worked up to her neck, rubbing the sore and tender muscles into a state of flaccid relaxation.

Claudia sighed. "I don't know. It's awful. The assets who were killed had been giving the CIA information about the electronic communications of the Russian government, so I think it must have been an electronic penetration. Why? Do you know something?"

"No," he answered lightly. "I checked out of curiosity and saw a slightly higher than average uptick in Russian attempts to penetrate the US embassy, but nothing that would explain where they got the info."

Omar Koss was *that good*. Nothing could have made it

plainer that Omar Koss meant business than seeing the memo in the President's Daily Brief today that two Russian assets had been killed.

"You said it's an electronic penetration?" he asked.

"The director of CIA isn't briefing me daily, but the scuttlebutt is that the two Russians were giving CIA operatives information about very highly classified programs inside the Russian government. Those included electronic communications. The Russians would have known they were communicating with CIA officers. They were exposed, then killed."

The map of the keys would have certainly allowed those kinds of communications to be visible, Mullinax knew. It would eventually come back to him. In fact, he was probably already being investigated. That was why he hadn't been to any of the meetings about the breech. The director of the NSA had attended, but he hadn't invited Richard. Did they already suspect him? Or was that just business as usual? He had no way to know; he had never participated in a meeting in which a spy was being flushed out. He felt the noose tightening around his neck.

"Ouch!" Claudia cried.

Richard realized he'd been unconsciously squeezing her flesh. "Sorry," he replied and used a softer touch. "I wonder who it is," he said lamely.

"I don't get it," she said drowsily. "I never understood the mindset of Aldrich Ames or Robert Hanson. I just don't understand why anyone would betray their own country."

"Me either," Mullinax replied. Now that he could sense the walls closing in, the promise of money seemed so slight ... a cheap, plastic reason for exchanging his honor. He wondered again if Claudia knew, if that was why she brought up Ames and Hanson: to see if she could suss out a motive from him.

She rolled over and cupped his chin, a beatific smile playing over her luscious lips. "Mmm, you're wonderful."

No, he decided, Claudia wouldn't betray him. Claudia enjoyed teasing him and sexually tormenting him, but she was a trustworthy person. And she didn't know about his involvement with Koss or the dead Russians. He lay down beside her and held onto her like a life raft. He hoped that somehow her goodness would protect him, as if purity and wholesomeness were transferable.

She soon wiggled out of his arms and began to pull on her clothes.

"Claudia, can we have dinner sometime?"

She emitted a little bubble of laugher. "Here?"

"Somewhere nice. A real dinner."

"Please don't tell me you've become sentimental about me."

"I adore you."

"Well, I adore you too. But that doesn't mean we should start dating." She threw him a maternal look. "Anyway, you're still a young buck. Get out there and date girls your own age."

He masked his disappointment and stood up to find his underwear. She watched him button his pants and pull on his shirt. He liked that adoring expression on her face, the awe she felt when she leered at his body. He wanted her to look at him as a man, not just a body, and gaze upon him with that same expression. As if she were looking at his heart or his soul.

Crazy. He was losing it. The stress was getting to him; that was all. He didn't need love. He just needed a little strength until Omar Koss got back in touch.

"You okay?" Claudia asked. A perplexed expression moved across her face like a shadow.

"I'm fine. Just tired."

Claudia set her shoes on the bed and stepped over to him. "Are you concerned the mole is in the NSA?"

He forced a casual smile to his lips. "I'm concerned about the espionage in general. My guess is that the mole would be in the CIA. There's never been a spy at NSA."

Claudia slid on her shoes, towering at almost six feet. "That we know about," she said.

FOURTEEN

Fallon left the office at six o'clock and arrived at Blair House twenty minutes later. Her father was not available, but her mother was in residence. She sent her personal secretary to inform Fallon that she would not be down for dinner.

Fallon was actually thankful for that. Kendra informed her that Evan hadn't been outside all day because it was too cold. Fallon buried her rage and dressed him in his coat, wrangled mittens on his hands, and wrapped an airplane themed scarf around his neck.

"Ready to go?" she asked.

He nodded his head solemnly.

Fallon snatched a cap off the dresser and led Evan into the hallway.

Tom, who had been standing at the door, looked at them with a little bit of alarm.

She felt guilty for going out. Tom had told her that the Secret Service was a little shorthanded right now with both her family and the current president to protect. New agents had been temped over from Pennsylvania and New York, and more were arriving through the next week, culminating in a massive force on inauguration day. Going out tonight was going to stretch them even further. Not to mention she still had media following her everywhere, accusing her of murder.

Tom had been with her since six o'clock this morning; she wondered if he was working overtime for her.

"You know, we can use his Secret Service detail if you'd like," Fallon offered. "You can leave."

Tom smiled at that. "I'm not leaving until you're in the house for the night."

"Okay then. We're going to the Kincaid Café."

Fallon and Evan climbed into a limo and the cars rushed through the District toward a small, nondescript café that was reliably quiet—a good place to take Evan, who was easily overwhelmed in loud places. Fallon looked at his sweet, open face, as curious as a little otter. She loved him passionately and protectively, and maybe it was just the stress of the week, but tears came to her eyes. She gently took Evan's hand and held it. He looked at their hands, then at her.

"You're crying," he announced.

Tom swiveled around in the front seat, searching her out in the dark.

"I'm okay," she whispered and wiped at her cheeks.

In the darkness of the SUV, she could see Tom's concern and it touched her very much, even through her embarrassment.

At the café, Fallon asked for a quiet corner, not near the kitchen, and they were seated at a table that looked onto a treelined residential neighborhood. After she gave her order—a steak salad for herself and chicken fingers for Evan—she looked up at Tom by the door. He looked exactly like what he was— an invincible Secret Service agent whose penetrating green eyes never strayed from her.

Something had changed between them; some tension had been relieved. Though questions remained, and they never discussed the future, she felt his affection for her, his protectiveness.

"Delta added a new route today, from Atlanta to Tulsa."

Fallon shifted into big sister role. She turned to Evan and smiled. "Did they? Why did they do that?"

"People in Georgia became curious about Oklahoma. The marketplace responded to demand and so they did that."

Fallon smiled. "What are you curious about?"

"We lived in Montana," he answered.

Fallon nodded. "Yep. You lived in Montana. Then you moved to Washington D.C."

The food was served, and Evan tucked in. He was unusually chatty this evening, though he didn't really talk in any logical order. Fallon made a note to call his pediatrician in Montana to get a referral for a better specialist in D.C.

She idly wondered if she could sneak away with Evan to the family ranch in Montana for a few days before the inauguration. But in the next instant she flashed to the stack of work she'd brought from Johnson Sloan Pruitt, still in the limo, and she knew she couldn't leave. Her position in the company was already tenuous. And the DOJ might think her leaving the state was a provocative act. Last thing she wanted to do was instigate them.

For better of worse, this was her life right now. She just had to suck it up and live it.

After they dropped Evan back at the Blair House, the limos headed on to Georgetown to Fallon's loft. Tom walked with her into the building. In the elevator she leaned against the peach marble wall and closed her eyes.

"Are you okay?"

"Mmm-hmm."

She became aware of his warm breath, then the slowly resolving pressure of his lips against hers. Oh *yes*. How she just wanted to sink into the experience. She made a low, gratified sound in her throat and lifted her hand to his cheek. At the brush of his tongue against hers, her nerves began to fire. Funny how even in her state of fatigue, he could do to her what spring did to cherry trees. Warmth bloomed low in her belly.

It was late and his cheeks were a little rough under her palm; she had never seen him unshaven before. She found it quite sexy. He pulled away as the elevator stopped. Fallon followed Tom to her door.

"Can you come in?"

"Not supposed to, sweetheart. But if you want me to, I can probably get away with a few minutes."

Fallon smiled, stepped inside, and held the door open for him. She dropped her purse on her bar and kicked off her heels. Tom towered over her. Strong, sexy, beautiful. She leaned gratefully into his broad chest. Tom hugged her, holding her tight in the warm safety of his arms and kissing the crown of her head. "You're so tired."

"Put me to bed?"

Tom exhaled softly into her hair. "God, woman, what are you doing to me? Making me risk my job …"

She pulled back and looked into his face. He was smiling, teasing her.

"Come on, Avalon, let's get you to bed."

He took her hand and led her up the stairs to the bedroom. She stood at the edge of the huge bed, swaying on her feet. Gently he kissed her lips again, and she allowed him to coax her mouth open, finding her tongue, drawing her into the kiss. His blunt fingertips began to unbutton her blouse, then gently pushed it from her shoulders. Fallon reached behind her back and unclasped her black satin brassiere, tossing it into a nearby chair. She stood very still, her breath frozen in her chest as she watched Tom's reaction. His warm hands gingerly held her breasts, his thumb brushing over her hardened nipples and sending currents of desire to her core. His fingertips played across her skin as if he thought she was made of fragile spun sugar. Down her sides his hands glided to her skirt. She stood still, letting him unclasp the buttons and tick down the zipper and finally tug it over her hips.

"Panties?" he asked.

Fallon shook her head. She'd begun sleeping nude again because she liked to remember Tom's kisses and touches on her bare skin. As he slid the scant garment down her bare legs, she studied his face and was surprised by the expression of awe etched on his features. He was gazing at her as if he'd never seen her naked before—as if he'd never seen any naked woman before. Awed and reverent.

"You are so beautiful."

She smiled and shook her head. "I'm not."

He held both her hands and looked down into her eyes. "You are the most beautiful woman I have ever known."

In the next instant, he swooped her up in his arms, making her yalp in surprise. He carried her as if she weighed nothing more than lace and tulle to the bed and placed her gently onto the white puff. He pulled the covers up to her shoulders, then turned off her lamp.

In the dim light from the hallway, Tom looked like a big, hulking, sexy Prince Charming. Arousal lit his face with that peculiar intensity, but he stubbornly refused to do more than admire her. That silly stubbornness. She suspected a broad swathe of it in his personality: a deep, broad bullheadedness. It seemed impossible that anyone would refuse him anything, but apparently he'd become practiced at getting his way … or denying himself, judging from the fact that he wasn't balls deep inside her right now. She wanted to laugh. Her body was exhausted, yet if he'd reached between her legs he'd have found her slippery and willing. He had a daunting effect on her. And she suspected that he knew it. She had never been good at masking her emotions and had no control whatsoever over the physiological magic of his gale force sexuality; pretending indifference to him was as impossible as growing wings. She was impressed by his restraint because a glance down at his crotch revealed a massive bulge that kicked up her heart rate.

He eased down beside her on the edge of the bed, his face suddenly grave. He began to pet her hair back from her forehead. The sweet, almost fatherly affection made her feel like a cat being stroked in the sunshine. She thought she heard him murmur something, but before she could reply, she was asleep.

As Tom left Fallon's loft, he felt he entered a switching station. Like Fallon, the past few days had been tiring, but he still had work ahead of him; he couldn't allow himself to be sidetracked by the sensual images of Fallon flashing in his mind, sending wild central nervous system flashes through his body. He'd wanted to lunge after her like a wild animal, but she seemed so out of it, so tired, that the lust had given way to those protective instincts. He had seen the open invitation in her eyes and politely declined so that she could rest. Sitting on her bedside, stroking her hair while she drifted off, he felt something even more ferocious than the furious intensity and possessiveness that seized him when they were making love: piercing, savoring gentleness. Affection shot through with elation.

Thoughts of Bethany drifted in. The pain was like a knife between his ribs. He hadn't been able to protect her that morning. He'd saved people, dragging them out of rubble, choking in the filthy air … but none of them had been Bethany. Even now, the loss was so acute that hot liquid dripped from his eyes.

In the years after her death, he had learned to love the agony. It had taken a while. At first he avoided it because it overwhelmed him and separated him from the rest of humanity—even his own humanity. Then he had come to rely on it because it was what he had instead of his wife. The raw pain was all he had left of that life and he protected it fiercely.

And it protected him. At least it had until Fallon. He felt shame at his own weakness and lack of professionalism—and the realization that his weakness was putting Fallon in danger. Until now, what separated him from the lowlifes he defended against was his professionalism and code of conduct. He was violating that big time with Fallon.

Maudlin bastard. He angrily wiped tears away. Get your head in the game, Bishop. This is why you don't fuck your protectee, why you don't get involved with people. No matter how sexy. Or lovely.

At his condo, Tom changed from his G-man suit into black cargo pants and a black shirt. He ran his hands through his hair so it spiked out in a million directions. He hadn't shaved since that morning, and a scruffy scrape darkened his jaw. He grabbed his weapon and a leather jacket, then walked out to his Jeep. He drove to an address in southern Maryland.

Deep in an industrial corridor, it was a nondescript warehouse on the Anacostia River, surrounded on either side by abandoned freight yards. Despite the general abandoned look of the area, he knew he was in the right place because the shale parking lot was packed with cars.

Outside the corrugated metal doors, two huge Viking-looking guys stood sentry. Tom confidently walked up to them.

"Invitation?" Ogre One said.

"Yeah," Tom replied. "I didn't print it out."

"Can't let you in."

Tom smiled thinly. "Fine. Tell them you turned away Phaze."

The ogre blinked. "Oh. You're Phaze?"

Tom didn't answer, just delivered a flat, challenging expression. Phaze had been Antoine Campbell's hacking name; it had once been legendary. But it wasn't very well known anymore. According to Tom's research, Antoine had changed it to something else after his arrest.

The ogre nodded knowingly. "Okay, go in."

Tom walked inside. A large dim room glowing with blue monitors opened before him. At the front of the room, someone was giving a presentation.

Tom had spent hours looking for anything he could find about Midnight Research, the hacking group the DOJ alleged Antoine Campbell had founded. He finally found a domain owned by the group, and on the domain was not a website but a menu tree of encrypted folders. Tom had asked Brett Hitchcock to decrypt them, and he had with no questions asked. Hitchcock had been taken aback by the sophistication of the encryption though. He'd managed to crack it but only after many tries.

In a folder labeled "Meetings," a text document listed a time, date and address. Nothing else. Tom wasn't sure what to expect. Even with his relative ignorance about hacking and hacking groups like Anonymous, he was surprised there were so many people in attendance. Maybe fifty people huddled around their laptops and tablets. Tom was glad he'd thought to bring one.

He took a seat at a long table where four other people were watching the presentation. They were so engrossed with what was being said that they didn't even glance up.

Tom opened his laptop, trying to understand what he was hearing from the front of the room. It seemed impossibly complex, abstract, and cerebral—a mathematical forest of numbers and symbols that he could not penetrate.

After the talk, Tom joined the group in applause. The lights came up and a girl next to him, who could not be older than seventeen or so, looked at him curiously. She wore her black hair in buns on either side of her head tied with small, fluffy red pompoms. She was dressed in a plaid schoolgirl skirt, biker boots, and a shirt that looked like it was made out of a sheer silver fabric that looked metallic. Yet he was the weird one.

Tom stood up, slowly making his rounds through the throngs. Several people surrounded the man who had given the presentation, and through the shifting crowd, Tom made out that he was gregariously entertaining them all, and he seemed well-liked. To his surprise the man looked up, directly at Tom. Excusing himself, he advanced through the fan club to Tom.

He smiled apologetically. "Hi. I'm Frank. I assume you're here to speak to me, but you aren't safe here."

"What do you mean?"

"You aren't safe here," he repeated. "This is about Antoine Campbell, right?"

Tom didn't answer.

"Right. Meet me at 21329 West Kendall Street in about twenty minutes. Leave now."

"Why am I not safe here?"

A thin, unhappy smile smirked across his face. "You look like a cop. And generally speaking, this is not a cop-friendly crowd."

Tom glanced around and realized there were a lot of hostile stares. But what kind of world had he entered where he wasn't safe because he was an agent? The two ogres from the doorway were stalking toward him. He suddenly realized that he had not come with his creds or his handcuffs. So much for thinking he'd be able to walk in and get whatever he needed in a roomful of nerds.

"Twenty minutes," Tom agreed and began walking away.

The address was a Waffle House. Tom made himself comfortable at a booth, where he ordered black coffee. Exhaustion was seeping into his bones though he was still wired from adrenaline and the buzz that Fallon always inspired.

The doors opened and Frank from Midnight Research

breezed in. He was short, Tom realized, and a little older than Antoine Campbell had been when he died. He slid into the booth and tapped his hands on the table like he was waiting for something.

"Why did you know the street address of this place?" Tom asked.

"I think better in numbers."

"Was Antoine Campbell the same way?"

The same cool smile crossed his face. "Antoine Campbell was even more agile with numbers than I am. He was incredibly smart. I have an IQ of one eighty. Antoine's was over two hundred."

"So he was still hacking illegally?"

The man shrugged. "I don't know."

"What is Midnight Research?"

"It's a group of technologists who share info about various systems, talk about encryption and decryption."

"So … what are you, like an identity fraud ring?"

He scoffed. "Not even close."

"What then?"

"Let me ask you a question. Was calculus invented or was it discovered?"

Tom, whose math education now seemed terribly inadequate, shrugged. "I don't know. You tell me."

"Basically we are figuring out the new maths. New, unimaginably complex encryptions. We sometimes practice on private systems, but we're the good guys. White hats. We don't steal. It's just the only way to get real-world experience."

"Did Antoine ever talk to you about the National Security Agency?"

"Sure, all the time."

"Was he hacking into the NSA?"

"That's the ultimate goal," Frank answered smoothly. "But the NSA has so many redundant layers, it's impossible right now. The first person who cracks the NSA will be a god among men."

"So Antoine never told you that he cracked the NSA?"

He chuckled softly. "No, that was still years off."

"Does Midnight Research make money?"

"Some of us do penetration testing for companies who want to see what their weaknesses are."

"Did Antoine do that? Did he have any clients you know of?"

"Yeah, the NSA. They offered him a million dollars if he could crack the servers before the end of the year."

Tom sat back in the banquette, absorbing the information. "What's a map of the keys?"

Frank smirked. "Please don't tell me you're a conspiracy theorist."

"Not at all. I don't even know what it is."

"It's a myth," Frank said. "Some people believe that there is a map of all the encryption keys that will expose the entire US government infrastructure. Like a skeleton key for a house that fits every door. Once you know the map of the keys, you'd be able to control the entire US government."

"Did Antoine Campbell ever mention the map of the keys to you?"

"Never," Frank said. "It's like an Area 51 type thing. Nobody takes that seriously."

Tom frowned, realizing something. "Antoine must have had research notes," he said. "And since he was a computer guy, he would have kept them in the cloud, right?"

Frank shrugged his shoulders. "I have no idea what he would have done."

"He would have used regular web-based programs like Twitter, Flickr, maybe Facebook too."

Frank took a sip of his soda. "So?"

"I will pay you to find his passwords for those websites."

"How much?"

"A thousand."

Frank smirked.

"Three thousand."

"Thirty five hundred. Cash."

Tom sat back in his chair. "Fine. I'll deliver it tomorrow."

FIFTEEN

The bitter cold made conversation almost impossible. Leah hunkered down in her pea coat, scarf, and cap and walked as fast as she could, matching Collin's long strides, step for step. They ducked into the Farragut West Metro, thankful for the weak heat. At the kiosk, she bought a ticket. She was not quite sure what was going on. Despite Collin's flirtation at Nordstrom, he was now unreadable, being charming at times but not reliably so. To make it even more awkward, when she tried to respond, he seemed indifferent. After dinner and drinks, he said, "I'll walk you to the Metro."

Leah felt like she'd made a fool of herself, though she couldn't think of anything she had done specifically wrong. She was just embarrassed for having thought he would be her Prince Charming. It was impossible trying to date. Interpreting statements and gestures, trying to decipher if he was interested in her or not. She wished she could just stop wanting to find a relationship. Indifference would solve so much.

After the machine spit out the Metro ticket, to her surprise, Collin fed some money into the machine. Unwilling to confess her hope even by asking what he was doing, Leah said, "Well, thanks ..."

He grabbed the Metro card and said, "I was going to ride back with you, if that's okay. To make sure you get home safe."

Leah smiled, hope flickering anew. "I'd like that." Together they proceeded through the turnstiles to the trains. It was warmer down here in the concourse, and Leah relaxed slightly as they sat on a bench and waited for the next orange line train. Collin made small talk, and Leah continued to try and figure out his intentions. He did not seem particularly romantic, but it was possible that was because they did not yet know each other well.

It was only a ten-minute ride to Court House but it felt much longer. She could not calm down, could not get a read on what Collin was doing or what he wanted. At the Court House Plaza apartment building, Leah swiped her magnetic entrance fob and they rode up to the twentieth floor.

Her apartment was tidy and plain, but the view was breathtaking. Collin drifted to the glass doors of the snow-covered terrace and peered out. Leah joined him, shivering in the cold. "It's pretty, isn't it?"

The Capitol Building and Washington Memorial were visible among the smattering of lights. The White House looked noble, blazingly white against the eclipsed sky. A necklace of airplanes landing at Regan National Airport sparkled along the horizon. She stood very still, contemplating the view as if it was the first time she'd ever seen it.

"There's a really pretty roof where the view is even better," she said. "This is the tallest building in Arlington, so you can see everything."

"Really? Can we take a look?"

"Sure," she said and led him to the elevators.

The roof, as Leah had promised, was extraordinary. A large pool was covered for the winter, and numerous chaises were laid out. As they walked to the balustrade, they left shoe prints in the snow.

Collin pulled her close to him and they looked out at the city in all its dazzling 360 degrees. "You could sell tickets for this view," Collin said with a little laugh in his voice.

"Actually they do on the Fourth of July. They give tickets to people because so many people come up here."

"You look cold."

"I am."

"Let's go back."

As they were coming inside her apartment, Collin said suddenly, "I'm glad somebody is looking into Antoine's death."

She had told him about the strange death of Antoine Campbell, that she was looking into it for a friend. It was, in fact, the only thing they discussed which had to do with her. They had discussed Collin's education and his career, his accomplishments on the soccer field, and his kindness to strangers, but the topic of Antoine Campbell, and indeed anything personal to Leah, had been avoided.

"So what have you discovered?" he asked.

"Not much," she replied. "Seems like his life was kind of a lockbox."

"That's a shame."

Before Leah could agree, he stepped forward and kissed her. Once she recovered from the surprise, she realized that she was enjoying it. She wasn't quite sure about Collin as a person, but wow, he was a good kisser. His lips moved to her neck as his hand cupped her breast. She did not resist. Nor did she resist when he suggested they find her bedroom immediately.

It had been a long time since she'd had sex, so when it was over four minutes later, she was inclined to keep any complaints to herself. Leah rolled on to her side and looked at Collin. He smiled, kissed her nose, and sat up. "That was amazing," he said and scooted out of the bed. Leah watched him dress in the semidarkness. He sat on the edge of the bed and put on his shoes and then belatedly said, "I have to get to work early tomorrow."

Leah nodded.

"Can I see you again?"

"Sure," she replied. Her voice was barely a scratch in the darkness. She flung off the covers and grabbed her sweater from the floor, yanking it on quickly because she didn't want him to see her naked anymore. As he tucked in his shirt, he looked at his reflection in the darkened mirror over her bureau. "Walk me to the door?" he asked, shifting his eyes to her in the mirror.

Wordlessly she stood up and, with her arms folded over her chest, followed him to the door.

"I'll call you," he said.

"Okay."

"Lock the door behind me," he said and leaned in to swipe his dry lips against hers. "You never know who is lurking around the corner."

Leah shut the door and locked it and took her phone from where it was charging on the bar. As she walked back to bed, she dialed Tom.

"I just had the strangest date," Leah said by way of greeting.

"You sound kind of ... odd. Are you okay?"

"I'm fine. Collin just left here. We had sex."

"Oh," Tom replied carefully. "Well, how was it?"

"I don't know. Weird. He seems to have pockets of time when he's affectionate and normal, and the rest of the time he's kind of a dick."

"And you had sex with this guy? Leah ...."

"I know. But it's been a long time. I miss the company of men."

"Well what else happened?"

"He asked me out for tomorrow."

"If you're feeling uncomfortable around him, don't go."

"It's not discomfort. It's a synchronicity issue, maybe. Or maybe the problem is me. I mean, he's very good looking, and smart, and I ..."

"And you are very beautiful and brilliant and deserve a guy who is going to rock your world."

"Tom, you're just saying that. I'm thirty-two and not married. It's fucking hard to find a man in this town ..." She felt the old hysteria welling up and fought to clamp it down, be pragmatic.

"Just be careful," Tom said.

"You're the second person who has said that to me in the last ten minutes. What do you think is going to happen? Somebody's going to throw me off a building?"

"Leah ..."

"I'm sorry. I'm just frustrated and I don't even know why."

"It's okay. Just relax this evening. Let's meet for lunch tomorrow, okay?"

"Aren't you working?"

"I can take an hour for lunch."

"Okay. Lunch then."

"I'll text you."

"Goodnight, sweet Tom."

Leah placed her phone on the bedside table and shut her eyes. Freezing rain tapped against her bedroom window. It had the potential to be a romantic sound if she heard it with somebody who cared about her and would hold her in his arms to keep her warm. Despite the dull ache between her legs, she felt vast and complete loneliness.

A familiar molten ache welled up in her chest. She pushed her face into her pillows as the sobs overtook her.

SIXTEEN

The next morning, while Fallon was en route to the memorial service for Antoine Campbell, Tom was standing at the door of Midnight Research. The office was in the basement of a narrow three-story townhouse not far from the Russian embassy on Wisconsin Avenue. Tom had the impression the location was not an accident.

Frank flung open the door. "You showed up."

"I'm surprised, too," Tom said sourly.

"Come on," Frank said and walked into the interior of the basement.

Tom followed him through a warren of dim, narrow hallways to a deep, cluttered room that he surmised was Frank's studio because there was a large desk upon which several computers were awake and working. A giant whiteboard on the back wall was covered in squiggles and symbols. No numbers that he recognized at all. Tom reached into the breast pocket of his jacket and pulled out the cash. He tossed it on the desk. "Find Antoine Campbell's research notes."

"They might not even exist," Frank said and picked up the stack of money. He looked at Tom sharply. "Why can't you get a warrant and get one of your government hacks to do this?"

"This is off the books," he replied evenly.

Frank smiled. "Interesting."

Tom ignored the unspoken questions. "Call me as soon as you find something. And obviously, this is between you and me."

"No problem."

Tom hesitated at the doorway. "By the way, if the FBI shows up here ..."

"Whoa, what the hell? The FBI?"

"Antoine Campbell's death has attracted the attention of certain people," Tom replied simply.

"The FBI though?"

Tom didn't tell him that he didn't believe it was the real FBI. He just said, "Yeah," and left it at that. "If they arrive, deny everything and get in touch with me."

"Should I be worried?"

"No," Tom said. He didn't feel as confident as he sounded, but he was glad when Frank became interested in the cash again. "Just … find the passwords."

He intended to drive directly back to Fallon's office to wait for her to return from the memorial service but changed his mind. He took Connecticut Avenue to N Street, turned left and saw the large white townhouse that was the Egyptian embassy.

He cruised two streets over and looked up at the building where Antoine Campbell had supposedly jumped. He parked at the curb across from the Four Seasons and looked up, thoughtfully measuring the distance between life and death.

He thought of Leah. He thought of Bethany.

Some cases you don't ever resolve, he thought. It was possible this was one of them.

Fallon wasn't sure what she hoped to find here, at the memorial service at Abyssinia Baptist Church. Nothing stood out. The mourners were a celebration of diversity: women and men, black and white and Asian and Hispanic, young and old. They were all dressed respectfully. From Fallon's vantage point, every attendant seemed to be there for no other reason than to mourn the death of a young man.

The interior of the church was beautiful. Beeswax candles burned, the scent of the melted wax mingling with the many flower arrangements. A gleaming black casket lay in the front center of the room, and it felt to Fallon like an accusation. She paused in the doorway, profound dread spreading through her veins like a disease. The air was redolent with candle wax and the abundance of flowers, perfume of the women, faint perspiration. A beautiful, melancholy scent. Low thrumming voices rose and fell against a melody of soft crying. No cameras. No famous people. Just grief, raw and exposed.

Fallon took a seat in a back pew. On her right was a large dark skinned man of indeterminate age. His chin was quivering and his chest would heave, and his wife would pat his arm, and he'd collect himself. Every person she saw was grieving, exactly as one would expect.

What, exactly, had she expected? That an obvious conspirator would be among the grieving—someone who wanted him dead because of his "national security" secrets?

The reverend, like most holy men, was an exceptionally good orator, and Fallon was immediately charmed by his familiarity with the congregation.

The service lasted one hour, ending with an invitation to join Antoine's friends and family at the home of his sister, Charlotte Campbell Mosely. Fallon wanted to meet Charlotte Campbell Mosely but hesitated accepting the invitation. Her presence might disrupt.

Reluctantly she asked Rowland to take her back to the office.

The moment they stepped back into the Johnson Sloan Pruitt offices, Ingrid Breyer appeared, summoned by some demonic energy that was bent on destroying anything good. Ingrid made herself an obstacle in Fallon's path.

"It's imperative that you are actually present in the office during office hours."

"I am here." Fallon said and strode past Ingrid to her office. Predictably, Ingrid followed.

"Also, I must tell you that there is some suspicion that you are not being completely honest on your timesheets."

Fallon wanted to laugh. After laying Antoine Campbell to rest, everything Ingrid was saying felt incredibly insignificant. "I will double-check them from now on," Fallon replied levelly.

Ingrid seemed a little deflated. Her eyes bore into Fallon, then realizing there was no more ground to be gained, she retreated.

Fallon began working on the outline for a deposition she was scheduled to give one of Robert Chandler's witnesses. The work was good; it kept her mind from wading too far into the sadness of Antoine's funeral and the infinite loop imagery from last night with Tom. Pleasurable, ecstatic, wonderful and … cowardly were the words she would use to describe last night. She had completely chickened out and not asked him The Question.

When he strode in a few minutes later, she was still wrestling with The Question, trying to figure out how to phrase it, how to time it. When she was around him, next to that sexy body and high-voltage intelligence, The Question seemed unimportant. But when he wasn't around, it ate at her. The only way to solve the problem was to ask. Tonight, she resolved. She would ask tonight.

"How are you?" he asked.

Fallon shrugged. "The memorial service put me in a bad mood, but I'm happy to see you."

Tom sat across from her, looking at her curiously. "You sure you're okay?"

She shook her head. "I don't know what's going on."

"I don't either," he said. "But we're going to find out. Don't forget that we're going to win. We are going to prove your innocence, and we're going to find out exactly how and why Antoine Campbell died."

"You sound so confident," she said.

"I am confident."

She impulsively squeezed his hand. "These people, whoever they are, are not fucking around."

"No, they aren't. Which is why we have to solve this."

Tom's phone buzzed. He read the text and frowned, and a stern line of concern appeared between his eyebrows. To Fallon he said, "Your computer was just found on the steps of the Lincoln Memorial."

Collin watched the Secret Service agents approach the steps where the jogger was standing guard over the computer, a swarm of dark blue suits, earpieces and dark shades. Excitement coursed in his veins. He liked watching the infidels up close, knowing that they could not see him. His fair good looks had been a blessing from Allah himself, a weapon to be used against them. Brazen *imshallah*. He'd been born for this, born for revenge.

And these infidels, in particular, interested him. Omar Koss might be an old fool, but his talk of patience did have some practical relevance: it was wise to study how the Secret Service reacted to something as simple as finding a laptop that had been seized in a search by the FBI.

How well he was getting to know them. These elite blue-suited crusaders who supposedly were invincible. FBI, Secret Service, they all looked absurd and pitiful—no match for his plans.

A technician was placing the computer in a plastic sleeve. They would find no physical evidence on the machine, or the spyware he'd installed, or anything of value that would tell them who had taken it. The Secret Service would no doubt examine it thoroughly, but they'd never find even a molecule that could help them.

The plan was officially underway. It filled him with anticipation; he could just imagine both the current president and the president-elect on television, begging for the return of the girl. And he, Collin, with the power of life and death in his hands.

The jogger who discovered the laptop was pretty. She reminded him of Leah, with her curly hair and slender frame.

On her replacement computer, Fallon watched the news conference online. Her father had taken time out of his incessant transformation-of-power meetings to stand beside the attorney general and the director of the Secret Service announcing to the press corps that a fake search warrant had been served on Fallon

Hughes, and she was not being investigated for any role in the death of Leo Jacobellis. Fallon frowned as she watched; nobody had bothered to officially notify her. Though it was a great relief, it would be nice to receive a personal phone call to let her know her life wasn't about to be ensnared in a murder trial.

Her father should get most of his retainer fee back from the lawyer. That should make him happy. She frowned, realizing he had not spoken a word to her since he wrote the check for her defense. Her mother, on the other hand, had sent a few emails and voicemails, which Fallon had not answered. She felt guilty about listening to them about halfway through before hitting delete. She simply didn't have the patience to concern herself with her mother's obsession with *Kill Shot* and her utter lack of concern that her son was being neglected. Fallon would not be able to keep her mouth shut for very much longer about Elizabeth's drinking. Eventually she would need to confront her mother.

After her experience with Leo Jacobellis, however, Fallon did not feel competent to handle her mother's addiction on her own. She would eventually need to beg her father again to become involved—a herculean task because he was quite happy with the quiet little wife who largely stayed out of his way and made him look good when she appeared on his arm.

Of course, now Elizabeth wasn't so content to be quiet. Two of the calls to Fallon's cell phone had been babbling missives about the script she was determined to accept with or without the permission of Preston Taylor Hughes.

Eventually, Fallon told herself. Soon. Soon she would take care of her mother. After the inauguration, perhaps, she would ask to speak privately with her father and implore him to do something to help his wife.

Fallon's buzzing cell phone nudged her from her thoughts. It was a text from Gwen: WTF? ARE YOU OK?

Fallon replied: FINE. CAN YOU MEET FOR DRINKS LATER?

Gwen declined; she was busy but would call later.

A few moments later, the phone on her desk rang. The kick

of dread in her stomach was immediate: it was Alan Johnson's extension. She shut her eyes for a second of prayer that she could at least speak to him without getting fired, then answered the phone.

Alan Johnson's assistant asked her to hold, then a few seconds later, Johnson himself took the line.

"Miss Hughes, it appears the concerns about the search warrant have been, well, unmerited. Your job is safe."

"Thank you. I appreciate that."

"Goodbye, Fallon."

Fallon dropped the phone back in the cradle.

She stared at the phone for a while, feeling nothing. She was supposedly free now, so why wasn't she thrilled?

It was early afternoon when Tom rode the Metro to DuPont Circle. As he strode into the café, Leah, already sitting at a table, looked up at him. He knew instantly that something had changed. She had that blank expression, dull-eyed and pale, that conveyed a story of agony.

Leah was sick again.

Tom arranged his features into an expression of gentle compassion and kissed her cheek. "How are you?"

"Okay."

"Have you ordered? Do you want some food?"

"I haven't ordered."

Tom ordered sandwiches, chips and sodas and then brought the meal back to the table. Leah took a bite of her egg salad sandwich and chewed thoughtfully. "Thank you," she said.

"No problem. Tell me how you're doing."

"I've been thinking. I wasn't supposed to be born."

"Oh, Leah."

"No, really. Hear me out. I've never accomplished anything. I matter to no one. It's a miracle that you put up with me, Tom."

"Leah, you are so wrong about all of that. You've—"

"I faked an orgasm with Collin last night. I realized that I've never actually had a real orgasm with a man, but I've faked hundreds." She wore a dark, abstracted expression as she said this.

He understood that she could no longer hear him. He had been through this often enough to know that her depression was like a tide of darkness inching over a planetary coast, blotting out every bit of lightness or hope. It pained him to see her this way.

"Leah, why don't you check in with Dr. Horner?"

She did not answer. She chewed her egg salad sandwich, looking at a place over Tom's shoulder.

"Are you going to see him tonight?"

Leah nodded and only then looked at him with a cold smile that sent a chill down his spine. "Yes."

"Why?" Tom asked.

"Because it's better than being at home alone."

"Leah, no." Tom reached across the table and took her left hand. "Please don't see him again. He sounds like a jerk. You deserve better."

"You don't get it," she said, and for the first time, he detected life in her eyes. "It doesn't matter who it is," she said, looking at him but miles away. "Any one of them is leading me to the same fate."

After the snack, Tom walked Leah to the Metro. He kissed her cheek, told her to check in with him in a few hours, and watched her board the train for the *Washington Post*. As soon as her train pulled out, he dialed her psychiatrist and left a message. He knew from experience that Dr. Horner would not call him back. Confidentiality laws forbade him from even confirming Leah was a patient. But Tom hoped that the psychiatrist would call Leah, and maybe Leah would open up to him and agree to come in for a session.

Just as he ended the call, another call came in. Tom answered. "This is Tom."

"Is this Agent Bishop?"

"Who is calling?"

"This is Karen Schwartz. You left a business card for me a few days ago regarding the death of Antoine Campbell."

"Thank you for returning my call. Are you at your office now?"

"Yes."

"I'm only a block away," he said spontaneously. "If you don't mind, I would like to stop in and chat with you."

"If it's no trouble …"

"None at all, Ms. Schwartz," he said, looking around for a taxi. "I'll be there shortly."

Ten minutes later, he arrived at the building where Antoine Campbell had jumped or been pushed. The same receptionist was at the front desk. Tom asked for Karen Schwartz.

While he was waiting, the receptionist said, "What's she really like? Fallon Hughes?"

"She is an indomitable patriot," Tom answered. Normally he would be a little more charming but his lunch with Leah was still weighing on him.

"Is she nice?"

"Yes."

"Is the president nice?"

He was saved from having to answer the question by the arrival of Karen Schwartz. She was a woman in her forties with brown hair and an attractive, alert face, framed by sexy librarian glasses. She shook Tom's hand then led him into a conference room.

"I'm afraid I don't have a lot of time," she said briskly. "I have a meeting in half an hour."

"I won't take up much of your time," Tom assured her. "Your receptionist mentioned that you saw Antoine Campbell jump. I'd like you to tell me what you saw."

"I was on my way back from my doctor's appointment," she said, and then a spontaneous smile appeared. "I'm eight weeks pregnant."

"Congratulations," Tom said.

"I had just discovered I was pregnant, in fact. As you can imagine, I wasn't paying very close attention to my surroundings.

As I arrived, I noticed a few cars parked weirdly on the street. I looked up and saw some figures on the top of the building. It was difficult to see clearly and as I said, I was distracted. I saw the figures on the rooftop interact and then one of them, Antoine Campbell, jumped."

Tom decided to proceed in chronological order. "What kinds of cars were parked weirdly on the street? Were they marked police cars?"

"No. One was a white Ford Taurus and the other was a blue late-model Volvo. But then a marked Maryland State Police car showed up at some point."

Tom did not react directly to that answer. "Did you see the drivers return to their cars?"

"No. As soon as he fell, I know it sounds awful but I wanted to get inside to get to my desk before they closed the building down."

"He fell?"

"Well, you know what I mean. He jumped. But it was strange. I did have the impression that he jumped ... facing the building. I can't be sure because it was sort of far away ... but it did strike me that he appeared to be falling backward."

"You said the figures 'interacted.' How did they interact?"

"I don't know. They just ... like, the police were trying to catch him, calm him down, and he wasn't having it."

"Did you see them push him off the roof?"

Karen Schwartz looked surprised but shook her head. "No. I saw them ... tangle. But I didn't see anyone throw him."

"Did you see him jump?"

"I saw him after he'd jumped."

"You saw him fall facing the building, but you didn't see him actually jump from the roof of the building."

"That's correct."

"Okay, Ms. Schwartz, that's all I have for now."

She looked relieved. She stood up.

"If you think of anything else, please call me."

"I will," she said and walked him back to the receptionist office. She said goodbye and walked back to her office.

Tom returned to Johnson Sloan Pruitt and, after checking with the control room, relieved Jason Slaney from his post.

As he entered her office, Fallon looked up at him with a sunny, melting smile that made his heart flip in his chest. It still surprised him, how transfixed he could become by her, arresting him even when his mind was on other things.

"You look happy," he said and dropped in the chair across from her.

"I am no longer suspected of murder," she said with a grin.

"That is terrific news."

"One problem down, eight million to go."

"What happened?"

"Nothing new. My mother wants to act in a violent movie about a former-ballerina-turned-dominatrix-slash-assassin, my father is occupied with an impending war in Russia, my little brother is probably sleeping for his fourteenth hour of the day, and I have no idea what a map of the keys is. Just your ordinary, average day."

She walked around to stand in front of him, reclining against the edge of her desk.

"How about we meet at Gwen's place? I'll bring over some wine and we have a nice, long …"

Fallon's eyebrow lifted.

"Talk," he finished with a grin.

Fallon laughed. "That sounds marvelous."

"Be there a quarter after eight. I'll be there at eight sharp. That way the Secret Service will never see me arrive. Just clear it with Gwen."

"Gwen's always at her fiancé's house in Massachusetts Heights. I don't think it will be a problem. Thanks for thinking of it."

"It was hardly a chore," he replied dryly. "Now for a more serious subject. I have a theory about Antoine Campbell's death. I want you to listen before you comment."

"Okay." She watched him expectantly, with private joy sparkling in her eyes.

"What if Antoine Campbell called the police, reported

his own car stolen, then led the Maryland State Police into the District, ran up the fifth floor of that building and then somehow knew about the weird fire escape issue, got to the roof. Then he jumped. And the Maryland State Police were witnesses, not assailants."

"No," Fallon said gently but firmly. "Why would he choose that building instead of the Verizon building?"

"Maybe he feared getting caught if he had that many more floors to get up."

"Feared being caught? Why? He was suicidal in this scenario. He has nothing to fear."

"Maybe he was really committed to dying."

"Why would he need Maryland State Police as witnesses? It was midmorning. There were a lot of witnesses to his death."

He liked this game, liked playing it with Fallon. She was smart. Tom was stubborn, the kind who would work doggedly on a problem until it was solved. Fallon, on the other hand, came at a problem with unusual angles, arriving at the unexpected conclusion. Their personalities meshed well together.

Based on what he was just discussing with her, Berringer's theory didn't fit the facts. What did fit the facts was the blue Volvo following Antoine Campbell. He called the police and told them he was in a stolen car to get them to move fast. In a panic, he then called Fallon, needing to document the truth somewhere, needing to tell somebody what he had discovered. Then for some reason Tom did not know yet, Antoine Campbell jumped out of his car and ran. He ran not to the Verizon building, which would offer certain death for a man hell-bent on destroying himself, but to a six-story building that had a hard-to-access roof. He could imagine Antoine Campbell running up to the fifth floor and hiding in that narrow little escape, waiting for the two men—and by now the Maryland State Police—to simply give up and leave him alone. But the receptionist said that the men had been on the fifth floor. Maybe they knew the building too; maybe they knew that cramped little nook where he would be hiding. They could not drag him back outside with him screaming. So they hustled him up to the roof. Maybe at gunpoint. Maybe they said they just wanted to talk to him. They crowded him. They walked toward him, making him walk backward, to the edge of the roof. He tried to dodge, and one of the men caught him and simply threw him off the building.

Tom could see it. That was more or less how it happened.

SEVENTEEN

Fallon's motorcade swept through a slightly run-down neighborhood with weathered homes and neat, postage-stamp yards just three blocks east of the US Capitol. On New Jersey Avenue, the vehicles halted in front of a small A-frame house with a big porch; unlike its neighbors, it wore a fresh coat of sage green paint. From the chimney on the side of the house, fragrant smoke puffed out.

It was midafternoon—Fallon's lunch break—but the sky was chromium, dimming by the minute. Fallon declined an umbrella, though the mix of snow and light rain was cloying and cold, and stepped carefully up the slick cobblestone flags to the front door.

A few moments later, the door opened to reveal a heavily pregnant woman. She was slim, despite the basketball belly, with a lovely face framed by mad corkscrew curls piled on top of her head and spilling down her cheeks.

A tentative smile came to her lips. "You must be Fallon," she said in a soft, pleasant voice. "I'm Charlotte, Antoine's sister."

"I'm sorry to meet under such unpleasant circumstances, Charlotte," Fallon said and extended her hand. The woman looked warily behind her to Tom and beyond, to the street, where the follow-up was parking behind the limo.

"This is Tom," Fallon said. "He's my associate."

Charlotte frowned. "Are you the cops?"

"He's Secret Service," Fallon said simply. "He's here for me; he's not investigating ... anything."

Charlotte's face was devoid of expression for a moment, as if she were simply absorbing this information, then she nodded shortly, deciding it was okay to proceed. "Why don't y'all come in. It's cold out here."

Removing his shades, Tom followed Fallon past the screen door into a clean, small living room with a new mint green sofa, glass tables, and a cozy fire roaring in the brick hearth. Everything was very clean and precisely placed in the room, but there were few decorations. No plants. A small framed picture of a large gathering of people was placed on the wall, but there was nothing else.

"We just moved in a few weeks ago," Charlotte said, answering the room's emptiness. "We're still unpacking, actually. It's tough, though, with the baby and Charles working all the time."

The hardwood planks creaked companionably under their feet as they followed Charlotte back to a yellow-tiled kitchen. The little curtains over the sink were open to the side yard and the house next door.

Charlotte put water in a teakettle and set it on the stove to boil. That accomplished, she addressed the two strangers in her kitchen. "Have a seat." She gestured at the round breakfast table. Fallon sat while Tom remained standing near the wall under a clock. Fallon liked this house; she detected happiness in it. Maybe it was the expectation of a baby.

Charlotte eased her heavily pregnant body into an armchair. "What can I tell you?" she asked.

Fallon looked over at Tom for guidance. He was the investigator; they should have planned this better so he led the questioning. "Well," Fallon began slowly, "first of all, I'm very sorry for your loss. It was … horrible." Such stupid words. She felt like a klutz, and she felt like she was in some way being rude, intruding on this woman's grief.

"Thank you," Charlotte said simply.

Fallon looked desperately to Tom. He nodded almost imperceptibly, encouraging her to continue. "Charlotte," Fallon said, "I spoke to your brother before he died. He called my office."

Charlotte's expression hardened, like she was bracing herself. She inhaled a small, sharp breath but said nothing.

"He wanted to discuss something with me and he never got the chance. I wonder if you might know … what he wanted to talk to me about?"

Charlotte's face paled. Some distilling emotion began to wash over her face and Fallon felt certain that they'd done the right thing by coming here. Charlotte did know something.

"What did he say?" Charlotte asked.

"Just that he needed to speak to me," Fallon said, hedging. "He did mention one thing I thought was odd. He said something about a map of the keys. Do you know what that means?"

She frowned. "No. I've never heard of that. I have no idea what it means."

"Do you know if he had any connection to Fallon?" Tom asked.

Charlotte began to shake her head. "He wasn't political or anything."

Tom Bishop, the experienced investigator, continued. "Do you know if he had any connection with anyone who might have been a national security threat?"

Charlotte shook her head. "No. I can't imagine Antoine being involved with anything having to do with national security. I mean, I know that he was doing some work for the NSA. But he didn't have access to anything classified."

"Did he ever mention someone named Richard Mullinax?" Fallon asked.

"That name does not sound familiar," she replied.

The teakettle whistled and Charlotte got up to prepare the tea. In silence, she served the tea. Fallon took a polite sip.

Tom placed his mug of tea on the table. "Did he ever talk about the president or anyone else in the executive branch of government?"

Charlotte shook her head. "No. As I said, he wasn't political." She touched her pregnant belly, for reassurance—for the child inside or for herself.

Tom asked, "Did he have any connection to anyone who might be a national security concern?"

Charlotte shook her head. "No. But …" She looked past

Tom and Fallon to the window over her sink. "I don't know what to believe anymore."

"What is it?" Fallon asked calmly.

Charlotte looked back at her. "Two days before he was killed he told me he was worried that he was being followed."

Fallon kept her expression neutral, trying not to appear too eager when she asked,

"Did he say who he thought might be following him?"

Charlotte put both her hands around her teacup, letting the warmth and rich aroma of Earl Gray warm her. "He told me that I wouldn't believe him," she murmured; the regret was unspoken but soft and luminous in her onyx eyes. "And I said he was right. I didn't want to know what he was up to. He hadn't been in trouble in years, but I recognized all the signs. He was being secretive, nervous."

"What kind of trouble had he been in?" Tom asked.

Charlotte shrugged. "The usual, I suppose. He'd been in jail for hacking, and when he got out, he seemed to change. He finished his college degree and started a little business."

Charlotte's pretty face was pinched with regret and sadness, raw grief roiling just below the surface.

Bracing herself, Fallon asked, gently, if it was at all possible that Antoine had killed himself.

Charlotte laughed bitterly, shaking her head. "He had never been suicidal, and he certainly was not suicidal when he was killed."

... *he was killed.*

A shiver ricocheted through Fallon.

Trying to appear at least outwardly calm, Fallon asked, "Why do you think he was killed?"

"It's obvious," Charlotte replied. "My brother didn't run off a six-story building miles from both his home and office to kill himself. He was not suicidal. He was murdered."

Charlotte's fierce words were delivered with the calm certainty of a scientific conclusion.

"Do you have any idea who would have wanted him dead?"

The room fell silent. Tears pooled and fell from Charlotte's dark eyes. Fallon felt the horrible impact of the question, despite Tom's kind tone when he asked it. Charlotte dabbed her swollen eyes with a tissue.

"What about his old cronies? Is it possible any of them had a grudge against him?" Tom asked quietly.

Charlotte shrugged. "I doubt it. It had been years since he had been in contact with them."

Tom Bishop appeared as the ultimate professional: compassionate, engaged, but all business. He was a comforting presence: tall and strong, bristling with efficiency and intelligence. He was the very definition of authority.

After ten more minutes of discussion gentled in deference to the woman's grieving, Tom Bishop thanked the woman for her time and he and Fallon stood to leave.

Tom handed Charlotte his business card. "Please give me a call if you think of anything."

Charlotte took the card and followed Tom and Fallon to the foyer of the small home. They thanked her again for her time and walked down the rain-slicked flagstones to the motorcade. Settling in the seat, Fallon looked back at Charlotte, so joyously round with child. Love exists, Fallon thought vaguely. It was an obscure idea, conjured seemingly from melancholy and a desperate desire to believe. Maybe, in the absence of those we love, the idea of love itself would do.

EIGHTEEN

President Ballard had invited the Hughes family to the White House for dinner with several members of the current administration. Tensions between the United States and Russia continued to worsen, and the president was eager to continue the dialogue between the two administrations, even if he had to do it under the guise of a friendly dinner.

In the President's Dining Room in the White House residence, the table was covered with a cream damask cloth. The lights of the candles softened the rich red and gold of the Reagan china and made the Kennedy crystal sparkle. The flowers were simple tonight but very rich: red daisies, red Floribunda roses, and green ivy in crystal pedestal bowls.

Fallon resented the part of herself that was impressed with all the pomp and circumstance. It was impossible for any American to not be a little awed by the White House and the history inside these walls, she conceded reluctantly.

Her parent's kabuki theatre of a happy marriage was in full swing. They were seated next to each other, and occasionally Elizabeth would lean into Preston and whisper something and they'd chuckle over a private, possibly sexy joke.

Elizabeth had two drinks—Fallon was counting—and it didn't show. It wouldn't show, Fallon knew from experience, until she'd downed five or six. Then the vases started flying. Then her mother would scream, pack her clothes, maybe run off for a few days. At least that was the routine in the old days. As First Lady, she wouldn't have that latitude.

"So," Elizabeth was saying to President Ballard, "Preston finally relented and I will be making *Kill Shot*. My character chops off heads with a samurai sword so I will need fencing lessons, of course. I am due on set on the first of March."

Fallon saw the planes of her father's face tighten, the smirk disguised as a smile. They had agreed to no such thing, Fallon knew, but her mother enjoyed embarrassing her father, pushing him into a corner where it would be impolite to correct his wife.

"You'll be redefining the role of First Lady," Caroline Ballard, the current occupant of that title, said graciously. "I'll enjoy seeing you do it."

And so it went, the standard desultory Washington, D.C. conversation.

Fallon mentally tried to hurry things along. She left work an hour early to be here; after leaving early yesterday she was going to get a reputation as a slacker. Whether or not she believed him to be guilty, Robert Chandler was relying on her and Sam Cahill in keeping him out of prison. Yet, once again, her father had insisted that this was for his career, so she had to show up. *What about my career?* More pointedly: *What about my life? My time?* She wondered what Tom was doing and squeezed her legs together to quell the sudden longing. She tried to reorient herself. Yes, she wanted Tom, but tonight, despite his seductive invitation, would not be just about sex.

Tonight would be about answers. She would ask the question she'd been privately pondering for years. She would ask why he left.

White-gloved waiters served dessert so unobtrusively they were practically invisible. Chocolate tortes with raspberry and crème Chantilly were served with sherry. Fallon accepted the sherry and drank it, while the torte remained untouched. Not accustomed to alcohol, the cumulative effect of the sherry and dinner wine was satisfactorily buffering.

A blind hour. The conversation dipped and swirled around her. When she was finally able to make a getaway, she could not recall even a single thing that was said.

Forcing herself to linger at President Ballard's dinner had been agony, but now as she arrived at the curb of Gwen's house, she felt the butterflies in her stomach. Excitement about seeing Tom was part of the reason. The other part was simple fear. She was scared to know the answer to the big question.

The door swung open and Fallon entered then shut the door behind her. Tom stood in the foyer, looking so beautiful she wanted to laugh or sing with pleasure. She, who had done a pretty good job of disguising her emotions for her parents and clients and even the media, of coming sixth or seventh—if at all—in the list of priorities, immediately felt that wild, buoyant joy that refused to be ignored.

Tom slipped her purse off her shoulder and placed it on Gwen's entry table, then took the sodden jacket from her shoulders and hung it in the closet. Only then, when she was comfortable, did he take her in his arms.

As soon as his lips touched hers, the grim energy of the evening dissipated like the end of a song. She melted against him, opening her mouth for him as he sensually stroked her tongue, hot and insistent. He pulled back. "How are you?" He spoke softly, conscious of the Secret Service outside the front door.

"Very good, now," she answered, mimicking his low whisper.

He took her hand and gently tugged her inside. Only then did she notice that Tom had lit some candles on the living room table and over the fireplace mantle. A bottle of wine and two glasses had been set out in anticipation of her arrival.

"There's some food in the kitchen," he said. "I stopped by the Italian Store and got a selection of antipasto. Are you hungry?"

"I nibbled at the White House but actually, I think I'd love some antipasto."

"Sit here," he said and strode into Gwen's kitchen.

Fallon sank onto the sofa and examined the wine. She loved Napa Valley chardonnay, and she briefly wondered if she'd revealed that in Greece. She must have, she realized, and she felt a certain bittersweet ache for the past, for the time spent apart. Occasionally during those years apart, she would grow frustrated with loneliness and think it foolish to keep herself in reserve. She should date! She should be open to others: Gwen was emphatic on this point. Fallon demurred, using her job as a convenient excuse to abstain from the dating derby. She never could verbalize that she simply couldn't move on because Tom had *mattered more than anyone else ever could.*

Her certainty on this point seemed justified and magnified tonight. He had thought of her; he remembered even the smallest detail.

Tom returned with a platter piled high with roasted vegetables, cheeses, meats and fragrant olives. "Oh my gosh," Fallon sighed with pleasure, "That looks incredible."

"Have some," Tom said.

Fallon selected a fat green olive and a slice of Asiago, cooing over the delectable combination.

Tom opened the wine and poured two glasses. He handed one to Fallon. "To us," he said.

Fallon clinked glasses. "To us." The chardonnay was a cold, wet kiss. She remembered that she'd had two drinks with dinner and reminded herself to go easy on the wine. "This is wonderful," she said. "Why did you do this?"

"Do what?"

"Come on. The candles, the wine, the food …"

Tom shrugged. "You've had a rough couple of days," he explained. "I wanted to do something nice for you."

She suddenly felt unaccountably shy, like he was answering a need directly from her soul, one that she herself could scarcely afford to acknowledge. She felt humbled by his perception and that he had taken it upon himself to remedy the plaguing stress.

"I wanted to …"

Fallon glanced up, her color rising. "Yes, Tom?"

He smiled reluctantly and set the wine glass onto the table. "I just wanted to see you happy and relaxed."

Fallon smiled then and spontaneously pivoted on the sofa, throwing one leg over his hip so she was straddling him. It was a heady feeling being atop all that muscle and power as he blazed from beneath her. The bulge in his trousers pressed against her softest parts. She gently ran her fingers through the rough silk of his hair, looking into his face and taking in every detail.

She was suddenly struck with how young he looked. No, not young. Vulnerable, she realized with wonder. It was a trait she did not associate with Tom at all, and it blindsided her. She had intended to say something flirtatious but the words evaporated. She felt his arms curl around her back and draw her closer. She bent her head and let their lips touch. The warm rose blush of his lips surprised her with their softness. She tasted the hint of chardonnay on his lips, the hungry heat of his breath as he delved deeper.

Fallon melted into him, surrendering entirely to his strength. His warm hands slid under her touch-me soft angora sweater, over the burning skin of her back, holding her close. Safe in his hot embrace, Fallon began to move seductively against him, and his hands moved down to the swell of her hips, pushing her into him so that she could feel his rigid erection through the layers of clothes. She sighed audibly and pulled back to look into his face. His eyes bore into hers with an intensity that shocked them both. He slid his hands to her breasts, cupping them reverently in his warm palms. The gentle stroking of his fingers through her lace brassiere was enough to make her nipples pucker, the desperate eagerness of her response undeniable.

She felt the clasp of her bra suddenly open and realized he'd unclipped it without her noticing. The excitement of his pleasure sent a jolt of affection through her. They were connected by an invisible current, she thought dreamily, the delight received multiplied by the delight returned. On and on, into infinity. He possessively pulled her against the powerful plank of his chest and took a taut nipple between his lips, gently teasing the sensitive flesh with the heat and wetness of his tongue. A heady twist of sharp pleasure spiraled through her as he sucked and laved the sensitive flesh. How unbearably pleasurable it was to be the focus of all Tom's concentrated affection.

Usually there was an undercurrent of danger and wild, untamed energy just straining to be released in Tom, but this time the gentleness and patience seemed heartrendingly genuine. Like he wanted to be fragile with her because he was feeling fragile. Like he cherished her.

Tenderness washed over her even as the intensity mounted and the pleasure grew. Her breasts felt hot, full of glowing light, and she had the strange thought that she might actually climax. If she just rubbed herself against the throbbing erection in his jeans … Oh no. Oh wow. She began to move more aggressively against him. Tom wrapped one arm around her narrow waist, keeping her tightly against the bulge in his pants. Suddenly, with a wrenching cry, the pleasure lifted and pitched her.

Fallon had resolved they would talk first, before any sex. How had she gotten so sidetracked? She could not go one more day without knowing. The awful timing embarrassed her, but she couldn't stop herself now. She squirmed out of Tom's warm, loving grasp and pulled her soft sweater down.

"We need to talk."

"Now?" he asked incredulously.

"Yes. We should have done it before."

The disappointment was all too obvious on his face. But to his credit, he was trying to be a gentleman about it, getting himself under control. "Okay. What do you want to talk about?"

Fallon arranged herself beside him. She stalled by taking another sip of the wine. She wasn't sure if it was the cumulative effect of the alcohol she'd had all evening or the literally intoxicating effect he had on her, but her head seemed to swim. The words she wanted to say seemed to dash in and out of her mind as she struggled to find the courage as well as the phrasing.

"Are you okay?"

Her heart broke at the concern in his voice. He grasped her hand, supporting her. "Why did you leave me on Paxos?" she asked. Her voice was tiny. It sounded wrong. Blasphemous. The question cleaved the night into two halves: Before and After.

She was scared of the answer. She hoped he refused to answer. Because she could not meet his eyes, she looked down at the wedding ring pattern on Gwen's grandmother's quilt that was lying over the arm of the sofa and absently traced the tiny seams with her fingertips.

The silence seemed to go on for several minutes, or perhaps several lifetimes. Right when she resolved that he was simply not going to answer, he spoke. "I was married," Tom said.

Fallon squeezed her eyes shut as the tears came. *No.* Everything in her body rebelled at this answer. An agonized high-pitched scream went off in her head. An icy chill permeated her skin, and she felt something like nausea well up inside her, but it was worse than that. She felt like she'd been poisoned. Like bleach was thrown on something living and vibrant and now it was shrinking and dying. But it felt so true. It was the answer she had been denying for all this time. The obvious truth.

She knew the damage infidelity caused. She'd seen it up close in her parents' marriage. She wasn't thinking specifically of her parents in that moment—no thought would hold, they all slid off her—but she felt, with a cold punch to the gut, that Tom was just like her father.

"I mean ..." He gently squeezed her hand. "Fallon ... I've never had this discussion before. I'm not sure how to." She let go of his hand as if it were a scorpion and scrambled to move off the sofa, but Tom grabbed her. "No, listen to me."

"Shut up! Just shut up!" The words trembled violently in a voice not her own. The agony and wretched anger in her shrill voice was humiliating. And yet she did not stop. She jerked her arm back so he could not touch her. "How dare you!"

"Fallon, listen to me." He followed her out of the living room, toward the foyer. "Fallon, please."

"Shut up!" she yelled at him. "I don't want to hear another word."

"You don't understand."

"I understand plenty. Shut up! Just shut up. I don't want to hear you, I don't want to see you. I can't believe you would do this!" She was shaking, her whole body coiled in rage. She felt betrayed and jealous and she had no idea why, but the emotions were tumbling out uncontrollably, or even understandably.

"Fallon, please listen to me," he said, and grabbed her arms. Instantly, she twisted out of his grasp and slapped him across the face. The sharp crack stunned them both to silence. She held her hands to her mouth, shocked. Liquid pain stung her eyes. "I'm ... sorry," she said from behind her hands, horrified. She had never struck another person in her life. Suddenly sober, she stepped to him, reaching for him to apologize.

He rocked back, recoiling from her. "No, you're right. Let's get dressed and go."

She had moved stiffly, wordlessly, her small body made smaller still by her cramped movements. She retrieved her coat, and without looking at him, walked out.

After the door closed, Tom felt incredibly alone. He had never felt so alone, except that first night when he knew without a doubt that Bethany had not made it out of the building. This kind of solitude felt like punishment.

He returned to the living room and blew out the candles. He lit a single lamp so that he could pour the rest of the wine down the sink and cover the antipasto platter to place it in Gwen's fridge. He assumed she would have more use of it than he.

After he had cleaned up, he sat on the edge of the sofa, trying to figure out what to think. The slap had shocked him and concerned him. But what had surprised him more was the reserve of anger that Fallon had accessed so quickly.

If anything, this nasty little scene just proved what he had known since Bethany's death. He was meant to be alone. It was better this way, in a nice cocoon of not expecting anything from any other person. It was certainly easier to be objective about life when you didn't have to consider anyone else. He glanced at the green LED clock on Gwen's microwave. It was late. He had no place to go but home.

Tom had finally sunk into an uneasy sleep when the phone jittered loudly on the bedside table. He grabbed the device, blinking at it, until the words dissolved into an impossible text:

FOUND SOMETHING.

It was almost three o'clock in the morning. Tom pushed himself up, got dressed, and drove back into D.C.

This time Frank was not frowning. In fact, he looked

jubilant. "It was so easy! We were totally overthinking it!" he exclaimed as they walked down the hall to his office. He handed Tom some papers from the printer.

"He took pictures of his notes and uploaded them to his Flickr page. He kept them private, obviously, but there they are."

Tom's mind was racing, trying to connect the dots that didn't seem to belong in the same stratosphere. He glanced over the pictures, some of the words hard to read, but the word Mullinax was visible.

The electric pulse of revelation zipped through him. He had been avoiding this angle because Richard Mullinax was a very powerful man. In order to accuse him of anything, Tom had to have his facts straight. He could not ask for a warrant based on Fallon's recollection of the dead man's call, and he knew even now, holding this in his hands, it was not enough probable cause for a warrant. But he felt like he had a new direction to pursue—the correct direction.

NINETEEN

Fallon was exhausted but could not sleep. Her mind was racing; she was alternately freezing and burning up, like she had some virus eating at her inside. The fact that Tom was married (might still be married, in fact) had receded somewhat in immediacy. Far worse was the fact that she had slapped him. Remorse kept her on edge, replying the scene over and over again. How stunned he looked. His pale cheek with that nasty red mark on it—a mark she caused! She cringed with guilt.

Just like my parents, she thought miserably and wiped the tears from her eyes. The screaming. The slap. Horrible. And more to the point: *just like my mother.* Elizabeth Hughes's drunken rants and irrational behavior had caused her family an incalculable amount of pain. Her father had too, with his discreet infidelities. She had seen her mother go insane when confronting Preston about his mistresses, claw at his face, scream, and throw things. Fallon had hated those fights. Yet she had allowed herself to do the same thing. Fallon wondered if it was possible her mother had gotten pregnant with Evan for spite. Had she done it just to prove she could? Could she be that destructive?

Reflecting on those fights, the answer seemed obvious.

Fallon had never been drunk before in her life, but now she wondered if some alcoholic gene was expressing itself in her behavior. No, she admonished herself firmly. That was far too easy an excuse. Tonight could be explained by one thing: she was simply out of control with rage. She had wanted some excuse to yell at him for leaving her on Paxos, and no matter his reasons, she was going to have an explosive outburst to punish him.

She felt absolutely wretched.

She threw the covers off and, after a moment's indecisiveness, padded downstairs. The big loft was inhabited by darkness. Normally the mementos from her travels made her happy; they gave her access to the freedom she craved. But tonight, in the shadowy, skittering light, the gaping African masks she'd bought in Botswana seemed like horrified witnesses to a terrible crime. Fallon shivered and turned on a set of recessed lighting over her work area.

She thought of sending Tom a text or calling him but knew he didn't want to hear from her. A little roil of panic rocked her as she acknowledged he might never speak to her again and would, of course, be completely justified.

Curiosity and jealousy—why not admit it, she had no pride after tonight's actions—gnawed at her. She wanted to know about the wife. The anticipated pain would help blunt the guilt and perhaps fade the grotesque memory of her hand striking Tom. Fallon typed "Thomas Bishop" into Google.

To her surprise, several listings came up. It took a moment to understand what she was seeing. She recognized Tom by the green eyes blazing off the page, but nothing else about him seemed familiar. The caption read: *A Secret Service agent carries an injured woman from the World Trade Center.* He wore a dark suit though it was barely recognizable from all the white dust that covered him. His face was streaked with white dust and dirt, a nasty jagged cut bleeding on his cheek, but his eyes were pure and angry—deep, vivid green, smoldering with anger at a world suddenly covered with nuclear ash. The woman in his arms was limp and pulped purple and red with blood, but she gazed up at him with what could only be described as devout gratitude.

Fallon had absorbed all of the assembled iconography of the attacks, but she had never seen this picture. An overwhelming sense of loss seared through her, leaving her grasping. Through her own stupid, impulsive, criminal actions, she had lost this brave, serious man. She was having difficulty reading the blurred words through her tears. She swiped the annoying wetness from her eyes and cheeks.

The answer she was looking for was found on the next page. It was just one throwaway line, captioning the same photograph as the famous picture of Tom, but it suddenly gave her more context to the man than anything else would have: *Agent Bishop personally rescued at least fifteen people. Bishop's wife, Bethany Bishop, perished in the attacks.*

The horror came back to her with a cataclysmic shudder as she acknowledged her own awfulness. *Fallon, listen to me.* She had not only refused to listen, she had assumed the very worst about him. She felt so very small.

She had to apologize, even if her words were flimsy and too minute to matter. Even if he never wanted to see her again, she had to apologize and at least convey that she knew she was wrong. So, so, so wrong.

Fallon dug deep for information about Bethany Bishop. She was a senior executive at a financial company officed on the 104th floor the North Tower. Personal memories of Bethany Bishop described a generous, accomplished woman who was loved by hundreds of people who knew her. She raised money for pediatric AIDS; she loved to sail; she collected antique blue glass.

These details hurt like bee stings. Fallon couldn't take any more, not just yet. She glumly stood up and looked around at her empty life.

At the wall of windows, Fallon pressed her forehead against the cold glass, looking through the lace of snow to the wide crescent of blackness: the Potomac was indistinguishable from sky. The world seemed full of violence, random losses, and cruelty. It refused to be ordered.

She felt incredibly guilty. Lonely, too, but she deserved to feel lonely. She tried to imagine Tom's loss but couldn't. She had been fortunate in that regard. The only person she had ever known who died was Antoine Campbell, and she didn't even know him really. He was just a voice on the telephone, begging for help.

Fallon shut her eyes. What a goddamned fool she was. To have been so eager to condemn him in order to justify her own rage. She had tried so hard to be the opposite of her mother and, in doing so, had become her.

TWENTY

The next morning, Fallon awoke completely calm. All her tears had been shed, and her mind was clear and clean. She operated with the hateful clarity of shock: it was ice-cold, precise, and implacable. The calm did not vanish as she got ready in the morning. It did not even leave when she opened the door and saw Tom standing there as he was most mornings. Seeing him, she felt the loss with her whole body, but her cold, protected machine mind knew it was unwise to burden Tom with her agony caused by her own character flaws. She did not want him to glimpse the pain and so the calm eclipsed her face, and she said nothing as they strolled to the elevator. She dared to glance up once and saw that he had been studying her. Shame filled her. Fallon urgently wanted to say something, but the right words refused to come, and so she left the silence intact.

For the first time she could ever remember, she was thankful for her work, which would consume her utterly. She attacked it with a certain cold ruthlessness she'd never experienced before. The calmness allowed her to think clearly. She dispatched inefficiency and ineptitude with remorseless action.

Her mother called her once to ask if she had her gowns altered. Fallon had become so accustomed to lying to her mother about even the most trivial matters in order to keep peace, but on this day, with a sense of strength, she said, honestly, "No, I haven't."

"I cannot believe you'd disappoint me this way," Elizabeth sighed and began to launch into a monologue about the responsibility of the First Family.

Fallon cut her off. "Mother, is your life so constricted and small that you care more about a ball gown than the fact that I was accused of murder or Evan is languishing because you don't care enough to find him a proper nanny and preschool program?"

After a stunned little pause, Elizabeth shot back, "You are just like your father."

"No, Mother," Fallon replied. "I am just like you."

She waited for a sense of regret, but it did not come. There was nothing. Just coldness. And under that, a sense of relief. She was finished enabling her parents' bad behavior. She'd spent her whole life attempting to please and appease them, to conform to their idea of what she should be. But those days were over. She knew she had just thrown down the gauntlet. Either they would all recover and be a normal family, or they wouldn't. Either way, Fallon was finished lying about what she wanted and who she was.

Tom Bishop was in the control room writing an email to Leah when Kevin White came inside. "The taps and traps caught two hang-up calls last night on Fallon's phone but the calls were unknown. The pen register came back unknown."

Tom mulled that for a moment. Circumventing the pen register and the taps and traps showed a very high level of technical sophistication on the part of the caller. Not that he was surprised. He remembered the meeting at Midnight Research and wondered if they had cracked the entire US government yet.

A sonar ping rippled through his mind. Something …

"Tom, there's something I'd like to ask you."

"Shoot."

"This is difficult to ask, but are you seeing Ms. Hughes socially?"

Oh shit.

Tom made a concerted effort to not flinch. Struggling to keep his expression completely neutral, he answered, "No." He hoped he was successful because there was a ferocious roar in his head, and he could not hear anything over it.

Kevin's eyes were probing, watching, waiting for some indication that he was lying. "No?"

"No. I am not seeing Ms. Hughes socially," Tom answered with more certainty. "Absolutely not."

"Okay then." Kevin stood up. "Well, I wanted to let you know about the pen register."

"Thanks. I appreciate it."

Kevin hesitated. Tom sensed Kevin's questions. Kevin was questioning his own instincts, which were fighting ferociously with his desire to believe that all Secret Service agents, particularly the agent most responsible for his protectee, would tell the complete truth when asked a direct question.

After Kevin departed, Tom looked back to the email he had been drafting and deleted it. It did not seem important now. Needing some air, he told the others he would be back soon and drove to the old Post Office building. He took the elevator down to the basement, to the shooting range. The monthly weapons requalification was one administrative task that every agent from the deputy director down to the guy hired just four weeks ago was obligated to complete.

Tom scanned the lanes and saw a female agent with whom he had spent a lonesome Thanksgiving in Norfolk, Virginia babysitting the president's brother. A freak snowstorm had blown through and there had been nothing to do but sit in the truck at the end of the street and talk for eight solid hours.

He remembered her name suddenly—Kayla Barnes. He'd have to say hello later.

Meanwhile, he claimed a lane, fastened his eye and ear protection, and began shooting. Normally he scored a perfect 300, but it quickly became apparent that today would not be like other days. His shots were all over the place.

As he reloaded, Kayla waved. She pulled off her ear protection and walked over.

The "No Talking" signs posted over the benches was mostly ignored but respected enough that the agents discreetly kept their voices down during the after-shooting banter.

"Hey, Bishop," she said. "You've been on the

grapevine lately."

"What do you mean?" he asked.

She pulled back the slide of her weapon, checking to make sure it was clear. "Just rumors."

"What kind of rumors?" Tom asked.

"Just that you might be taking the service in 'Secret Service' a little too far with Avalon."

A fine flush washed over him. The Secret Service, like any organization, paid attention to rumors, and this one was tantalizing enough to be investigated seriously if it caught fire. Not to mention it had the distinct disadvantage of being true. Or it had been, for a while.

Tom realized Kayla was watching for his reaction, which meant the rumor had gained some traction. He smirked. "She's hot. Keep those rumors going."

Kayla laughed. Tom was relieved—she seemed to dismiss the idea of by-the-book Tom Bishop fooling around with his protectee. She moved on to other gossip.

After ten minutes of catching up, Tom washed his hands and returned to his government vehicle, a white Chrysler Sebring. Once on Pennsylvania Avenue, he swerved into the parking lot of a convenience store and turned off the ignition.

Fuck. Everybody knows.

Tom Bishop was not a man who panicked often, but a distinctly trapped sensation was descending upon him. Tom had been a Boy Scout growing up; he'd been a United States Marine officer. And now a Secret Service agent. He had built his life on a foundation of honesty and trustworthiness—just like the Secret Service motto, *worthy of trust and confidence*. He wasn't worthy of those—or of honor, that most sacred part of himself. Sneaking around with a protectee did not exactly comport with the image he had of himself. The fact that it was definitely over did not help matters.

He decided quite suddenly that he would go back home to New Jersey for the weekend. It had been a while since he'd been back, and since the inauguration was coming up, travel would become increasingly difficult. He had so much time saved up he could spend six months away from the office—with pay—but decided a weekend would suffice. He would come back feeling clearer, knowing what to do about the problem of Fallon Hughes.

TWENTY-ONE

Years ago, Tom's parents retired to Florida, but Bethany's parents, the Cabrerras, remained in their rambling old house in Red Bank, New Jersey, where they had a wide circle of friends and family. When Tom called to tell them he would be in town, they invited him to dinner, as he knew they would.

Badsea Drive: the first time Bethany had turned the corner into the cul-de-sac, to introduce him to her family, he had been so anxious—just flat out scared. He had never bothered to meet a woman's parents before, but Bethany was special. Bethany was the One. The beautiful white Colonial with the red door and black shutters, and towering trees in the front yard, was the place most important to her, and he could immediately see why. It was a place that simply felt simply like home: warm, welcoming, infused with family history.

During that first raucous dinner with her family, he had discovered that Bethany was right: there was absolutely no reason to worry. They welcomed him warmly, laughing with him like he had been part of the family forever. After her mother's homemade peach cobbler, Bethany had taken him outside to the pristine snowfield that was the backyard. They had built a snow gremlin, complete with branches for arms and a rock for a nose. Her father had joined them outside, and together they stood staring at a large tree. It was covered in snow. It was bare, except for one tiny green fruit on a low limb, which Tom believed was a fig. The fig was covered with snow, but it still managed to hang there, enduring the wind and the snow. "Some things last," Bethany's father had said. "That is comforting."

• • •

As Tom turned off the ignition in the driveway, another wave of nostalgia pulled him under. He had always felt comfortable here and remained so even after Bethany's death. At least, it had been comfortable before he met and became involved with Fallon Hughes. Now he was not sure what he felt about anything, which was part of why he had come. He wanted clarity. Part of that, he admitted only very reluctantly, was that he wanted to feel his bond to Bethany, to test it and see if it was as strong as ever.

Taking a big breath to steady himself, Tom knocked at the front door. Inside the house, he could hear one of Bethany's nieces yelling, "Mommmmmmm-eeeee!" Other small children's voices faded in and out like bad radio reception.

The white sheers over the windows fluttered as Mrs. Cabrerra peeked out from the side of the door, and a moment later, the door swung open. "Tom," she breathed and enveloped him in an embrace. She smelled like crushed tomatoes and basil and felt like home. As he held her, he asked, "Are you making pasta, Mary?"

"Lasagna," she answered, pulling back. She was in her early fifties, but when she smiled like that, she looked like a girl in her mid-twenties. Joy transformed her, made her eyes sparkle and her face glow. "Come in out of the cold," she said and closed the door.

The house was exactly the same. Warm with a fire roaring in the fireplace, the yells of kids, the smell of cooking. The only thing foreign was he.

Bethany's brothers, Brian and Sean, had come with their wives and children. Her sister, ten months older than Bethany, had brought her husband and new baby. She was sitting at the bar, eating green Provencal olives and talking to her father. When she caught sight of him, a lovely, wide, warm smile spread over her features. Tom felt the old, cellular-level grief wash over him. Grief and confusion—a feeling of displacement, like he'd gone back in time. Carolyn and Bethany looked so much alike: they had the same beautiful olive complexions, bright brown eyes, and winsome smiles that felt like benedictions.

Carolyn slid off the bar stool and hugged him. He shut his

eyes for just a moment, smelling her hair, enjoying her female form against him. It felt so much like holding Bethany that he wanted to say her name aloud, wanted to kiss her and tell her he loved her and missed her so much that sometimes he felt his heart was being ripped out of his chest.

The moment passed. He said hello to his brothers-in-law, and his father-in-law, and made the obligatory cooing noises at Carolyn's new baby, Bethany-Anne. Carolyn gently placed the baby in Tom's arms, and Bethany-Anne looked up at him with that drunken-sailor, cross-eyed expression that was at once adorable and silly. Unaccustomed to being around very small babies, he was not prepared for the protective affection that washed over him. The baby weighed less than ten pounds, practically light as air in his arms, staring up at him as if he were God. Gently, Tom touched her silky brown hair and then felt her smooth cheeks with the back of his knuckles. He tickled her soft, oval feet and kissed her starfish hands. He could see Bethany somewhere, indistinct, but very much alive in the niece that she would never know. Before becoming too emotional, he gently placed the baby back in her mother's arms.

Mary Cabrerra was a proper Italian wife. While the lasagna finished baking, she had set out a beautiful antipasto buffet on the bar with selections of sliced meats, olives, artichokes, hearts of palm, and four different cheeses. Carolyn offered red wine from a carafe but Tom declined; alcohol sometimes made him nostalgic and melancholy, and the last thing he wanted to do was spend the whole evening brooding over Bethany. Instead, he took a bottle of spring water from the fridge. Shutting the door, he recognized a photo among the Monmouth County emergency numbers, a Chinese menu, and magnets. All the siblings were smiling at the photographer—natural, happy smiles, not the stiff smile eked from a photographer demanding a good shot. With an ecstatic smile and fire-bright eyes, Bethany was connecting directly with the photographer, who happened to be Tom Bishop. Between home and heaven. The stamp on the bottom right corner was barely visible: 15 June 2001.

Paleontology. Artifacts everywhere. Mementoes still had

the ability to surprise him, knock him momentarily off center. If only he had been able to save her. If only he had been useful on that day. But he had not been able to protect his own wife. He was punished for it every day.

Tom stayed through dinner and dessert, until the children were getting cranky. Mary Cabrerra walked him to the door and embraced him. He held on to her, loving her enough for both himself and Bethany. When he pulled back, he saw that she was no longer trying to hide her emotions; big, luminous tears wet her eyes.

"Will we see you again before you leave?" she asked.

Tom tried to discipline his voice, to sound casual. "Sure. I'll stop by before I leave town."

Mary Cabrerra smiled wanly. "Good. We miss you around here."

And then the cathode burst of love and ache in his chest, which he could no longer disguise. Bubbles of emotion deluged forth as tears came to his eyes. "I miss Bethany," he said, as much to her as to himself. It sounded good to his own ears. It sounded honest.

"Me too," Mary said and wiped her eyes. "She was very special."

"What the hell am I supposed to do?" he asked. Even he wasn't sure what he meant. There were so many things happening all at once. He felt like a conquered country, adjusting its borders and trying to rewrite the laws in a language he didn't understand. Mary Cabrerra was not only a mother, she was Bethany's mother, and even if she could not know every aspect of Tom and Bethany's marriage, she understood that his loss was equal to hers.

"You just live," Mary replied calmly, "the best you can."

At first blush, it sounded like the myriad platitudes he'd heard after Bethany's death. Casserole Brigades would come round, bringing their "God has a reason for this" and "time heals all wounds" bromides as if they were nuggets of divine wisdom when, in fact, they were worth less than the gum on his shoe. But when Mary spoke, it sounded true. Like it was something she had discovered herself, through years of hard work: that every person must create the journey for his own redemption. He could be nothing but grateful that she would share it with him.

Tom hugged her again and promised to call more often. Then he drove away in his Jeep.

Forty minutes later, the smudgy skyline of New York City came into view. His eyes scanned the southern tip of the island; there was nothing for his gaze to snag. Still so strange, the buildings evaporated like white morning mist, as if they'd been a collective delusion. Ducking into the Lincoln Tunnel, he emerged into the city, which was like driving into a photograph.

His old apartment was in a beautiful historic building in the center of Chelsea, seen with the random immediacy of a snapshot. Those huge, vaulted windows that Bethany had so loved remained bare. The new owner must also like the exposed, urban feel, the way the sun poured in during summer, leaving great slashing sun marks on the pale blonde floors. The effect had reminded him of other sunlit apartments: Paris and Istanbul, where he and Bethany had honeymooned. Everything self-referencing, a never-ending echo chamber of Bethany. Bethany's city garden, right outside the bedroom doors, a patio full of flowers—particularly her orchids. Difficult to grow, she'd enjoyed the feeling of accomplishment when they bloomed. Tom had teased her for taking credit for an act of nature. She had liked to sit out there in a glade of sun and read, sometimes with a glass of mother vodka. In those awful days right after her death, Tom had tried to find the peace that Bethany had so obviously experienced out there. After a while, he stopped trying to relax, knowing it was futile, though the vodka remained.

He had almost begun to believe that love is the guilt you feel for not being enough for the people you cared about. Guilt was the only emotion he knew during those dark days—love and guilt were all mixed up, relying on each other for definition. And he was guilty. Even more guilty for reaching a point where he could not bear to think about Bethany anymore: trying to outwit the poison air, the memories, and that grinding saw of sorrow.

Had to get rid of it, had to drive out of the blackout, escape.

As soon as it was offered, Tom accepted the transfer to protection that would send him south to Washington, D.C. Technically it was a promotion but it felt like retreat. He had plenty of money; his lifelong habit of savings, plus the settlement from the September 11 Victim Compensation Fund allowed him to leave immediately and worry about selling his apartment later.

He fled the city like a refugee, leaving his friends baffled and surprised when he called them, weeks later, from his condo in D.C.—the condo that had no memory. Blank slate, fresh start.

The W Hotel at Union Square: $429 per night for an indeterminate number of nights. The room cool and sleek as a doctor's office. Tall windows of the fourteenth- floor room faced south, toward All That Is Missing. Tom pulled the cinematic draperies closed, undressed, and slept for fifteen hours.

TWENTY-TWO

Where are you?

Fallon blinked back sleep and squinted at her alarm clock; the numbers blurred in indecipherable red squiggles. "What time is it?" she mumbled.

"Ten," Gwen said with a touch of petulance in her voice. "You were supposed to be here thirty minutes ago."

Oh no. The room was slowly coming into focus. Panic gripped as she realized what was happening. It was Saturday. The wedding and inaugural gown summit that they'd planned weeks ago. "I overslept, sweetie. I'll be there in ten minutes."

"Hurry! Make them use the lights and sirens if you have to!"

Fallon bolted out of bed, yanked on jeans, brown leather boots, and a white button-up shirt. Mentally berating herself for her tardiness, she brushed her teeth, swiped on deodorant, and grabbed her purse. Tugging on a knee-length black car coat as she ran out the door, she realized she wasn't even fully awake yet and her hair was a disaster.

Jason Slaney, standing post at her door, looked startled.

"Hi," Fallon said breathlessly. "I'm in such a rush."

Jason Slaney radioed down to the limos as they hurried down the hallway to the elevator. Fallon fluffed her hair and wondered if she was dressed appropriately for a wedding shop. She suspected jeans were not appropriate. Too late to worry about it now.

She slid her shades on and flung herself onto the backseat of the limo, barely noticing Kevin White slam the door behind her. It was a very short drive to Virginia Street and the Vera Wang boutique at the Watergate complex, but every second seemed to take forever.

Gwen was browsing shoes and handbags, still dressed in her street clothes, when Fallon arrived. "Big night?" she asked archly.

"I'm so sorry," Fallon said, hugging her friend. "You haven't started yet, have you?"

Gwen, pacified now that Fallon was here, replied, "No. We were waiting for you. You are late, but you're here, at last."

"Well, scoot. Get your gown on!" Fallon replied brightly. She was feeling defensive, and every movement seemed exaggerated to compensate for her lateness. Her over-effusive blather, exaggerated grin, and frantic eyes were certain giveaways of her guilt. Fallon urged herself to calm down. Gwen would forgive her for being late, but a ruined day would be much harder to overlook.

She sat on a huge white brocade salon chair and waited while Gwen and the attendant went into the changing room. A few moments later, Gwen emerged in a silky strapless gown of the palest, most luscious cream color that Fallon had ever seen. Fallon stood up, her hand to her mouth, as tears spontaneously sprang to her eyes. "Oh my God," she whispered.

"Do you like it?" Gwen asked.

Fallon wanted to answer but she could only stare. Her friend was beautiful. And there was more than that: she was not only beautiful, she was *getting married*. The reality of it had never been as vivid as it was that moment, and a mosaic of memory and emotion kaleidoscoped through her: images of them playing on the kindergarten carpet together, the awkward middle school years, the emotional high school years, college … and now Gwennie was becoming a wife.

"Say something. You're scaring me," Gwen said and looked down at the length of her body encased in the finest bridal silk.

"You are absolutely breathtaking," Fallon said and stepped closer to touch the fabric at Gwen's hip. "You are gorgeous. The gown is gorgeous."

Gwen twirled in the multiple-aspect mirrors, checking out her backside. "It's not bad, but the waist is still a little big. Late nights at the hospital have kept me skinny."

"You look beautiful," Fallon said. Her heart was so full of emotion she could barely utter the words.

The attendant went to find a pedestal for Gwen to step on, and while they waited, Fallon used the moment to collect herself as she casually browsed the racks of gowns. Beautiful laces, flowing silks, gorgeous patterns. Fallon selected one that she liked and looked at the beading. Turning to the mirror, she held the gown to her body and inhaled deeply. She had a flash of an image, wearing a dress like this one, walking down an aisle on her father's arm to Tom Bishop. Impossible now, of course, but oh what a sweet dream. Crystalline tears appeared in her eyes. Funny, she thought she was all cried out.

"Are you getting married too?" the attendant asked from behind her.

Fallon spun around, startled and embarrassed at being caught in her private moment. "No," she said, a little too emphatically. "No, I'm just ...."

The attendant, an older lady with a brusque manner but a kind smile when she cared to crack it, gave her a friendly look. "Happens all the time."

Gwen stepped up on the pedestal and the attendant straightened out the dress, fussing with the hem.

Fallon picked up a veil and placed it on her head, the beautiful gauzy material flowing over her shoulders and hips, trailing behind her. "How do I look?"

Gwen smiled. "Gorgeous."

In the mirror she caught a glimpse of Kevin White and Jason Slaney standing in the corner, and she blushed deeply. Undoubtedly they would tell Tom she was acting like a ditz in the bridal boutique. How embarrassing. Fallon quickly put the veil down and turned her attention to Gwen, who was watching the whole thing in the mirror. The second their eyes met, they started laughing until they cried, until the seamstress told Gwen to shut up or she'd get poked with a needle.

TWENTY-THREE

Though it seemed the only thing anyone could talk about, Fallon dreaded the inauguration. She wanted to avoid any situation in which she might be forced to see Tom, and she could not stomach the thought of her mother now. Behind the shield of her cold calm, she even managed to forget Antoine Campbell to some degree. It was ridiculous to worry about so many people—her mom, Antoine Campbell, Evan, even Tom— and have absolutely nobody worry about her. That emotional energy was best spent caring about someone actually paying her to care: she worked relentlessly on Robert Chandler's case. Since she understood now that life was worse than unfair, it was diabolically corrupt, she worked intently to see that the hedge fund billionaire would be acquitted.

It had been a week since she had talked to Tom, and six days from the inauguration, when her phone rang with a vaguely familiar number.

"Hey, Fallon!"

She recognized the voice as Travis Hill, a young and too-ambitious-for-his-own-good political consultant that her father used for polling. One quasi date eight months ago and he still called or emailed often enough that instead of simply writing him off as a bad date, she'd had to reluctantly reclassify him as a friend. At least a friendly acquaintance.

"I thought of you because I have two tickets to the Kennedy Center on Friday evening and I know how much you love opera."

Opera? She didn't love opera and almost asked what made him think so. Before she could utter the question, he invited her to tonight's performance of *Carmen*.

Excuses ticker taped through her mind. She did not find him attractive; she was very busy with work; he was not Tom Bishop.

But this was perhaps the very reason to see *Carmen* with Travis Hill: if Tom Bishop was not appropriate, maybe Hill was … or maybe she had just lost her ability to filter out the losers. Travis Hill was a blowhard who pursued with an intensity that left her unsettled; only in retrospect did she realize he was simply a political animal, more interested in her father's administration than in Fallon. Still, all other things being equal, a date with him was probably more productive than crying all night, sulking around her apartment until she collapsed from exhaustion. It would be healthy to get out there and try to find some semblance of a romantic life, even if it killed her. The fact that Tom would have to follow her around all night, seeing her up close and personal with another man, did not escape her notice either. It was this fact that prompted her to accept the date. She demurred from *Carmen* but suggested dinner, which seemed to make him happy.

She tried to psyche herself into being excited about the date but only succeeded in giving herself an ulcer.

Collin Whitcomb was thrilled about Fallon's date with Travis Hill. The spyware installed on Fallon's laptop automatically sent every email directly from her account to one of Collin's. It was utterly untraceable—and invisible to the user. Without it, he would not have discovered Fallon's plans for a date on Friday.

This was the opportunity he had prayed for. Collin stood up and walked downstairs to the basement where Malkhazi was polishing his weapon.

"I have good news," Collin said modestly.

"Yes?" Malkhazi grunted.

Collin told him of the opportunity that had presented itself. "Soon Ayrzu will be free." He frowned, contemplating. "But then we will have to think of a way to outdo ourselves."

TWENTY-FOUR

On Friday evening, Fallon walked next door to warn Cameron Chapman that she would be ready to leave in five minutes. But it wasn't Cameron on post; it was Tom. Caught off guard, the cold calm receded for just a moment. He looked so handsome that her instinct was to smile and run into his arms. She had to deliberately remind herself that she would never do that again. The icy calm returned, enabling her to utter the first word's she'd said to him in over a week: "We're leaving in five minutes."

Before he could even acknowledge her statement, she walked away.

She gathered her purse and her coat, and Tom followed her to the elevator bank. Her phone rang with a call from Travis Hill.

"I wanted to make sure we're still on schedule," he said.

"Absolutely," Fallon replied. She was surprised her voice sounded approximately normal; the coldness had not prohibited her acting ability. "Just come right up to the sixth floor."

"Are there going to be any surprises? You know, the Secret Service …"

"They're totally laid back," she assured him. Passive-aggression is what it was. Fallon knew it and was too depressed to even be ashamed of it.

Tom stood post at Fallon's door. A man turned right at the elevators and began walking directly toward him. Tom stepped up to him. "Secret Service."

"I have a date with Fallon Hughes."

Tom used the moment of surprise to look the guy over. Like so many in Washington, his political ambitions gleamed from him; he wore a suit as pricey and conservative as Tom's, his hair was coiffed and shiny, and he had a used-car salesman smile.

Getting past his own emotion, Tom asked himself the central question: *date or potential assassin?*

"Okay," Tom said, forcing his voice to sound neutral. "We weren't told anything about this. I need some identification."

Tom watched the man's hands as he reached inside his jacket, scanning his waistline, looking for a sign of a weapon or something out of the ordinary. *Nothing. Back to the hands.*

Auto Sales handed Tom a Montana driver's license. Travis P. Hill of Helena, Montana. Tom quickly connected the license to the Hughes White House: a staffer, perhaps, or an aide. Bile rose up in his throat.

"Move back by that door over there, please." The man watched as Tom keyed the mike on his wrist. "Security room, Bishop."

"Go ahead."

"Did you receive a call about a visitor by the name of Travis Hill?"

"That's a negative."

"Copy. He's here claiming to have a date with Avalon. Could you come up for a sec?"

"You bet. On my way."

When Jason Slaney arrived, Tom indicated the visitor. "Watch this guy for a sec, would you?"

"Sure thing, man."

Tom stalked down the corridor to Fallon's unit and knocked on the door with more force than was necessary. A moment later, the door cracked open. His heart sank. She looked absolutely breathtaking. Her silky blonde hair was soft and wavy to her shoulders. Smoky, smudgy eye makeup made the blue of her irises pop. Her lips were nude, the clear gloss sexier than a swipe of color would have been.

She was wearing a lace slip dress the deep color of merlot, setting off the golden glow of her skin. And damn, there was a lot of skin. Her bare arms, the lush swells of her breasts, long legs made to look even longer with round-toed high-heels the same color as her dress with satin ribbons tied in sexy, sweet little bows around her slender ankles. But nobody was going to be looking at her ankles. What the hell was she going to do with this moron?

A furious energy welled inside him. He wanted to stalk down the hall and smash that asshole's face in.

Snapping into his agent role, Tom cleared his throat. "Sorry to bother you, ma'am," he said through gritted teeth, and held the driver's license out for her to see. "Your date is here." He tried not to emphasize *date* and struggled to keep the question out of the statement. He wasn't sure if he succeeded because a storm of white noise was filling his ears. He wanted to ask a thousand questions and have her deny everything.

Since she slapped him, they had not spoken. Tom had taken her silence for hurt, at first, and slowly decided it must have been anger. She was still angry with him for a completely wrong conclusion she had drawn about his awkward explanation for why he left her in Greece. He'd wanted to speak to her, but after visiting New York and seeing Bethany's family, he had decided it was best to keep things professional with Fallon until they could be made nonexistent.

It was painful, though. Painful to see her face without animation, without a smile for him. Painful to be proven correct by fate. They were simply not compatible.

Not that there was a fireball's chance in Halifax that she would be more compatible with Travis Hill of Helena, Montana.

Fallon looked down at the hallway where Jason and Hill were standing. She waved and called out, "I'll be right there." She looked back to Tom with an impertinent, happy smile. "Yes, he's invited."

The door shut softly and Tom walked back down the hallway. "Thanks, man," he said to Slaney, dismissing his friend.

Alone in the hallway, the guy turned to Tom, a cocky smile on his face that made Tom want to punch something—preferably the guy. "So you're Secret Service, huh?"

"Yes."

"Are you guys armed all the time?"

"Yes."

"Seems like a pretty nice job."

"It has its advantages."

A moment later, Fallon opened the door. She smiled at Travis Hill. "Don't mind the three piece police," she said lightly, indicating Tom.

"You look beautiful." He leaned in to kiss her cheek. "And you smell wonderful too," he added.

Seized by a force even darker than mere jealousy, Tom was going to strangle him. Right here in the hallway, he was going to grab the bastard by his throat and squeeze until he quit struggling.

Fallon smiled politely. "Thank you."

She locked the door and tucked the key in her purse. Pointedly avoiding eye contact with Tom, she looked fawningly up to Travis Hill.

Tom walked behind them and spoke into his wrist. "Avalon limo, we're moving to the elevators."

Travis turned and looked at him. "I thought the mikes in the wrist were just for movies."

Fallon grabbed his elbow, guessing accurately that Tom did not want to discuss Secret Service methodology with Travis P. Hill.

Fallon kept avoiding him, even in the elevator, and it was for that reason that he knew she was hyperaware of him, and that brought him some measure of satisfaction.

A black Porsche so young it still had temporary tags on it gleamed under the faux gaslights in front of Fallon's building. Travis opened the passenger door for Fallon and she slid inside, looking straight ahead. Tom walked past the German automobile to the limo and got into the passenger seat.

The Porsche's speed remained five miles over the speed limit through the ancient streets of the District. Turning left on M Street, they passed the yellow-windowed building where Antoine Campbell had jumped to his death and then arrived at a chic Mexican-Japanese fusion restaurant that had just opened.

At the curb, Travis got out and opened Fallon's door, then

gave the keys to the valet. Tom got out of the SUV as the valet approached. He flashed his commission book and said, "These two vehicles will wait by the curb."

"Yes, sir," the valet replied and promptly turned and walked away.

In the restaurant, Fallon and Travis were shown to their table. Slaney stood discreetly behind Fallon. Tom remained in the entryway, hands folded in front of him.

Fallon seemed to have forgotten he existed. She had shrugged off her jacket and was all luminous skin and long shiny hair as she leaned forward, allowing Travis a good eyeful of her magnificent cleavage.

Was she actually going to sleep with that jackass? That mouth-breathing, premature ejaculator?

With despair, he allowed himself to reexamine the incidents and accidents that had brought him to this moment. It seemed to him that that all the wrong turns he had taken linked back that pivotal day: New York City, September 11, 2001. If he had protected Bethany that morning, he'd still be in New York. Maybe he and Bethany would have had a child by now—the subject had come up in the last year. If he had protected Bethany that morning, Tom would not care why Fallon was hanging on to every word of that clown.

He waited for the inevitable feeling of guilt—the same sense that he was betraying Bethany with his attraction to Fallon. But it didn't come.

Just now, watching Fallon, he realized that maybe he was starting to come to terms with the loss. Maybe it was like that sometimes; you just get so used to grieving, so used to being *without* that you shut yourself off from the possibility of ever healing. During that time, women had found something attractive in his emptiness, but he could not reciprocate with anything more than cursory politeness. He had come to believe that his ability to connect emotionally had been cauterized. He had nothing to give any woman.

But that didn't seem true now. Fallon was not only a complication or a problem to be solved. She was a truly decent, good human being who was presently grinning at the smarmy bastard, her head tilted, her long, ladylike fingers loosely twirling her hair. The guy kept stealing glances at her cleavage, and Fallon would tilt her head, giggle, adjust her position, and then continue to flirt.

This was progress?

Tom scanned the dining room, noticing that a few of the patrons were stealing glances at Fallon, and even at him, guessing he was the Secret Service detail.

The waiter delivered the bill for the evening. Fallon's date discreetly paid.

Tom lifted his wrist and spoke into the tiny microphone. "Avalon departing."

Travis helped her into her coat, and Fallon looked up adoringly at him as she pulled it close around her. He kissed her cheek and as she giggled, her eyes met Tom's. Tom didn't look away; he was too full of rage to look away and too full of jealousy to miss even a heartbeat of this stupid Kabuki theatre. She was beautiful and even angelic in the soft light of the restaurant. Her thick honey-colored hair looked very bright against the black cashmere of her coat. Everything about her seemed so glamorous and alive. And she was holding the hand of Travis P. Hill.

She had the attention of every person in the room now, though she didn't seem to notice. Travis was taking her arm. She blinked like she was coming out of sleep, as if noticing for the first time that she wasn't alone with Tom, in private.

As she walked past him, Tom smelled the rich fragrance of her perfume and her date's bitter scotch.

Tom glowered from the passenger seat of the limo as Travis opened the door of the Porsche for Fallon. She leaned up against him and kissed his cheek, then climbed into the tiny car.

Beside him, Rowland was pushing buttons on the music console. "You mind country?" he asked.

Tom gave a quick dismissive gesture that vaguely indicated

he could listen to whatever he wanted. It didn't matter. Tom was not able to concentrate on anything other than the sick, sinking nausea in his chest and the wild, random energy in his arms that kept making his hands ball into fists. This is what he said he wanted. He had told himself that he could not try to split his loyalty between Fallon and Bethany anymore. That horrible scene, watching her cry after she'd struck him …. Seeing the tears fall from her eyes had pained him. Made him want to gather her up and kiss them away. He felt that awful swimmy, panicked sensation in his throat like he was drowning.

Rowland pounded his palms lightly on the steering wheel in time with the music. "She looks hot tonight, huh?"

"What?"

"Avalon. She was smokin'."

"Yeah."

Rowland glanced at Tom in the darkness of the cockpit. "You okay, man?"

"Yeah, I just have a headache."

"Late night last night?"

Tom looked at him blankly, and then understanding the other agent's meaning, simply shook his head.

They drove in silence for a while; Tom was too intensely focused on the fury growing in his gut to make chitchat with Rowland. He wanted to throw furniture or smash somebody's face in. He wanted to insert a microphone in the lining of Fallon's coat and hear what she was telling that asshole in the Porsche. On the other hand, maybe he didn't want to know.

Yes he did. He wanted to know.

They once again got on the George Washington Parkway and headed toward McLean.

Kyle Rowland looked in the rearview mirror and saw the follow-up vehicle, and in the left lane was a speeding gray SUV, and several car lengths back was an identical one.

"Check it out," Rowland said.

Tom looked in the side mirror and saw the two vehicles. "How long have they been with us?"

"Noticed them about a mile back. Not too long."

The car to the left eased alongside them.

The sound of Jason Slaney's voice buzzed in his earpiece. "What do you guys make of the two late-model gray SUVs?"

Tom had a bad feeling about this. In an abundance of proactive caution, he advised Slaney to speed up and move to the shoulder to protect the right flank of the Porsche. To Rowland he said, "Edge this guy out. Let's get to the Porsche's left and Slaney will get to their right. We need to get that car off the road."

He hoped Travis was a calm driver and would stay steady.

The gray SUV had advanced nearly parallel with the primary vehicle, but because of the light rain and reflections on the black smoked windows of the other car, Tom could not make out anything until he saw the windows being lowered. A black automatic weapon appeared. As Tom reached for his Sig Sauer, an explosion rang out and splinters of glass rained inside the car.

"Fuck!" Rowland shouted, fighting the steering and trying to take cover as Tom returned fire. Rowland did as he was trained to do and turned the wheel into the other car.

The impact was loud and rough, the SUVs crunching metal on metal. The Secret Service follow-up passed them to protect the Porsche and its precious cargo as the primary and the gray SUVs spun to the left. Travis, however, had seen the commotion and moved to the shoulder of the road—the absolute wrong thing to do.

Slaney saw the second gray SUV right behind the Porsche and moved to cut him off, but the windshield suddenly exploded in a fresh hail of gunfire.

The primary smashed hard against the retainer wall. In the driver's seat, Rowland was slumped over the steering wheel. Tom's training compelled him to ignore Rowland, fling open the door, and run toward Fallon. Cars had stopped on the freeway; wreckage and glass lay on the street. As he ran, a man with an automatic weapon was firing at him and he felt that particular coldness along the neck that was death drumming his fingers, waiting. Tom was underarmed with just his Sig Sauer. He fired off several rounds, striking the man, but another shooter had appeared. Tom saw him with sudden clarity, as if he would have to retell the events in court one day, and he wanted to get the details exactly right. He lined up the man's head with the sight of his weapon and pulled the trigger. The bullet entered cleanly between the eyes, and he dropped.

But still the hail of bullets came. None of his guys were firing. Slaney? Rowland? Kevin White? He was alone, barely covered behind a van that had come to a stunned stop, and the only sound of gunfire was coming from the bad guys.

He saw Fallon's blonde hair and realized she was struggling in the man's arms. Bullets flew at him seemingly in a wall of projectiles. He could not get a clear shot of the kidnappers, so he tried to shoot the shooters.

A bullet grazed his shoulder, momentarily shocking and paralyzing him, and he dropped his weapon. Falling on the ground, he reclaimed his weapon as a bullet whizzed over him, where his head had been seconds ago. Keeping a very low, fast profile, he ran toward the SUVs. He changed the magazine, but it was too late.

He grabbed his radio and began barking orders, trying to tell the dispatcher what happened. He saw a figure in the Porsche and he ran toward it.

Flinging open the door, he saw that Travis was dead, or very close to being dead. In the dim light of the overhead cockpit light, Tom saw a trail of blood leaking from Travis's slack lips. "Hang in there, buddy," Tom rasped. "I'm trying to get you some help."

Behind him, somebody moaned. Tom spun and saw Slaney walking toward him. His white shirt was saturated with blood. His skin was diaphanous and gray. Shocky.

"Sit down," Tom ordered.

"They got her?"

"Yeah," Tom replied. He lifted up Slaney's shirt and saw a clean red hole ripped about two inches above his navel. Tom applied pressure. "Talk to me," he said.

"I feel bad," Slaney said. The light snow fell onto Slaney's face, but his eyes didn't instinctively squint.

"Keep talking. You're doing fine. Just stay with me, Slaney."

Through the pounding of his heart and the scream in his head, he heard sirens wailing in the distance.

TWENTY-FIVE

"Israel and its ally, the United States, have done irreparable harm to their image as peaceful nations," said a Russian spokesperson. "Under no circumstance will any person look upon the USA as a benevolent force in the world again. The unprovoked missile attack by Israel on the city of Moscow has killed hundreds of people. Soon Israel and the USA will know the full force of Russian might. This cowardly attack will be answered."

A serious charge. Missiles launched from Siberia could strike D.C. within twenty minutes; hearing the threat spoken extemporaneously ratcheted the tensions on both sides. The Russians surely understood that if they attacked the American homeland, the retaliation would be devastating.

Without any warning at all, scud missiles had been launched from Tel Aviv, striking Moscow during morning rush hour. Within minutes, the Israelis declared they had no knowledge of any missile launches. "We have no cause to start a war with Russia," one diplomat said, though he reluctantly admitted that the missiles had indeed been deployed. They were launched without the approval or knowledge from anyone inside the Israeli government, the diplomat assured the reporters and other diplomats around the globe.

Their denials were viewed as a ploy to offset a Russian counterattack, but Claudia Wells believed them. Israel was not known for being an aggressor, particularly toward Russia, a vast and well-armed country capable of flicking Israel off the map with a single well-aimed missile.

The mood in the Situation Room was grim. The conference included President Ballard, intelligence chiefs, the secretary of defense, secretary of state, and President-elect Hughes's own cadre of advisers, including Richard Mullinax and his superior, the director of the National Security Agency. The inauguration was three days away, so anything that happened now would affect both administrations. Ballard believed it was imperative to craft a strategy with the incoming administration for handling the Russian threat, but it was becoming clear they had very different ideas about how to proceed: Ballard desperately desired to leave with a generally positive legacy intact. Hughes wanted to begin his presidency with a very decisive statement.

"If Israel is attacked, we must come to the aid of our ally," said Hughes. "There can be no equivocation about this."

"It would be foolish to attack Russia with US bombs, particularly since Israel is denying responsibility for the attack," replied Ballard. "If Israel needs defense, she can look to other European nations. The USA should not become entangled. We don't want another Iraq on our hands."

Claudia thought of the two dead Russians who had been feeding the USA information. She idly wondered if Russia had somehow created that situation for show, if the two informants were still alive and well. Or perhaps alive and being tortured in Lubyanka. No, some American spy deep in Moscow would have been able to verify that if there was any possibility. They were dead.

"I have no doubt that Israel will use nuclear weapons if Russia makes any gesture toward a counterattack," said the current National Security Adviser.

The opinions circled the table, but Claudia remained silent, pondering the circumstances of the last week. With a sudden turn and click, she saw the answer.

"I think someone is trying to draw the USA into war," Claudia said, realizing the words sounded absolutely reasonable as she spoke. The table went silent. Serious faces peered back at her, questions but no real doubt in their eyes.

"The two assets murdered in Moscow were victims of a mole somewhere. They were helping the USA and were killed when their identities were discovered. Is it possible they had information that could have prevented the missiles from striking

Moscow? And now Israel has launched missiles at Russia without any provocation at all. But maybe it wasn't actually Israel. Maybe it was meant to look like Israel. Our systems have been deeply penetrated at high levels." A most dangerous penetration, Claudia mused, not bothering to become entangled in the question of how extensive it was or who was behind it. It was enough to know that the problem existed.

A sudden knock on the door was indistinguishable from it opening. The conference looked up, shocked that they'd be disturbed at such a critical moment; one simply did not open the Situation Room door without having been expressly invited to do so.

Blake Henley looked over the table, his face white with shock. "Sir," he blurted, "the director of the Secret Service is here to see you. He says it is urgent."

Both Ballard and Hughes began to ask what it was about.

"Sir, Mr. Hughes, Fallon has been kidnapped."

TWENTY-SIX

As the lone survivor of the ambush, Tom Bishop felt overwhelming guilt as he replayed the events in his head over and over again. Fractals of images flashed at him, and other endings supplanted the true, fatal ending. He could have told Rowland to speed up. Or to slow down, to make the other SUVs slow down so the follow-up could have climbed the shoulder and flanked the Porsche.

His training had been good but inadequate. The Secret Service was notoriously underarmed. On the morning of September 11, as agents were ordering tourists to leave the White House gates, the director had ordered that agents carry only their issued Sig Sauers; they were not to be photographed with the bigger MP5 submachine guns. This, as the United States was under direct and immediate attack. Since that morning, agents were instructed to carry the minimum firepower—their pistols. So when the worst happened, when for the first time in Secret Service history, a protectee was kidnapped, and on American soil to boot, the agents responsible for her safety simply did not have the firepower to respond adequately.

Not only could they not save Fallon, they could not save themselves. Responsibility for the largest loss of life in Secret Service history rested firmly on Tom's shoulders.

If only he'd had more bullets, more power ... If only ... Tom shook away the thoughts. Useless little fantasies. He had one task as a Secret Service agent and he had failed. He had not kept Fallon Hughes safe. She had relied on him and he let her down. And now she was who-knew-where, at the hands of well-armed terrorists.

Images of Beth came roaring back, interfering with the

perception of the present and the past. Desperately he tried to blot it out, but the comparison remained. He clenched his jaw so tight he heard it crack. He raged against his own failure. An internal black tide of self-hatred roiled through him, toxic and cloying. He couldn't save Bethany. And now he couldn't save Fallon. He was grotesquely offended by his own incompetence. Several people—other Secret Service agents, some of the FBI who were investigating in unison—told him that he was brave. They said he didn't have a chance against the firepower of the terrorists. He heard the words but didn't hear them—they seemed to be muffled, delivered from the bottom of the ocean.

It was like when the Secret Service had commended him for his bravery on September 11. He had wanted to laugh out loud. Bravery? He wasn't brave. He saved those people because he had no choice; he was a federal agent and they were dying. Anyone would have done the same. The one person he wanted to save more than any other languished in the top of the tower with the promise that help would never arrive. When the building pancaked, his life crumbled and sank with that building.

His fragile, nascent sense of the possibility that life could go on had been erased when they took Fallon.

Bravery? He wanted to laugh in their faces.

He had recited his version of events dozens of times in the last hour. He'd spoken with Metro Police sketch artists, though he knew that was a futile effort. The shooters would not be recognized by concerned citizens calling a crime tips hotline. He had spoken to his supervisor and director of the Secret Service, rehashing the details until they became rote words.

But had had not expected to speak to President-elect Preston Hughes. Tom had been on his detail during the long campaign to become president. Tom was the number two man on the team and he felt that he had gotten to know Preston Hughes pretty well; he was essentially a good man who wanted to bring some sanity to Washington, D.C.

Tom felt ashamed being in his presence.

He had acted unethically. He had become personally involved with Fallon against his own better judgment; he had not treated his job with the earnestness it deserved. All he wanted was a chance to make it right by finding Fallon and bringing her safely home.

"Tell me what happened," Hughes said.

Tom repeated the same facts he'd been uttering all night, and in the retelling he noticed his voice was arid, professionally distant, as if these things were happening to someone else. Someone else was being spattered with Rowland's blood. Someone else held Slaney's gaping wound, the warm slick red bubbling between his fingers. Someone else walked over the shattered glass and metal strewn over the George Washington Parkway, looking around at the dead agents who had been his coworkers, and the empty passenger seat of the Porsche where Fallon should have been. It had been smeared in blood, and he was eager to know if it was her blood. And eager not to know because he could bear affirmation that it was.

Internally, he felt like something essential was being hurt—his honor or his very goodness.

When he was finished, the president-elect nodded, as if he were satisfied with that answer.

The silence protracted out, making the point that his words were inadequate.

"Sir," Tom said finally. "I need something from you."

"Something from me?" Hughes's eyes squinted in disbelief. Deep, raw helplessness scrawled itself over his features. A possible war with Russia he could handle—it only involved death. But his daughter at the hands of terrorists? What could a president do that a father couldn't? Nothing. He was utterly powerless.

"Sir, I think I know who did this. I need you to make sure the Secret Service doesn't put me on administrative leave." After a pause, he added, "Please, sir."

Something in his voice or his earnestness sharpened Hughes's attention. "What do you know?"

"Fallon was involved in … I don't know what. I was investigating. I don't know much right now, but if you give me until inauguration day, and you give me access to the resources

I need, I promise I will bring Fallon back, safe and alive." He wasn't sure where the words were coming from. He only knew that he couldn't live without her. He had to get her back because it was the right thing to do and because he loved her.

"You can't promise that," Hughes said bitterly.

"I can promise I will get further than anyone else would. Sir, I have… personal reasons for believing so strongly."

The president-elect studied his face, and took in a little breath, as if he understood the subtext of Tom's statement. His gaze bore into him, as if willing Tom's confidence in his ability to be well placed.

Hughes already looked worn. Tom remembered after making love with Fallon, she told him that her father was disappointed in her. He didn't look disappointed now. He looked devastated, shattered into a million pieces. But when he heard Tom's words, he grasped at the hope that Tom was offering. Reluctantly, Preston Hughes nodded. "You have three days."

Tom entered Secret Service headquarters and proceeded directly downstairs to the evidence room. A technician brought out the weapon that had been recovered from George Washington Parkway, among the shattered glass and jagged plastic that resulted from the assault. The gun was enclosed in a plastic envelope; it would be sent to the FBI for further processing. He had been eager to get a good look at it before it got swallowed in the jurisdictional skirmishes between the Secret Service and FBI.

On a day that was full of shocks, this was another.

It was a K6-92 Borz submachine gun. Originally made by Armenians, it had been modified for Chechens and used in their war with Russia. An ugly, bulky thing, it was extremely deadly.

Not too many of them either, certainly not much demand in the US with the sexier Kalashnikovs the MP5s easily available—and cheaper too. That might mean that the weapons were smuggled in for personal use, as opposed to purchased illegally in the USA.

Looking at the weapon that killed his coworkers made

stars bulge in his mind. Fury and grief welled up, shivering at the breaking point, and he forced himself to take a breath. He busied his hands by taking several pictures with his BlackBerry.

Secret Service received intelligence briefs weekly, and he tried to remember last time he'd heard of a Chechen threat in the USA. There was a warning that al Qaeda was attempting to recruit "Western-looking" Muslims for missions in the US, but some instinct honed from years of intelligence work told him that this wasn't al Qaeda. It wasn't spectacular enough—a small mission, two cars, no more than three men. Taking the soon-to-be First Daughter, who until today did not warrant a full security detail, seemed small for their usual scale. They liked to go after huge targets. Though, of course, they'd decapitated Daniel Pearl and he wasn't a big shot in the US media or government. Lastly, it seemed like a crime of opportunity.

Tom's unspoken best guess was that this was a sleeper cell of terrorists of the Chechen flavor, who had been inside the US for a while, looking like Americans, acting like Americans, and generally being Americans. Waiting for an opportunity to present itself.

It was urgent he interview the one person he'd been avoiding—the one person who possessed crucial information. If he did not get it, he had not the slightest doubt that the interviewee would be joining one terrorist and Tom's coworkers in death.

The government Sebring shuddered at eighty miles per hour, and he slowed to accommodate traffic. He remembered telling Fallon that traffic from Maryland to D.C. was heavy even in midday just two weeks ago. Had it been longer than that? It seemed like years ago. The only thing that felt completely real was this moment, with its nervous tension and mounting fury.

I-395 was jammed. He hit the steering wheel, detesting the space to think. Adrenaline was still pumping and he fidgeted with the heater and the radio. Finally he got on the shoulder and hit the gas.

Turning off the freeway, he saw the large black cube that was the National Security Agency. It was one of the fortresses around D.C., a government building protected with many layers of security. He had no official pass to get beyond the gates—no search warrant. Oh well. He would burn that bridge when he came to it.

Tom drove into the parking lot, remembering when he had escorted the vice president here a year ago. But at the time he didn't have to park his own car. The parking lot, like the lot at the Pentagon, was vast. He chose a spot at random and walked toward the doors.

A bank of turnstiles impeded him. A Marine guard came out and Tom presented his cred book. The Marine looked at it. "Is someone expecting you?"

"It's an unofficial visit," Tom replied smoothly.

The Marine handed back his passport and waved him through.

He rode in the elevator to the third floor and asked a secretary if he might speak to Deputy Director Richard Mullinax.

She picked up the phone to dial and Tom walked past her to the door and opened it.

Mullinax was meeting with two people, one in a military uniform. "Sirs, you will need to reschedule," Tom said.

Both looked to Mullinax, confused at the impudence of this man. Tom pulled out his creds. "Secret Service. Would you like me to question you in front of them?"

Mullinax was young, Tom realized. Too young and immature for the job he had. He looked genuinely alarmed by Tom's sudden appearance in his office. He attempted to disguise the fear with benign indifference, and failed. "Obviously this is important," he said lamely. "Gentlemen, let's reconvene later."

After a moment of confused stares, and packing up their documents, they left, and Tom shut the door behind them.

"Who was Antoine Campbell?" Tom demanded.

"Who are you, barging in here like this? Do you know who I am? Do you have a warrant?"

"Do I need one?" It was a bluff, and it worked. He could

see Mullinax mentally back down.

"I don't know what you want," he said weakly. A posturing little man.

"What's the map of the keys?"

"I have no idea."

"You're lying."

The door opened and two Marines built like refrigerators entered. "Sir, you need to come with us."

"I'm going to find out what you're doing," Tom said. He jerked his arm back from one of the Marines who had gripped it. He saw cold fear glint in Mullinax's eyes. Pure terror, like the hand of death was already squeezing his throat. That was all the validation Tom needed.

Escorted out of the building, Tom sat in the car for a moment, thinking. It was late in the evening. Since Mullinax was scared and jumpy, Tom guessed he would be leaving very soon. He was too spooked to stay in one place long.

His suspicion was proved correct when he saw Mullinax walk out the door and head toward a glossy black Mercedes. Tom drove out before him, watching in the rearview mirror as Mullinax pulled out of his space and headed for the gates. Tom turned left, toward the freeway. Mullinax followed. Once on I-395, Tom slowed down and let Mullinax pass. He was careful, staying several cars back and one lane over.

Mullinax drove eight miles over the speed limit, heading toward D.C. As Tom tailed him, he allowed his mind to unspool.

For the first time since the ambush, Tom let himself really think about Fallon and know explicitly what she was going through. The images tortured him. It was like Bethany all over again. His eyes overfilled with unshed tears and he angrily wiped them away.

He loved her. Despite his best efforts at keeping some distance, he'd fallen hopelessly in love with her. In fact, he had been in love with her since that first moment in Paxos when he saw her at the harbor. It was sunset and thousands of sailboat masts had been thrown into stark relief. And Fallon had simply been watching the water, the sailboats. It was one of the most beautiful images he'd ever seen.

He fought so hard to stay loyal to the idea of Bethany. He wanted to be the man Bethany believed him to be. He had somehow got in this crazy cycle of loving Fallon, feeling guilty, and cutting Fallon off, rather than simply doing the hard work to try and make peace with Bethany's death. It seemed like such a silly waste of time now. He would always love Bethany. But he also knew that he had behaved in a way that Bethany would have hated.

And he loved Fallon now. He knew that he loved her more than anything—even more than his career. He would resign so they could be together, he thought suddenly. He would do anything.

But first he had to find her.

After half an hour, the Mercedes ramped onto Route 50. Tom was concerned that Mullinax would recognize him and start to get suspicious. He was probably paranoid by now and if he noticed Tom's government car following for too long, who knew what he might do.

He called Cameron Chapman. The surprise and grief in her voice touched him, but he refused to acknowledge it. He was on mission.

"I need a big favor. You available?"

"Of course."

"I need to do surveillance on someone who has already seen me. I'm on Route Fifty heading west in the District."

"I can pick him up in about five minutes; I happen to be very close by."

"Excellent. It's a black Mercedes. Stay close. He won't recognize you. He's scared though, and he's going to be looking for stakeout cars."

"I'm on my way."

Tom glanced in the rearview and saw Cameron's blue government issued Chevy Malibu. He called her phone. "Our target is in your lane, about three cars up from me. Black full-size Mercedes sedan. Get up to him and I'll fall back."

She passed him, keeping her eyes forward as if she didn't

know him, and Tom fell back a few car lengths. The Mercedes moved right, exiting on Connecticut, which would turn into Route Fifty again as soon as he got into Maryland. His blinker came on at the Clarendon/Court House exit.

"You follow. I'll take a few streets up and then come back."

"Copy that," Cameron replied. Tom watched them exit then exited at the next opportunity. He turned around and circled back.

"He parked at the Motel Fifty on Route Fifty," Cameron said. "And he just knocked on the door of Room 7. It's on the bottom floor, facing east."

"Good work, Cam," he said. "Thank you." He glided to the west side. "I'm here now," he said.

"You want me to stay for a while?"

"No, I have this," he replied.

She hesitated and then said, "Call me if you need anything."

Tom drove around to the east side and watched Cameron steer out of the lot, back onto the access road. Tom parked in a space under a tree. The sky was dark and a light snow had been falling all day; if Mullinax happened to glimpse the car, Tom would be hidden among the darkness and reflections of the rain and branches.

He turned off the car and zipped up his coat and watched the door.

Nearly two hours later, the door opened and Mullinax emerged. Tom watched him climb inside his sedan and then leave. As soon as he was gone, Tom swung open his car door and hurried to the door. The motel was shoddy and old; the doors were operated with keys instead of cards. He twisted the copper knob, but it was locked pretty solidly from inside. Tom knocked. A rustling soft noise was followed by deliberate silence. Someone creeping to the door to look through the peephole. Tom gave them five seconds. "Open the door," he growled.

No answer. Tom body slammed the door, the wood cracking up the middle to the jamb. He shoved it again, reached inside and unbolted the door.

The room was dimly lit by a grungy overhead light that cast a sickly yellow pall. In the scant illumination, a woman stood against the wall, terrified. She was naked, her toned flesh and red hair momentarily stupefying Tom.

Claudia Wells, R-Virginia. The Vice President-elect of the United States.

Though he recognized her, she certainly did not recognize him. "Who are you?" she rasped, bringing her arms up to cover her breasts. "Get out, I'll scream …." Her voice was shrill, the fear mounting.

Tom shut the door, locked it, and said, "Ma'am, I'm with the Secret Service."

"I told them I didn't want protection until …"

"I'm not your protective detail."

She grabbed her dress from a hideous puce chair, then hurried into a bathroom and shut the door. Tom glanced around the room. A shoddy place for a lover's tryst. Old cigarette fumes lingering in the wallpaper, water damage on the sagging yellow ceiling, and orange shag carpeting gave him the creeps. Apparently neither Claudia Wells nor Richard Mullinax was the romantic type.

A moment later, Claudia Wells returned with her clothes on. She looked scared: her eyes wide, her arms folded across her chest. She was attempting to feign self-assuredness, but Tom noticed the quiver in her lips before she spoke. "What is this about?"

"Richard Mullinax," Tom answered simply.

She opened her mouth as if she were about to deny knowing him, but Tom's appearance in her room obviated the need for denials. She slowly sank to the edge of the bed. "What about him?"

"Has he ever mentioned a map of the keys?"

She thought about it and shook her head. "No. What is that?"

"How about Antoine Campbell? Has he ever mentioned Antoine Campbell?"

"No. What is this? Who is Antoine Campbell and what is a

map of the keys?"

Tom attempted to ascertain whether she was telling the truth. She had something to hide by being here with Richard Mullinax, but he had never met a person who would sacrifice a glorious political career to protect an extramarital affair. She was probably being truthful, but it was best to make his power position clear from the start.

"Aren't you married?"

She pinked to the ears and cast her eyes downward.

"I see."

She looked up at him, her eyes and cheeks burning. "Are you going to announce this to …"

"I don't care who you're sleeping with, Claudia," he said.

"Then why are you here?"

"Mullinax is involved in some bad stuff. I don't have enough to ask a judge for a search warrant, so I'm trying to find out more."

"I will tell you whatever I know. But my husband and Preston Hughes can't know about … this."

"I don't have any reason to tell anyone about your adultery. Did Mullinax ever mention Fallon Hughes?"

"No, he hasn't. Why? What do you think he has done?"

"Fallon Hughes received a call from a young man who told her that Mullinax was giving away the map of the keys. Half an hour later, that man was thrown off the roof of a building. I believe he was killed for attempting to warn someone about Mullinax's activity. And now Fallon Hughes has been kidnapped. Mullinax has something to do with it."

Her eyes were wide saucers and her face had gone pale. "He wouldn't," she whispered.

"I want to find Fallon Hughes."

Claudia's brows were creased with uncomprehending anxiety. Finally she shook her head, as if becoming clear about something. "I feel very secure in saying he would have absolutely nothing to do with Fallon Hughes or the death of anyone else."

"You are probably wrong about that," Tom replied evenly.

Claudia stood up and gathered her coat and purse.

"Where do you have to be?" Tom asked.

"White House to meet with President Ballard and Mr. Hughes. We're trying to avoid war with Russia."

"But you stepped out to meet Mullinax."

She looked indifferent for a moment, but the corner of her mouth turned down, and the façade cracked. "Oh God," she moaned, then put her hands over her face. Tom realized that she was crying. He felt nothing. It alarmed him; just a few days ago, he would have cared about the emotional state of another person, but something had died inside him. Something warm was now small and cold. He watched her, thinking only that she was hindering his progress toward finding Fallon.

"Go to your meeting," he said. "I'll be in touch. Give me your phone number."

She wiped her eyes and recited the number while Tom keyed it into his phone.

"If I call, I expect you to answer."

She nodded. "I will."

"And if you tip off Mullinax, your little affair with him will be the last thing you ever need to worry about."

She shook her head and looked up at the water-stained ceiling, wiping the slight smudge of mascara under her eyes. "You don't have to worry about that."

Tom stood behind the curtains and peeked out the edges. Nobody waiting. "Wait five minutes or so before you leave," he told her, then strode out.

He got into his government car and got back on Route Fifty and headed back into Washington, D.C. He fumbled with the heater and then sat back in his seat. A light snow continued to fall over the federal buildings and monuments.

TWENTY-SEVEN

Leah Lennox awoke to the sound of a scratching sound on the door. She lifted her head, realizing she'd fallen asleep on the sofa with her chenille throw over her legs. Her whole body was stiff from sleeping on her cramped sofa. Her eyes felt sandy and rimmed in ash. Flinching from a sudden crick in her neck, she sat up. Disoriented, she noticed darkness pressed against the windows. Was it night or morning? She noticed that she had a Word document open; she'd fallen asleep while working.

She listened in the silence, trying to figure out what woke her up. Her breath was labored; she heard its cadence in the cold silence of her living room.

Footsteps outside her door hurried away. Pushing herself up, she wrapped the blanket around her shoulders and padded silently to the door.

Through the peephole, she saw a brown package propped against the door. Her instinct was to open the door and grab the package but she hesitated. It was too early or too late for a FedEx or UPS delivery. The United States was on the edge of war with Russia, and closer to home but no less terrifying, Fallon Hughes was ambushed yesterday. She felt raw, perceiving danger and threats in everything. It could be a bomb. The knowledge struck her at once crazy and serious enough to actually pursue.

Why would anyone bomb her? She cracked open the door and peered down the hallway but saw no one lingering.

The package was about the size of one of her Amazon. com book deliveries, but there were no markings on it that she could see.

She closed the door and grabbed her phone from the kitchen. She glanced at the clock on her microwave. It was not yet six o'clock in the morning. She must have slept hard for those few hours; she was still disoriented.

Tom answered on the first ring, as if he was waiting for a call.

"How are you holding up?"

"I'm fine," he answered stiffly. She knew he wasn't but he didn't want to talk about it. He was action-oriented, not inclined to talk when he was feeling emotional.

"Somebody just left a package for me on my front door. I'm afraid to pick it up."

"Does it have anything on it?"

"No. I don't think so. It's just a brown box."

"I'm at the office. I can't come over. I can call the Arlington Police."

Hearing him say that instantly made her feel foolish. "No," she said automatically. "No, that's okay. I'm just being overcautious. Don't work too hard," she said. She meant to sound casual, sort of like "take care," but once the words were out of her mouth, she realized it was the wrong thing to say. "I mean …"

"It's okay," Tom replied.

After goodbyes, and wrenching out a promise that he would call her later, Leah hung up and went back to the door. She picked up the package and brought it inside.

She experimentally put her ear to it but didn't hear a ticking bomb. She used her kitchen scissors to cut the tape, and opened the box. A DVD fell out. On the surface were the words LEAH LENNOX ONLY.

The cryptic delivery and the words filled her with trepidation. Fleetingly, she thought of her loneliness: how now, shivering in her kitchen, with a strange package, it would have been nice to have a man to soothe her jangled nerves. To care if she was blown to smithereens. Collin certainly didn't qualify.

Turning from those thoughts, she returned to the living room and inserted the DVD into her ancient MacBook Pro laptop. A movie screen appeared.

It took a moment to understand what she was seeing. A

woman was tied to a chair, arms tied straight down against the chair back. Her eyes and mouth were covered with strips of black cloth. Behind her, the room looked indistinct and gray. Leah's first unchecked impression was that the woman appeared to be in a warehouse or some industrial setting.

It was Fallon Hughes. Leah's shaking hand flew to her mouth to hold in a gasp.

"Fallon is okay as you can see," a voice said. Russian sounding, Leah thought. "This is for the reporter, Leah. As you see we have Fallon Hughes. We are invisible so do not attempt to find us. Our demand is simple. We want Mahomet Ayrzu in exchange for Fallon Hughes. If we do not have an agreement from the president by midnight, we will kill her and the next video you see of her, she will be headless."

Leah blinked, unsure of what she was seeing and hearing, but panic was spreading through her like an ink stain.

A hand and forearm, appearing to be that of the cameraman, moved to Fallon and removed the gag.

"Tell them your message."

"Leah, tell Tom I am okay and that I am so sorry for assuming the worst about him."

The video abruptly ended.

Electrified, Leah shot up and grabbed the phone and dialed Tom again.

"What was in the box?"

"A DVD," she answered breathlessly. "A movie. It has Fallon on it. She said to tell you she's okay and they asked for somebody I've never even heard of. Why would she say tell Tom she's okay? Please tell me what to do. I am really freaking out."

"I'm at the Washington Field Office," Tom replied levelly. "I want you to get here as soon as you can. Bring the DVD. I will pay any speeding tickets you get on the way."

• • •

Both teams were convened in the Situation Room. All their nerves were frayed, but Claudia was so on edge she was practically vibrating with fear. She'd bitten the skin around her thumbnail so that now it was a disgusting, bloody mess. Besides the Russians and Fallon Hughes's kidnapping, she had another issue to be concerned about. Tom Bishop. If he betrayed her, her career would be over, as well as her marriage. Hours later and she could still feel his eyes burning into her skin, his disapproval of her adultery obvious in the way he looked at her. She felt nauseated by it; she needed a shower because Richard was still all over her.

After making such a mockery of her position until this point, she was determined to do better. To be strong and moral and do the right thing. Problem was, she had no idea how to go about it. Should she confess to her husband? Should she demand answers from Richard?

She attempted to avoid Richard's insistent stare throughout the meeting, but now she finally glanced up at him. He looked tense, but they all did. The United States was on serious war footing; everyone in the room seemed to have aged at least five years. He shifted his gaze to her and for the first time since she knew him, she felt cold disgust. At herself, mostly, but Tom Bishop's words were still echoing in her mind. She attempted to analyze the situation objectively. One thing she had found odd was that Richard had so quickly dismissed the possibility that the mole could be in the NSA. It seemed obvious to her that the NSA was one of the first places that would be investigated because the two events that deepened the tensions with Russia were the Russian assets being assassinated, and Israel attacked Russia but said they had no knowledge of how the missiles were launched.

Both of those things would require some kind of electronic interference. Fact: Richard had access to the most sophisticated electronic systems in the world. He had seemed incredibly uneasy that Claudia would even suggest the NSA's involvement. Was he attempting to deflect attention from himself?

Claudia could not fathom why Richard would want to go

to war with Russia, but the possibility that he was involved left her disoriented. Had he betrayed those assets? His country? If he was capable of giving information to the Russians, he was capable of anything. Including killing the man who called Fallon Hughes with a desperate message about the map of the keys.

A cold electrical current seized her heart. Richard Mullinax was the mole. She knew it in a flash of epiphany, all the questions suddenly answered, all the pieces fitting together. There was not a doubt in her mind.

She was seized with an irrational desire to simply accuse him, here in the meeting with the president and the president-elect looking on. She forced the discipline to maintain her professional veneer.

"What is the news?" President Ballard asked. Before him was a notebook, pen, and a half-full heavy crystal water glass with a presidential seal. Claudia, across from him and two seats over, stared at it as a focal point, trying to keep her face neutral as the world began to take on a dizzy quality around her.

The secretary of defense said, "Sir, the entire Russian electronic grid is shut down. And we just received a memo from a source inside Mahmoud Ahmadinejad's regime that they too are in blackout."

Claudia bit her cheek to keep from blurting out what she was thinking. She needed to talk to Tom Bishop again. Urgently.

The meeting droned on. Finally the president said they'd had enough for today and asked to reconvene at seven tomorrow.

Claudia grabbed her purse and left the West Wing without any of the usual lingering, the rallying for a few moments alone with the president. She wanted out of the White House complex and fast.

At the Kremlin, there was increasingly frantic activity as the reality of the situation became clearer. The official smooth assurances of retribution notwithstanding, there was internal knowledge that delivering on promises of destruction would be met with overwhelming force—possibly nuclear missiles launched either from Tel Aviv or from the United States itself.

But to do nothing was madness. The great nation of Russia could not sit idly by while enemies launched missiles into Moscow. The dead now numbered in the hundreds. Yet in his secret heart, Dmitry Medvedev had not believed a single readiness report in years. The ancient nuclear stores were degrading at nearly five percent per year, and the older ballistic missiles could easily be intercepted by the Americans' missile shield. To launch and fail would be more humiliating than withstanding Israel's original attack.

FSB Chief Moldovan appeared silently in Medvedev's office while the leader paced. The president stopped and regarded him with his infamously furious, rodent-like gaze. "What is it?"

"Sir, our entire missile system has been disabled."

"Disabled?"

"The entire city has experienced a power outage. Our backups have failed, our entire defensive system is completely black, off the grid."

TWENTY-EIGHT

Omar Koss deplaned at Stockholm-Arlanda Airport and proceeded outside to the queue of taxis. Snow was falling, gentle and calm. It was midnight here, dawn in Washington D.C. Like a pilot, much of his life was distilled down to time and weather. A taxi driver peered at him through the windows; it was late, there were few passengers, and the well-dressed businessman holding a chic leather travel bag no doubt looked like an easy fare.

Omar examined the taxi. The tires were worn; the black paint job with the words TAXI STOCKHOLM looked legit. It was a habit, looking for the tiny thing that would give away the enemy.

He climbed inside.

"Do you want me to put the bag in the back?" the driver asked in Swedish.

"No, thank you," Omar replied, also in Swedish.

The taxi steered away from the curb. "Where to?"

"Bromma Airport."

The driver looked at him in the rearview mirror. "You fly again tonight?"

"Important business," Koss replied with a weary smile. An easy smile, the kind that signaled a businessman's fatigue and weariness on the road, rather than what it masked, which was fatigue and weariness from his time in Russia. Corrupting their entire internal grid had been extreme, but it prevented them from attacking the United States.

He had no doubt that his old enemies in the GRU or FSA would come for him. If the taxi driver was still here when they arrived, he would be interrogated painfully and then killed. For his sake, he hoped the driver called it a night after he dropped

Koss at the airport.

The drive south from Arlanda Airport to Bromma took only thirty minutes; traffic was nonexistent. Koss leaned his head against the seat, allowing himself to rest for a few moments. When he opened his eyes, they were driving up to the small terminal of Bromma.

He paid the driver and stepped into the terminal. A woman behind the counter smiled at his appearance. "Good evening, Mr. Banks. Your aircraft is ready. The crew is already on board."

Koss used several aliases. Banks was his favorite when he was traveling with an American passport. Edward Banks thanked the lady and walked out to the apron that stood in front of the VIP receiving area. A Gulfstream G-600 was warming its engines, exterior lights blazing and the door open in anticipation of his arrival. No other airplanes were readying for a trip this late.

It was exactly what he had ordered but as he stepped onto the stair, his instinct told him something was wrong. The lady. He had flown through Bromma many times, but he didn't remember ever seeing her. He had a photographic memory that did not rely on extraordinary beauty or ugliness; he absorbed and filed everything.

He glanced back and saw her at the glass doors of the terminal. She wore a jacket over her airport uniform. It was heated comfortably inside, he thought. The jacket would cover a multitude of weapons at her waist. She pushed the door open. "Is everything okay, sir?"

The flight attendant appeared in the doorway. "Mr. Banks," she purred. "Welcome aboard."

He caught the glint of light on the dark metal of her gun the moment she brought it from behind her back. Automatically his leg violently struck out, kicking it from her hand. As she moved to find it, the two pilots, who had been waiting inside the body of the plane, appeared.

The lady from the desk was instantly behind him, the cold barrel of a pistol shoved against his spine. With the two pilots advancing he would have to be crude. Omar spun around, grabbing the woman's head between his hands, and snapped her neck hard to the left. Her gun fell to the ground with a clatter one second before her lifeless body did the same.

Two pilots were coming for him. He reached into the leather duffel bag and pulled out the MP-5. Even in the snowy semidarkness of the airport, his shots were deadly accurate. Though he disliked killing, he was good at it. One of the best in the world, in fact. Humanely, he aimed for the heads, and they vanished in a spray of red mist.

He would leave the front desk lady lying where she fell but thought it best to carry the flight crew with him on this particular trip. There would be questions in the morning as more business flights arrived, and leaving four bodies on the tarmac would alarm the locals. He would have to dispose of the corpses at some point, but that was a problem he could easily solve. He would call some associates to take care of the mess.

He dragged the dead bodies inside, to the very back of the plane. Respectfully he laid them on the floor, as not to stain the plush leather bulkhead seating with viscera, and then covered them with blue woolen blankets found in the overhead compartments.

He had not planned on flying tonight—he was exhausted already—but he had to get to D.C. and this was the most expedient way.

He fastened himself in the cockpit, taxied to the runway, and launched the jet into the sky. Once he got above the snow clouds, the G-600 was smooth as silk—practically flew herself. In seven hours he'd be at Dulles. That gave him time to wonder if the dead people in back were Russians who had beat him to the airport, or if perhaps they were a team of Georgians; he'd worked in Tbilisi recently. Oh hell, there were enemies all over the globe, some even in the Unites States, who wanted him dead. He would have to investigate later. Right now, he just wanted to get home.

Omar Koss landed at Manassas Airport where a team was waiting for him with a car. He normally worked alone but in this instance it was nice to have someone clean up the bodies for him. There were two of them and they reminded him of FBI agents with that corn-fed earnestness. He hated FBI agents.

"There are three bodies in the back," he said and handed them the keys. "Return it to Dulles after you clean it."

"Yes, sir," the pretty female said sarcastically. She wasn't yet accustomed to being ordered around. That would change soon enough.

He slung his leather duffel into the passenger seat of the Crown Victoria and headed east on Route 66 toward D.C. It was already evening again and he had not slept in two days. While in Russia he had been so typically focused on his mission that nothing of the outside world penetrated his cone of concentration. So when he turned on the radio and heard for the first time that Fallon Hughes had been kidnapped, he knew with an instinct honed to a finely sensitive instrument that Collin had become impatient. Koss frowned, angry with himself for not managing him better.

That probably explained the dead bodies in the plane; Collin, perhaps to delay him, had ordered a team to kill him.

Stupid, foolish kid. Omar felt a sudden great weariness. The stupidity of people, and the cruelty, had ceased to faze him long ago. But because he knew Collin, and he understood the situation better than Collin, he allowed himself to feel almost sentimental about Collin's ignorance. He would have to kill the kid. It was such a waste.

The Central Intelligence Agency had used decoy companies for many years, but after September 11, they became a vital part of the covert program in order to draw terrorists by operating false weapons organizations.

Most of these operated in the Middle East, the most famous of which was Brewster Jennings where Valerie Plame had worked. After the Plame affair, Brewster Jennings had been shuttered, and another one had popped up, headquartered in Kuwait.

One organization, blandly named Sutton Layes

International, operated in the United States. Omar Koss was a "contract employee" of Sutton Layes, a fictional status, a pretense created by bureaucrats that offered no legal protection from activities he knew to be illegal. Only twelve people operated inside SLI. For security reasons, Omar knew none of their names. A squad of support staff in a classified CIA facility in downtown Washington, D.C. was his only connection to his ostensible employer.

While still working officially for the CIA, a gaggle of the world's foremost psychology authorities had interviewed the potential operators for attributes such as innovation, ruthlessness, and the ability to genuinely thrive on stress. Independence was prized over teamwork since many of the missions were single or two-man missions, requiring expert technical, physical and social skills.

The fact that SLI was small and secretive made its resources almost limitless. Its missions to eliminate terrorists were classified NEED TO KNOW. And there was no one, save for the president and the director, who needed to know. Even the operations group never knew the details of any missions. They were trained to simply get the resources to the operatives who called in.

About a year ago, intelligence from Gitmo was indicating that someone inside the US government was selling electronic capabilities to anyone who had the funds to pay for it. In an effort to find out how much was compromised, Omar had simply put himself in the right place at the right time, and sure enough Richard Mullinax had contacted him with an appalling proposal: he wanted to sell the map of the keys.

Omar Koss was not a law enforcement officer so he could not arrest him. All he could do was try to disrupt his plans while simultaneously attempting to learn more about his contacts. Koss had been close to turning over the information to the brass at the CIA and hope they would get it to the FBI for prosecution—sometimes that happened and sometimes it didn't, depending on the current goals of the administration. In any case, the circumstances had become complicated in the last twenty-four hours when he was in Russia, and he knew that any potential Mullinax prosecution had just been delayed.

Mullinax had gotten impatient: he'd had those Russian diplomats killed; he'd launched a warhead from Israel into Russia just to show what the map of the keys could do. People were dying now. War was imminent—or it had been until he'd taken the whole damn country offline: a crude solution, admittedly.

Omar drove into D.C. and the first thing he saw was the Washington Monument. It was one of his favorite views, a gasp of blue sky and the monolith rising from the ground, circled with crisp American flags. A certain simple happiness wrapped itself around his heart. Even with all the death, it was good to be home.

TWENTY-NINE

She had resisted. She thought it important that her family knew she had resisted with all the power and strength in her body. She'd tried to claw their eyes out, the way she'd learned in a women's self-defense class she and Gwen had taken two years ago. She'd twisted from their steely trapping grasps, she kicked and screamed and fought, but they subdued her with a shot of something delivered with a pinch into her neck. It acted quickly, making her weak, almost paralyzed, and the blindfold was wrapped around her head with no protest at all. Her hands were tied with plastic flex ties but she wasn't sure when they'd bound them. They drove for a long time, switching cars twice. Blind, she tried very hard to imagine the map of Washington D.C. so she knew where she was going, but she lost her sense of direction almost instantly. It seemed like they had driven in circles, then they took her out of the car. Another car had driven her in silence on what she thought was a freeway; the car wheels on asphalt made a constant, lulling rhythm.

When they stopped abruptly, she was yanked out of the car. She stood in the freezing cold, hearing a whipping sound. *Whoop whoop whoop.* After several moments, she realized she was hearing the rotary blades of a helicopter. Rough arms picked her up and she wanted to struggle, but her body wouldn't resist. Her mind still struggled somewhat, but her body was limp and useless. Whatever impotent flailing she managed certainly had no effect at all. They put her inside the helicopter. The helicopter lifted, hung for a moment and swayed before rising through the air.

It was cold inside the helicopter. She shivered. Nobody spoke. When she tried to speak, she realized a gag was tied around her mouth. She slumped against the seat, trying to figure out where she was and where she was going, but it was so hard to think. Everything felt so far away, as if it were happening to someone else. Foggy images of Tom and Evan and Travis and her parents shifted through her mind. There had been a crash and the men grabbed her. She saw Tom—this she did remember—she saw the expression on his face as if time had stood still. The frantic activity had slowed, the roar of traffic and the constant barrage of gunplay had ceased, and she looked across four lanes of skidding, car-slamming traffic. Under a light post, Tom Bishop stopped in mid-fire and looked directly at her. She said his name. She was sure he heard her. She saw the stunned dread on his face when he realized they had her, the frozen alarm evident in his intense green eyes.

In the blackness behind her eyes, she clung to the image. It disintegrated.

It was impossible to know how long they were in the helicopter. It seemed like they flew in circles again, specifically to disorient her.

Finally they landed and then Fallon was gathered from her slumped position in the helicopter. It was freezing cold. She felt wetness and remembered it was snowing. The peaceful sound of sloshing water made her think she was on a boat or maybe at a beach house. They picked her up. The stink of their sweat made her gorge rise in her throat; the rough arms around her felt like prison bars. Slowly, heart pounding, she stumbled along. They entered a shelter; the temperature was a little warmer than it was outside; there was no sharp, slicing wind, at least, and the sloshing water was gone. Almost immediately she was taken into an interior room. It echoed slightly as the door opened and had the particular feeling of being empty, like the basement of a funeral home, she thought—but the thought had no weight. It flitted and was gone.

They pushed her to the ground and threw a wool blanket over her. The doors slammed shut. She thought she was alone; there were no voices at all, not even outside the room. No rats snuffling through ancient wooden beams. For that matter there was also no feeling of stale air, the way some basements can be stale.

The floor felt like poured concrete; it was very cold against her butt and back. In only her small merlot-colored lace dress, she shivered violently. She pulled the blanket over her head, trying to create a small cubicle of warmth.

She didn't know how long they left her there. Maybe she slept. Or maybe she was sleeping now, dreaming of this incredible cold because she could not recall ever feeling this particular bone-piercing freeze in real life.

At some point she became more awake. The drugs were wearing off, the haze receding. The cold remained. The gag and blindfold were making her claustrophobic; she ordered herself to stay calm. The more awake she became, the more she began to panic. She focused on breathing, like she did in yoga. In through the nose, hold for eight, exhale slowly. As long as she could breathe, she would be okay. Something her father said during the campaign came to her. He told her the story of Bay of Pigs. He said that President Kennedy was having a meeting with his cabinet and he would listen to every person until he became emotional. When he raised his voice, or began to look hysterical, Kennedy calmly asked him to leave because he simply did not trust the judgment of anyone who could not control his emotions. You're not thinking when you're emotional, her father intoned. In desperate times, the best thing you could do was force yourself to stay calm so you could think.

She tried to take heed. The memory of the words calmed her. Deep breath. She would not cry. That would only wet her blindfold, and it would be hard to breathe through the gag. Calmly dragging in a deep breath, she held it for eight and then let it out for eight.

A giant reservoir of love opened up inside her, deep as the Marianas Trench. Tom and her family would miss her if she did not get out of here, and she hoped that they would be okay. Evan especially. Her sweet little brother—the thought of his gentle innocence made her throat constrict and her heart boil. She hoped her father would learn to take care of her mother. She hoped her mother would finally let herself be loved.

And Tom …. The pain in his eyes when she'd slapped him was compounded by unimaginable degrees when Travis arrived. She felt ashamed for flaunting her date and trying to make him jealous. So juvenile, so stupid. Hopefully he would know that she loved him, despite the way she had acted. She hoped he would see to her heart, the way he always had before.

One day he would find a woman he could love without any guilt or reservations at all. She wanted him to have that; he deserved that kind of relationship. She wished so sincerely that it could have been her.

The breathtaking snowcapped mountains of Shelby, Montana came back with vivid clarity. *Home.* She would have liked to see the vast blue sky one more time, the majestic glaciated peaks of the Tetons. She would have liked to see and do so many things.

Suddenly the door swung opened with a loud bang. She heard their voices for the first time. There were many of them, more than ten, she thought. She identified their language; it was Chechen. A ray of hope began to shiver through the black fog when she recognized it. It was not the same dialect she knew from her time in Jordan, but she understood it well enough. Plus, she had lived in Tajikistan for a while and spoke Tajik and Russian, both very similar to Chechen. They were Chechen Muslims who practice the same extreme form of Wahabism as practiced in Saudi Arabia and other places in the Middle East. Reluctantly, she understood what this meant for herself. They regularly slaughtered Westerners. They killed a school full of babies and children earlier in the decade. They decapitated an oil executive last year and ghoulishly filmed it and uploaded it to the Internet. They meant to kill her. A lump appeared in her throat and she bleakly willed it away, impotently reminding herself to stay calm.

Someone roughly yanked her up under the armpits and dropped her on a chair. She was then tied to the chair at her wrists and ankles. Her legs were numb from the cold; the chair was cold.

"You will say a message that you are okay," someone said

in English.

She didn't reply.

She heard some scraping, people moving around.

Then she heard: "Fallon is okay as you can see. This is for the reporter, Leah. As you see we have Fallon Hughes. We are invisible so do not attempt to find us. Our demand is simple. We want Mahomet Ayrzu in exchange for Fallon Hughes. If we do not have an agreement from the president by midnight, we will kill her and the next video you see of her, she will be headless."

The blindfold was suddenly ripped away. Blazing white light hurt her eyes; she blinked and squinted, unable to see anything but dark figures in front of the light. She barely made out the green recording light of a handheld camera. She began to speak quickly, to say all she could because she didn't believe she'd ever have another chance. She wanted to speak directly to Tom, to let him know she was thinking about him. If she was going to die, she wanted him to know that she did love him: that was the overriding message.

The blindfold was again wrapped tightly around her head. They left her alone in silence after that.

How long ago was that? An hour? Twenty-four hours? She couldn't guess. Time had begun to spin and blur, to become a measure of nothing. She thought of her father and Tom. Maybe they would somehow find her before she outlived her usefulness to the terrorists. Her job right now was to stay calm. Just breathe. In for eight. Hold. Out for eight.

THIRTY

On Air Force One, winging toward New York where its passenger was to deliver a presentation at the United Nations in a last ditch effort to rally support for sanctions against Iran, President Ballard read the classified brief that had been placed on his desk. It included a probability study to determine who was responsible for the attack on Fallon Hughes's motorcade, based on the concept of "chatter." The Deputy Director of the National Security Agency had pointed out an uptick in Iranian chatter in the hours after the attack. Of course they were chattering more; if Preston Taylor Hughes had his druthers, they'd be choking on bomb dust on January 20.

The same countries that were always suspect were analyzed, giving potential motivations for them to take the young daughter of the not-quite-in-office president-elect. Russia, Ukraine, Afghanistan, Iraq, China, Pakistan .... The whole damn world had a motive to toy with the USA, but after eight years in office, Ballard didn't think this was some state-sanctioned act of terrorism. A small cell of terrorists that had a grudge about Mahomet Ayrzu executed the kidnapping; there was no mystery here.

There was nothing of value in the brief.

And now for the difficult call. He indicated for his secretary to dial the number.

Preston Taylor Hughes picked up the line.

"This is a call from Air Force One. Please hold for the President."

He was meeting with Jerry Chambliss and his online media

coordinator in the Blair House Library. Setting the handset aside, he asked his personal assistant to shepherd everyone out while he spoke to the president. Hughes braced for news of a nuclear attack—some big act of revenge, from Russia with love.

But the news of Russia was not to materialize. Instead, Ballard came on the line and explained he only had five minutes before the plane landed in New York. "So I'll come right to the point. Unfortunately, the United States simply will not authorize exchanging Mahomet Ayrzu for Fallon Hughes. To do so would jeopardize relations with half a dozen countries around the globe as well as undermine the confidence of the American people in their government. On national security grounds, we simply refuse to even engage on the subject."

Ballard had the good sense to sound a little apologetic, but it made no difference. Preston clenched his teeth, wondering if this was sick payback after a bruising political defeat.

"At this point, the best we can do is stall. Frankly, with the Russia situation, we simply cannot become distracted ..."

"Distracted?" Hughes cut in.

"I understand your anguish, Preston."

Preston Hughes felt disgust for his predecessor. Saving his legacy was apparently more important than protecting American lives. He was counting down the hours until he could fly back to his home in Vermont and live out his days giving speeches and building his presidential library. It was a time-honored tradition, of course, to avoid controversy in the last months of a presidency. But to Hughes, this felt less like punting the issue than simply running from it, and that stank of cowardice.

"My foreign policy advisors believe the most prudent course of action is to attempt to stall with the people who have captured her. We simply cannot acknowledge the existence of Ayrzu."

"For Christ's sake," Preston said, "this is not the time for prudence. Use him as bait. Promise to hand him over if they return Fallon."

After a short, deliberative pause, Ballard said simply, "The United States's policy is not to admit that he exists."

"That is *your* policy," Hughes corrected, "not the United States's."

"It is the policy of the United States not to negotiate with terrorists. I realize this is emotional for you, but I believe the best course of action is to appear on television and explain that there is no such person as Mahomet Ayrzu in our custody."

"What do you expect them to do to her," Hughes demanded. "Just let her languish? No. They are going to torture and kill my daughter. They have leverage and they know it."

"We can do some behind-the-scenes work to see if we can broker a deal, but as a matter of policy, we can't open negotiations with terrorists."

Preston finished the phone call and then rose to his feet. He paced the library, thinking. The first whiff of the limits of presidential power unpleasantly settled around him. There had to be a way to get Fallon back. His only biological child. She had been a sweet, startlingly beautiful little golden-haired girl who loved her daddy more than anything in the whole world. Then somehow, by minutes he could no longer remember, she grew into a beautiful young woman whose mind was as independent as his own.

When he ran for president, he had envisioned himself masterfully solving world problems. Yet he could not solve even his own domestic issues.

He shut his eyes, thinking about Fallon and the things he had missed in her life while he pursued the presidency. Was it worth it? The boy, Evan, would grow up in the public eye and eventually he would have to morph from publicly known figure to just a normal kid. Or as close to normal as possible.

Preston largely ignored Evan simply because it was painful to be around the evidence of his wife's betrayal. But Preston would have had to be blind to not know Fallon meant the world to Evan. He wondered if the boy realized what was happening, if he asked where Fallon was. A jab of pity and genuine sadness staked him through the chest.

Preston resented the feeling of helpless that was engulfing him. This frame of mind would not help Fallon. He would focus only on what could be done to bring Fallon home.

With the official position being that the US would not negotiate with terrorists, Tom Bishop was his only hope to bring his daughter home alive. He hoped Tom didn't negotiate with them. He hoped he killed them.

The entire security apparatus of the government had been compromised. Omar Koss had stopped the Russians, but with the map of the keys on the open market, it was impossible to know who was watching America's systems. Unfortunately there were many individuals and countries with a motive to interfere with America's ability to track intelligence assets and programs; the most prudent course of action was to act as if every single one of America's enemies was watching.

The problem with alerting the president was that Ballard had never liked the Sutton Layes program. Twice he had attempted to axe it, only to be persuaded by the secretary of defense and the CIA chief that Sutton Layes was vital to national security. There was very little advantage in admitting a screwup and giving him a reason to shut the program—and Omar was under no illusions about his own career, if it came to that. The map of the keys was never supposed to get out. Antoine Campbell had been right to be alarmed enough to alert Fallon Hughes. Koss, who was without sentimentality about people, felt genuine sorrow for Antoine Campbell and anger about his death. Collin had acted impulsively, stupidly. Antoine Campbell could have been silenced in other ways—he did not have to die.

Koss had originally written off the young radical, but he did have some good Middle Eastern and Chechen contacts, so he strung Collin along long enough to get the read on several of those contacts. One was Malkhazi, who had one very good contact for highly enriched plutonium that Omar was keenly interested in. Because Collin had expressed desire to kill Fallon himself, and because Malkhazi was probably the most dedicated terrorist in Collin's phone book, Omar made the easy assumption that Malkhazi, or someone close to him, had Fallon Hughes.

Thus at ten o'clock on the morning after the kidnapping, a very fortuitous thing happened. A video of Fallon Hughes was broadcast on television. She said an odd thing. "Tell Tom I'm okay." Not "tell my family I am okay." But "Tom."

Listening to the news broadcast, Omar heard the name Leah Lennox, identified as a reporter for the *Washington Post.*

And thus, one of America's most covert operatives, a man whose face and name had never been uttered anywhere in any media, showed up at the 15th Street offices of the *Washington Post* and asked to have an audience with Ms. Leah Lennox.

Leah was frightened of the giant man who stood up as she entered the conference room at the *Washington Post* office. He was huge. Six feet four or five, built thick. All muscle. His face was impassive and expressionless.

"Mr. Jones?"

"My name is Omar Koss," he said. His voice was low and soft and precise. Factual. He did not smile. *Spare* was the word that came to her.

"Oh. Was Jones a ... pseudonym?"

"Miss Lennox, sit down."

There was simply no question of arguing with him. She sat.

"You have a tape of Fallon Hughes. Why did they send it to you?"

"I'm sorry, Mr. Koss. I can't ..."

"Miss Lennox, I do not have much time. The security of our government has been compromised. Any information you give to the FBI, CIA, NSA, even MPD or anywhere else is exposed directly to our enemies." He slid across a credential that identified him as a CIA employee.

Leah picked it up and examined it. Looked legit. She had seen Tom's Secret Service credentials many times, and this small booklet looked a lot like that. She slid it back to him, eyes wide with shock.

"I believe I can return Fallon Hughes to her family, but I cannot use the FBI's massive surveillance assistance, and certainly not the NSA's electronic expertise, or even a small, specialized team of operatives from the CIA. If you do not assist me, it is inevitable that Fallon Hughes will die."

Leah's eyes had gone huge. "Inevitable," she whispered.

"Yes, ma'am. You have to trust me."

"My friend Tom …"

"Tom from the video?"

"Yes. My friend Tom is a Secret Service agent. He was on Fallon's security detail. I know he would never betray our government."

"Do you know where I can find him?"

"Probably Secret Service headquarters. I think they're analyzing the video for clues about where she might be."

"You need to come with me." He started to stand up again.

"I can't. I have to work …. The Russian situation …"

"Miss Lennox, Fallon Hughes is in the custody of a man who wants to chop off her head."

"I … I …" She floundered; there was no answer to that.

"Bring your iPad and let's go."

Leah sat in the passenger seat of Omar Koss's Crown Victoria, dialing Tom's number. He didn't answer. She left a message. Koss would not talk. He would not turn on the radio. He just drove. The air became heavy with awkwardness. Leah kept glancing over at him, fascinated and scared of him. He was not conventionally handsome, but she felt sort of magnetized by him. But he was also terrifying.

"So do you track terrorists for the CIA full time? Or do you have other tasks?"

He didn't answer.

"I see." She looked out the window. "Who do you think has Fallon Hughes?"

No answer.

"Who is Mohamet Ayrzu?" After another silence, Leah asked, "Do you have a hearing problem?"

He looked at her. His face was utterly impassive, his eyes

hidden by dark black shades.

She nervously took out her phone and dialed Tom again. This time he answered. "Hold on," she said and looked at Omar. "What should I tell him?"

"Tell him to meet you at the Starbucks on H Street."

She relayed the message. "He says he can't."

Omar grabbed the phone. "Meet us at the Starbucks or I'll kill your friend. Come alone." He hung up and handed the phone back to Leah.

Leah stared at him with fury and fear, completely confounded. "That's not nice," she said finally. "You don't just threaten to kill people."

She thought for a moment that he was going to apologize. Instead, he asked, "Is that him?"

On the sidewalk, Tom was walking from Headquarters to the Starbucks. He looked so handsome; even after all he had been through, he looked so invincible. Her heart swelled with pride.

"Jump out and tell him to get in the car."

Leah did as Omar instructed. Tom hesitated. He approached the car and opened the passenger door. "Who are you?"

"Get in the car. Watch your feet. My gun is in that bag on the floorboard."

Tom tried to understand what this stranger was saying but it sounded crazy. He could not ask the FBI or even his own agency for assistance? "It's compromised," Omar said plainly. "The map of the keys is out there. It's going to take hundreds of billions of dollars to fix the damage caused by this. But more importantly, for the foreseeable future, assume that everyone you speak to is operating against you. Your entire chain of command is suspect. Your radio transmissions are being monitored; everything you type into a government computer, every secret we have is being bought and sold right now around the globe."

Tom tried to absorb the impact of what Omar Koss was saying. Under the horror of the situation was a grim sense of pride: Fallon had been correct. She had known, with some otherworldly sixth sense, that Antoine Campbell had not been an attention-seeking lunatic. And his call to her suddenly did not seem quite so random. He would have known that the government systems were not secure. Fallon, a lawyer whose father was the president-elect, was near government without being a part of it. She would have seemed an infinitely safe and reasonable person to contact. *Good job, Antoine Campbell.*

"Ballard is going to kick this down the road and deny, deny, deny. The last thing the US wants is for news of Ayrzu's existence to become part of the dialogue of terrorism. Ballard is in CYA mode and not going to be any help at all. That means we have the choice of actually freeing the terrorist in exchange for Fallon, which I am not wont to do, or finding her ourselves and taking her from them. The problem with the second scenario is that we will have minimal support, and it could be bloody. The operations people at Sutton Layes will be able to give us some logistics assistance, but there is no backup."

Tom did not think twice. "I'm in. Let's go."

"I'll go too," Leah said.

"No," both men said in unison.

"Fine. If you kick me out of this car, I will go straight back to work and file a front page story about what both of you just said." From her purse she pulled out her iPhone, which had been recording the conversation. She was still smarting from his threat to kill her, so she looked Omar with a particularly smug smirk on her face.

"When did you get so sneaky?" Tom asked, dismayed.

"Since I started covering politics for the *Washington Post.* Now are you going to let me tag along or am I going to write a big story about—"

"Or I could kill you," Omar said tonelessly.

"Quit threatening to kill me! Is that the only trick you know?"

"No you couldn't," Tom said smoothly, his gaze locked on Omar.

A car behind them honked; they were double parked and blocking traffic on G Street.

"Where do you live?" Omar asked.

"Court House," Tom replied. Omar put the car in gear and headed toward Arlington.

"I wonder if the FBI has asked for the video footage outside my building," Leah mused as the towering Art Deco structure came into view. "The DVD was hand delivered to my door. Maybe someone showed up on the video."

"Secret Service didn't request it," Tom said.

"Maybe it's still there," Leah said.

Omar parked along the curb in front of Tom's building and they walked across the street to Leah's building. Tom approached the concierge desk with a smile; they knew him in here because he visited Leah almost every day, and the person at the desk was actually a woman he and Leah had given some chocolate chip cookies to over Christmas.

"Martha," he said sweetly. "I've got a special request today."

Leah hung back, watching him use his charm to procure the video. She glanced to Omar, who was attempting to avoid the video cameras in the lobby, looking down at his device. It didn't look like an iPhone or a BlackBerry. He was strange and scary, but he was also interesting. His body was dangerously sexy; standing beside him, she felt positively dainty.

He glared at her with his neutral poker face and Leah looked away.

"Thank you," Tom said. To Leah and Omar he said, "Come on," and headed toward the elevator bank.

"Why are we going to my place?" Leah hissed. "What's going on?"

Tom remained quiet until the elevator door slid open and they stepped inside, Omar following. Tom pressed the button for Leah's floor. "She said she'll record this morning's tape to DVD but it will take about half an hour. I figured we should wait here."

Leah opened her door and glanced around, cringing when she saw her mess of papers stacked all over her desk, an empty bottle of water on her living room table, and that nothing had been dusted in months. In her haze, none of it had seemed important, but with guests over, she suddenly realized how sloppy she had become. She'd stopped caring about things, she realized in dismay.

"Sit wherever," Leah said.

Omar went to Leah's desk. "Can I use your computer to receive some email?"

She looked at him suspiciously then said yes.

Omar used his encrypted cell phone to dial the operations desk at Sutton Layes. He trusted the people at Sutton Layes, if for no other reason than it was one entity that could not be cracked with the map of the keys; they existed outside the government structure and were therefore invulnerable to attacks.

A female voice answered without any official greeting. Just the standard, "Hello?"

Bridget. Koss liked her; she was a levelheaded analyst who maintained her calm composure under even the most extreme pressure. He didn't say her name—as was the protocol—but he was pleased that she had picked up.

"I need a look-down over the George Washington Parkway and surrounding areas for the last forty-eight hours."

"I was wondering when we'd get this call," she said lightly.

"Get a drone, flying high and silent," he said. That was also blatantly illegal, and completely justified. The FBI and Secret Service were no doubt right now trying to locate witnesses who saw the crash. Eyewitnesses would give stunned descriptions of the assailants, each disagreeing with the version of events before it. One person would claim the attackers were Teutonic ectomorphs; another would be positive they were swarthy mesomorphs. One would say there were two; another would say no less than fifty. And because they did not know what else to do, the government investigators would give equal credence to every single one of those people who in reality knew nothing at all. The brain doesn't record information well during a crisis, a phenomenon that Koss often used to his advantage. In this most significant case, the FBI and Secret Service would scramble to investigate thousands of leads that would ultimate point them directly to a big fat dead end.

This way was much faster.

"I'm on it," Bridget said.

"Expect some low-quality pictures in the next half hour," Koss said.

"Standing by," Bridget replied and hung up.

Leah's landline rang; it was Martha alerting her that the DVD Mr. Bishop requested was ready.

Tom left to get it and Leah looked over at Omar, who was intently involved in his handheld device. "What are you doing?" she asked.

"Waiting." He set the phone down and looked at her.

Leah held his gaze. She stood near the wall, biting her thumbnail. She was a funny little thing, a scared bunny with big eyes ... and just five minutes ago had brazenly recorded him and threatened to write a report on his activities. Those flashes of confrontation intrigued him. A lot.

He had the strangest thought that she would hate him if she knew what he did most of the time. If she'd seen him kill the "flight crew" in Sweden, she'd have been outraged. On the other hand, she would have probably been completely impressed if she'd watched him disable Russia's electronic grid.

Leah walked into the kitchen. "Do you want something to drink?" she called from the fridge.

"Sure. When you were in the news room did you hear anything about Russia? Are the lights back on over there?"

"I haven't heard that. Why, did you blow their power grid or something?" She shut the door and handed him the water. Her playful smile faded. "Oh my God. Did you ...?"

The door opened and Tom slammed inside. He held a silver DVD in his hands. "Move over," he said to Omar. Omar stood up and Tom slid the disk into Leah's computer.

They gathered around the monitor and watched the grainy black-and-white video of the front of Leah's building. At 5:51 a.m. a man walked into the lobby. Leah gasped. "That's him.

He's holding the box."

The man was only on the video for two seconds. Tom replayed it and paused on the three-fourths profile against a muzzy background. Omar squinted, trying to see more than what was on the screen. Nada. He'd send it to Bridget; she would analyze it with sophisticated face-reading software, and with any luck, the guy would turn up in the database.

"Move over," Omar said to Tom. He copied the video to Leah's desktop, then navigated to a website that had an incredibly long URL made up of seemingly random letters and numbers. Any attempt to determine in the origins of the domain would come up empty. A traceroute would lead any casual observer to believe it lead to a server in Russia, with a masking attempt. Even a more sophisticated attempt, say from the Mossad, the FSB, Istakhbarat, or even other divisions inside the CIA, would come up with nothing. In reality, it was a server located in Alexandria, Virginia: one of hundreds residing in the server farm at the Sutton Layes building.

Omar uploaded the video for Bridget.

Tom walked to the sliding glass door that led to Leah's balcony. He was no doubt thinking of the video the man had delivered. Fallon, tied to a chair, with terrorists barking like hyenas around her.

"Are you okay?" Leah asked. She hugged him and rested her head on his chest.

"Yes," Tom lied.

Leah's cell phone on the desk sounded like a machine gun in the quiet room. Omar glanced at it. To his shock, the name Collin Whitcomb appeared on the screen.

"You know this person? You know Collin?" Omar said. He was on his feet, holding out her phone to her.

"I wish I didn't. Let it roll to voicemail."

The ringing suddenly stopped. Omar looked at the screen, then back to Leah. "How do you know him?"

"He approached me a week ago at the mall. I hate him," she said passionately. "He's awful."

"Who is he?" Tom asked.

Omar dialed Bridget again. "Find the location of the last person who just called … Leah, what's your number?" She recited the digits to him, and he relayed them to Bridget. A second later, he asked, "Who is your carrier?"

"AT&T," she answered.

Bridget replied coolly, "I see that phone. I'm looking up the last calls placed to it."

Omar waited impatiently while Bridget collated the information. "It's a black hole," she reported. "There's nothing."

"Damn it."

"But I have some raw satellite images from the kidnapping. I can give you a sixty percent assurance that one of the men is Djvebe Malkhazi. We are still attempting to ascertain the identities of the others."

It was all the confirmation Omar required. Sixty percent was usually enough to justify a scud missile strike overseas. But this was the USA. There would be no missile play.

"See what you can find about Malkhazi's movements over the past twenty-four hours. Go several layers deep, in fact. Check out his known cohorts, et cetera."

"Give me five minutes."

"Make it a fast five minutes," Omar said and hung up.

Tom turned on Leah's television. The kidnapping dominated the news cycle, pushing everything else off the electronic front pages of the cable news channels. There was little other news to report, each segment rehashing the previous ones, talking heads trying to inject fresh insight into the story. Pictures of Fallon appeared on every channel, images of her walking out of her office building just days ago when she'd been accused of murder and older images culled from tabloid and fashion magazines.

Tom turned it off, unable to stomach the onslaught, and turned his attention to Omar.

All his career, he had worked by the book. Warrants, probable cause, justifications, assurances, civil rights—all these things he willingly and enthusiastically embraced, even when he was certain the suspect was guilty. But Omar was concerned with none of the trappings of a restrained government. Tom grudgingly admired the productiveness of Omar's work and the complete lack of roadblocks, particularly since Fallon would be the beneficiary of it.

Fallon Hughes was the only thing in the world that mattered. Her safety, first of all. But after that was secured, if she ever wanted to talk to him again, he would make a full confession. He would wash himself clean with the truth. He would explain about Bethany. He would explain that he had been uncertain that he could ever love anyone again, until he met her. His love for Fallon had grown larger than the regret and sadness he felt over Bethany's death.

He shut his eyes for a moment, trying to assure himself that she was okay. She was alive. They wouldn't kill her as long as they believed they would get Ayrzu in exchange for her.

"What's the story with Ayrzu?" Tom asked Omar.

"Last I heard, he was being held in a private prison in Syria, but that was over a year ago. Who knows. He could be anywhere; we have classified prisons all over the globe. There is no chance Ballard will release him, if that's what you're thinking. And don't even think about him anyway, because if it is Malkhazi who has her, I promise he has no intention of actually seeing an exchange."

Tom swallowed the rage that welled in his throat.

A moment later, Omar's phone rang. "A credit card number of a known Chechen rebel formerly connected to Malkhazi, currently in Tbilisi, had been used to make a purchase in Virginia Beach about twenty hours ago. Looks like a Wal-Mart."

"That's him," Omar said. "Get some drones over Virginia Beach and call me back when you find him." Omar glanced at the fat platinum watch on his wrist. It was ten o'clock. "And get a helicopter ready to go at the South Capitol Street helipad." Even with a helicopter, that would be cutting it close. Virginia Beach was at least three hours away by almost any method of transit. "And some good weaponry."

"Your favorites?"

"Yes. Double them."

Omar hung up. "Looks like Virginia Beach," he said.

Tom and Leah began to speak at once and Tom placed his hand over Leah's mouth to hush her. "Where in Virginia Beach?"

"Still searching, but let's get to the helipad."

"I'm coming too," Leah chirped.

"All right," Omar said. They left the apartment and headed for Omar's car. Leah slung herself in the back. Tom took the passenger seat. They were silent as they drove to the helipad.

It was late and there were many places he could have gone, but Richard Mullinax refused to leave his office. The president had returned from New York and had reconvened his meetings on the state of Russia, but Mullinax had not been invited. His boss, the Director of the National Security Agency, had been invited, of course. He did not know if others previously invited had been cut out, but he sensed disaster. Every hour seemed to add to the sick confirmation that his career was over.

He could not understand why they were toying with him. If they knew what he had done, why did they not arrest him? Perhaps they were attempting to gain more knowledge of his activities. They would not find it. He had destroyed his personal computer, bashed it over and over with a golf club until it had broken apart into pieces small enough to hoover up. Then he'd driven to Alexandria, where he threw away some in a Dumpster, and to Towson, where he threw away another chunk in another anonymous trash bin, and to a Wendy's in Arlington where he'd thrown away the rest in the restaurant bathroom. The hard drive he had soaked in his bathroom sink with bleach, and then taken it apart, destroying each part as thoroughly as he could, then throwing away the parts in three other Dumpsters.

They wouldn't find any way to connect him to Omar Koss or Antoine Campbell, no matter where they looked. Maybe he wouldn't get arrested after all. Maybe he would still be okay. He vacillated between the two poles—certain he would be caught, and then, just as abruptly, certain he wouldn't. He fought, even now, to believe he would survive this.

He had stopped trying to reach Omar Koss, aware that his phone calls to Omar's number could be traced, if it came to that. He still hoped that Omar would contact him. Maybe he could ask Claudia to contact him.

No, she wouldn't do it. Richard was troubled about Claudia. Maybe she was too close to the power—she would have sided with them. At the last meeting he had attended, she had looked across the conference table at him blankly, as if she didn't know him. Her stoicism frightened him. Two calls to her had not been returned.

Isolated, he realized. They were isolating him.

It was possible they were even watching him in his office. He sat very still for a moment, attempting to appear relaxed and normal while he tried to imagine how likely that was, and what, exactly, they would know after the last two days of his admittedly erratic behavior. In the silence he heard a sound, like a tick, in the reception area outside his door. His blood froze in his veins. His breath suspended as he listened for it to repeat. Was someone out there? Someone was out there. He knew it. He rose on shaky legs, but aware he might be on camera, didn't creep like he wanted to. He walked to the door. Opening it, he saw the empty reception area where his secretary parsed visitors. But the secretary was gone; it was late. He took a step out of the reception and looked around. Nobody. This area of the building was usually not manned in the late hours. This was the senior executive area, the brass. There was no reason for anyone to be here. Himself included.

He wondered if it was a test, if someone had been sent here to draw him out. He shrank back inside the reception area, angry at the games they were playing with him. Spontaneously, he sat down in the receptionist's chair. Her computer was on but asleep; it would require a password to activate and any bad password attempts would be logged on the server. He wondered if he dared try it. While considering it and trying to figure out what her password might be, he opened the desk and found the usual things. Pens, paperclips, tape. No obvious cameras or recording devices.

"Hello, Richard."

Richard jumped, his body going cold and wet instantly, as if struck by lightening. The director's aide smiled apologetically. "I'm sorry—I saw your light on and thought I would stop by."

"Oh, yes," Richard replied, aware that his voice sounded high and scared. He didn't sound like an innocent man. "Hi. I'm looking for a damn Post-it."

Despite his own clumsy acting, the aide seemed to believe him. He stepped inside. He was an older man—sixty, this year—and a lieutenant general in the Army.

"It's late," Richard said. "Why are you …. I mean, is everything okay?"

He smiled. "Just fine. I was wargaming the mole problem with a few peers at the CIA and here in my group. I guess I let the time get away from me."

Richard's throat went dry. He looked at the man for any hint that he was toying with him, but he seemed to be forthright. Of course, if he were sent here to sound out Richard, he would be smooth as butter. They wouldn't send someone broadcasting suspicion and unease, someone whose very presence sent Richard scurrying for cover. Richard intuited that he was in the presence of a very powerful foe.

He smiled stiffly. "I've been doing that myself," he said. "Wargaming."

"I guess you've heard there is some suspicion that the mole is here in the NSA."

"I had not heard that. I heard rumors it was someone at Central Intelligence with access to Soviet analysis."

The aide frowned slightly. "Anything is possible at this point." He glanced around the reception area and said, "Well, goodnight Richard."

"Goodnight."

He watched the aide walk away as raw nausea welled. He felt like he'd been sucker punched in the gut. He got himself to his desk, trying to catch his breath. A fine cold sweat sizzled on his feverish skin. He had to get out. If they were this close, there was no reason to continue the façade. Rising to his feet again, a wave of dizziness struck him in a swoon. He paused, shutting his eyes and willing the sick feeling away. The needle. It was going to feel like this, he thought, and a visible shudder moved through him.

He grabbed his briefcase and walked out, forcing his posture to remain tall and firm. He walked fast down the funhouse maze of glass and fluorescent lights, trying for the sake of the cameras, and, in this quadrant, late night workers, to look merely busy, like he was going somewhere important; he had no time for chitchat.

Walking through the turnstiles, he felt a sudden liberation. He nodded to the faceless Marine guard and pushed open the heavy glass door. It had continued to snow, and the frigid air and wet flakes felt wonderful on his fevered skin. He lifted his face slightly as he walked to his car.

Once he got on the road, he began to shake. *Everything is fine*, he told himself. *Everything is just fine. Just drive normally.* He heard another sound, a little fragment of radio static. *Was that a signal burst from a transponder? Was it possible they were this far ahead of him?* He glanced behind him as he drove. Nobody behind him.

Maybe it was just a problem with the radio. It was set to the classical station, and when he turned it on, the car filled with the beseeching voice of a cello. The radio was fine. Maybe hadn't actually heard it. Maybe he imagined it. Maybe.

A white Taurus fell in behind him. It occupied the middle lane, but it stayed with Richard past several exits. Were they were blatantly following him now? He knew the first rule of countersurveillance: never show that you know you're being followed. If you know you're being followed, you have a reason to be looking for a tail, and thus any escape or evasion is usually a sign of guilt. He badly wanted to get off the freeway and maybe stop in at a gas station to see if the white Taurus would follow but forced himself to stay steady. He tapped his hands on the wheel of the Mercedes, then shut off the radio. But then he heard the snatch of sound again, so he turned it back on.

He mouthed, "Oh God," afraid there were sound recording devices in the car.

He didn't want his followers to see the red brake lights flash, so he gently removed his foot from the gas and let the car begin to slow, just by a few miles per hour, not really noticeable in normal traffic. But to Richard's horror, the Taurus didn't pass. It remained the same distance behind.

"Fuck you!" Richard suddenly shouted. Even his rage sounded scared. "Fuck you!" he said again more forcefully to the guys listening in his car, and the ones following him, and the whole system. Fuck them for not trusting him.

At his exit, he swerved off the freeway and watched the Taurus continue on. Someone else would appear behind him—a classic four or six man operation, which meant he was being advertised internally as a pretty big fish. He supposed that was something.

They would not follow onto the narrow residential streets because there was too much risk of being made. Richard drove into the parking structure, then hurried into his building.

He had hung very heavy black drapes over the windows to keep out the directional microphones, cameras, and other gadgets which were no doubt assaulting the condo windows every second of every day. As he came inside, it was pitch black, like a deep cave. He turned on all the lights to let them know he was home and walked directly into his office.

He sat very still for a while at his desk, thinking. It seemed that he still had a tiny bit of leverage. He could still embarrass them all—all the ones listening, the ones who thought they were so much smarter than he. He had hundreds of thousands of dollars of United States technology aimed at him right now and unknowable numbers of federal agents. With attention like this, what better time to leave his mark on the world?

His mind flashed to Tom Bishop, who had stormed into his place of business, his blustering threats still echoing in Richard's ears. That was when he had really known they were on to him. If he had to pinpoint a moment, it would be then that it became impossible for him to live out his days on some beach with beautiful ladies and billions of dollars partitioned away in various investments and accounts. He had been running since then, running from the needle that he now understood was inescapable.

Killing Tom Bishop would be difficult. An easier target might be that journalist, Leah Lennox. The newspapers had reported that Fallon Hughes's kidnappers had sent Leah the video and in the video, she had mentioned Tom. The newspapers said that Leah was a dear friend of Tom.

The fact she was a reporter would provide the perfect ruse. The fact that she was a friend of Tom was a pleasant coincidence. While his nascent plan was primarily one of revenge, he couldn't discount the fact that people would always wonder what was it about Leah Lennox that led her to be in such a terribly wrong place and the wrong time.

Leah Lennox stepped out of the car. Tom gently grabbed her arm and pulled her into a hug. "You can't go," he said into her hair.

She pulled back and saw with disbelieving eyes that he was serious. "You tricked me?"

"I can't lose you. I can't even risk it. Please drive Omar's car back to your building. I'll call you from—"

"I can't believe you would lie to me like that."

"Leah, you're a reporter. You're not a cop. Go home, and please be careful."

Leah's phone rang.

"Is it Collin?" Omar asked.

She shook her head. "The number is private." She answered. "This is Leah."

Tom listened to Leah's side of the conversation, growing increasingly bewildered. Omar stood nearby, looking out at the Anacostia River and the flow of headlights on the Frederick Douglass Bridge. Tom suspected he was missing none of Leah's conversation.

Tom looked back at the helicopter, urging Leah to finish.

Finally she hung up. "Okay, you guys go on." She held her hand out for the keys to the car.

"Tell me," Tom said.

Leah smiled slightly. "I have a meeting with none other than Richard Mullinax, Deputy Director of the National Security Agency. He invited me to his home for an exclusive story. He said he can get me access to … some stuff."

"Stuff like what?" Tom asked.

"Documents or people?" Omar added.

She pursed her lips. "Both, actually."

"Have you ever talked to him before?" Omar asked.

"No."

A look passed between the two men. "Don't go," Tom said suddenly. "There is something really wrong about this situation."

"You don't want me to go with you to help get Fallon Hughes. You don't want me to get this story, which Mullinax said will make my career. Would you like to assign me a bedtime too?" The sharpness in her voice was accompanied by a frustrated shake of her head. "I'm not a kid, Tom. I can take care of myself."

"He's setting you up," Tom said bluntly.

"He would hardly be the first source in the government to try and manipulate the press for his own agenda." When she saw the doubt in Tom's eyes, she softened her tone. "Do you have any idea how badly I need something like this? An exclusive that will blow away the entire press corps?"

Tom looked back to the helicopter, feeling time slipping away.

"He's a trapped animal, Leah," Omar said. "He's dangerous."

"I can handle myself."

"Like Fallon Hughes handled herself?" Omar said.

Tom winced. Fallon should never have had to handle herself. It was his sacred duty to protect her and he had failed.

"You think you know what you're doing. You don't."

"Go with her," Tom said suddenly. "Go with Leah to see Mullinax. I'll be fine by myself."

"I do not need a chaperone to do my job," Leah said stridently. The ambition in her eyes conveyed her iron will.

Omar seemed to consider it for a moment, weighing Leah

alone with Mullinax and Tom alone with terrorists. A nearly imperceptible nod was the only indication of acquiescence.

Leah looked wounded.

"I'll see you soon," Tom said, and to cut off any more conversation on the subject, he sprinted toward the helicopter. The rotary blades were spinning; Tom ducked and climbed inside. The pilot said, "He isn't coming?"

"Just me," Tom replied.

"Roger that."

The helicopter began to lift and Tom shut his eyes. He still hated heights and hated flying. But for Fallon, he'd endure anything.

THIRTY-ONE

Leah wanted to watch the helicopter until she couldn't see it anymore, but Omar told her to get into the car. She sank into the front seat and turned the heater up. Omar slammed the gas pedal and headed toward Maryland.

Gazing out the window, she thought about Richard Mullinax. "Why do you think he's a bad guy?" Leah asked.

"He sold some secrets," Omar said simply. "He got a lot of people killed."

Leah absorbed the information silently. She had more questions—that journalistic instinct was always working—but she held back.

Omar's face was lit only with the light of the dashboard. His profile was surprisingly noble and Leah had the distinct feeling that Mullinax's activities actually *hurt* Omar. Not only on a professional level but on a deeply personal level, like he had offended Omar's personal code of honor.

"Oh my God," she whispered. "You're a Boy Scout."

"What?" He looked at her with a confused expression.

"You're actually a good guy."

Omar smirked and shrugged his big shoulders. "I guess that depends on what you mean by good."

His phone buzzed. He picked it up and read.

"Ugh, that is so dangerous," Leah said and grabbed the device from him. "Please just drive. I'll read it." She frowned. "It says, 'PACER has detected unusual heat signatures located east of Virginia Beach at latitude 36.852N and longitude negative 75.978W.'" To Omar she asked, "What does this mean? What is PACER?"

"It's a drone. It means they've located Fallon in a boat off the coast of Virginia Beach. Call Tom and tell him. Call the last number dialed and ask for a Zodiac boat and a truck to be waiting for Tom when he lands."

Leah did as Omar ordered. She hung up the phone just as Omar turned into the drive of a swanky high-rise condo building.

The hallway was well lit. Leah wished for a moment it was filled with scurrying rats and flickering lights to betray Mullinax's dark and cannibalistic soul. But it was well lit and well decorated, well-off in general. Mullinax's condo was at the end of the hallway, a corner unit.

Omar kept his profile thin against the wall beside Mullinax's door, and Leah knocked. A few seconds later, she heard someone on the other side and assumed he was looking at her through the peephole. "Who is it?"

"Leah Lennox."

A series of locks was unlatched, and finally the door opened. She had never seen him in person. She was surprised that he looked like a male supermodel, all high cheekbones and pouting lips. He looked rather ill though. He appeared to be sweating and his eyes were rimmed in red, like he had been up for a week without sleep. Leah was repulsed by his appearance but could not look away. Omar's words were ringing in her ears and she kept reminding herself she was in the presence of a powerful traitor.

Mullinax didn't notice her focused attention on his gruesome appearance. He was staring past her, at Omar Koss. And he had gone ghost white under the film of greasy sweat. "You ..."

"Hello, Mullinax," Omar said smoothly. He stepped beside Leah and entered the apartment, walking past Mullinax as if he wasn't even there. The man knew how to dominate.

The condo was a miracle of opulence: Onica, Cartier, Waterford. It seemed strange for a bureaucrat to care so much about delicate, beautiful things. Leah wondered if the ornaments had been bought with dirty money.

As Mullinax followed Omar into the living room, Leah noticed he wasn't wearing shoes, perhaps so he wouldn't make a sound on the polished oak floors as he approached the door.

Secondly, she noticed heavy black drapes over the windows.

Tom's instincts had been right. She felt the creeping sense of something off now that she was inside his domain. Instinctively she hung back just a little bit as Mullinax was speaking in a stage whisper, frantically gesticulating to Omar. "You betrayed me!"

"You betrayed our country," Omar said smoothly.

Mullinax, who was not stupid, had been so blinded by greed that he had failed to see the obvious: Omar was not on his side. The sudden realization caused him to physically stagger backward, as if Omar had struck him. Slack-lipped and wide-eyed, he stared at the larger man with fury and disbelief. "All those things we discussed …"

"You discussed. I listened."

A weird laugh bubbled from his gnawed lips. "This is actually perfect," he said. He looked to Leah with that weird, unfocused stare, and took a few steps toward her. "This is so perfect. I'm glad you're here. Come on, follow me to my office."

Omar put himself between Mullinax and Leah and they followed Mullinax into a large wood-paneled office. It looked like a library at a stuffy old gentleman's club with leather oxblood club chairs, heavy wooden tables, and leather-bound books. Expensive-looking art hung on the walls.

Mullinax sat down behind his huge desk, his bearing like the captain of a ship. Despite his unhealthy appearance, he smiled pleasantly as Leah and Omar sat across from him.

She remembered her surprising question at the Hughes press gaggle. The confrontational style of her question had caught him off guard and he'd evaded answering. She thought that in this environment, Mullinax would not be able to avoid answering. Before he could take control of the meeting, Leah asked, "Is it true you sold secrets to the Russians?" She didn't know if it was really the Russians, or even exclusively the Russians. Omar had not indicated the buyers of the secrets Mullinax stole. But she knew very well that two Russian assets had been killed, and that the United States and Russia were still teetering on war, though a little less so than a few days ago when the entire Russian electrical grid was taken offline. It seemed a good guess.

Mullinax eyed her skeptically. "Is that what you think?"

"You called me here to give me an exclusive. I must assume it was for something big. The facts seem to fit."

He laughed a weird high-pitched laugh that went through her like a scream. The man was truly evil. "You want your exclusive. You want the story that will make your career." He smiled at her, almost fatherly.

"That's why I was called here, isn't it?"

"I didn't know you were bringing him." He cut his eyes to Omar.

"I'm sure he won't mind if you tell me if you sold US secrets to Russians."

"He knows the truth," he said. He seemed to be indicating there was more to the story—some mysterious "truth" that would justify his actions or absolve his guilt.

"Well why are we here? It's very late. If you've changed your mind, I'd just as well go home."

He sticky gaze fixed on her, his eyes like bright wet stars.

A few tense seconds passed, then Leah said, "Okay, I'm done. Clearly you had no real reason to call me here."

Leah stood up and Omar followed.

Mullinax stood up. "I said you'd get a story that makes your career."

"Yes. Where is it?"

"Here's your story," he said.

She had an impression of movement in the corner of her eye and realized that Mullinax's hand had come up shoulder level. In that first chaotic instant, she thought he was reaching across the desk to strike Omar. But his hand went to his temple. Omar suddenly grabbed her—a feeling like being flash-frozen with some exotic cartoon weapon because suddenly she was in his arms, her face pressed into the hard wall of his chest, and she literally could not move. At that exact moment—with a million questions buzzing in her head—she heard a loud crack that reverberated in her bones and left her dazed and stunned: the percussive bang of a pistol being fired in an enclosed area.

She jumped instinctively, but Omar held her tight, not letting her move. The acrid smell of burnt metal whiffed through the room.

The silence was horrible. She wiggled to breathe.

"It's over," he said into her hair. "Don't look." He loosened his steely embrace, and human nature being what it was, Leah glanced to the last place she had seen Mullinax standing. All she saw was grotesque red splatter over the bucolic painting of a Spanish countryside.

The Atlantic was a smooth black expanse, with flickering white caps where the waves tumbled onto the shore. Through the snow-flecked windows, Tom searched out the blackness for a light or a shape that looked like a craft anchored at sea where Fallon might be held, but there was nothing to see. The world from up here looked infinite, a vast void. He would have to trust Omar Koss's intel and believe that Fallon was somewhere out there, beyond the blackness, waiting for him. It was already eleven forty. Twenty minutes until the terrorist's deadline.

The helicopter descended on a pad not far from the beach, where the truck that Leah promised was waiting with a small Zodiac boat on a covered trailer. After a few moments of searching, he found the keys in the cup holder and pushed the truck into gear.

He backed the truck up to the pier and cut the engine. He pushed the seat back to give him more room and changed into the black clothes that were on the seat beside him. Only then did he open the duffle bags that were waiting on the floorboards. A gorgeous, beautiful, darkly glinting cache of weapons glimmered at him like a mirage. Tom's heart caught in his throat. If only he'd had this firepower when the killers attacked Fallon. He could have mowed them down like the guys in the movies, in a spray of red mist, leaving only bloody chum where their bodies once stood. If only. He holstered his Sig Sauer below his hip and a second pistol in a cross draw shoulder rig.

Grim and strained from repressing regrets, he took what he

needed. It felt strange not to have backup. He would have to go in there with only his heart and guts and desire to kill. In the heat of the moment, that felt like plenty.

The fishy, salty air seemed incongruent with the cold wind and spitting snow. His mind flashed to Paxos, the sultry midday heat, and Fallon lying in his arms as the ceiling fan cooled their spent bodies. He shook the image away, needing focus.

He lowered the black inflatable boat to the icy bite of choppy water, then clambered inside and started the powerful motor, which smoothly hummed to life. An auspicious beginning. Getting a feel for the small craft, he guided it carefully through the harbor, impressed by the way it zoomed easily over the choppy surface. He plugged in the coordinates in the GPS that Leah had given him and continued toward open water. Looking back toward shore, he could not see a thing.

The boat struggled as he proceeded farther out to sea. The waves were very rough and the boat was not designed for deep water, certainly not in such inclement weather. Tom struggled to steer on the correct coordinates as the wind easily blew the light craft off course.

The sea was vast and rough and empty as it churned beneath the tiny boat. He struggled to see and steer through the back spray of freezing salt water. Squinting his stinging eyes, he looked for any hint of the boat that Koss promised would be anchored out here, but he saw only more snow and sea. He grew increasingly tense as midnight stalked toward him.

Then, just as he was beginning to think the intelligence had been wrong, he saw a shape just ahead, a hulking shadowy structure that could not be the sky or the sea. With no outboard lights, the yacht was perfectly camouflaged by the night.

He wished he had some infrared or FLIR devices so he could see where everyone inside was located. *God let Fallon be okay.*

As the Zodiac approached, he grew concerned that the motor was too loud. Hopefully the slush of the waves and the whipping wind would be enough to cover the sound because if he turned off the motor, the little boat would immediately skiff off the waves in the whim of the wind.

He was amazed at how large the vessel was. Three stories tall and very long. It was practically a floating city. Anyone on the upper levels certainly would not hear the motor, but he had no idea who was lurking on the lower levels.

Laying low in the boat, he advanced to the side of the ship. He expected the slice of gunshots whizzing at him any minute.

As the Zodiac skimmed the fiberglass wall of the yacht, Tom slipped the MP-5 from its case. His gaze followed the overhang of the boat, his eyes blinking against the falling snow. No people. Sitting up, he slung the MP-5 over his chest with a strap. He slid in the shadows to the rear of the yacht. The boat drifted on the current away from the ship, and Tom cursed silently, willing the ocean to cooperate. He navigated back to the edge of the yacht, then grabbed the steel rung of the outboard ladder. He stood up in the Zodiac, stepped onto the ladder, and let the Zodiac go. Tom watched it drift off, becoming invisible as the chop swiftly carried out toward deep sea. Presently, there was no place to go but up. He climbed.

At the top, he paused to survey the deck of the ship. A wandering guard took a last drag of his cigarette and flicked it overboard.

He stood with his back to Tom, looking out at the snowy nothingness. Tom quietly launched himself up, took two giant strides across the deck before the man could even register his surprise, and latched his forearm neatly around his throat. Using a small knife, he stabbed him cleanly in the heart. He jabbed upward and felt the resistance of the blade punching through fat, cartilage, and muscle. He heard a dripping sound, like a toilet running, and realized the man was gushing blood. Tom hustled him to the railing and threw him over, hoping he'd sink instead of float. In the darkness, the blood on the polished wooden deck wasn't terribly visible, but anyone missing the guard would come to search and inevitably discover it.

There were no nearby towels or rags to clean it up. So be it, he thought, and pocketed the knife.

He approached the glass doors that led to the main cabin. The lights were off. It appeared to be an empty room. He slid the door silently on its tracks. Stepping inside, he shut the door to prevent the room temperature from changing. He paused, listening for voices or for the sound of Fallon calling for him, but there was nothing other than the lapping of water against the ship. He walked silently through the cabin to the staircase and realized he had entered on the second floor, which meant the boat had four stories. More space to cover—and the clock was ticking down.

Trying to decide whether he should start with the top floor or the bottom, he heard the male voices he had been expecting. Tom froze, listening to determine which direction it was emanating from. He gripped the powerful MP-5 in his hands and proceeded soundlessly upstairs.

Inside the stairwell, he rose on his tiptoes to scan the scene. The voices might have been from the television. A man was lying on the sofa with his eyes closed, apparently asleep. Tom lifted his foot and quietly placed it on the next step, aware of every muscle contracting, every breath that sounded like the sawing wind in his own ears. Standing motionless on the top step, he took in a plush white and purple room that reminded him of a nightclub. Glossy tables, a wet bar that was lit from underneath, plush white sofas.

"Khalid!" Someone shouted from beyond the wet bar.

Tom dove behind the sectional sofa. The man on the sofa sat up, blinking sleepily. "Yes, I am here." He looked around, like he'd sensed Tom's presence, his smell, or the swirl of the air or the way the boat shifted, slightly, when Tom landed.

Tom willed himself to be as small as possible, to keep his heart from pounding so hard.

"What is happening in here? Are you asleep?"

"No, I was praying."

"Where is Aziz? I paged him on the radio but he did not answer. He is useless."

"I will check."

"The plan is good. If everyone would just adhere to the plan we would have no problems."

"We will have no problems, Faisal."

"Find Aziz. Tonight there can be no surprises or mistakes."

Tom heard one man walking toward the stairs, but one stayed. He felt his footsteps on the floor approaching him in his hiding spot, and then a gasp. "Who are—"

Tom's actions were instantaneous. He lifted the weapon and fired a silent shot into his head. Tom shot up and grabbed the man's shirt before he fell back with a thud. Tom eased him down and then began to drag his body toward a closet door.

From the back deck: "Faisal! Come quick!" So young Khalid had no doubt discovered the blood puddle on the polished wood flooring.

Tom shut the closet door as the younger man appeared. His eyes grew wide when he saw Tom and he reached to his side, as if to grab a gun, and realized, too late, that he did not have it with him. Tom shot but missed, the bullet whizzing by the guy's head to lodge behind him in the wall. He was a blur as he ran back downstairs, screaming. Tom shot again and he fell, a black-red mark appearing on the wall in front of him. Tom could hear a disturbance from upstairs. Someone calling, "What is happening?"

Tom did not want to risk going back onto the deck to drop the body overboard; he sensed the people upstairs would be looking over the upper deck, curious about the shouting. Instead, he dragged the leaden body through the salon to a bathroom. He placed him on the floor of the shower, closed the door, and listened.

They were coming. It sounded like a stampede of a hundred people, but he knew it could not be more than twenty or so. Tom gripped the small device in his pocket and hurried toward them. He heard the *thwap* of a silenced weapon before he saw the people holding the weapons. Tom tossed the flash-bang grenade and shut his eyes.

In the small, enclosed area, the percussion was devastating. Tom swayed on his feet, momentarily blinded. Regaining his equilibrium, he vaulted himself up the staircase and began to yell, "Fallon! Fallon!"

He knew they were behind him, dazed and blind for the

moment, but they would recover and come for him; he had seconds to find Fallon. They knew where Fallon was, and they might kill her just to spite him, so he moved quickly. A man suddenly jumped on Tom's back, strong hands squeezing his throat. Tom jammed the barrel of the gun backward into the man's face. His grip loosened slightly but Tom bashed him repeatedly until he fell away with an anguished moan.

Panic erupted down below decks. He heard them yelling. Then splashing. Were they jumping ship? Into freezing water? The flash-bang would stun anyone with the noise and blinding flash, but it wasn't deadly. He carefully moved to the stairwell, then crept down, and he felt a massive wall of heat advancing like a wave. Then he realized the back half of the ship was on fire.

Tom ran to the bow of the ship and took the staircase upstairs to the very top level. "Fallon! Are you here?" There was a Jet Ski and a kayak and a small Boston Whaler but no place where she might be hidden.

He ran back to the second level, screaming her name. He heard no reply. Frantically he flung open doors, searching every crevice he could find. That left only the two bottom floors. He again used the front stairs to run down. He bypassed the floor with the fancy club furniture and plunged into the dark hallway. As he landed on the bottom step, he felt cold water and realized he was up to his ankles in seawater. The fire was causing the boat to sink. And it was burning hot and fast. Even down here, thick black smoke burned his eyes and his throat. He resisted reaching for a light because he didn't want to spark another fire. He found the small penlight he kept in his pocket and struggled to see in the weak illumination. The beam only reached two feet in front of him and with the restricted beam the room seemed not very big. He trudged in the darkness deeper into the bowels of the ship, the water rising to his calves. It was sloshing up high against the walls.

"Fallon!" Using his left hand to keep the beam in front of

him, he ran his hand along the walls, looking for a door. The fiberglass and sheetrock were hot, burning rapidly. His heart was pounding; his throat felt like it was closing up. Smoke curled into his eyes, irritated his lungs.

His foot struck something and he realized he'd walked into a wall. There was an enclosed square room in the center of the room. Flashing the beam onto it, he saw an engraved silver plaque: ENGINE ROOM.

Desperately he pushed against the door but it would not open. It was flat; there was no handle. "Fallon, if you're in there, stay away from the door." He lifted his weapon and fired at the lock. Pushing against the water, which wet him to the knee, the door finally opened. A giant wall of hissing heat burned his eyes. Hissing and crackling blood orange and black flames were consuming what had been the back wall of the ship.

In the center of the room, only feet from the conflagration, Fallon was tied to a chair, blindfolded and gagged. His soul transformed at the sight of her. He wanted to fall to his knees and give thanks to a God he had not believed in since September 11, 2001 that she was alive. He trudged through the rising water to her and ripped off the blindfold. Dazed, she looked up at him with wide, blinking, terrified eyes. But in the next second, she recognized him. Amazement and love and hope blazed out at him in that instant. Tom worked at the gag and finally got it loose. She was crying, her whole body shaking. "You came," she gasped over the noise.

Tom used the bloody knife to cut the heavy nautical rope at her wrists and ankles. She was wiggling, trying to get away from the fire, but her squirming prevented him from getting a clean cut.

"Stay still," he yelled, grabbing her ankle.

Finally he sliced through, tossing away the ropes. Fallon stood up on legs as fragile as a newborn foal's. She collapsed against him as if she had no stamina of her own. She was hurt, almost helpless. Nothing he could do about it now though but be the muscle for her.

The thick black smoke was becoming overwhelming. He

grabbed the blindfold. "Breathe through this," he instructed. He placed it over her mouth and nose. "Good girl."

He scooped her up in a fireman's carry and waded through the freezing water back to the door. The engine room had been waterproofed and had held back a deluge, but when he entered the hallway again, the bottom floor of the boat was submerged. He could not carry her to the stairs; he would drown. "Hold on to me," he said and placed her gently in the water.

She clung to his back as he led the way through the black and watery chamber. He gripped the handrail of the stairs; it was hot. Fallon wrapped her legs and arms around him, and he carried her up. The rear of the boat was underwater. He could no longer see the place he boarded or the place the two bodies had been discarded.

Tom hurried with Fallon to the front steps. The fire was bad on the starboard side. The sound of it was terrifying: chewing everything in its path, the crisping and popping, the roar that drowned out everything else.

Keeping himself focused on the only objective, he kept to the port and climbed up to the bow of the ship. The water was quickly rising, and even in the cold, open air the smoke was horrendous. Fallon was coughing, gasping for air.

She leaned over as if she was heaving, and Tom saw a bloody mark on her neck. Gently he lifted her hair and saw a deep red slice into her tender magnolia skin. She would need stitches.

"They were telling me how they would behead me," she said with dazed simplicity.

Tom stuffed it down. He'd deal with it later. Right now he had to get Fallon off this sinking ship.

At the edge of his blurred vision he saw something white in the water. He blinked, thinking it was moonlight throwing shapes on the waves, but then realized there was no moonlight tonight; it was snowing. It was the edge of the Zodiac creating a slight wave as it floated near the yacht. It had gone in crazy circles since he let it go.

Tom would have to jump in the water, swim to the Zodiac, and pull himself inside, then steer it close to the ship so Fallon could make her way into it. That fire looming behind her looked ferocious, but he had no choice.

"What is that?"

"It's our way out of here. Stay here. I will—"

"No. We're going together."

There was no arguing with Fallon. He nodded. "We jump, swim, and I'll get you into the Zodiac. Do not let go of my hand."

She looked sick, but she nodded.

Tom walked with her to the edge of the boat, which was now almost entirely on its starboard side, rocking and heaving in the choppy waves. The black water swirled and heaved, terribly rugged. Meanwhile, they were tottering perilously high on the side of the ship. Tom could detect the craft already starting to descend into the sea, and once it really began to sink, it would create a powerful draft, sucking them and the Zodiac down with it.

"On the count of three." He gripped her hand. "One. Two. Three."

The icy shock of the water left him breathless, blindsighted. It was barely above freezing, and the air was even colder; snow still fell. He felt that peculiar sense that there was no bottom beneath his feet, and he struggled to swim up while holding Fallon's frozen hand. He had to move quickly, even as his cramping limbs ached from the sudden penetrating cold. Fallon's teeth chattered loudly and her hair was instantly frozen. Her skin had paled to a translucent, sickly white. Holding her with one arm, he reached for the Zodiac. Grasping it with his shaking arm felt like a miraculous victory. But they were far from safe. Once the ship went down, they were going to get dragged down too. They had to get far away, fast. Fallon hung onto him and then flung one leg over the rim. She was numb too; her limbs weren't working. Her foot barely caught the edge of the boat, then fell back into the water.

"One more time," Tom said. Holding on to the Zodiac with one arm, he awkwardly pushed Fallon up, trying to get her top half inside and let gravity do the rest. To his great relief, she tumbled inside. She crawled toward the edge and held her arm out for him as if to help. God, she never stopped caring, did she? She was so weak, he would have yanked her back into the water. Tom flung his left leg over the ledge and launched himself inside. He grabbed the steering wheel and pointed it toward the shore.

It suddenly became a thousand times darker, and Tom realized that the yacht had sunk; the fire was extinguished in the waves. He felt the pull of the massive form in the water, the vacuum created by the displaced ship, but the Zodiac was far enough away that it wouldn't get dragged into the vortex. He listened for voices, for cries for help that would go unanswered as the terrorists drowned, but there was nothing. The wind and waves covered a multitude of sins.

Fallon was no longer shaking. Very bad sign. Tom positioned her in front of him so he could steer the boat and share his body heat. "We're almost there," he said into her ear. They weren't. They were at least twenty minutes from shore. He hoped she didn't glance at the GPS; he'd be busted.

He was so cold. He had never been so cold in his life. He could not feel his feet or his hands or ears or nose but he was more worried about Fallon. She had begun to shake a little bit again, which was good.

Finally, they entered the safety of the small harbor, where the wind eased up a little bit. The high, splashing, freezing, splattering waves were gone, replaced by calm water, snow, and total blackness.

Tom steered the boat to the pier and cut the engine. He stood up on shaking legs and placed one wet boot-clad foot on the pier, holding the boat in place so Fallon could get out. He held her waist and helped her step out of the unsteady rocking boat to the pier. She swayed dangerously. Not good. In one swift movement, Tom scooped her up. With her body sagging against his, he carried her to the truck. She leaned against while he opened the door; she simply had no stamina of her own at all. Tom, alarmed, gently placed her in inside with the heater blasting at her like jet engines. She was deathly pale. He began to rip the thin lace bodice of her pretty lace.

"What are you doing?" she asked between clenched, chattering teeth.

"I have some blankets," he said. "You're going to freeze if you stay in those clothes."

He threw the sodden dress onto the floorboard, followed by her underwear. Her skin was ice cold and white as alabaster. He gently wrapped her naked body in warm fleece blankets. He wanted to hold her, give her his heat, but he didn't want to wet the blankets that were keeping her alive.

"What about you?" she asked through chattering teeth.

"I'm okay. We need to get you to the hospital to be treated for hypothermia and whatever is wrong with your leg."

"I don't need the hospital. Just let me warm up."

Tom belatedly noticed the towels stocked behind the driver's seat and wrapped her hair in one.

"Tom …"

He saw unmistakable love in her pale face. It was so raw and unshielded that it nearly broke his heart. She never had to say another word; he knew what she was thinking, what she was feeling because he felt it too. He thought of all the time and energy he'd spent trying to keep her at bay, keep himself apart from her, and he felt like a fool. Never again. Now that he had her, he was going to keep her close to him, forever and always.

A teary smile came to her face. Tom was getting the feeling back in his hands. Painful, searing feeling, but it was something. He pulled the blankets tighter around her shaking body, trying to keep her warm.

Fallon reached from beneath the folds and laced her fingers through his.

He held on tight, all the way to Washington.

THIRTY-TWO

Tom had been in the Oval Office many times, but never as a guest. He stood outside in the busy vestibule, watching the goings-on with an outsider's interest. The new president had brought in a new cabinet; only two days into the Hughes administration, everyone appeared flush with excitement and eagerness. A young female with square glasses and her hair in a knot on top of her head marched importantly behind the new Chief of Staff, nearly stumbling over herself to keep up as they turned down the hall.

Tom wondered if all this activity was genuinely constructive and these young guns were focused on the right things. The entire US intelligence apparatus was still in disarray, with secrets spilling forth to the open market. It would take years to figure out who knew what, and even longer to repair the damage.

A studious young guy whose eagerness reminded him, grimly, of Travis Hill appeared at his side. Tom blinked, trying to steady his aim.

"Sir," the young man said, "the president is ready for you."

Tom stepped inside the Oval, sensing that Hughes had called the meeting in this storied place because it was still a novelty to have it at his disposal. Elizabeth Hughes had redecorated the Oval in pale blue, beige and pale yellow. He took in the blur of art and bronzes, the subtle signifiers of rugged Montana individualism that Hughes had run on.

Tom stared blankly at the man across the room, unsure of what was about to happen.

President Hughes stepped from behind John Kennedy's desk and indicated a powder-blue sofa. "Have a seat."

Tom sat.

"How are you feeling?"

"Well, sir."

Hughes sat across from him. "I really want to know." His gaze met Tom's candidly.

Tom was suddenly at loss. It had been a long time since anyone asked him that question. And it wasn't something he spent a lot of time pondering in the dark of the night. Self-pity wasn't his style. But the president wanted an answer. Auditing himself, he would have to say physically he was in top form; he'd escaped Malkhazi's goons unharmed. His emotions, however, were a morass of confusion and angst. After he delivered Fallon to Gwen at Georgetown University Hospital, she'd declined to see him. He'd been abruptly pulled off her detail, ostensibly at Fallon's request. Now he was back on VP Claudia Wells's rota. But none of that was the president's business.

"I'm fine, sir," Tom repeated.

The president's expression didn't change. "You've been put on administrative leave for six weeks. After the administrative leave, you will decline to return to protection."

"When did I decide that, sir?"

"Then," the president continued as if he hadn't heard him, "I would like to personally offer you a position on a new task force."

Tom frowned. "Sir?"

"It's a new program under the direction of the office of the National Intelligence Director. The short version is that you'll have an opportunity to play a little offense instead of defense. You'll be working with Omar Koss."

Preston Hughes let that sink in for a moment. At first glimpse, it was damn attractive; Tom rather liked the way Omar Koss played at national security.

When Tom didn't reply, the president continued. "There is a lot to clean up after Fallon's kidnapping. Djvebe Malkhazi and Collin Whitcomb are at large. They've managed to disappear in the last twelve hours. We need them found and punished."

The notion that the men who killed Antoine Campbell and kidnapped Fallon could still be at large sickened him. And inspired him. "I accept, Mr. Hughes," Tom said.

Preston Taylor Hughes smiled his seductive TV smile, and in that moment Tom could see a trace of Fallon. It pained him.

"Good. There is one other item I need to speak to you about. Something else that I consider more important."

"Fallon."

"Fallon," the president repeated, nodding his head. "I owe you …" To Tom's astonishment, tears appeared in Preston Hughes's eyes. "I owe you a great deal," he said. "You did your job. You saved my daughter."

To his horror, he felt himself go swimmy, the past weeks' emotion trying his limits. "I'm sorry," Tom murmured suddenly, free-floating emotional wreckage, responding seemingly at random. "I'm sorry I did it wrong. I'm sorry about Slaney and … the others. I'm sorry I didn't stop it all."

"You did it just fine, Agent."

Tom inhaled deeply, trying to get hold of his emotions. Thankfully, the president charged on.

"I have to ask more of you, Tom."

"Yes, sir?"

"Convince your friend Leah to keep what she knows about Claudia and Richard Mullinax secret. In exchange, she will have full access to my White House."

"How do you know about Leah?"

The president smiled. "You have a lot to catch up on."

That was no doubt true. "Anything else?"

"Yes, actually." He looked to Tom, meeting his gaze squarely. "I owe you an apology. I was the one who blocked you from seeing Fallon at the hospital after her recovery from the boat."

Whoa. Game changer. He had not understood her refusal to see him, and it had hurt him grievously. Over the last few weeks, he'd come to accept Fallon's choice. It served him right. But it didn't make the absence any easier.

Profound happiness began to flood through him, warm and alive.

"I believed at that time that you were a bad influence on her. I wasn't pleased that you were lying to your employer, sneaking around to see her. It seemed like another bad choice she was making, driven from passion rather than reason. I've come to realize I was wrong.

"I've given up trying to understand my daughter, but I've never given up loving her. Her brief absence has made me realize just how much our family has relied on her to hold us together. I'm ashamed to say that, but it's the unvarnished truth. I realized when she was kidnapped that I had never actually asked what she wanted in her life. She was always a bit … airy-fairy, if you know what I mean. Into art and yoga and travel, things that seem trivial to me. I disregarded her wishes and pushed her toward law school, as if she was mine to conform. Because she is a bit of a people pleaser, she went along with it and has become everything I said I wanted, at least on paper. She's miserable. She doesn't sparkle like she used to when she was teaching yoga and planning trips to Thailand or the Dalmatian Coast or some other far-flung dot on the globe."

The president's lips pinched, as if remembering something painful. He then resumed, his voice as matter of fact as before. "I'd very much like her to be happy. She deserves happiness, and I believe you made her happy."

It took a moment to understand what Hughes was saying. Once Tom got it, he felt a little embarrassed. Hughes had been right a few weeks ago, but not now. There was no way Fallon would forgive him for abandoning her again. He was grudgingly resigned to that fact. "Thank you for your blessing," he began, "but that is all in the past."

Hughes squared his chin. "If that is the case, then so be it. I'm not going to mess up my relationship with Fallon more than I have by meddling in her private affairs. But you did make her happy. And I'd like to see her happy again."

Fallon kicked off her shoes under her desk and sat back in her chair to take a sip of coffee. It was half past nine o'clock in the evening; most associates had called it a day. She, however, was still at the office, chasing an acquittal for Chambers.

But not totally. Her thoughts shifted to Tom, as they had frequently since he rescued her. She'd been delirious with cold and terror; her injury had been serious. A nasty row of stitches still crisscrossed the back of her neck where the kidnappers had teased a sword over her skin, slicing into the muscles to prove their willingness to kill.

Tom had appeared like a dream, strength and competence personified. In her state of trauma, she'd nearly told him she loved him. And he shut her down. Thank God. It was his last gentlemanly act: not allowing her to humiliate herself in that most desperate time.

He'd dutifully delivered her to Georgetown University Hospital. After her neck had been stitched and her fractured rib had been braced, and she was finally warm enough to feel her extremities, she'd asked Cameron if Tom was okay: Was he here? Was he being treated for hypothermia? Cameron informed her that he'd left but other agents had arrived.

Of course Tom had left. That's what he always did. Why should this time be any different?

It felt like she'd swallowed acid.

However, in the intervening weeks, she'd settled into a sort of dull acceptance of the facts. He didn't want her. Fine. She'd cried enough tears. It was time to move on. These words sounded like Gwen and though they had the cold, concrete quality of truth, they weren't comforting. In fact, they hurt like a bitch.

She shut her eyes, struggling to maintain her equilibrium.

There were times when she could still feel him, as if they were connected by invisible magnets. Even now, she felt him. For just one deliciously sinful moment, she sank into the sensation, imagining the air was charged with his rich cologne and the electricity of his powerful body, feeling the air altered as if a jet had just zoomed through the room.

Fallon suddenly stilled as goose bumps rose on her skin. She really did feel like she was being watched. She felt the subtle electromagnetic pulse of another human being in her vicinity.

She opened her eyes, all suspense and expectation, and stared at the empty office where she had illogically believed that

Tom would be. The conviction of his presence was so acute that she felt his absence with such a sudden intensity that she could have wept.

He had always shown up when she most needed him. He was so expected, so rooted in her heart that she could scarcely believe that he wasn't there, waiting for her too.

She hadn't given any thought to what she would say or do if he were actually there. All she had seen in her mind was that one second when she would see him and nothing else would matter because he made everything—her whole life—brighter.

She exhaled shakily and looked back at the work on her desk: the stacks of documents to vet, the research that had leeched hours of her precious and singular life and would leech yet more. A pit in her stomach settled and felt like despair.

The sudden detachment she felt for her work repelled her.

She began to type again, forcing words onto the page, wishing she believed the passionate arguments she put forth. The stubborn fact was Chambers was guilty. In private consultations, he'd come close to admitting his guilt himself. Even so, Fallon was obligated to design sophisticated legal arguments that would negate this reality.

"Garbage," she muttered to herself and deleted the latest paragraph. Weak legal thinking mixed with lackadaisical writing would just result in more fallow hours of soul-breaking labor.

She glanced up; her vision skewed. There, in the doorway, stood Tom Bishop.

He stood with his hands in his pockets, slouching sexily against the doorframe, looking so damn gorgeous it made her heart thud.

She could have laughed at the timing. But she only gazed, afraid that any sudden moves would ruin the very pleasant hallucination.

"I thought I'd find you here, working late," he said.

Okay, not a hallucination. She nodded dumbly, mentally scrabbling for ballast.

He smiled softly, teasingly. "Why do you work so much, Fallon?"

"To get ahead," she answered, finding her throat suddenly dry.

"Do you get paid more if you work more?"

"No."

"Sounds like a scam."

Fallon cracked a smile. It *felt* like a scam. Since being discharged from the hospital, her job seemed like a vast façade, something to occupy her time so she didn't think too deeply about the joylessness of her days. She'd always assumed that lawyering would become more fascinating the more senior she became. But she never seemed to achieve big goals, and the small achievements she did manage didn't bring anything like satisfaction. That Tom should see her unhappiness made her heart hurt.

He dropped that sexy pose against her doorframe and sauntered her office. "How is your neck?"

"I'm okay. Healing."

"Really?"

She met his eyes candidly, surprised at the prompt. "Yes," she answered carefully, suddenly feeling as tight and constrained as if she were wearing a whalebone corset. "I'm fine."

Tom nodded thoughtfully—not really believing her, but allowing his question to be dismissed. He sat in the seat across from her. "I came here to apologize."

She began to shake her head—to head him off because she couldn't bear an emotional scene at the office—but protestations would not come.

"I'm sorry for a lot of other things," he said matter-of-factly. "I have a list of violations that dates back to Paxos."

She sat mutely, remembering the similar shock she'd felt when she saw him for the first time in five years. Same head-spinning awe. Same sense of wonder.

Her whole body felt like she was standing on a fault line, like anything could happen.

Tom's gaze met hers squarely, pupil to pupil. "I owe you some answers as part of my apology. So here goes. I left you on Paxos because I was still hurting for my wife who had died and

I wasn't ready for ... well, for you. I should have told you that I was unprepared instead of acting like an ass and leaving. But to do so would have meant my feelings for you were more serious than I wished to credit.

"Mostly I'm sorry for having been such an indecisive jerk these past weeks. I wasn't sure what I wanted, and you showed up again, this new happiness ... and I panicked. I felt like happiness would be a betrayal to Bethany, my wife. I know now that she would hate the way I've behaved. I know it is hard to believe but I'm not always a selfish, uncommunicative oaf. I'm capable of being a good husband and partner, though I can't blame you for being skeptical."

Fallon's stupefied silence protracted out an uncomfortably long time. She became aware of the silence, the buzzing emptiness of the darkened outer offices and the fact that they were pretty much alone. She'd never heard such honesty from Tom, possibly from anyone. He was speaking to her like an equal, not a protectee. Like a lover.

Just when she was about to ask why he was saying this now, Tom spoke again.

"Your father sent me away from the hospital," he said flatly. "In case you were wondering why I wasn't there and why we haven't spoken in these weeks. It was because I was told you didn't want me there."

"I did ..." Her voice was a strangled whisper.

Tom's lips narrowed to a sealed, flat line. There was something about his manner that seemed to suggest regret and pain. It passed so quickly that she wondered if she'd imagined it.

But the anger lingered in her blood. It was the last straw. She would have to renegotiate the terms of her relationship with her father. She wanted a more authentic life; she detested being his prop for political purposes.

"I love you," Tom said.

The fault line heaved. That woozy, tilt-a-whirl feeling came cartwheeling through her, and there was no possibility of refusing it.

"You mean more to me than anything. I almost lost you,

and if I had, it would have killed me."

"I'm right here," Fallon said, tears springing to her eyes. "You didn't lose me."

"I'm not sure what it's worth to you, but I love you and I want to make you happy every day for the rest of our lives. Though I don't really deserve it, I want you to give me an opportunity to do that. No sneaking around. No lies. No misunderstandings about our feelings."

Tom stood up and walked around the desk, pausing just close enough to make her body respond in the way it always did. He did to her what spring did to cherry blossoms.

"Can you forgive me?"

Fallon nodded her head, not trusting her voice in that moment.

Fallon began to smile—she couldn't help but smile— and Tom caught her lips to his. She buckled to the pleasure and twined her arms around his neck as the joy swept her up in its magic.

Tom pulled back and looked into her eyes. "Is that a yes?"

"It's a yes."

"In that case …" Tom reached inside his pocket and pulled out some papers, folded into quarters, and handed them to her.

"What are these?"

"Two e-tickets to Paxos, Greece."

Fallon bit her bottom lip, looking at the tickets with teary, lovestruck eyes. The whole world was waiting. Open and inviting, and she could see it all with Tom. She hadn't dared dream of so much.

She glanced over at the work on her desk, the same work that never seemed to diminish, the same work that was giving her an ulcer.

It was immediately obvious in that moment that she was done with it. She had no idea what she would do instead, but she desperately wanted to find out.

The future seemed as wide open as the blue Mediterranean horizon. She could do anything, and she'd happily do it all with Tom Bishop by her side.

"When can we leave?"

"Anytime we want."

Just when she thought she couldn't take any more happiness, her heart squeezed and tears began to pool again. "Okay, Bishop," she said, grinning wildly. He held out his hand for her, and she laced her fingers with his. With her other hand, she grabbed her purse from the desk.

"Ready, set, let's go!"

ABOUT THE AUTHOR

After spending most of her life in Washington D.C., Cara now lives in a remodeled Victorian schoolhouse in southern England, which will no doubt make an appearance in future books. She lives with her husband and cat, both of whom provide an endless source of amusement and inspiration.